THE DELIVERER

BOOKS BY SHARON HINCK

The Dancing Realms series
Hidden Current
Forsaken Island
Windward Shore

The Sword of Lyric series
The Restorer
The Restorer's Son
The Restorer's Journey
The Deliverer

The Secret Life of Becky Miller
Renovating Becky Miller

Symphony of Secrets

Stepping into Sunlight

Dream of Kings

THE DELIVERER

THE SWORD OF LYRIC
BOOK FOUR

SHARON HINCK

The Deliverer
Copyright © 2015 by Sharon Hinck

Published by Enclave Publishing, an imprint of Oasis Family Media, LLC

Carol Stream, Illinois, USA.
www.enclavepublishing.com

ISBN: 978-1-62184-049-7 (print)
ISBN: 978-1-62184-050-3 (eBook)

Cover Design by Kirk DouPonce
Edited by Reagen Reed

Printed in the United States of America

To the One who keeps His promises

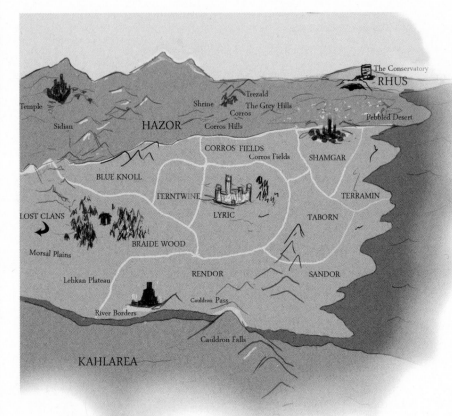

The Conservatory
RHUS

Temple

Sidian

HAZOR

Shrine
Trezald
The Grey Hills
Corros
Corros Hills

Pebbled Desert

CORROS FIELDS
Corros Fields

SHAMGAR

BLUE KNOLL

TERNTWINE

LYRIC

TERRAMIN

LOST CLANS

TABORN

Morsal Plains

BRAIDE WOOD

Lehkan Plateau

RENDOR

SANDOR

River Borders

Cauldron Pass

Cauldron Falls

KAHLAREA

PEOPLE OF THE VERSES

"In every time of great need, a Restorer is sent to fight for the people and help the guardians. The Restorer is empowered with gifts to defeat our enemies and turn the people's hearts back to the Verses."

CHAPTER
1

LINETTE

FRANTIC POUNDING INVADED my dreams, and I bolted upright on my pallet. Angular shadows tilted toward me. The strident scent of stone and metal was unfamiliar and. . . wrong.

Hazor. I was in my quarters in the palace, deep inside the capital city of Sidian.

"Linette! We need you." Nolan's normally stoic voice gasped from the outer hall. He banged again, and I pulled on my songkeeper's robe as I raced to the door. I triggered the magnetic lock, and the door slipped sideways into the wall.

Under his dark bangs, Nolan's eyes were huge. His chest heaved. Panic splashed dozens of scenarios through my thoughts. Had King Zarek revoked his protection? Did we need to flee for our lives? Or had Nolan heard dire news from the clans?

"The baby," Nolan said, breathless. "Hurry."

"Is Kendra in trouble?"

"Bleating like a caradoc."

I'd kept my worries hidden as her time to deliver the baby neared. Now all my apprehensions burst free. My hands shook as I knotted my belt.

Nolan raced ahead of me down the hallway, disappearing at the first sharp angle. The hall doubled back on itself briefly, then bent sharply again. The odd design might make the path more difficult for invaders, but tonight the palace's frustrating architecture made me want to fire a syncbeam straight through the walls.

I ran to catch up as Nolan opened the door to Tristan and Kendra's rooms.

Inside, Kieran spun to face us, bootknife in hand, muscles tense. He waved us into the room, then stepped to the door, checking both directions of the hallway before putting away the knife. "What took you so long?" he snapped at his son. Turning to me, he glowered. "We don't know what to do."

And he thought I did? We were in a strange land, far from any healers. "When did her pains start?"

Kieran and Nolan exchanged helpless looks. They'd clearly be useless. A groan carried from the inner room, sending an anguished expression across Kieran's face. Poor man. He could count the people he cared about on one hand. His sister Kendra and his friend Tristan were two. No wonder he was worried.

I brushed past him to the inner room. The lightwall within was dimmed to a gentle level. I expected to find Kendra writhing on her pallet, but she stood with her palms braced against the wall. Tristan rubbed her back and whispered something in her ear. As a tremor moved through her, I heard another groan. Not from Kendra, but Tristan.

When he noticed me, gratitude chased away a measure of his fear. "Thank the One you're here. How can I help her?"

Kendra straightened, drew a slow breath, and smiled at me. "I told them not to wake you. I'm fine. But since you're here, would you please make these men calm down?"

Tristan's eyes showed white like a panicked lehkan's. Kieran and Nolan's gazes peered anxiously from the door. My lips twitched. "If you think I can calm them, you're overestimating my skills."

She managed a short laugh, but gasped as a pain took her. Tristan reached to support her, but she waved him away.

He turned to me. "Do something."

"Would you like me to call Havid?" I asked Kendra. The older songkeeper and her husband had come to Hazor with us—although whether they were more help or hindrance was a matter for debate.

Kendra snorted. "That old crone? No, I don't want her here."

I'd probably feel the same way in Kendra's place. But that left only one woman from the clans to assist her. Me.

After the pain eased, Kendra prowled the room, taking slow steps, her arms wrapped around her middle. I tugged Tristan's arm to get his full attention. Once he met my eyes, I summoned my firmest tone. "I can't give Kendra all my focus if I have to keep reassuring you three men. She needs peace and confidence. Can you do that?"

Tristan, a toughened guardian who could wield a sword against the fiercest enemies, swallowed hard and barely managed a nod.

Then he pulled me nearer the door. "I was thinking," he whispered. "Maybe we should call for one of Zarek's practitioners."

Kendra marched across the room and whacked Tristan's shoulder. "Don't be an idiot."

"But if they could help . . ."

"My baby is not coming into this life with dark arts and—" Kendra broke off to wince and press her hands against the wall again. Her muscles strained as if she wanted to push the stone outward and expand the room. Sweat beaded her forehead.

Arguments wouldn't help her through this. "Nolan, go get my rondalin. It's in the cubby in the great room of my quarters. Kieran, brew some clavo. Keep it weak, but make plenty. Tristan, we'll want more blankets."

As the men scattered, Kendra drew a deep breath, released the wall, and hugged me. "Thank you." She paced the room a few times. "You have attended births back in Braide Wood, haven't you?"

"Of course." I smoothed the blankets on her pallet and didn't meet her gaze. This wasn't the time to explain that I'd simply provided small comforts and music. Only experienced mothers assisted with the actual birth. I'd kept to the background where I belonged . . . and where I wished I could be now.

She sank onto her pallet and leaned back against the wall. Kendra was one of the strongest women I knew. She had the sharp mind of a transtech and the courage of a guardian. But fatigue shadowed her eyes, a frightening reminder of how haggard she'd appeared after the Rhusican poison. Frailty lingered in her slim frame.

I sat beside her and rested my hand on her swollen abdomen. "When did the pains begin?"

"All . . . night." Her breath caught and her hands dug into the pallet. "Didn't want to . . . wake Tristan . . . but now . . ."

"Now it's time," I said, forcing reassurance into my voice. "And I'm here to help."

The tightness grabbing her belly finally eased. She adjusted to find a more comfortable position. The humor she'd shown at the men's fussing had faded, and her eyes welled with uncertainty as she focused on me. "We tried for so long. We thought this was a blessing we would never have. What if . . . what if I can't? Maybe we aren't meant to have a child."

"You already do. We just need to help him enter the world." I gathered her hands in mine and buried my own worries. Doubt could bleed into a soul as quickly as Rhusican poison, diluting the joy and trust meant to live there. I needed to cling to truth for both our sakes. "The One cradles you in His love. He never looks away."

"Not even in Hazor?" Kendra managed a breathy laugh, then sighed. "I wish we were in Braide Wood."

"I know. But yes, even here. Even on our hardest roads. Especially then."

Nolan cleared his throat from the doorway, a bundle in his arms that he thrust in my direction.

"Thank you," I said, taking the round stringed instrument from its protective wrap.

He spared me a shy smile before backing skittishly out of sight. I settled on the floor near Kendra and tested a few strings. The tone was as smooth as warm water. "I hope I can remember the order of the welcome songs. It's been several seasons since I attended my last birth."

Kendra smiled and rubbed her belly. "Play quickly. I'm ready to meet this baby."

I began the first of the traditional songs, relieved when the music helped Kendra relax. She braced herself during the next pain, but this time no fear tightened the lines of her face. My own worries gave way to the beauty and strength of the songs. So often in recent seasons I'd felt small and useless. I didn't have the political knowledge and craftiness of Kieran, or the strength and courage of Tristan. Our time in Hazor had only highlighted the limits of my gifts. But in this moment, my calling had value. I could help in a way no one else here could.

With the aid of music, even the men calmed. Tristan kept Kendra supplied with clavo to sip, blotted the sweat from her face, and wrapped an extra blanket around her shoulders. Kieran and his son stayed out of sight but always in earshot in case we needed anything.

As the tempo of both birth pains and music increased, Tristan held Kendra and sang softly in her ear. At times she seemed barely aware of our presence, lost in a deep private struggle, but worry and fear remained at bay.

My fingers ached. My shoulders and arms grew sore and numb. Still I played and sang. Had all births taken this long? I struggled to remember. In the small, dim room, time became meaningless. My heart ached to ease Kendra's pain, and the words I sang pleaded for the One to protect her. In the recent seasons, she had become a dear friend—my only real friend in this foreign place. I couldn't face the thought of losing her.

At last, it was time to set aside my rondalin and help Kendra deliver her child. I summoned my memories from other births. The older women of Braide Wood said that in most cases babies knew their path. I hoped they were right.

When my music stopped, a muddle of other sounds took over the room. Ragged breaths, groans, nervous questions called from the outer room, murmured reassurances. Finally, in a flow of blood and water, a wrinkled, slippery baby emerged.

A girl.

Even as I worked to gather her safely, I laughed. She'd already subverted the predictions of her father. He'd been sure the baby would be a son.

I wrapped her in a soft blanket, rubbing her skin, coaxing sound from her tiny lungs.

The small bundle gave a surprised hiccup, then turned red-faced with a hearty squall. I handed her to Kendra and sank back on my heels, awestruck. Pure new life had burst into the world, and we were witnesses. Tears ran down my face, relief and joy mingling. I wished I could compose a brand new song to honor the infant's arrival, but at the moment her squawks were the most beautiful music I'd ever heard.

Kendra's arms encircled her child, and she nuzzled the top of her head as Tristan knelt beside her with his eyes glistening. Kendra pulled her focus away from the baby and reached a hand toward her husband. He pressed his forehead against hers. "She's beautiful."

"Her name is Emmi," Kendra said. Joy shone along with the sheen of moisture on her face. "And Tristan, do you realize what this means?"

"We're parents?" he answered, letting his daughter wrap her tiny perfect hand around his finger.

Kendra giggled. "Well, yes. That's the main thing. And now we can finally return home to the clans."

My heart sank. Hazor was about to become even more lonely.

CHAPTER 2

LINETTE

THE DARK GRANITE of the city's wall glared down on me. Massive carvings of distorted figures and vicious faces added to the morning chill, making me feel small and vulnerable. I struggled to shrug off the heavy darkness that plagued me with increasing persistence as our time in Hazor lengthened, but it was soaking into my bones. I was supposed to be a songkeeper on a grand adventure, yet every day the music in my heart grew more muffled. How long before I heard only silence?

I pulled my gaze away and turned to Kendra. "Are you sure you need to leave?"

Kneeling beside a canvas bag, she unearthed her cloak and sent me a sympathetic smile. "Are you sure you need to stay?"

The question I'd grappled with for weeks.

I helped Kendra to her feet, and we both checked on the downy head poking from the pack strapped to her chest. Emmi's snuffling baby sounds coaxed a small smile from me. "Kieran thinks our work here isn't finished." Out of loyalty, I tried to keep the doubt from my voice.

Tristan, Kendra, and Emmi were heading back to Braide Wood. Back to piney scents, to giggling children playing among the trees, to warm meals with even warmer friends. Back to our home.

I turned away and tugged at my hood, tucking stray strands of hair under cover. A soul's true home rested in the One who never changed. I should be able to find contentment even in this foreign land. Yet no matter how hard I sought that elusive peace, the sense of danger grew each day.

"About time." Tristan's grumble carried from the nearby gates, where he'd been watching for Kieran. The two men strode toward us, both intense and war-hardened.

Kieran frowned up at the jagged battlements, his face as angular as the wall carvings. Passing over me, his gaze settled on his sister and brother-in-law. "Be careful to cross the pass before dark tomorrow."

Tristan tossed his head back and laughed—a laugh with the power to scatter worries. "You just can't stop yourself, can you?"

Kieran scowled. "Stop what?"

"Trying to manage everyone around you."

"If you'd show a little more sense, maybe I wouldn't have to." Kieran feigned a deeper frown, but a trace of a smile slipped out.

Tristan's arm circled Kendra, and he rested his other palm on Emmi's head with all the beaming pride of fatherhood. "We'll be fine. You're the one who should be worried. It won't be safe for you here once King Zarek finds out."

Another twist of anxiety tightened under my ribs. I could join the argument. Tell him it was time for us to leave. Or would that be abandoning our calling? Not that Kieran would take my opinions seriously anyway.

He squinted into the distance and raw yearning touched his features. Then he shrugged. "Nothing to worry about." He gave a slight smile, more bleak than confident. "Hazor's king has more to concern him than gossip from the clans."

Tristan turned to me and winked. "Linette, keep him out of trouble, all right?"

My face heated, and I stared at the ground. "I'll do all I can to help. And so will the other songkeepers." When I pulled my gaze up, Kendra was watching me with a knowing smile.

Flustered, I drew a folded cloth from my pocket and handed it to Tristan. "You'll go to Lyric as soon as you can, won't you? Jake will need your support. And tell him I'm asking the One to be with him." If the messages could be believed, Markkel and Susan's son had been poisoned by Medea and manipulated by Cameron. Then Jake had broken free to lead the guardians against a Kahlarean invasion. As a show of encouragement, I'd embroidered him an emblem of Rendor clan to wear on his tunic as he continued to provide leadership in Lyric.

Kieran shifted and muttered something, but when I glanced at him, he turned away. Emmi made a mewing sound and Kendra started swaying side to side in the instinctual dance of all mothers. Light glowed in Tristan's eyes as he watched his wife and child.

No wonder Kieran had scolded. Tristan was so in love with his family that he didn't look capable of fighting off a stinging beetle, much less the larger dangers prowling the canyons between the city of Sidian and the border.

The men grasped forearms. "Go with the One." Kieran's words were gruff. I gave Kendra one last hug. Then the little family set out on the road to the mountains on the border of Hazor and Braide Wood.

As I watched them stride away through the grey light of morning, my chest contracted with a hollow ache.

Kieran stood beside me in silence.

After years of adventuring alone, he'd clearly savored the past seasons. Constant banter and debate with Tristan had made Kieran almost cheerful at times, and no new uncle could be more proud. Today his shoulders slumped.

A good songkeeper would have the perfect encouragement to offer, but I couldn't dredge up a single useful word. I stared up at the dark gates of Sidian. Beyond them, we challenged generations of darkness in a frightening culture. Well, frightening to me. Fear wasn't part of Kieran's vocabulary. But the dangers were growing. "Maybe Tristan was right—"

Kieran's jaw tightened. "You of all people should understand why I can't leave." He rubbed his shoulder—one of the old scars that bothered him at times. "The One asked me to stay. Nothing else would have kept me from Lyric when I heard what Cameron was doing."

"I know." I wrapped my arms around my embroidered silk cloak, wishing instead for the rough woven textures of a handmade cape from Braide Wood. "But keeping this secret from Zarek is dangerous." I stepped closer. "We should sit down with him and explain what's happened. I'm sure he'd understand—"

Kieran's bark of laughter sounded harsh in the quiet emptiness outside the city. "Right. Serve him some clavo, recite a few Verses, and tell him I'm a fraud. That's a great plan."

His sarcasm stung.

Be patient. He's the One's chosen. "Would you at least consider it?"

"Consider taking strategic advice from a songkeeper? And a barely grown one, at that?"

His taunt was so unexpected I couldn't form an answer.

He raked a hand through his hair. "Linette, I was exploring Sidian when you were still playing cover-and-ambush in Braide Wood. I know what I'm doing."

If he'd thought I was too inexperienced and naïve, why had he asked for my help in Sidian? I struggled to gather the strands of my dignity. "I'm not a child. I was old enough to be life-pledged." The words brought a familiar stab, a twisting pain behind my ribs.

Kieran's condescension instantly changed to pity. I wasn't sure which reaction I hated more. He rested a hand on his sword hilt, as he often did when uncomfortable. "I know. I didn't . . ." He shook his head. "Let's go." His restless energy propelled him toward the gates. "Nolan will be awake and hungry—as always."

I followed, relieved at the change in subject. "He's a growing boy."

Kieran's snort showed what he thought of that description. "If I'd known he'd be as hard to keep fed as a herd of lehkan . . ."

I scurried to keep up with his long strides. "Yes?"

He rubbed his neck and hid a smile. "I'd still take him in and count myself lucky."

"He is sweet."

"Sweet? Yesterday he sneaked into Zarek's armory and stole a dagger. Said he needed a spare. He's reckless, devious, suspicious. Always into something."

Like someone else I knew.

By the time we reached the palace, I had forgiven Kieran's latest flare of annoyance with me. In the past seasons, I had learned that his temper blew from major to minor keys as quickly as the music of a spice-wood flute. The weight of his calling pressed him night and day. He needed support, and if that meant enduring his cutting words, I simply needed more patience.

"Will you stop by after the rains?" His tone was offhand, but he paused in the front hall, waiting for my answer.

I pushed back my hood and twisted a strand of my silver-blonde hair. I hadn't found time to put it into traditional Hazorite braids this morning. "If you like. Nolan arranged another meeting for me with the messengers this morning. I can give you a report later."

His eyes narrowed in calculation. "If they could learn the Verses and travel to all the villages, we'd make real progress."

"I'll do what I can. At least they'll be ready if King Zarek allows it."

Kieran gave a curt nod. "He's holding court today and wants me there. I'll ask him again."

"Go with the One," I said quietly. But Kieran was already striding away.

I walked toward the wing of the palace that housed the king's messengers, slowing my pace. Change comes gradually to hearts and countries. Rushing wouldn't alter that. Years of songkeeper training had formed patience in me that Kieran would never have—patience that seemed to annoy him. In fact, everything I did seemed to annoy him lately, and I hadn't figured out why.

I shook off the dark mood and entered the gathering hall to find that Nolan had faithfully spread word about this morning's meeting. Clusters of youths surrounded the tables. The boys looked up from table games. A few frowned and slouched back in a show of disinterest. Others smiled, bringing light and eagerness to their faces. They were so young. Most hadn't seen their families in years—given or sold to the king as disposable commodities. Their self-reliance and loneliness tugged at my soul.

Dylan and I had talked often about the children we'd hoped to have one day, young lives to be treasured and guided and loved. Another pang of loss twisted my heart. The attack at Cauldron Falls still cast a long shadow over me, for there I'd lost not only the man I loved but also the children we would never have.

A tapestry of a bloody war scene covered the back wall, so I pulled out a bench and settled facing the doorway. I greeted the children warmly—the children who might not be my own but needed my love—as they gathered around me.

When I'd begun meeting with them a few weeks ago, Nolan's endorsement had eased the young messengers' wariness. My attempts to play a Hazorite long-whistle helped them accept me even more. The mouthpiece was tiny, and the holes were covered and uncovered in complex combinations to change the pitch.

Two of the boys pulled out their whistles and brandished them over their heads. "A reel!"

Time to endure some good-natured teasing. I took my whistle from a pocket of my tunic. Grinning, the boys drew deep breaths and dove in to the music. They had taught me the melody yesterday, but I struggled to keep up. By the time the song ended, I was breathless and laughing.

The other boys cheered and called for another song. For a wonderful moment their faces lit with the innocent energy of children, instead of the grim, fearful expressions they usually wore.

I lowered the long-whistle. "Time to review our lessons."

Young voices groaned and muttered protests. A couple of the boys wandered off and made a point of resuming table games at one side of the room; but several settled around me. One boy who couldn't be more than ten plopped down near my feet. "Let's sing the one about getting power."

I ruffled his dark hair and smiled into his eager eyes. "It's not about getting power. It's about honoring the One for His strength and kindness."

The messengers exchanged looks. A few rolled their eyes. The boys were glad to learn new songs, and their skills at memorizing made them ideal students. But though they mimicked the words, they viewed the Verses as little more than stories to tell around a heat trivet on a cold night.

Holy One, show me how to lead these boys to You.

I played an introduction on the whistle, and the boys cheered and applauded. Then I set the instrument aside, and they joined me in singing one of the songs of feast days.

Awesome in majesty, perfect in power,
One to Deliver us, He is our tower.
Enemies circle us, darkness descending;
He is the Morning Light, love without ending.

Lord of the Verses that teach us Your way,
Guardian of seasons and Chief of each day,
Looking with mercy on each need we bring,
You give us strength through the Songs as we sing.

Their voices rose with enthusiasm. Some throats cracked as they wavered between the lighter registers of boyhood and deeper tones of approaching adulthood.

"Will singing these Songs really give us power?" one teen asked as the last note faded from the hall.

A younger boy bounced up to his knees. "Or speed? Will it make us faster?"

Another messenger gave him a playful punch. "Nothing will make you faster." He turned toward me. "Besides, you have to sing at the Lyric tower. That's where the One lives, right?"

I fought back a sigh. Like their king, these boys were intrigued by what magical powers the One might grant them, what advantages

He offered over their hill-gods. "He lives everywhere. The tower is just a special place where we gather to worship Him."

"Like a shrine," one of them asserted.

Movement by the doorway caught my eye. Nolan slipped into the room and lounged against the back wall, observing my efforts with a grin. Slim build, eyes framed by dark lashes, and a black thatch of hair that needed trimming—in recent seasons, Nolan had grown to look even more like his father.

I beckoned him forward. "Nolan has seen the Lyric tower. Let's ask him. Is it like a shrine?"

A hint of red brushed across Nolan's cheeks, but he sauntered in and planted himself next to me on the bench. "It's not like our shrines at all. Or like the hill-gods."

The boys listened to him intently. As part of the agreement to serve Zarek and the people of Hazor, Kieran had bargained for Nolan to be freed from his role as a messenger. But to these boys, Nolan was still one of them—a messenger who had survived capture by the "barbarians" of Braide Wood, endured Zarek's prison, traveled to the mysterious city of Lyric, and now had been claimed as son by the Restorer.

"Messengers! Report to the king's court." A herald in the doorway barked out the command, and the boys scrambled from the room.

My brief opportunity evaporated. Once again, I'd made scant progress. Who knew whether they would all return safely from their tasks?

Nolan seemed to sense my melancholy. "They'll be fine." He ducked his chin down and peered up at me through his bangs. "He was grumpier than usual this morning. Is he worried about his sister?"

"He has a lot on his mind."

Nolan shrugged. "He'll be happier tonight."

"Why?"

"He's agreed to spar with Zarek after court this morning."

My breath caught. "He can't do that."

A grin stretched slowly across Nolan's face. "You're welcome to tell him."

I winced. "You know he won't listen. But if Zarek learns the truth . . ."

Nolan's smile disappeared. "I know." His hand moved to the dagger tucked in his boot sheath. "That's why I plan to be there."

Even worse. I had as little control over Nolan as I did over Kieran. "All right. Then I want to be there too."

Nolan opened his mouth to argue, but I cut him off. "The One sent me here to help, and I can't help Kieran if he's dead."

"I don't think it's a good idea." His jaw clamped shut with a stubborn thrust.

I gave him a sweet smile. "Then I'll have to tell him you were gambling with the other messengers last night."

Nolan gaped at me. "How did you know?"

I held my smile and waited.

Finally his eyes narrowed and he gave a grudging nod. "I'll find you when court is over." He hurried toward the door and disappeared down the hall.

I sat down and pressed my hands against my face. I'd blackmailed him to get my way. He and his father were rubbing off on me.

The old songkeeper proverb said it best. If you want to blend into the chorus, sing in the same key. Here in Hazor, it seemed that deception and manipulation were the keys of choice. How long could I remain here before the music of my soul completely changed?

CHAPTER
3

LINETTE

SCRAPES AND CLANGS echoed in the training hall below us. Crouched behind storage containers on a small balcony, Nolan and I watched as Kieran dodged another vicious swing of Zarek's blade. His sword blocked a heavy overhand blow, then he jumped back and waited for the king's next move, feigning nonchalance.

I bit my lip. Bracing my hand on a crate, I leaned to the side to follow the action. Why had I insisted that Nolan bring me along? This dangerous sparring squeezed my lungs until I couldn't breathe.

"So the messengers could travel through Hazor." Kieran side-stepped in a relaxed crouch. "Share the Verses. That will cut down on the disagreements you've been dealing with." He feinted to Zarek's left side, then attempted to slice past his opponent's guard but failed.

"The messengers are busy with my work." Zarek charged forward. Steel flashed as if he planned to carve Kieran into one of the sculptures on the city walls. For a time neither man spoke, as the sparring grew more intense.

Beside me, Nolan's muscles were tight and alert. If Zarek's intent turned lethal, he'd probably leap from the balcony to help his father. I rested a hand lightly on the boy's back, trying to steady us both.

The two men below us pulled apart, both breathing hard. Zarek propped his sword against a bench, removed his gold-embroidered

THE DELIVERER

tunic, and wiped his shaved head. Gleaming with sweat, the powerful muscles of his upper body displayed his strength.

Kieran blotted the loose sleeve of his tunic against his forehead.
"You could . . ." He took a few breaths. ". . . spare a few messengers—
if you're serious about steering your people in a new direction."

Zarek frowned at the challenge and picked up his sword. "If I
weren't serious, you wouldn't be here. Your body would be buried in
small pieces in the fields outside of Lyric." He traced a small pattern
in the air.

Kieran raised his weapon. "Funny. That's not how I remember it.
I recall having my blade to your throat."

Why did Kieran insist on taunting him? Did he have a death
wish?

Zarek's teeth flashed. "And I seem to remember having your city
surrounded."

Kieran dipped his head in a nod of acknowledgement. "But the
One had other plans."

"Let's see whom he favors today." Zarek exploded forward and
their swords engaged. The tempo became more aggressive as they
circled around the practice room.

I squeezed my eyes shut, grabbing Nolan's arm. A loud series of
clashes ended in a sharp hiss of indrawn breath, and my eyes popped
open.

A red stain spread across the white linen of Kieran's tunic where
it clung to his ribs. I gasped, and both men glanced upward.

Nolan pulled me back into the shadows.

Zarek frowned. "I think we've got voles in the rafters. I'll have to
send someone to clear them out." He turned back to Kieran, resting
his sword irreverently over one shoulder like a farmer's test gauge.
"Are you going soft? You used to give me more of a challenge."

Kieran winced. "Maybe you've improved."

Zarek's laugh rumbled through his chest. He clapped Kieran on
the back, causing him to stumble a step forward. "I'll consider your
request for messengers." Abruptly, he grabbed his tunic and left the

room, hurrying to the next thing that drew his attention. Kieran often complained about Zarek's boundless energy. I could see why, though at the moment I could summon only relief.

As soon as the king's steps faded, Kieran staggered to a bench and slumped down. He hugged his ribs and let loose a string of curses.

I quickly covered Nolan's ears, but he pulled back, whispering a protest.

"Nolan." Kieran's voice was as sharp as his blade. His upward gaze blasted in our direction, seeming to see through our hiding place. "Get down here."

Nolan swallowed hard and straightened, looking over the top of a crate. "Coming."

He placed a finger over his lips and motioned for me to stay hidden, but I wouldn't let him face Kieran's temper alone. I followed him down the ladder.

When he saw me, Kieran's frown darkened. "Have you completely lost your mind? What are—? No. Don't answer that." He moved his hand away from his side. Blood soaked the fabric. "Since you're here, I could use some help."

The floor seemed to wobble, and the walls of the room shrank inward. Over the buzzing in my ears, I barely heard Kieran's words.

"Nolan, grab her. She's going down."

I fumbled for a bench and sat, trying to breathe. "Don't be . . . silly. I'm . . . fine."

"You look kind of funny," Nolan said with adolescent bluntness.

I shook my head, but the effort made my stomach lurch. "It's nothing."

"Help her back to her rooms." Kieran's tone flattened.

"No." I stared at the floor, avoiding the sight of blood, and worse, the ridicule in his eyes. "You can't leave here dripping blood all over. Someone will tell Zarek." I turned to Nolan. "Find something to use as a bandage."

Nolan dug through a storage cubby and unearthed a towel. I unwound my fabric belt. "This should work to hold it in place."

I glanced toward Kieran, who calmly blotted blood from his side. Dizziness prickled my head like the needles of a pine branch. I shoved the belt into Nolan's hands. "You bandage him. I'll keep watch."

I stumbled to the doorway, leaned against the frame, and checked both directions of the hall, drawing in slow, deep breaths.

"You worked at the healer lodge in Braide Wood," Kieran said.

I couldn't tell if he sounded exasperated or simply puzzled. "I helped. Mostly with the mind-poisoned. I'm not a healer."

Nolan coughed to cover a laugh at my queasiness. "I'll patch this up better when we're back at our rooms. He'll be fine."

I'd seen the wounded after the battle of Morsal Plains—helped them without a qualm. Delivered Kendra's baby without a problem. Yet Kieran's relatively minor injury made me woozy. Why couldn't I maintain my composure now? I kept my gaze on the hallway, humiliation heating my skin. "The way is clear. You can go now."

The men slipped past me. "Sure you're all right?" Nolan paused in the hall.

"I'm fine. Take care of your father." *And leave before I embarrass myself further.*

"I still want to meet after classes this afternoon." Kieran's tone was unreadable. "Unless you're not well."

"I said I'm fine." My snappish tone surprised me.

Kieran chuckled. "Good. See you later." He and Nolan sauntered down the hall as if the threat of discovery added fun to their day.

I felt a sudden impulse to knock their heads together. Clearly I was absorbing too much of the violence of this culture. If I stayed in Hazor long enough, maybe I'd understand the appeal of banging at each other with swords. I frowned at a rack of wooden practice weapons.

Leather gauntlets hanging from a peg triggered a flare of memory: Dylan on his lehkan, charging across the plateau at the end of a day of training, his smile bright under a face smudged with dirt, his strong hand reaching down to snare a flower. He had pulled up before me in a skidding of hooves. Bounding off his mount, he presented the small red-bud stem to me while other guardians nearby cheered and I blushed.

With a deep breath, I pressed my grief back into its cubby. I had work to do.

An afternoon of classes with a group of tradeswomen from the city restored my equilibrium. They seemed genuine in their curiosity and asked challenging questions. The Verses' call to keep the night separate from the day was a sticking point for them, since they all counted on Sidian's huge outdoor lightwalls to keep the shops in business half the night.

My passion kindled as I explained the love behind His Verses. At times, I felt as if the melody of our Maker flowed through me while we talked. My time with the women helped me remember my purpose. By suppertime, as I wove my way along the jagged corridors to Kieran and Nolan's rooms, my doubts and anxieties had faded like a stray sour note.

Kieran answered my knock and waved me inside. He turned to a side table, where steam rose from a bowl over a heat trivet. I sank onto the couch.

Garish banners appliquéd the angled walls of Kieran's common room. He hadn't bothered making any changes to the palace apartment that Zarek had given him. He probably couldn't describe the décor if he were asked. But he undoubtedly knew every exit, obvious and hidden, and the location of each weapon. His sword never strayed far from his side.

I tucked my legs under me and studied a particularly ugly sculpture. The stone was polished, exquisitely threaded with variegated colors. But the image of faces contorted in rage and pain made me shudder.

A longing for Braide Wood welled up in me like mist in the Lyric tower. I missed simple log homes. I hungered to compose songs under the trees near the healers' lodge, or pray with Lukyan while afternoon rain pattered his roof, or join the tower musicians on feast days. I was tired of the harsh lines of the buildings in Hazor, the crowded city, and the wary people.

Kieran handed me a steaming mug, then began prowling his room.

I bit back a sigh. Sidian clavo tasted stronger than the clans' and had a bitter tang, but I sipped without complaint. I wouldn't burden Kieran with my homesickness.

"So do you think Royan and Havid will keep their arguments out of class tomorrow?" He didn't hide the frustration in his voice. The other songkeepers with us, an older married couple, seemed to delight in arguing—about interpretations of the Verses, about how they should be taught, about each step in the work here.

Once again, it fell on me to be a peacemaker. "They only fight because every detail matters to them so much."

Kieran made a snarling sound in his throat and stopped to face me. "Well, it's not helping. The Hazorites are confused enough. Maybe Zarek threw too much support behind our work. The people are substituting the One for the hill-gods because they think they have no choice."

He was tired. Zarek's invitation to teach the Verses had been a rare opportunity, but one that carried weight. Kieran looked leaner than usual and hollow-eyed. With the constant intrigues at the palace, he probably slept with his bootknife in his hand and one eye open. Each day was a balancing act on a thin truce with the king. And I'd seen the longing in Kieran's eyes when he looked toward the mountains. I knew he was as homesick as I was.

"Be patient. Look at how much you've done already. The shrines are all closed." For a renegade with little knowledge of the Verses, he'd brought tremendous change, especially through his friendship with King Zarek.

He resumed his pacing, tight and focused as a mountain cat.

His anxiety was contagious, and I fought to keep my voice calm. "The One isn't asking you to carry this alone." Couldn't he sit still for a moment?

As if he heard my thoughts, Kieran slouched onto the couch near me. "I know." He propped a foot on the low table. "But it's not what I expected."

His quiet honesty tugged at my heart. Hard work and danger weren't the challenges that strained him the most. Shortly after arriving, we'd gotten word that Cameron had declared himself king in Lyric. Kieran's newfound faith had been shaken. He'd prepared to return to the clans, but the One appeared to him and told him to stay in Hazor. In spite of the direction, the inner struggle almost tore him in two.

He turned to me with a wry smile. "After everything that's happened, a couple of idiot songkeepers shouldn't get to me."

I raised my eyebrows. "I think I should be offended."

He stretched. "You may be a songkeeper, but you're no idiot." His expression hardened. "Most of the time."

He wasn't going to ignore my clumsy spying earlier. "I'm sorry. Nolan was worried about you, and I didn't want him getting into trouble."

Kieran shook his head slowly. "I'm sure there's logic I'm missing somehow."

"These matches with Zarek. Why do you take the risk? If he hadn't hurried off today, he would have noticed you didn't heal."

"I can't tell what he's thinking lately." Kieran rubbed his temples.

"Headache?"

He dropped his head onto the couch back and closed his eyes. "Yes." He sat in silence for a few minutes. "Tell me it's making a difference."

"I've already told you that."

He squinted at me. "Then why? What did I do wrong?"

Good. Honest doubts. He hadn't talked about his loss of Restorer powers for a long time. "Who said you did anything wrong? Did Susan do something wrong when the Restorer gift lifted from her?"

"No. But she needed to go back to her world. It made sense that the One chose a new Restorer."

I grinned. "You didn't think so at the time."

He frowned. "Point taken. But once I offered my life to Him . . ."

"He used you to save Lyric and to remove poison from Jake."

He made a dismissive gesture with one hand. "But if I did what I was supposed to do, then why . . . why did He take away the gift?"

"Kieran, He still speaks with you. He's given you an important role. That hasn't changed just because Jake is the Restorer now." I paused, searching for the right thing to say. "Susan told me that she began to find peace when she stopped demanding explanations."

He sat up and met my eyes. "And you? Have you stopped asking for reasons?" He studied me in the way he watched everything around him. Intent. Absorbing and analyzing every detail. He saw too much.

I set my mug on the table and edged away. "We aren't talking about me."

Quiet spread over him. "You never talk about him."

Of course I didn't. Because if I talked about Dylan, I might shatter. I might start crying and never stop. And Kieran needed me. Hazor needed me. The One needed me. I couldn't afford to be weak.

"Linette?" His voice was rough, insistent.

Why was he tormenting me? Whole days went by when I didn't think about Dylan. At night when I tried to remember him, his face blurred as if I saw him through tears. I was afraid of forgetting him. Of betraying his memory.

How could my memories of Dylan be fading? I had no trouble remembering the moment when Tristan told me—the details of that searing pain. A giant fist had reached inside of me and wrenched away every bit of life and joy, leaving a husk of chaff—and little else. I wasn't the same person.

But I couldn't explain all that to the man beside me. I folded my hands in my lap. "The One is perfect in His love and purposes. That's all I need to know." My voice was prim, hollow. When I dared to glance at Kieran, undisguised disappointment shadowed his face.

I stood. "I should go."

"Maybe you should." Then he sighed. "Linette, I wasn't prying. I was asking because of Nolan."

"Nolan?"

"He doesn't talk about Shayla." He shifted, then winced from his recent injury. "I thought you'd know . . ."

Shame burned my face. Kieran wanted to help his son with grief about his mother's death, and I shut him out with songkeeper clichés.

Dear Maker, I keep doing the wrong thing.

Nolan darted in from the back room and skidded to a stop. "Linette? Can you stay for supper?" He noticed our tension and glanced at Kieran uneasily. Nolan still moved with the agile speed of a sixteen-year-old messenger, yet he was often awkward around his newfound father, as if he were wearing boots that weren't quite the right size.

Kieran's eyes softened as he looked at his son, but the planes of his face remained hard. "She can't stay."

I'd been dismissed—relegated to the ranks of the annoying song-keepers that Kieran barely tolerated. And I deserved it.

Nolan threw me a questioning glance.

My lips forced a smile. "I'll see you tomorrow." I crossed to the doorway and slipped out, then hurried along the hallway, trying to outrun my failure. When I reached my room I shut out the confus-ing world of Hazor and fell to my knees. My throat felt thick as I sang a feast day litany over and over, the melody scarcely above a whisper.

"Where can we seek Him?
He seeks us.
What can we give Him?
What He first gave.
Holy One, we answer Your call.
Holy One, we give You our lives.
Holy One, change our hearts."

Slowly, my heart calmed. Tomorrow I'd find a time to broach the subject of his mother's death with Nolan. I'd diffuse the ten-sion between the other songkeepers and protect Kieran from that unnecessary conflict. And King Zarek planned to visit the class I taught for the palace women. Perhaps I could find out if Kieran was in any danger from him.

Food held no appeal, so I didn't bother with supper. As I curled up on my sleep pallet, I tried to conjure images of Dylan riding across the plains near Braide Wood. Instead, I kept seeing Kieran's dark eyes—glaring at me in annoyance, flickering with inner doubts, and assessing me with cold disappointment.

Holy One, I want to go home.

CHAPTER
4

LINETTE

KING ZAREK HAD arrived. Energy surged higher in the room, and the palace women focused on the door behind me. Eyes grew wider, spines straighter. Some smiled coyly, some swallowed nervously. I turned to welcome him, and his gaze raked me with a raw appreciation that made me grateful for my long, full song-keeper's robe.

Even so, heat flushed my neck and my confidence wobbled. Teaching under the king's observation no longer seemed like a good idea. I managed a pleasant nod. "Thank you for coming." Turning back to the women arranged on comfortable chairs and cushions around me, I caught several courtesans sending covert winks and giggles in the king's direction as he came farther into the room and took up a position against the side wall where he could watch everyone.

I folded my hands in my lap. I was not here to impress a human king. If I became distracted, the other women would get nothing from our conversation. "Let's review the creed. *Awesome in majesty . . .*"

"*Is the One eternal.*" I felt some measure of relief that they remembered the response. We continued in unison.

"Perfect in His might and power, the only truth and only source.
He made all that is, and loves all He made.
His works are beyond our understanding."

The tangible power of the words never failed to move me. My heart steadied, and my gaze moved around the room as my students continued reciting the basic tenants of faith. One young woman closed her eyes, her face glowing as the truth washed over her. Others nodded.

I glanced over at Zarek. He watched closely, arms crossed and brow furrowed. At least he had stopped leering.

"In every time of great need, a Restorer is sent
To fight for the people and help the guardians.
The Restorer is empowered with gifts to defeat our enemies . . ."

I shot another glance at the king. How did he feel about this prophecy when he had so recently been one of the enemies? His face gave nothing away.

"And turn the people's hearts back to the Verses." The women finished and looked at me.

"Very good. The next part of the Verses is more challenging. It talks about a promise that we don't fully understand.

'We wait in the darkness for the One who brings light.
The Deliverer will come.
And with His coming all darkness will be defeated.'

"Some of the songkeepers believe that the Deliverer will be a final Restorer who will create a world with no more wars."

Zarek made a sound like a chuckle.

I pressed on. "My teacher, Lukyan, believed that the Deliverer will defeat more than the darkness of the world; he will also give us a way to be rid of the darkness within ourselves."

"We are full of life force, not evil," said an older woman who was a practitioner, a type of healer in Sidian.

Another woman leaned forward. "Maybe some. But I've known a few people that carry evil within their bodies."

Nods and murmurs of agreement rose from the group.

"But darkness isn't so bad." A hawk-faced girl addressed the others. "We gain power from touching darkness."

"No," I said quickly. "We weren't meant to carry darkness." That stirred more debate and eager questions. I forgot all about Zarek as I shared my understanding of the One's intent and how He planned to restore us one day. Music hummed in my heart—echoes of the last time I joined the songkeepers in tower worship. How I wished I could take all these women there so they, too, could feel the mist lower onto their faces and hear the gentle whisper of their Maker.

"Interesting tales." Zarek's deep voice drew instant attention. "But you all have places to be, don't you?" The women scattered like a burst of feathered moths from a cluster of ferns, a few murmuring quick good-byes, some barely glancing at me.

I rose, keeping my gaze on the polished black floor. "I'm sorry. I was told you approved this meeting time. It wasn't my intention to keep anyone from her work . . ."

Zarek strode farther into the room and took a seat on the bench where I'd been teaching. He gestured at me to join him. "If Restorers arise only at times of specific need, what happens when the need has passed?"

I perched on the edge of the bench and tucked my hands into my sleeves to hide their tremor. "Whatever the One chooses to do next." *Don't let me say the wrong thing.* "Early in the last generation, Kahlareans invaded Sandor clan near the sea. Oren was called by the One and spoke to the Council, giving them courage to unite against the threat."

The tension in my fingers eased as I continued the history lesson, pretending the man beside me was another young messenger curious about clan legends. Oren, Illias, Mikkel.

Zarek shifted, drawing my attention back to him.

"And the one before Kieran?"

My heart warmed, and I smiled. "Susan. Her husband came from Rendor, but he found her from beyond the clans. She was different from any Restorer that came before, not a guardian, but more like a healer or songkeeper. She was one of the few who didn't die in battle."

The king's eyes narrowed. Was it curiosity or some darker intent? "Did she pass her gifts to Kieran, then?"

"I . . . I'm not sure. The day after the battle of Morsal Plains, she returned to her home. That might have been when . . . but . . . Kieran didn't tell me about his Restorer signs until much later." Sweat prickled along my hairline. "You should ask him."

He stretched and rose to his feet, then braced one foot on the bench and leaned toward me. "You have a true gift for patient explanation. Not like Kieran."

"I was trained as a songkeeper. But he—"

"Will you meet with me tomorrow morning?" His expression seemed open, sincere. No different from the young messengers or palace women I taught.

Kieran had warned me to stay out of Zarek's line of sight as much as possible, but Kieran didn't trust anyone. Yes, the king made me uneasy, but I didn't want my fears to hinder me from an opportunity to help someone searching for truth. "Of course. I'm happy to answer any questions I can."

The king rewarded me with a broad smile. "Tomorrow, then." He strode from the room, several guards falling in behind him. I used my sleeve to blot moisture from my forehead. Had I done the right thing?

The door to Kieran's apartment was braced open when I arrived that evening. As I often did when the songkeepers gathered to meet with Kieran, I walked straight into his common room.

And stopped short.

Between the low couches on the left side of the room and the eating area to the right, a barely dressed Hazorite woman was wrapping herself around Kieran. He was trying to pry her off but didn't seem to be making much progress. I took a step back, ready to slip out before they noticed me. Then I hesitated. Kieran looked like he could use some help.

I cleared my throat.

He looked my direction and blanched. "Zarek's idea of a thank-you gift." He peeled the woman away and held her at arm's length. Was that a blush creeping up his neck?

Seeing him flustered tempted me to grin, but I kept my face expressionless. "Should I come back later?"

"No!" His voice was edged with panic. "Would you stop?" He swatted the girl's hand away as she walked her fingers over his biceps.

She moved in closer. Really no more than a girl, all huge eyes and myriad black braids, she leaned in and gazed up at him. "Don't send me away. The king would be displeased with me." Behind the overt sensuality she'd been taught to portray, fear edged her words.

Kieran pushed her back. "Tell him whatever you want. But you can't stay here." There was definitely heightened color over his cheekbones.

Her eyes pooled with sudden tears, and Kieran scrambled around the common room table, adding more distance between them.

Amusing as Kieran's discomfiture was, I took pity on them both and stepped into the room. "What's your name?"

"Ria." The girl spared a glance in my direction but returned to studying Kieran.

I put an arm around her and guided her to the couch. "Ria, you know that Kieran is here to teach your people."

She nodded, finally pulling her attention away from him. I poured orberry juice from the pitcher on the low table and gave her the mug. She took a long drink, her hands shaking. "King Zarek is grateful. That's why he sent me."

Kieran made a strangled noise, but I ignored him.

"That was generous of him. But Zarek doesn't understand the things the One asks of us. He asks His people to keep their bodies pure. To only give them to one person—and only in a life-bond of marriage." An annoying blush warmed my face as I struggled to explain this while Kieran hovered in the background.

Her eyes widened. "But the hill-gods want us to give our bodies to them. It gives them power, and then they give us power. Or did. Until the king closed the shrines."

Poor child. "Ria, were you working in the shrines?"

She shook her head and the narrow braids bounced around her face. "Not yet. My parents sold me to our shrine in Trezold, but when that closed, I was sent here." She dropped her chin. "This is my first assignment. If I'm sent away, Bezreth will give me to the prison guards . . . or worse."

Like a darting minnow, she slipped past me and threw herself at Kieran's feet. "Please keep me."

He choked and managed to free one leg, pulling back as she clung to his other ankle. "Let go. Look out for my bootknife." He threw me a pleading look. "Do something."

Now he wanted my help? Yesterday he'd told me he didn't need strategic advice from an immature songkeeper.

Forgive me, Holy One. I'm supposed to humbly serve. As Kieran dragged a few steps back, bumping into a side table, giggles welled up in my throat.

Nolan bounded in the open apartment door. "Linette, one of the messengers asked—" He pulled up short. Kieran's skin mottled, and he reached down to pry Ria off his leg. She clung like a stubborn strand of waterweed. Nolan's eyebrows disappeared under his bangs. "Who's she?"

Laughter strangled me, but I covered it with a cough. "Her name is Ria. Your father is trying to explain the Verses to her."

Nolan looked ready to comment, but Kieran shot us both an icy glare. "Enough." The bite in his voice finally convinced Ria to release his leg, but she remained huddled on the floor, crying into her hands.

"Am I to presume we aren't having our scheduled meeting?" Royan's gravelly voice came from the doorway. My laughter died as he cast a withering sneer at the sobbing girl and Kieran's red face. The songkeeper from Blue Knoll had criticized every aspect of Kieran's work in the past seasons. Now he'd have more to complain about.

I hurried over to Ria and coaxed her up from the floor. "Shh. It's all right. We'll figure this out."

Kieran raked a hand through his hair, leaving short black tufts standing on end. "Come in. I want the report on—"

"No." Royan crossed his arms. "I fail to see any way that this is helping our goals here." With a sniff, he turned on his heel and left.

I groaned.

Kieran looked ready to fling a dagger after the retreating man. "This gets better and better."

"Really, who is she?" Nolan's eyes lingered on Ria's bare shoulders.

I angled her away from him. "A gift from Zarek."

"A gift that we're returning," Kieran added quickly.

Nolan's large, dark eyes gleamed. "If you don't want her, can I have her?"

Kieran turned and grabbed Nolan by the scruff of the neck, jerking him toward the door. "Go tell Royan and Havid that we'll meet tonight during supper. I need their report on their trip outside Sidian."

Even with his father's forceful shove, Nolan had trouble tearing himself away. Once he was out of sight, Kieran faced us. Shards of black obsidian glinted in his eyes. Ria shivered, but his glare targeted me. "Any ideas?"

"You can't send her back. Who knows what would happen to her?"

"You're not suggesting I keep her."

"Of course not. I'll take care of her."

"Good. And keep her away from Nolan, too." The tightness of his jaw eased. "Thank you."

Of course he could relax now. His problem had just become my problem.

"I'm happy to help." Tempted to storm off like Royan, I managed to cover my irritation with placid songkeeper sweetness, although the effort nearly strangled me. *Don't complain. It's why you're here. Songkeepers serve where they're needed. No task too small. No task too large. Lukyan told you that a hundred times.*

I forced a smile onto my face. "Come, Ria. You'll be safe with me until Kieran can explain why he can't accept the king's gift."

I settled the young palace girl in my rooms, then hurried back to help calm the waters with the other songkeepers. When I reached Kieran's apartment, he and Nolan were sitting alone at the common room table. Nolan crumbled bread into piles on his plate while Kieran glared at a spot on the table. Tension pulled through the room like a rondalin string tuned too tightly.

I took a deep breath, trying to assess who needed help first. "Where are Royan and Havid?"

When Kieran didn't answer, Nolan gave a sullen shrug. "They're packing."

"Again?" I pulled up a chair and sat across from Kieran. "They didn't honestly think you were keeping a shrine girl here, did they?"

"Who knows what they think?" Kieran's arm circled his ribs.

"Should I speak with them?"

"Let them leave. They're miserable here." He tilted his chair back and glowered at the ceiling. "And you should go back with them."

A gasp caught in my lungs. He'd lost patience with me, too? Had I made too little progress in my work in Sidian? As much as I'd longed to leave with Tristan and Kendra, I wanted to make a difference here first. I glanced at Nolan, but he kept shredding pieces of bread and staring at his plate.

"No." The word burst from my lips and surprised me.

Kieran lowered his chin and stared at me.

I met his eyes. "You might not believe me, but I'm seeing some results. And today King Zarek asked me to meet with him."

His chair's front legs crashed back to the floor. "What?"

A songkeeper wasn't supposed to be smug, but Kieran wasn't the only one doing some good in Hazor. "I'm getting good questions from the palace women and building friendships with the messengers." I glanced to Nolan for support, and he nodded. "And tomorrow I'll talk to the king—"

"Send him your apologies. Better send a messenger tonight. Make some excuse. A fever. Some sickness. You're pale enough. He'll believe it."

I tugged the sleeves of my formal robe and folded my hands on the table. "Why would I do that? Zarek is hungry for truth."

Kieran's frown grew darker. "Zarek is hungry for a lot of things."

I wasn't about to avoid a wonderful opportunity clearly provided by the One. Kieran was probably frustrated that he hadn't made more progress with the king on his own. He and Zarek had a strange, uneasy friendship. Sometimes I thought that it was the king's unwillingness to accede anything to Kieran that kept Zarek noncommittal about the One. If he could talk with someone new, someone who didn't trigger his pride, perhaps a breakthrough would come. And perhaps Kieran would look at me with more respect. I wasn't a first-year apprentice.

I stood calmly. "May the One bless your house. Ask Him for favor as I meet with the king tomorrow."

A string of curses followed me out the door. Good thing Royan and Havid weren't in earshot.

CHAPTER
5

SUSAN

"WHAT'S FOR SUPPER?" Jon blitzed through the living room, threw himself into a clumsy pivot, and shoulder-checked himself against the wall. How could a ten-year-old make the whole house shake?

I set my fistful of silverware on the dining room table and shook my head. "Jon, not in the hou—"

His foot moved, and a soccer ball flew into the dining area toward my face.

I snatched the ball out of the air. Another second and Mark would have had to replace the glass china-cabinet door. Again. "Stir fry and brown rice. And take this outside." I hefted the ball to toss it back to him, but the scrawled letters on it caught my eye. Jake. Jon was using Jake's old soccer ball. My throat clogged.

Only a few years ago, Jake had been the grade-schooler charging through the house shouting questions about the dinner menu. Now he was so far away—

Don't go there.

Kids grew up and left home. It was a normal part of life.

My daughter Karen's messy room already sported new piles of college brochures, and even little Anne was too busy to snuggle when she got home from third grade each day.

Jon's face, capped with a mop of hair, popped around the door-frame of the living room. "Why can't we ever have cheeseburgers?"

43

I tossed him the ball and shook off my melancholy. "Stop complaining and call your sisters for supper. We need to eat early. My Bible study group is coming over tonight."

I went back to setting the table. Five places at supper. Five blue-and-white plates. Six chairs. I tucked forks beside each plate and skirted the extra chair, pausing to rest my hand on the polished maple. What was Jake doing right now? Did he think of us often? Was he safe?

Friends talked about the adjustment they had made when their firstborn headed to college. But at least that was a normal adjustment. If only my pain were that simple. No one besides Mark knew our family's secret.

Jake could be in real danger, and I had no way to find out. No way to send him a text of encouragement. No cell phone call that could reach him. Mark and I had agreed to wait one month. The month was almost up, and I stared at the calendar a dozen times a day.

"Hi, honey." Mark's arms circled me from behind.

I sagged backward into the secure warmth and swiveled my head for a quick kiss. "I didn't hear you come in. How was your day?"

Mark nuzzled my neck. "Better now." He turned me to face him. "How are you?"

His question wasn't a casual formality. He was still worried about me. When I drove Jon to his soccer games, I'd stand in the shadow of the trees on the edge of the park, avoiding the carefree conversations of other moms. When I sat at the kitchen table to help Anne with her spelling, I'd feel her tug my sleeve minutes later and realize my mind had drifted again.

"Susan?"

I blinked. Mark's grey-blue eyes studied me with concern. A few silver flecks shone in the blond waves of his hair. It had torn him apart when Medea and Cameron pulled me through the portal. I kept reassuring him I would heal, but frequent nightmares undermined my efforts to convince him.

I smoothed a curl at his temple and forced a smile. "I had a good day. Really. Where are you taking the kids tonight?"

"I thought we'd stop at the hardware store. We need washers for the bathroom sink again, and they have some linoleum on sale that might work for the basement."

My lips twitched. "Jon and Anne will love that. What else are you doing?"

"Hey." Mark stepped back and folded his arms, pretending to be affronted. "You know the faucet has been leaking again."

"Yes, dear." I sashayed back into the kitchen. "Any excuse to visit the hardware store."

He charged after me and tickled me until I shrieked. I beat him off with a plastic serving spoon, laughing myself breathless.

"Are we eating or what?" Karen's dry voice sounded from the doorway. "I'm supposed to be at work in an hour." Slouching against the doorframe with sophisticated nonchalance, my daughter rolled her eyes, but couldn't completely hide her affection.

We tumbled into chairs and joined hands for a brief prayer. Comfortable chaos burst out seconds later.

Anne piped up first. "Mommy, my guppy died. When can we get a new one?"

Jon's voice overlapped hers, as it often did. "Dad, the coach wants to schedule an extra soccer tournament. I forgot to bring the papers home, but you have to sign them. Hey! Anne's foot touched my chair. Tell her to stop."

"Mom, you really should do something about them. They're always fighting." This from Karen, who refused to believe that she and Jake used to act the same way.

I poked at a piece of broccoli and smiled. Food disappeared, a glass of water spilled, Anne howled, Karen sighed. Mark tried to tell me about his day but wasn't able to finish a sentence without interruption. I savored every second.

Months in Rhusican captivity had expanded my ability to appreciate the bits and pieces of average days.

Suffering crushed the very breath from the body, but somehow in the dust left behind, a space remained for gratitude—especially for the beauty of ordinary moments.

Soon the meal had been inhaled, and Karen helped me shove plates into the dishwasher. She closed the dishwasher door and sighed.

She seemed a little more withdrawn than usual, and I debated whether to ask about it. Approaching a teen was tricky. She might bite my head off, but, then, that was just another scar of motherhood to be worn cheerfully—like stretch marks.

"Sweetie, is anything bothering you?"

She turned away with a shrug, but didn't leave the kitchen.

I waited.

"It's lame. I don't want it to bug me . . ."

"But?"

She faced me, dark brows drawn together. "Jake hasn't called once since he left for college. And his texts are so short. I mean, I knew he'd be busy and all, but he promised to stay in touch . . . let me know what it's like."

Pain squeezed my heart. I'd been so worried about Jake that I hadn't noticed the toll this was taking on Karen. Jon and Anne cheerfully accepted our explanation that a work-study opportunity had opened up and Jake had left early. When they groused about missing their chance to say good-bye, I distracted them with art projects to give him when he came home. But Karen . . .

"Honey, you mean the world to him. You know how guys are. He's not the best communicator. And he's probably so wrapped up in all the new things . . ."

The deceit had to stop. Mark kept Jake's cell phone hidden in our bedroom closet. He thought answering an occasional text would keep Karen from undue curiosity, but this couldn't continue.

She shrugged again. "Yeah. Gotta go. See ya later."

"Let's talk more when you get back from work." I caught her for a quick hug.

She pulled back and grinned. "Right. Like you could be coherent after ten p.m."

"Let's go," Mark called from the living room.

Everyone scrambled out the door just as my friend Janet pulled up in her mini-van. I always looked forward to our small group study, but tonight I felt desperate for the comfort I gleaned from my friends. I put a kettle of water on the stove while Janet unwrapped a plate of brownies. The doorbell rang and she hurried to let in the others.

"Denise can't come," Beth called from the living room. I carried in a tray of mugs and teabags as she tossed her jean jacket across one end of the couch. "Her kids have the flu."

"They're sick again?" Janet pushed some magazines aside and set out her plate.

Corina kicked off her shoes by the door and settled into her favorite chair. "We need to pray for her. She must be exhausted. They just got over strep."

"It's the back-to-school germ fest." I ducked out to get the hot water and filled everyone's mugs. Mingled scents triggered a series of vivid memories in my mind, like a movie trailer: holding a mug of clavo in Shamgar, braided spice trees in Lyric, the cloying smell of wintergreen in Rhus. I coaxed my attention back to the present.

After some animated minutes of catching up, we opened our study guides. We'd moved on from Deborah to study Gideon, Samson, and Ruth. Now we had reached Samuel and David.

Corina read the story of Goliath as we followed along in our Bibles. She grew starry-eyed as she looked up. "What I wouldn't give to fight battles for God."

I choked on a sip of tea. My thoughts swirled with images of tense battle plans, impossible odds, clashing swords, blood, and death. Not fantastical imaginings, but memories. Memories as vivid as the solid details of my scuffed furniture and stained rugs.

When faces turned my direction, I kept coughing and waved to the group to ignore me. I used to tell these friends anything, but now my secrets created an invisible wall of loneliness that closed me away and threatened to smother me. Is this what Mark had lived with all these years?

If I told them the truth, they'd call the men in white coats.

Come to think of it, heavy-duty psychiatric drugs held some appeal.

The discussion moved on, and I drew little boxes in the margin of my journal. My pen traced one square over and over until I poked through the paper.

"I gotta tell you, I get tired of hearing folks whine about their problems." Janet's voice jarred me back into the conversation. "If people obey God and keep a positive attitude, things always work out."

Indignation surprised me like a sudden pinch. "That's a little simplistic, isn't it?"

Corina stared in my direction, open-mouthed.

Careful, Susan, don't say too much. But I couldn't hold back. "Even when we're following God, we aren't immune to the suffering that's part of this world." Not to mention *other* worlds, but that was another issue.

Janet crossed her arms. "I think people cause a lot of their own pain." The smug tone reminded me she'd had few experiences that wrenched the soul.

My irritation faded. I didn't need to argue about the reality of pain in a Christian's life. Janet would face her own dark valleys one day. *And Lord, when that time comes, give me the grace to show her compassion and never say, "I told you so."*

Beth gave me a worried look from her place beside me on the couch. She patted my leg. "Let's go on to the next chapter."

I turned my journal pages, looking for a fresh sheet to take notes.

Deborah. The pencil sketch on the paper stilled my hand.

Months ago, a lifetime ago, I had slipped into the attic for time alone to prepare for one of these Bible studies. Deborah, a prophetess who led her people during a time of need, had inspired the drawing.

Later, Jake had left a note in the corner. "Cool sketch, mom."

Tonight something moved across the page.

I shrieked and dropped the notebook. "A bug!" Must have been a spider. Maybe it dropped down from the floor lamp next to the couch.

The others looked at me as if I weren't the only one contemplating the white coats. Sheepishly, I reached down to retrieve the book as they resumed the study.

I cautiously opened the journal. No squashed bug marred the paper. My image still stood beneath the sign "Oak of Susan," with the picture of a rough-sketched warrior approaching. The lines seemed to shiver.

Eyestrain? I pinched the bridge of my nose and dared another glance. This time I didn't look away.

The penciled man moved across the page like a first-draft animation cell. He held out a sword toward the woman in the picture.

My alter ego took the sword. Dark shapes shaded the margins, looming toward the two figures under the tree. The sketch of the man turned to look at me from the page. Jake!

His eyes pleaded for help. The shadows surrounding him grew fangs and continued to move closer to both figures, threatening and dire.

Impossible. Pictures didn't change themselves and move. Drawings of darkness didn't crowd in from the edges on their own. My journal couldn't be bringing me a message.

But then, portals to alternate worlds weren't supposed to exist either.

My heart raced. Jake needed us.

"Excuse me a second." I interrupted Corina in the middle of her thoughts on a verse, launched from the couch, and ran into the kitchen. I had to talk to Mark—now. Where was my cell phone? I rummaged through the basket on the counter where we tossed keys and mail. No, no, no. My purse. I found it and dumped the contents. My hands shook as I snatched up the phone and dialed. "Mark, get home now. Something—"

"Susan, are you okay?" Beth hovered uncertainly in the kitchen doorway.

I cleared my throat and tucked the phone out of sight. "I might be getting that new bug that's going around. Do you think anyone would mind if we wrapped up early?"

Her gaze traveled to the contents of my purse. "Do you need some aspirin? You're awful pale."

I shook my head. "Just . . . just tell them. Please."

I begrudged each agonizing second it took for the meeting to break up and for Mark to get home.

The second he walked in the door, I pulled him out of earshot of Jon and Anne.

"What happened? Are you all right?" He'd been asking me that a lot lately, but there was a new layer of concern in his voice. "You don't look so good."

I lifted my gaze to meet his. "Mark." Fear strained my throat. I held the journal out to him. "No more waiting. Jake's in trouble."

CHAPTER
6

SUSAN

AFTER WE TUCKED our two youngest in bed, my husband and I conferenced on the couch. Mark rubbed his thumb along the sketch in my journal, picking up a smudge of pencil lead on his skin. "Susan, there's nothing here."

"But I saw it. The picture changed."

He tugged the book from my hands. "Come here." He nestled me against his side and pressed a soft kiss against my temple. "You haven't been sleeping well since you got back."

I pulled away from him. "You think I imagined it."

He didn't break eye contact, but he didn't answer, either.

My jaw squeezed and muscles tightened all the way down my neck. "You believe in a portal and an alternate world and Restorers. So why can't my journal send me a message?"

"It's not that I don't believe you—"

"Mommy." Anne whimpered from the entry to the living room and rubbed her eyes. "I had a bad dream." She squinted against the lamplight and took another tentative step forward.

I opened my arms, and she flung her gangly body onto my lap. Sometimes eight-year-olds still needed to be rocked and lullabied. I whispered soothing words against her hair, drawing peace from the act of comforting her. Her wavy blonde hair smelled like strawberry shampoo, and her skin was flushed from restless sleep. A few stray scabs from summer's mosquito bites still peppered her coltish legs. She tucked her bare toes into the hem of her nightgown, curling into a tight ball on my lap. The pull toward the portal suddenly seemed ridiculous. Could I seriously consider leaving her again? And Jon and Karen and Mark? But if Jake was in danger . . .

"Maybe you should talk to someone." Mark rubbed the evening stubble on his chin, producing an irritating sandpaper sound.

Scrape the soft places of my heart while you're at it.

My arms tightened, and Anne squirmed. "Talk to someone?" Where exactly would I find a counselor who knew how to deal with the trauma of Rhusican torture?

He glanced at the top of Anne's head and pressed his lips together. "Let me put her back to bed. Then we can talk."

The last thing I needed was his oh-so-patient and rational lecture about how I wasn't dealing with everything I'd been through. Or the probing questions born from his intuition that I'd hidden the worst. He lifted Anne from my unresisting arms. She was already drowsing.

When he disappeared down the hallway, I stared at the closed journal on the table.

The living sketch wasn't our only problem. For days now, I'd felt an impression of danger—a low crackle of anxiety in the background like a banked fire; but tonight the worry kindled into full flame, and urgency burned in my marrow.

Mark had hidden the portal stones. Maybe in the garage. More likely in the basement. In the past he'd hidden one among the jumble of his workbench. I needed to find them. Jake needed me—with or without Mark's help.

I shot from the couch, ran down the hall, and scrambled down the basement stairs, scraping my ankle on one of the bottom treads when I slipped. My stockinged feet found purchase on the cold concrete.

I pulled out a drawer of screws and scooped them into my hands, letting the bits of metal fall through my fingers. Nothing was hiding beneath them, or in the next drawer. I yanked a third so hard it came all the way out of the storage unit. I upended the drawer and pawed through reels of speaker wire, boxes of nails, paint stirrers, and sheets of sandpaper.

"Planning on a midnight painting project?" Mark asked from the foot of the stairs, sounding genuinely confused.

"Where did you put them?" I jerked open an overhead cabinet and clambered up onto the bench so I could reach the top shelf.

"Them?" He walked over to the workbench.

I pulled out a power drill kit and handed it down to him, reaching farther along the recesses of the shelf. "The portal stones."

Mark hissed in his breath as if he'd dropped the heavy tool on his foot. "This is your idea of discussing our options?" He reached for me.

I slammed the cabinet door closed. "What's to discuss? Jake's in danger. I've tried to tell you. You don't know—"

"I'll tell you what I know." He helped me down, and his hands tightened around my waist. "They nearly killed you."

The surge of adrenaline bled away, and I sagged, resting my forehead against his chest. "I'm fine. I made it back."

"You say things in your sleep. You wake up screaming." His chin leaned hard against the top of my head. "Do you really think you've been hiding how bad it was? I know I can't understand it all, but I want to help. Tell me what you need. Tell me what to do."

"I don't know." The hoarse whisper was the voice of a stranger, even though it came from my own throat. "I thought if I could be strong you wouldn't worry. So that if I needed to go back—"

"Go back?" He stopped breathing.

I felt the stillness of his body every place we touched and eased back so I could see his face. "Don't pretend to be shocked. You agreed. We need to find out how Jake is. The month is almost up."

"He could come back any day."

I groaned internally. Classic Mark. Denial was his favorite solution. Don't think about a problem, and it will go away.

My brain never worked that way. "We can't keep waiting. I can't explain how I know, but Jake is in danger."

"You aren't going back. Not without me."

"The portal didn't let you through last time."

He pulled a hand through his wavy hair. "If you're right, if your journal is telling you something, then . . ." He opened a metal tool-box under the bench and reached inside. "I've been working on something."

I caught my breath. When I'd first come home, he'd mentioned messing with the inner workings of the stones, hoping he could realign the portal so that it would let him through again.

He held up the smooth, grey stone in his palm, the camouflaged panel hidden by his fingers. "I thought I'd need a way through to find you. You came back before I solved it, but since then I've kept experimenting."

"You could have broken them."

He shook his head. "Jake doesn't need them to come home. He knows where the portal is in the grove."

"But . . ." A rush of vertigo made the walls waver, and I leaned against the workbench. "Does it work?"

He rubbed the back of his neck. "I'm no transtech. Besides, none of the transtechs I knew have seen anything like this. It's all guess-work. If we need to go through, it might let us."

"There's no 'if' about it."

A low whisper rose in the distance. Almost like the hiss of air through ductwork—except our furnace wasn't on.

I gripped Mark's arm. "Listen."

"I am listening. You think we need to—"

"Not that. Listen."

He frowned, but held his breath along with me. Silence swelled around us. Then scratching noises came from Jake's room, a fright-ening sound I'd heard before, as if a radio were tuned between sta-tions yet distant voices carried through the static. My eyes widened. "You hid the other stones in his room?"

An electrical tingle brushed my skin like a breeze. I let go of Mark and walked toward the open door of Jake's basement bedroom.

"Wait." Mark grabbed my arm. "We need to talk about this. What about Karen, Jon, Anne? You'd just leave them?"

I tugged away from his grip. "That's not fair."

"No, it's not. But it's real. What if we can't get back?"

Turning to face him squarely, I put my hands on his biceps as if touch alone could convey the desperation flooding my heart. And not just about Jake. I hadn't forgotten the dangers, the loneliness, the fear. The first time I'd been pulled through the portal, all I could think about was finding a way home, frantic about what was happening to my family while I was gone. "That's why you have to stay here."

He crossed his arms. "Not an option."

Mark had reverted to the guardian-trained councilmember of Rendor clan. Adamant, courageous, uncompromising.

A man I would always want by my side.

"If you're right," he said, "and Jake is in danger, then I'll go. But I need you to stand by in case anything goes wrong."

Did he think I would let him risk his life passing through the portal again? Based on some untested recalibration? Of course I'd rather go together, but even if the danger to him weren't so clear, we couldn't risk having us both trapped on the other side. I had to think of the other children.

I had to do this alone.

My hands tightened on his arms; then I let go. I stepped across the threshold into Jake's room. Whispers rose in volume. Urgent, compelling—the sounds a giant might hear if he pressed a stethoscope to a city and listened to the mix of tiny, overlapping voices.

"Mark, I can't explain it. I just feel . . . desperate. Like I don't dare wait. This isn't because of the nightmares, or lack of sleep. I'm not unhinged. You've got to believe me."

His eyes fell into shadow as he joined me in the room, away from the harsh basement light. "Then I should align the stones and try to go through. If it doesn't let me through, we aren't going. Understand?" Mark's gaze was hard as flint, and I braced myself for a long argument.

Before I could say anything, static raised the hair on my arms and the walls of Jake's room rushed away and disappeared into an unseen horizon.

Mark's mouth moved, but I couldn't hear him through ears plugged by swelling air pressure. I tried to ask what was happening, but my breath was trapped in my throat.

No, no, no! We need to make plans. I need supplies.

An implosion of wind seemed to rush at us from all directions. Mark fought against it and grabbed me in a bear hug with the one portal stone still clutched in his fist. I had a brief impression of his arms around me, but then he dissolved, as insubstantial as the rest of the room.

Had he been swallowed by the portal—stolen from me forever?

Lord, no! You can't take him!

The energy field danced a current across my skin. I was no longer in our basement, but tumbled and spun through a vast nothingness. Curled against the noise and chaos, I blindly reached out for my husband, but touched only emptiness. I screamed but heard nothing over the shrieking wind.

Finally the universe stopped spinning. The jet-engine roar in my head stilled, and I felt ground beneath my feet. Summoning a dreg of courage, I straightened and opened my eyes.

Utter blackness surrounded me. I stretched my hands out into the void, turning, floundering for something to hold. Blind, disoriented, I took a step forward and slipped, crashing to my knees on a hard surface. Wet. Cold.

"Mark?"

Silence, darkness, and the smell of decay were my only answer.

CHAPTER
7

LINETTE

IN THE MORNING, I struggled to plait my hair into the many thin braids so typical in Sidian. Since coming here, I'd adopted Hazorite styles to show my respect for their culture, but that didn't mean I'd mastered the tiny strands interwoven with metallic fibers. I could have asked Ria for help, but she was still sleeping—exhausted from her tearful conversation with me last night.

My fingers tired of knotting strands of hair, so I stopped with only a few completed and rummaged in a cubby for my clothes. I picked up a long satin tunic with elaborate silver threads woven around the edges, an appropriate choice for meeting with Zarek today. But the lush colors seemed to symbolize everything harsh and unfamiliar about this land. I tossed aside the tunic and instead put on a brown, fine-woven sweater and trousers, and the unadorned robe I wore for informal gatherings in Braide Wood.

As I knotted the fabric belt, a light tap sounded at my door. Kieran always reminded me to keep my door locked, and I'd made it a habit. He might be hopelessly paranoid, but his advice had saved me several times from drunken soldiers who stumbled down the halls at night.

This morning the door slid aside to reveal Nolan. He ducked his head—awkward and endearing at the same time. "G'morning. Kieran sent me with a message: 'Zarek asked me to meet with a division of the soldiers camped outside the walls, and I may be gone until the rains. Don't go to see the king until I'm back at the palace and can come with you.'"

His words rushed out in one breath, with the inflectionless delivery typical of messengers. He sucked in a gulp of air and looked at me, waiting for my answer. After a quick scan of my informal attire, the worried pinch around his forehead relaxed. "Oh, you've already decided not to see the king. I'll tell him."

"Have you eaten? Would you like something?"

He grinned, sauntered into the room, and grabbed a small melon from the bowl in my common room. As a guest of the king, I was provided with more food than I could eat.

Nolan sliced a wedge of fruit with his bootknife and talked around a large bite of melon. "Where's Ria?"

"Still sleeping." I sat across the table from him and poured some juice for each of us. No bitter Hazorite clavo when I had a choice. "Nolan, I'm sure your father has talked to you about this, but we need to treat Ria with respect."

"She's a shrine girl," he said dismissively as he wiped juice from his chin with his sleeve.

"Yes. And she's precious to the One. Like every person, slave or king . . . or messenger."

He rolled his eyes. "It's how things work here."

I'd heard plenty from Ria last night about how things worked. How her family had sold her into an uncertain future. I shook my head, dislodging an unfinished braid. "Promise me you'll treat her like . . . like a sister."

He shrugged, and I decided to try a different trail. "You've been a great help to your father. Your mother would be proud of you."

He stilled. Then slowly, deliberately, he carved another slice from the fruit in his hand. Then another and another. But he set each slice on the table instead of eating them. Finally, he tucked his knife in his boot-sheath and wiped his hands on his pants. He nodded toward the fruit. "Help yourself. I'd better go. He's waiting."

I stopped him with a touch of his arm. "Sometimes it helps to talk." The one thing Kieran had asked of me was to try to help

Nolan talk about his grief. And I was about to lose the opportunity. *Give me the right words.*

He glanced at me sideways, then grinned. "What's wrong with your hair?"

I sighed. "I don't have enough hands to weave in the threads. It's harder than learning to play the long-whistle."

He laughed—such a rare sound from him that I forgave myself for not being able to draw him out.

"You want help?" he asked. "I used to braid the ones in back for my mother."

My heart caught in my throat, and I fought to reply with the same casual tone. "If you have a moment."

Hands still sticky from the melon, he plaited the first unfinished strand with nimble fingers. "It's not that hard. My mother could do her braids in no time . . . until she got sick."

Maybe if he stayed preoccupied with fixing my braids, he'd keep talking. "How long did she have the fever?"

He knotted off a piece of thread and moved to the next section. "Not sure. She didn't tell me right away. And I was gone a lot."

I ached for him. "You were so young."

"I was twelve when they conscripted me." He sounded offended.

"Practically ancient."

He snorted. "It wasn't bad. I was fast. They mostly used me in Sidian. Not like some messengers that have to travel to Corros or Trezold or Grey Hills. They don't always make it back."

"Did you see your mother much?"

His hands paused for a second, then resumed the rhythmic winding and tugging. "They kept us in the palace." He stepped back. "There. You try."

I fingered a last unbraided strand and slowly knotted it.

Nolan snickered. "Well, it's a little better."

A quick shake of my head tested the braids. "Thank you. And anytime you want to talk . . . songkeepers are supposed to be good at listening."

Color rose up his neck as he backed toward the door. "Sure. Well. I'll let Kieran know you got his message."

He left, still assuming I'd agreed to Kieran's order to cancel my appointment.

Should I have admitted I still planned to see the king? I could make a bigger difference in one meeting than in hundreds of classes with the women of Sidian or even the young messengers. Yet my spirit felt unsettled. I could hear Lukyan's grandfatherly voice in my head. *The value of a choice isn't measured by the act alone, but by the motives of your heart.*

My motives had been such a confusing mix lately. If I waited for all my intentions to line up, I'd never take any action. Some of my desires stood up to any songkeeper standards. I truly ached for the people in Hazor. So much darkness, so many lies. I was willing to take any risk, make any sacrifice if I could change that.

But less virtuous reasons also compelled my choice to meet with Zarek. Kieran had made me feel like a worthless fledgling who should return to safe and familiar arbors. I yearned for his respect. Was he waiting for me to make my own decisions? To stop acquiescing to his?

I also wanted to justify my presence here. Needed to. If Kieran sent me back to Braide Wood, the loss would drown me. I'd pass the small cottage Dylan had built, or see the trail where we would slip away for a stroll after supper, or run into one of his friends at the healer's lodge.

As homesick as I was, I wasn't ready to face that. I wanted to stay here—to have worthwhile work to fill my days. A good discussion with the king would ensure that.

A firm rap on the door interrupted my thoughts.

A king's herald stood in the hallway. Wiry as a messenger, he wore a leather vest over his tunic that hinted at a military role. The heralds weren't technically soldiers, but were still trained fighters. In this violent culture, Zarek surrounded himself with people skilled in every weapon.

"The king awaits," he said simply.

I nodded and followed. "Of course."

He escorted me along the jagged corridors, heading one direction, then making a brief backtrack at a diagonal before continuing forward. Each sharp-edged corner reminded me that I was in a foreign place. Instead of the central hall where Zarek held court, the herald led me deep into another wing of the palace and to huge double doors covered with grotesque carvings. The men standing guard were undisguised soldiers: swords, daggers, armor, and heavy foreheads that seemed carved into a permanent glower.

The herald stopped. "Linette of Braide Wood to see the king, at his request."

One of the guards touched a lever recessed in the stone wall, and the doors slid apart with a magnetic gasp.

My stomach tightened. What if I said the wrong thing? What if Zarek were in a bad mood today? This wasn't a good idea. Kieran understood court politics better. I should have waited until Kieran and I could meet with him together. I should have—

The herald cleared his throat. He gestured me through the door. When I didn't move immediately, he gripped my elbow and marched me inside.

Kieran had visited Zarek's private quarters often for fermented orberry wine and games of Perish. He'd described the huge slab of stone that formed the common-room table, and the austere, military atmosphere. He seemed to respect Zarek's lack of decadent luxuries. I thought the space seemed barren and cold.

Seeing no sign of the king, I cast a questioning look at the herald. He backed from the room. The doors slid closed after him.

"Come in." I whirled toward the voice. Zarek stood in front of a curtain that moved slightly, as if touched by a breeze. His sleeveless tunic was unadorned, but shone as if woven from pure metallic thread. An armband circled his right bicep, and an ornate dagger was wedged in his belt.

I gave a small bow. "I'm honored to meet with you."

His teeth flashed. "I'm sure." He scanned me up and down, and shook his head. "Are you as innocent as you sound?"

"In-innocent?" What did he mean? "I'm no criminal."

He gave a howl of laughter. "Dear girl, I wasn't accusing you of that. Sit, sit."

I perched on a chair, keeping the stone slab table between us. The curtain behind him shifted again. The cold of the granite floor seeped through the leather of my shoes and up my legs. But I shivered with something more than physical chill, something I'd felt before—this sense of a presence, foreign and dark, rippling in the air.

Zarek settled across from me. "Has Sidian been all you expected?"

I shook off my unease. "I didn't know what to expect. But your people have been so welcoming and curious."

He studied me for a long moment. "The other songkeepers didn't seem to find it so. I hear they've returned to the clans. But you're different. Tell me about yourself."

"Royin and Havid are much more experienced. They met during their apprenticeship and—"

"Stop. I asked about you."

My stomach tensed. I was here to find out how far Zarek's understanding of the One had developed, but I was quickly losing control of the conversation.

His smile broadened. "In my nation, when the king asks a question, he is given an answer."

My fingers fluttered in a rhythm of a feast day song, and I clenched them in my lap. But the melody lingered in my mind, strengthening me. "I was born in Braide Wood. My first teacher was Lukyan. He's the eldest songkeeper of the clan. When I was old enough, I apprenticed in Lyric. That's where I met Royin and Havid. They've been life-bonded for twenty years and—"

"And you?"

I glanced up. Zarek's broad forearms rested on the table. He was still smiling, but I didn't know how to read his eyes. Another whisper of cold stirred across my skin. "I . . . I don't—"

"Life-bonded. You must be alone to leave everything and come here."

My eyes stung, surprised by the sudden pain his words stirred. "I was pledged." I swallowed, unwilling to desecrate Dylan's name by speaking it here. "He . . . was killed by Kahlareans."

"The skirmish at Rendor?"

Kieran was wrong; Zarek continued to be very well informed about the clans. Who was feeding him information? I shook my head. "Before that. At the Cauldron Falls outpost. Syncbeams from across the river."

"I'm sorry." His rich, deep voice softened to a gruff rumble—a glimpse of unexpected gentleness. He reached for a pitcher, filled a mug, and slid it toward me. "And what led you here?"

"Well, after he told the Council he was the Restorer, Kieran—"

"Ah." He gave a knowing smile. "I understand."

I stiffened, then took a slow breath, willing away my irritation. "When the Restorer asked for help from the songkeepers, I agreed to come. The Council was surprised that the One was calling the Restorer to serve Hazor, but it made sense to me."

"Because the One is switching his allegiance?" Zarek poured another mug.

"No. Because the One loves everyone."

The king raised one eyebrow, furrows marring the slope toward his bald head. "Even Kahlareans?"

My stomach clenched. Did He cherish the enemy who had taken Dylan from me? Could I ever embrace His love for them? I clutched the mug in front of me and groped for one of the Verses. "'He made all that is and loves all He has made.'" But in spite of the words, pain stung the raw places of my soul. *Holy One, I'm drowning in this place. I don't belong. I shouldn't have come.*

"My apologies. That was an unkind question. Grief shakes even the strongest truth."

"Shakes it but doesn't change it. Good plans can unfold from even the worst pain." A warm current throbbed through my veins, and I could breathe again.

Zarek lifted his mug. "To plans."

Orberry wine was worse than Sidian clavo, but I didn't want to offend him. "To the One and *His* plans." I managed a small sip. The sour liquid pinched the inside of my mouth.

Zarek drained his cup and slammed it to the table. He didn't expect me to follow, did he? I tried another swallow, and the juice burned in my throat.

"So you ran here to escape your grief. Have you succeeded?"

Put so bluntly, his assessment stung. I *had* longed for distraction from the pain. But my grief wasn't the only reason I'd come here.

I met the king's eyes. "I came here because I wanted to help the people of Hazor. There are others here with grief to overcome, and I hope I've been able to serve."

"I'm sure Kieran has appreciated your help." He waited for my response with a carefully bland expression.

I sank back, relieved to move away from myself as the central topic. "He's faced a lot of challenges. Your people have different thoughts on . . . well, everything." This might be a good time to explain why Kieran couldn't accept Ria as a gift, but my face heated as I tried to form the words.

The king rose and strolled the perimeter of the room. "I've paid careful attention to everything Kieran has said. And I've wondered. Wondered why the One would have sent the Restorer to Hazor when the clans of Lyric were still threatened. Kahlareans, Rhusicans. Your people have been in danger."

He walked toward the doors, and I turned my chair to keep him in view.

"Uniting under a king was a smart step, but from what I understand, Cameron couldn't hold power. And in the meantime, your clans were successfully invaded. Doesn't make sense, does it?"

A dull ache throbbed inside my temples. "The One continues to protect the clans. And He called us to come here and offer you truth—"

"And I accepted a trade." Zarek's powerful arm reached for a lever beside the door and jerked it with unnecessary force. The magnetic seal gasped apart, and the doors slid open. Two guards dragged a bound prisoner into the room. A sack covered his head, and the man twisted in the grip of the soldiers, making muffled, angry sounds.

Panic welled up in my chest, freezing every muscle in my body. Even before a guard pulled the sack off the man's head, I knew who the prisoner was.

Kieran.

CHAPTER
8

LINETTE

KIERAN SQUINTED AS the bag was pulled from his head. When he saw me, his eyes flared, but whatever he said was lost behind the rough fabric gag binding his mouth.

I lurched forward, but Zarek shoved me back into my chair. "No need for dramatics. We're going to have a conversation."

Kieran's eyes narrowed over the gag, and Zarek chuckled. "Remove that," he told one of the guards. "And you can untie him."

As soon as he was freed, Kieran worked his jaw side to side a few times and rubbed his wrists. He shot a stinging glare in my direction, sending a stab of shame through me as sharp and poisonous as a venblade. He'd told me not to meet with the king today. Why hadn't I taken his advice?

Deliberately turning from me, he gave Zarek all his attention. "If you wanted to play games, you could have invited me to spar. Or I could beat you at Perish again."

All trace of humor vanished from the king's demeanor. "Show me the wound."

"The what?"

Zarek signaled the guards. One grabbed Kieran from behind, the other lifted his tunic and slit the bandage wrapped around Kieran's ribs. The soldier wrenched the fabric away in one harsh move. Kieran hissed in a sharp breath as the fresh scab tore open and blood ran down his side.

My lungs tightened, the air in the room too hot and thick to breathe. I'd warned him of the dangers. Why hadn't he listened? Or was this my fault, too? Should I have been more insistent that it was time to leave Hazor?

Kieran ignored me, ignored his injury, and faced Zarek as though he were in control of the situation. "Your point?"

Zarek answered with a bitter half-smile. "I would think that's obvious." Then his lips flattened. "We had a bargain. But that has changed."

"Nothing's changed."

"So if I slit your throat, you'll heal?" Zarek drew a dagger from his belt.

"No." Kieran's confident posture sagged. "I meant that nothing important has changed. The One asked me to give you my service, to answer your questions about Him. I can still—"

Zarek slammed him in the ribs with the blunt handle of the dagger.

Kieran gasped and doubled over as far as the guard's grip on him allowed.

"Stop this!" I sprang forward and flew between Zarek and Kieran, rounding on the king. I held out my hands. "Please."

Zarek's mouth curved up slowly.

"Linette." Kieran ground out the words from behind me. "Get away from me. Now." The hardness in his voice jabbed like a blow to my own ribs. Even now, he still didn't want my help.

Zarek's smile grew. He gently drew me to the chair again. I didn't resist, my knees unsteady. Everything was tumbling out of control. All our work—the allegiance we'd nurtured, the good we'd tried to do—was crashing into pieces. How could I stop this? I wasn't a guardian. I had no weapons.

The king rested a hand idly on my shoulder, and I sensed the deep current of betrayal and rage coiled inside him. "I knew your word couldn't be trusted," he said to Kieran.

Kieran strained against the grip of the guards. "Zarek, let her leave. You promised her safety."

Zarek looked at his one-time friend with venom. "And you promised me the services of the Restorer. It seems we were both deceived."

My heart raced, and every swallow threatened to choke me. Why hadn't Kieran been honest with him? He could have prevented this moment. Why had he been so stubborn?

I fought to think of some way to salvage the situation, but my head throbbed. The shadows in the room seemed to close in like fog, invading my vision and my mind. Bereft of anything to say or do that wouldn't make things worse, I begged the One to save Kieran. Begged him to . . . My thoughts grew blurry.

Zarek studied Kieran. "When did you stop being the Restorer? Is there a new Restorer? Where is he? How many guardians protect him?" He fired the questions like blasts from a syncbeam.

Kieran paled but drew himself up and met the king's eyes.

Careful, Kieran. Don't antagonize him.

"The sign of healing stopped soon after I came here." As if he'd heard my thoughts, Kieran answered Zarek with a rare tone of respect. "I should have told you. But because it didn't change the reason we—"

"Is there a new Restorer?"

Kieran, clench-jawed and silent, dropped his gaze.

The king fingered one of my braids. "It's regrettable, but Linette is about to deny a request from the king. An offense that demands her death."

My heartbeat stumbled and the chill seeped more deeply into my body. I tried to pull away from Zarek's hand, but my limbs had become strangely heavy.

Kieran strained against the guard holding him. "Leave her out of this."

"That's your choice. Answer my questions, and perhaps I won't make my request."

"What can I do for you?" I meant to speak quickly, but my words slurred. "I'm happy to grant you a request. Just let him go."

Zarek ignored me. "Last chance," he said to Kieran.

Kieran sent a tortured look my direction. His eyes reflected every inch of his old identity as the outcast son of Braide Wood. Desperation. Regret. Pain.

He didn't need to plead for my understanding. I knew he couldn't answer Zarek's questions. I didn't want him to. We wouldn't put others in danger. We'd both rather die. Still, as Dylan used to tell me, reality was far different than theory. My stomach turned hollow as I met Kieran's eyes and shook my head.

Kieran's eyes flared, and his chest heaved. "I'd answer if I could, but the ways of the One aren't always clear. Let me—"

"Liar." The king spit out the word. "You've tried my patience long enough, Restorer. Or whatever you are. I'm done." His hand left my shoulder and slid along my neck. "Linette, will you serve as one of my courtesans?"

I gasped. For a moment the fuzziness that clouded my thoughts receded. "You know that's impossible. I'm happy to serve you. I can teach. I can work in the kitchens. I'll scrub floors. Ask me anything else."

Zarek didn't bother looking at me. His intent had little to do with making me suffer. His bitterness was directed at Kieran, who struggled against the guards, sinews cording on his neck.

"Don't do this." The growl in Kieran's throat was more threat than plea.

Zarek grabbed my chin and tilted my face up. Anger glinted in his eyes like the silver threads in his onyx table. "Linette, you refuse the king? Then you die. And during your last breaths, remember it was Kieran's choice."

I jerked my head away from his grip and struggled to my feet. "My life and my death are in the hands of the One." It was a battle to speak clearly, but I had to confront Zarek with the power of truth. I had to reassure Kieran that I didn't blame him. But my legs wavered and I grabbed the chair for support. The floor rippled, and waves of dizziness swam through my brain. What was wrong with me?

The curtain near the back of the room moved, and a hunched old woman hobbled forward, hooded cloak shadowing her features. The darkness I'd felt earlier returned. Deep currents of something fetid and evil circled the room.

"No!" Kieran choked, all color leaving his face.

Zarek smiled at the reaction. "Linette is fortunate. She benefits from Hazorite law. The high priestess can claim the condemned for the shrine. Bezreth has been kind enough to offer this girl a place in the Sidian shrine."

Bezreth drew closer. Amber irises framed her pupils, the rings so thin they were almost invisible. Set in her wrinkled skin, her eyes were black as bitum sap—pits that swallowed all light. I needed to run, but could only sway on my feet.

"How much did she drink?" Her sibilant voice hissed like liquid spilled on a heat trivet.

Zarek frowned. "Only a few swallows."

The sour taste in my mouth threatened to choke me.

I backed away from them. Rough hands grabbed and held me. More guards. Where had they come from? The two who had brought Kieran into the room were still holding him, despite his efforts to break free.

Bezreth seemed to float toward me, smiling an ancient toothless smile. Rumors were that she'd lived for five generations. Certainly some sort of prehistoric evil inhabited her.

I recoiled, struggling in spite of the strange weakness draining my muscles.

Bezreth pulled a silver wristband from her tunic, tapping one nail on the wide metallic surface. "Welcome to the sacred service of the hill-gods." She examined a fabric layer inside the bracelet, then grabbed my arm and wrapped the band over my wrist. It closed with a click.

Almost immediately, my panic and nausea dissolved. From a confusing, distant place Kieran shouted something. Words pummeled the air, but I couldn't translate them. I squinted against the chaotic shapes. The room was full of noise and people and swirling darkness. A girl with dark braids appeared beside the high priestess. She seemed familiar, but I couldn't remember why.

Bezreth nodded toward me. "Better, yes?"

The old woman understood. She knew I'd been chilled, feverish, confused. Her wristband was helping me. I felt so much better now. Calm.

"Thank you," I whispered.

Through the haze of my vision, Zarek shook his head at me with something like regret, but then turned back to the others with barely restrained rage. Poor man. He was so angry. I tried to reach out toward him, but couldn't move. Why couldn't I make my body obey simple commands?

"Why?" The hoarse, desperate cry came from the other man . . . I struggled to recall his name. Kieran, wasn't it? Another confused, distressed soul. I tried to speak, to reassure him, but my lips had grown numb.

Zarek's shape, blurry but still large and easy to identify, stepped closer to Kieran. "I give my trust rarely. I'm seldom wrong. When I am, I correct it."

The fog in my head told me that none of this mattered. I pushed against the heaviness, fighting it. Could Kieran hear the pain beneath the king's anger? If I could convince my throat to produce sound, maybe I could stop Zarek from his bitter path.

Bezreth joined the king and pointed at Kieran with a gnarled finger. "Let me have him. Only *his* blood will fully appease the hill-gods."

Zarek crossed his arms. "No. I've granted your other petitions. You get the songkeeper. That's enough. His crime is against me. His death will be by my hands."

Death? The king was going to kill Kieran! The heavy effect of the armband lost its grip for a few heartbeats. The scene blinked back into focus. Zarek still clutched his jeweled dagger, and the blade glinted. Kieran didn't even watch his approaching death. His chest heaved, sweat dampening his face and hair as he stared at me. Raw fear and desperation burned across the space between us. And something deeper. Something tender I'd seen before in Dylan's eyes.

If only I could tell him. I had to stop this . . .

Then my failed efforts no longer mattered. Soothing numbness cradled me. My head lolled forward and I sighed, unable to remember what I'd wanted to do. Bezreth's men drew me toward the curtain at the back of the room. I had no will to resist.

A howl, feral and broken, rose behind us.

Kieran.

A shiver ran through my spine. I stumbled.

The young girl squeezed my hand. "It's all right. You're a shrine girl now. We'll take care of you."

A corner of my mind resisted. This was wrong. Someone needed help. Who was it? I needed to go back, to fight.

The curtain fell closed behind us, shutting out whatever had so worried me. The farther we walked down the hidden passageway, the harder it was to cling to my memories.

Bezreth paused before a steel door, guarded by more soldiers. One of them toggled a switch, and the door slid aside.

The girl beside me leaned closer. "One of the ancient kings built this hall so that shrine girls could be sent for at his command." She glanced at a side passage and a closed door, also heavily guarded. "Those are his private rooms. Bezreth promised that one day she'll send me."

The girl was bright, eager. She wanted me to feel happy for her. Yet sorrow poured through me. Something wasn't right. I didn't belong here. Who was I? What was I doing here? My head drooped forward, and my chin rubbed against the knobby weave of my robe and the scent of caradoc wool.

Braide Wood.

Memories woke inside of me. My mother gathering the collar of my cloak under my chin and resting her forehead against mine. Lukyan's aged smile. Mist lowering against my upturned face inside the Lyric tower. The music.

Bezreth turned suddenly. Her skeletal hands gripped my face and the blackness of her eyes filled my vision. "Your past is gone. You belong to me. I speak for the hill-gods and they have put you in my care."

Deeper and deeper her gaze pulled me in. Darkness swallowed me, permeated every memory and wiped it away, as if an armored hand slid the lever of a light panel in my soul. Dimmer, dimmer, everything faded.

She smiled, pale gums appearing amid the deep crevices of her wrinkled face. "That's right. Come with us."

She was ancient, far wiser than I was. I bowed my head and followed her.

The heavy door slid closed, sealing me into my new life. Beyond, jagged steps led downward to a passage beneath the palace. Red panels of light cast blood shadows on the stone floor.

The girl beside me continued to whisper as we walked. "The high priestess has prepared for the past two seasons for this return. The shrine isn't ready for the hill-gods' visit yet, but she restored the homes for the shrine girls. I'm sorry about lying to you earlier."

"Earlier?"

"About the king sending me as a gift. It was an idea of the high priestess."

I winced and rubbed my forehead.

"Oh, that's right. She explained you wouldn't remember." Her gaze skimmed my bracelet. "It's best to forget anything that came before. I'm Ria."

I nodded and stopped trying to place her. Our walk ended at large metal doors with burnished carvings. Contorted faces. Claws, fangs, wild eyes. They repulsed me. Were they supposed to? The girl beside me didn't seem bothered by them.

When the doors slid apart, we walked slowly forward. A sweet scent pervaded the air in the next hall we entered, with undertones of something sour and metallic.

"We're under the shrine now," Ria said in hushed tones. "You won't be able to help with ceremonies right away, so your room is at the far end. Just do what you're told and remember what an honor this is for you." She slipped away, and one of Bezreth's men propelled me farther down the dark hall.

We passed alcoves recessed into the stone, each one fronted by wire fence barriers. I caught glimpses of young women alone in many of the rooms . . . some on silk pallets, some pacing their small space in embroidered robes. As we went deeper into the cellar beneath the shrine, the girls were more unkempt. Many were bruised, hair matted. One girl saw us and threw herself forward, shrieking.

An electrical charge flared across the wire in front of her room. She fell backward. Helpless whimpers followed us down the hall.

"In there." The guard motioned toward an empty alcove. I stepped forward and wire fencing slid out from the wall on one side and caged me in.

Still feeling unsteady on my feet, I sank to the floor and leaned against the back wall, hugging my knees, as far from the electrical current of the wire as possible. My wrist itched and I glanced down. A wide band of silver rested against my pale skin. What was that for? Was it supposed to be there? I twisted it, then lost interest. Tucking my hands into my sleeves, I rested my cheek against my knees and let my thoughts drift into inviting nothingness.

CHAPTER 9

SUSAN

"MARK!" MY VOICE echoed, and my breath rasped in my ears. I blinked several times, but still saw only blackness. The air smelled musty. Either we'd lost power, or I'd gone blind, or . . .

The terrifying possibilities throbbed inside my skull. Speculation would only drive me into panic. *Think, Susan. Think.*

From my knees, I reached out to orient myself. The cement beneath me was hard and damp, as if a basement pipe had broken. A faint drip sounded in the distance. The leak in the laundry room faucet? Mark had been trying to fix it for weeks.

"Mark?" My head ached. Holding my breath, I strained to hear any other sounds and caught a soft exhalation. Someone, or something, hid in the darkness.

I had to know. I crept toward the sound. The spot where I expected to touch Jake's bed held only bare concrete.

I wasn't in our basement anymore.

Anything could be waiting nearby in the dark. Cold sweat beaded on my forehead.

Desperate to get oriented in the horrible, heavy blackness, I crawled onward, feeling my way. A stone dug into my knee, and, with a cry, I fell forward against something soft and warm. It moved beneath my hand. I shrieked, and the emptiness swallowed the echoes. Heart pounding, I clamped a hand over my mouth, pushing back the rising terror.

A low groan emanated inches from my hand.

"Mark? Mark, is it you? Please let it be you."

"What were you screaming about?" My husband's grumpy voice washed over me like a warm tide, carrying me back to shore.

"It is you!" I threw myself across him. "Oh, thank you, God. You're here." I patted him, finding the contours of his shoulders, neck, and head.

He swatted my hands away. "Stop poking me. Why is it so dark? What happened?"

"I don't know. You were the one playing with the portal stones."

"I wasn't—" He shifted. "Never mind. Would you let me up?"

I eased back, but kept a grip on his arm, my only touchstone in the hollow, unknown space we inhabited. "Can you see anything? Or is something wrong with my eyes?"

"It's not you," he said quietly. His hand found my arm and followed it upward to my shoulder, and then rested his palm against my face. "I can't see either. We could be anywhere."

"Or nowhere," I whispered.

He pressed his forehead against mine. "Susan, trust the One."

I clung to his quiet confidence, breathed in the comforting scent of his skin. Where did he find so much strength? We were lost, blind, and buried in a dank, dripping space, and he still took time to offer me reassurance.

Something scuffed along the ground in the distance. I flinched. "Did you hear that?"

A pebble tumbled and more shuffling sounds drew closer. I turned toward the noise and caught a hint of gauzy light that hadn't been there before. Mark stood, pulled me up, and pressed me against his left side. He'd instinctively left his sword arm free, even though neither of us was armed.

Hazy blue illumination bounced around a bend. The rough-hewn tunnel gradually took shape, revealing slopes of tumbled rock rising on all sides, like piles of Easter eggs in hues of grey and blue.

A small figure stepped around the bend and stopped with a squeak. Shorter than our daughter Anne, the tiny person stared at us with huge eyes in a blue-tinged face, holding what looked like a glow-stick.

Had we tumbled into yet another alternate world? Nothing here was familiar. Dampness oozed through my stockinged feet, and I curled my toes under, longing for sturdy boots.

"Who are you?" The figure's high-pitched voice was breathy and feminine. As she moved closer and held up the glow-stick to see us better, I realized her skin wasn't blue. Her pale complexion had simply reflected the hued light, an effect heightened by the fluorescent aquamarine striations adorning the cave walls.

Mark's hand squeezed my shoulder with unnecessary force, warning me not to speak. "We're lost," he answered simply.

A whispery giggle. She took another step closer and stared with unblinking eyes that looked permanently surprised.

More footsteps approached. "Galena? Wait for—"

A taller shape entered the cavern, spotted us, and gasped. She ran and scooped up the girl. Her long hair also had a bluish cast until the light moved and I realized it was as white as her skin.

The girl squirmed. "Mama, they're lost. What are they, Mama?"

I held out my hands, devoid of weapons, and smiled. "We're sorry we disturbed you. Can you tell us where we are?"

Mark tugged me back, breathing through his nose like a bull ready to charge. What was his problem? They seemed harmless.

The woman with huge eyes and almost no chin returned an uncertain smile. "Tremolite tribe. Where are you traveling?" When neither of us responded, she gave a worried glance at Mark's angry stance and eased away a few steps. "I heard a scream. Do you need help? Perhaps you should come with us to our grotto."

The woman and daughter backed farther away, rounding the rock wall and taking the light source with them.

"Wait!" I called.

Mark's fingers dug into my shoulder.

I reached up to rest my hand over his. "What's wrong? We can't just stand around in the dark."

"Kahlareans," he whispered.

Dry ice bit the lining of my lungs. In my worst nightmares I still saw bulging eyes over shrouding masks, heard the hissing argument of the Kahlarean assassins dragging me into the forest, felt the burning paralysis of the venblade. The mother and daughter had the same pale skin, toothless gums, and large eyes, but they couldn't possibly be the same sort of threat as grey-clad assassins.

The soft glow of fluorescence in the walls was fading quickly and Mark took a reluctant step toward the tunnel. "We must be in Kahlarea. Not a good place for us to be."

"Well, duh." Minutes earlier I'd have given anything to find Mark in this dark place. Now his grim assessment irritated me.

Mark ignored my sarcasm. "We can't let them know who we are."

"Okay. Fake names. You be Fred and I'll be Ethel."

Even in the fading azure glow, I saw Mark's mouth twitch. "I think we can come up with something better than that."

I crossed my arms. "Hey, I'm not the one with experience at aliases."

He stiffened, and I wished I could call back my words. I'd forgiven him for hiding his identity for so many years. Mostly. But digs like that would make him think I hadn't. "I didn't mean it that way," I said softly.

He pulled away from me. "No, you're right. I'll handle it." He moved forward, not bothering to offer me his hand.

"Fine." I tried to rekindle my crankiness, to keep the fear at bay, but dread pounded inside my ribs as we felt our way around the rock face and followed the light of the glowing stick bouncing along ahead of us. I watched my footing to avoid stubbing my toes, but the surface of the path was well worn and smooth beneath my socks. Ahead of me, Mark moved more confidently. He was still wearing tennis shoes from his trip to the hardware store.

After a short walk, Galena and her mother led us into a large cavern, where hundreds of iridescent blue icicles dangled from the ceiling. They created a glow on the uneven cavern walls. Muted fabric draped across small alcoves, and I glimpsed sleep pallets inside one.

A man crouched beside a collection of heat trivets. His knobby fingers emerged from grey sleeves as he ladled stew from a bowl. His physique, his eyes, even the smoothness of his motions triggered memories of my past encounters with hooded creatures and drawn swords. If we'd met him first, I would have caught on much sooner that these people were Kahlareans.

The scent of chowder and raw fish tweaked my nose.

The man looked up and dropped the ladle. Stew splashed onto the heat trivets, spitting and sizzling.

"Travelers, Papa," Galena said cheerfully as her mother set her down. "We found them in the blue cave."

"I'm Lazul." The man stood and exchanged a look with his wife. "Would you like to share our meal?"

"No," Mark said sharply. His body language radiated hostility, and not without cause. His history with the Kahlareans contained even more bitterness than mine. They had killed his father in battle, assassinated his mother years later, and hunted him until he'd had to flee through the portal.

Even though Lazul's small family had little in common with the assassins, polite conversation wouldn't come easily to Mark.

The woman's large eyes bulged. "We have plenty. The grenlow fish were swarming yesterday." She cast a nervous look at Mark's stony profile.

I eased away from my husband. "Thank you for offering, but we've already had dinner." I spoke softly. Sounds rang harshly against the stark walls. No wonder Kahlareans spoke in whispers.

The woman's receding chin almost disappeared as her lips curved shyly. "Do you need help?"

We needed far more help than they could realize, but I shook my head and waited for Mark to take the lead.

He finally cleared his throat and forced out a few words. "How far are we from Cauldron Falls?"

The man and woman looked at each other, their large, unblinking eyes communicating something I couldn't translate.

Lazul sighed and squatted beside the heat trivet. "How did you come to be lost? We've heard of the banished, but none has made their way this far into Kahlarea before."

The Council and their practice of banishment. If they had sent out some sort of Peace Corps to surrounding nations instead of the worst of the clans' criminals, the tensions might not be running quite as high.

"Just tell us how to get to Cauldron Falls," Mark gritted out. His neck muscles hardened into tense ropes.

The man spooned stew into a small mug and handed it to his daughter. "Several days and nights of hard travel. Where are your provisions?"

"We'll manage," Mark said. "Which way?"

"You'll need light to leave the cavern." The woman pulled her daughter close. "I can guide you out."

I smiled warmly. "Thank—"

"No!" Lazul stepped in front of his family, matching Mark's suspicion and hostility. "I'll take them." He moved silently toward the back wall of the grotto and pulled on a long vest with numerous pockets and pouches. He tossed a light rod toward Mark. "How did you make your way so close to our grotto without lights?"

"We got turned around. Lost our lights." Mark kept his head down as he mumbled his evasions and studied the smooth, five-foot long stick. A few twists made it glow. "I'm grateful your daughter found us."

Lazul sucked on his lower lip, increasing his resemblance to a frog, but he nodded, and his knobby fingers eased their stranglehold on his own light rod. "This way," he said, moving off toward a narrow passage opposite the way we'd come.

"Thank you." I looked back and waved at the mother and daughter, then started forward.

And crashed into Mark's unmoving back.

"Susan. The portal stone. Where is it? It was in my hand when we came through."

"I . . . I don't know. I don't remember seeing it, but I wasn't looking. And there were all kinds of stones in that cave."

By now, Lazul had noticed we weren't following. He returned, his broad, hairless forehead creased, and his eye ridges raised. "The way out is this way."

Ignoring him, Mark strode back through the cavern, past the heat trivets. "We have to find it."

The mother and daughter squeaked and moved out of his way. Lazul and I hurried to catch up.

"What is he doing?" Lazul's harsh whisper had no trouble reaching my ears as he kept pace with me.

The raspy sound sent pinpricks down my limbs and stirred flashbacks of assassins arguing. Who knew how a mild-mannered family man would react if he felt threatened? Those vest pockets could hold venblades. Why couldn't Mark try a little harder to put these Kahlareans at ease? "He just realized we left something," I said, glancing over at him. "Can you show us back to the cave where your daughter found us?"

Lazul's face creases hardened.

"Once we find it, we won't cause you any more trouble. I promise." Hard to sound soothing and reassuring while loping behind Mark, who was storming forward like Indiana Jones brandishing a torch.

Mark ducked under a cluster of stalactites and stopped when two tunnels branched off. "Which way?"

"Left," Lazul rasped. "But—"

Mark strode onward and I scurried after him. Lazul followed us, making swishing noises with his tongue that might have been a Kahlarean version of grumbling.

"Yep, this is it." Mark pulled ahead as we broke out into the cavern. He held the light up, and turned in a slow circle, studying the piles of thousands of rocks on every side. They looked as if they'd been caressed to smoothness by eons of flowing water. Any one of them could have been the portal stone.

Mark picked up a rock, examined it, and set it to one side.

Lazul squatted by the tunnel entrance, braced on his staff. His swishing sounds progressed to a throat gurgle that held a hint of threat. Overhead, the fluorescent strands in the roof of the cave absorbed the glow of our light rods.

I shifted a few egg-shaped rocks back and forth. "Our host is getting upset," I said in an undertone. "Let's get out of here."

"We need to find it." He stooped and grabbed stone after stone, glancing at them and tossing them behind us.

The ugly clatter echoed against the cavern walls, and I winced. "Why? We know where the..." I glanced at Lazul. Was he far enough away not to overhear? I cupped my hand and brought my lips closer to Mark's ear. "We know where the portal entrance is outside of Lyric. That'll take us home."

Mark stopped. "And then we'd never be able to come back."

Would that really be so horrible? Couldn't we find Jake and take him home and live happily in our own world, with the portal closed to us forever?

As if he read my thoughts, Mark grabbed two more of the thousands of rocks in the pile closest to him. "Susan, we can't leave it behind."

I squatted beside him to help, lowering my voice again. "Well, we can't stay here looking for it. We don't know what's happening back home. We don't know what danger Jake is facing in Lyric. And if we wait around in Kahlarea, they may figure out who you are. We have to get back to the clans. We have to cross the river."

"Enough." Lazul stretched upright at the entrance of the tunnel that led to his grotto. He pointed one bony arm in our direction. "You are disturbing the grubs. We must leave."

"Grubs?" I looked at the back of the stone I'd just pulled from the pile. A flat white worm clung to the surface. "Eww!" I flung it down.

Lazul took a few steps forward, then retreated. "Careful. Do not wake them."

I didn't like the sound of that. Even Mark stopped his frantic search. "Are they like ground crawlers? Poisonous?"

Lazul flapped his arms. "No, no, no. But they don't like to be disturbed."

Mark snorted and turned back to the next mound of stones. "Well, sorry for irritating the little worms, but I have to find—"

I grabbed his arm. "Um, Mark?"

He frowned at me, then slowly straightened.

All around the cavern, stones began to clack lightly against each other, as if a mild earthquake were humming deep inside the bones of the earth. White goo seeped out between the seams of the stones, gathered, and lifted to float like a growing spider web.

Hampered by the dim light, I had to squint to understand what I was seeing. Thousands of the grubs slithered out, stretched, joined, and levitated into a threatening, undulating curtain over our heads.

Mark grasped my hand and we backed slowly toward the tunnel entrance. "Lazul, what should we do?"

No answer. I took my eyes off the massive organism and glanced behind us. Our guide had disappeared.

"Mark?" I choked out. The slimy white sheet swayed back and forth across the cave ceiling and began to descend. "I think we'd better—"

"Run!" he shouted.

CHAPTER 10

LINETTE

THE DIM ROOM became a forever place. I couldn't remember how I'd come to be there. Sometimes I dreamed of vast skies, scented trees, and soft mist that brushed my skin. A vague sense of being someone else teased me, but when I tried to follow those thoughts they slipped away.

Then I would open my eyes. Black walls glowered at me, and the mesh door spat stinging electricity if I got too close. The tiny window far above my head let in the soft hint of first light, along with distant sounds: mini-trans on a nearby road, whirring insects, gruff voices. The unfamiliar sounds unsettled me, even though I'd been assured that this room beneath the shrine was my home.

During my first days there, Bezreth visited me often. She told me about the training I would receive to serve the hill-gods. Ceremonies, sacrifices, rites that I was meant to embrace, but that instead made my stomach turn. She reminded me of my purpose over and over, as my clumsy brain struggled to comprehend. Bezreth was my one certainty. High priestess, teacher, mother. She brought food and reassurance.

She also brought the medicine that I needed to survive. Each day she pulled off my wristband and slipped a new strip of drug-patch into the lining. When it clicked closed over my forearm again, tranquility seeped through me, banishing stray, disturbing memories.

One morning a melody woke me, drifting in from the sliver of window above my head. A long-whistle trilled and skipped through a playful chorus. My soul rose up in answer. I left my pallet and stood on tiptoe, reaching toward the music, as if my fingers could grasp it.

New thoughts flickered to life. I belonged with someone . . . somewhere else. Somewhere with music, and broad grey skies, and tree limbs that braided a shelter over quiet homes. Yearning welled up in me. Where was that place? How could I find my way back? I couldn't dredge up a name or remember a single clear day of life before I'd come here, but the song stirred my spirit.

"You seem restless." Bezreth's whisper crept past the mesh gate, twined coldly around my ankles, and sent dread up my spine.

I turned to face her, my back pressed against the wall for support. The music had drifted off. What had I been trying to remember? A dull throb in my skull ate away my ability to think. I pressed a palm against my forehead.

"Poor child." Bezreth opened the gate and stepped toward me. Her gummy smile stretched in her gnarled face. "Are you feeling more confusion today?" She removed my wristband, replaced the drug patch, and clamped it back onto my arm.

I stared dully at the silver band. I'd seen it before. What did it mean?

"Let your worries float away." Bezreth's hoarse voice no longer sounded harsh, but gently wizened with age. "All you need to remember is that you are safe in my care. As long as you wear this band, you'll get better. Soon those tortured thoughts will never disturb you again."

The ache behind my forehead faded. She was right, of course. She was always right. "Thank you," I whispered.

She squeezed my forearm until her nails dug into my skin. Numbness began to swirl through me. Her husky voice took on a hard edge. "You would die without a new patch from me. Within a few days. I'm the only one keeping you alive."

When she left, I curled up on my pallet, breathing slowly as another day drifted past and blended into another night.

Sometime in the last watch of the night, I woke to heavy feet tromping down the hallway. Drunken laughter. Pen doors slamming. A girl moaned, and her whimpering lingered long after the other sounds quieted.

When Bezreth felt I was ready, footsteps would come to my room in the night. I would be expected to welcome the visits that fed the cravings of the hill-gods. But for now, I pressed my hands over my ears. Dark horror crept through me. When would Bezreth's medicine finish making me strong?

The next morning, the music returned with the birds. The sweet sound of a familiar tune soared and then plunged into me, pulling me along with it, awakening a fragile link to a deeper self—a truer self. Memories rose so close I could almost push away the water-weeds clogging the surface and find my past revealed in bold colors.

But then Bezreth's feet shuffled down the row. Her rasping voice interrupted the music as she stopped at each pen to speak with the girl inside. Murmurs were punctuated by a squeal of joy. The high priestess had selected someone to serve in a shrine rite, and the girl's excitement carried through all our rooms.

When she opened the mesh door of my room, I dully held out my arm. This time after she changed my drug patch, she traced one fingernail down my face. "I think you're ready to spend time with your sisters. Follow me."

A hint of interest rose for a moment, then faded back into the sea of indifference. "If you think it's a good idea."

She led me along the hall, past jagged stairs, beyond two huge guards, then to a large room filled with comfortable chairs, pallets, and dozens of other girls. Many of them sat quietly staring into the distance. Others carried on conversations in small clusters around the room.

Ria sprang up. "Over here."

I knew her. Relief washed over me at the flare of recognition, and I happily took a chair beside her. Ria picked up a length of fabric and began to stitch metallic thread onto a stole. She kept her focus on her work until Bezreth withdrew from the room.

"Guess what?" she whispered. "Bezreth told us that the shrine will be reopened before the end of the season. And she's been so pleased with my service that I'm to be one of the first shrine girls to serve."

She seemed excited, so I tried to smile.

"Oh, I forgot. You wouldn't know. Bezreth and the priestesses made sure the rites continued, but all in secret. The shrines had been closed because of the king's bargain with—" She glanced up at me. "Never mind. He's gone now. It doesn't matter." She held up the stole. "What do you think? It's for one of the priestesses."

Silver threads wove through a tumble of crimson. The design looked like blood spilling toward the maw of stone depicted along the hem. What did I think? Some dark reaction welled up but disappeared before I could identify it. I smiled weakly at Ria. What had she asked me?

Ria sighed. "The drug patches. You're barely awake."

"They don't bother you?"

She showed me her bare arm. "Don't need them."

But Bezreth had said we needed them to stay alive . . . or I needed them . . . or . . .

I picked up a skein of thread and held it for Ria, forsaking the painful effort to think.

Just before lunch, Bezreth came into the room followed by two robed priestesses who carried wide, flat baskets of stones. No, not stones. Carvings. Angry, drooling faces like the ones on the doors I'd passed through when I came here.

A chill brushed over me. Hill-gods. Or an image of them. Was there a difference? Surely Bezreth had explained it to me, but I couldn't remember.

The old woman moved around the room, stopping before a girl. She picked up a statue and weighed it in her hand, stared deeply into the eyes of the girl, then handed it to her. She continued around the room, followed by the young priestesses, and stopped by Ria. The girl held her breath, her body so tense her tunic quivered.

Only a few of the stone images remained in one of the baskets. Bezreth looked at each of them as if greeting friends, then chose one and presented it to Ria.

Ria's face lit and her braids bounced as she grabbed the statue. "Thank you, high priestess." Her voice squeaked, but then she composed herself and bowed her head.

Bezreth turned to study me. My heart beat faster. My life had been given to the hill-gods, yet I still hadn't been found worthy to serve them in any way. Not even to scrub the floor of the shrines.

She turned away and handed a statue to someone else.

I shrank into my chair. Inadequacy gripped me, vaguely familiar, as the chance to prove my worth again passed over me in favor of others more worthy.

A form stopped in front of me. "Linette."

I looked up, startled. Bezreth stared at me, her lips stretched in a smile that chilled me. "Congratulations. You've been here long enough. It's time for you to be of use to the hill-gods."

A feeble sensation twisted in my stomach, then faded. "I'm glad," I said, but my voice sounded dead in my ears. Where was the euphoria, the fulfillment I'd longed for? "I want some way to serve."

She poked my chest with one gnarled finger. "You will. Tonight."

I dipped my chin, trying to hide the fear that roiled again, this time with more strength.

She chose the final stone statue from the basket, communed with it briefly, then handed it to me. The sculpture depicted a leering face framed by clawed hands, frozen in a moment of attack. Loathing washed through me like a swallow of the bitter clavo I was brought each morning.

"Let it speak to you," she said.

But I could barely look at it.

The high priestess cupped my face in her hands and forced me to look into her onyx eyes. "You'll have the honor of serving one of Zarek's generals. Do whatever he tells you. Understand?"

A deeply buried part of me recoiled in horror at the night ahead. Why? This was what I'd waited for. This was a shrine girl's purpose.

"Understand?" Her dark eyes filled my vision and her sour breath surrounded me. Bezreth communed with the hill-gods and held the power of life and death.

I swallowed back the tremor in my throat. "I understand."

CHAPTER
11

LINETTE

RAIN. THE RAIN didn't change. Each afternoon water stippled against rock outside my window, splashed into puddles, and then dwindled to gentle drips. Cleansing, soothing. I always welcomed the sound. The rain brought a soft scent that briefly scrubbed away the undercurrent of sourness and decay in these underground chambers, scouring off the cloying sweetness of perfumes used throughout the shrine.

But today, the comfort of rainfall was short-lived. The light in the small window deepened to a slate grey too soon. Near the mesh barrier penning me in, the hill-god statue sat on the floor. Bits of static occasionally crackled from the wires and arced toward the vicious face on the stone, as if the hill-god were drinking in the power.

I struggled to muster my courage, but each time I looked at the carved image, I turned away. A shrine servant brought supper, but the fried bread stood untouched, along with the ceremonial goblet of lehkan blood.

No wonder Bezreth had waited so long to choose me. Too fearful. Unworthy. Any other shrine girl would have been thrilled with the honor—and one of Zarek's generals, no less. I smoothed the long white tunic I'd been given. The finely woven fabric felt odd against my skin, and I longed for a robe to cover my bare arms.

Enough. Time to stop staring at the darkening patch of sky and embrace my purpose.

With a steadying breath, I picked up the image and stared deeply into its face. The stone burned cold and empty against my skin. My muscles ached from holding it at arms' length.

Night advanced like the rock beetles that occasionally skittered across the cold floor of my room before disappearing into small crevices. If only I could follow them and hide.

Before men fought and beetles stung . . .

A wisp of melody came to mind, words emerging from some tiny cubby still unlatched.

"There was a time,
A time rich with days,
Before sad and lonely songs were sung.

"There was a day,
A day rich with time,
Before men fought and beetles stung."

I let the words flow, singing softly so the girls in the nearby pens wouldn't hear. I lowered my hands, shifting my gaze from the snarling stone image back to the window. When had I sung those words before? How was I remembering them? I'd certainly not learned them here at the shrine. The progression of notes didn't follow patterns like anything I'd heard in this place—not even the light reel that the unknown musician played in the distance every morning.

Another thread of memory whispered through my mind. An old man leaning on his walking stick, saying, "Music helps us remember, Linette. That's why the songs are so important."

Whoever he was, he must have been right. Though Bezreth told me I should have no memories from before my first day in the shrine, still the melody produced words, images, understanding.

"Flowers bloomed in the pebbled sand;
Ground-crawlers didn't torment the land;
The mist caressed like a mother's hand
In those days when the earth was young.

"There comes a time,
A time of new days,
When new songs dance on our tongue.

"There comes a day,
A day after time,
When all the battles will be won.

"The mountain cat will sheath her claws,
Rescued from the enemy's jaws.
We'll sing the truth of the Deliverer's laws
And leave the mourning songs unsung.

"Some day, One day,
On the day of the One.

"Clay pits no longer will swallow our dreams,
No comrades fall amid battlefield screams.
Music will flow in eternal streams,
Like the days when the earth was young.

"When new songs dance on our tongue,
And the battles are all won . . .

"Some day, One day,
On the day of the One."

Something flared deep within me, a rekindling of passion once familiar. The One. He was the unseen companion I'd struggled to remember. No wonder I'd felt confused, haunted, tangled in darkness. I didn't belong here. I belonged to Him.

The image in my hands leered at me.

With all my feeble strength, I flung the stone against the corner of the room. The harsh clang jarred the air. Not a single chip broke loose, but my fear of the lifeless image shattered.

I would never serve the hill-gods. I still had no clear memories before coming here, no conviction about who I'd been. But I couldn't do what Bezreth commanded.

At that moment, heavy footsteps moved down the hallway. Doors slid aside. Men's voices growled.

My heart pounded and roared in my ears. My fists clenched. *Not now. Not when I know the truth.*

Panicked, I reached for the mesh door. The surge of electricity sizzled and slapped me back, sending me stumbling onto my pallet. Would I survive if I threw my entire body against the wires? Would that be a better option than what Bezreth had planned for me?

"Holy One, deliver me." As soon as the words escaped my lips, a doubt seized my stomach. Were ordinary people allowed to speak directly to the One? These past weeks I'd been taught that no one would dare approach the hill-gods unless Bezreth bestowed a stone image on them. Only Bezreth survived true conversation with the spirits inhabiting the shrine. But what about the One? I ached to remember, ached to fight through the fog and grasp truth. "Forgive me if this is wrong, but if You are the One who was before time," I whispered, "I know You can hear me. Please give me strength."

I held my breath. Few men ventured down to the far end of this hall. We were the least worthy, the newest arrivals.

Tonight as doors slipped open and closed, footsteps moved rapidly past all the other doors toward my room. I backed against the far wall, a fist of dread squeezing my throat. I would explain that I didn't belong here. I would reason. I would beg. I would fight. But I wouldn't surrender.

A figure in military dress stopped outside my door. "This one," he barked. The faceplate of his helmet hid his features, but his eyes burned in the dim light.

An accompanying shrine slave worked the lock and lever. The door slid open.

The man advanced and reached toward me. My plans to reason or beg flew from my mind. I screamed.

Even as the sound rushed from my throat, I realized my foolishness. No one ever came to the rescue of a shrine girl screaming in the night.

He grabbed my arm and pulled me toward the open door. "Let's go."

I clawed at his arm, kicked, broke free, and looked wildly around the room. He blocked my path to the door. *Holy One, save me or kill me. Don't let this happen.*

He rubbed the arm I had scratched as if it were nothing more than a beetle's bite.

The burly slave hovered in the hall. "Having trouble?"

The soldier in my cell growled. "I'll handle this. You're dismissed."

With a shrug, the man lumbered away. I wanted to dissolve into the rough wall behind me. I crouched lower, and my hand found the goblet of lehkan blood.

The general grabbed at me.

Launching forward, I swung the goblet in an arc that sprayed blood across the walls and struck the side of his head.

He stumbled away and blasted out some curses I didn't remember hearing before, even among the guards that worked beneath the shrine.

I dodged around him and out the door.

But I hadn't hit him hard enough. Steel-banded arms grasped my waist and pulled me back. I writhed, drove my elbow back, and struggled with desperate gasps of breath. I smelled the salty tang of his skin, the earthy scent of leather, and the sour remnants of lehkan blood.

"Stop!" He whirled me around to face him.

I squared my chin. "Let go of me."

To my shock, he released me. I quickly edged back as far as the small cell allowed. He advanced a step, his helmet streaked with lehkan blood, making his blazing eyes even more terrifying.

His jaw tightened. "We don't have much time . . ."

All the better. Maybe I would be able to fight long enough for him to give up. Then I read the determination in his eyes, and my stomach clenched.

He reached for me again.

As soon as he touched me, I exploded into motion. Kicking, scratching, pounding against his leather armor. His limbs were hard as the stone walls.

His fingers dug into my arms. He shook me hard, making my teeth clack and my head snap painfully. "What's wrong with you? You're coming with me."

My ears rang. The bones of my neck ached. I gulped in a shaky breath. I had been praying for a way to escape. Leaving here could bring me one step closer to that goal. Just buy some time. Go along until you're out of this place and can run.

I stopped straining away and stared at the floor, a compliant shrine girl. "I'm sorry. I was told we would stay here. All right. I'll come with you."

His hand manacled my arm as he led me to the door. He leaned out and checked the hall. Odd. Who was he trying to avoid? Bezreth had myriad rules, and it was rare for men to take shrine girls from their rooms, but I couldn't imagine a general worrying about rules.

He lunged from the room, dragging me behind him. I struggled to keep up with his long strides as he whisked us past the other rooms, where dark shapes moved in the shadows. By the time we reached the end of the hall, I had to run to match his pace.

We reached a set of jagged stairs. Ria had once pointed out the foot of these stairs because they led to the main palace and the king's chambers. The man propelled me upward in front of him without speaking. When we reached the top, a hall branched off in three passages. I searched my memory. Had I been here before? Nothing looked familiar.

My throat tightened so much my breath escaped in a whistle. "Wait."

"Now what?" He stopped, but his gaze kept moving, scanning the hall in each direction.

"Are you Zarek? Or are you taking me to him?"

He let go of me as if his fingers had been scorched. His eyes turned even harder than when I'd fought him in the cell or hit him with the goblet. "The king? No." He tore the helmet from his head, revealing dark hair spiked with sweat and a scar puckering a line of skin over one brow. "Something wrong with your eyes?"

Humiliation, my constant companion these past days, forced my gaze to the floor. "Forgive me. I can't remember anything before I came to the shrine. I thought you might be taking me to the king."

While one part of me strove to keep a conversation going, beneath my down-swept lashes, I quickly scanned the halls, the doors, searching for the best means of escape.

The general settled his helmet back on his head. "Sorry to disappoint you. This way." He gripped my arm with barely leashed anger.

What had I done now? There was no time to think about it as he urged me into a run down one hall, and around a zagging turn that forced us in the opposite direction for a few yards. Tapestries and stone walls passed in a blur. He dragged me at a pace that made my ribs heave for air.

The corridor angled again and revealed a long straight hall with doors framed by two armed guards.

He tightened his grip on me. "Don't make a sound. Understand?"

I managed a nod.

"Open it," he ordered the guards as we approached. Seeing his high-ranking uniform, they snapped to attention. One of the soldiers slid a lever, and the door skimmed open a heartbeat before we reached it.

The general didn't even pause. We passed through and into a broad courtyard. I tilted my neck to catch a glimpse of the black sky—so much wider than the small piece I had seen from my basement cell every night.

Still he didn't stop. We passed a fountain, through massive carved doors, and into a spacious plaza. Light panels as tall as houses cast a harsh illumination over a melee of people and animals shoving their way past booths and open storefronts.

Where was he taking me? Perhaps Zarek's generals had private homes outside the main barracks of the palace. Did it matter? Wherever he planned to take me, I needed to escape before we reached his destination.

We wove around milling people and past stalls. Under the glare of the outdoor lightwalls, vendors sold a dizzying array of goods in the center of the square. The mixture of scents overwhelmed me. Burnt caradoc meat, sickly sweet perfumes, and most pervasive of all, the sour smell of fermented orberry wine.

Shoppers cast curious glances toward us but sidled quickly out of our way. The general pulled me through an alley and onto a dark and isolated side street. As the lights and sounds behind us dimmed, fear wrapped around me like the black cloak of the night sky.

He paused to glance back at the empty street behind us. Seizing my chance, I flung myself toward the ground in a dead weight. He didn't completely let go of me, but he was thrown off balance. I kicked out at his legs, then gasped as my foot bruised against his shin-guard. As I twisted my body, I managed to wrench my arm free, roll, spring up, and run.

Another dark alley ahead beckoned me. Now I exploded forward and ran with every fragment of strength pent up in my body during weeks of captivity. Nothing else mattered. Only each pounding step. Only each breath I could gasp while I was still free, still whole.

But over the throb of my pulse, the sound of his pursuit advanced every bit as fast. I tore out of the alley, around a corner, and down another dark corridor . . .

And faced a solid wall.

He was right behind me. I couldn't turn back. I pressed my palms against the granite, as if I could coax the brick to part for me. The general pulled to a stop behind me. His breath heated the back of my neck. Every muscle in my body clenched.

Summoning a last shred of courage, I turned to face him.

Once again he pulled off his helmet and this time tossed it aside. My pulse throbbed under my jaw. *Holy One, please, please save me.*

He raked a hand through his short hair. In the pale cast-off light from the square, it almost looked like the edge of his mouth twitched upward. "I really didn't expect you to be this difficult." He was barely out of breath.

My lungs continued to fight for air, panting, exhausted. Heat and cold ran through my veins. The drugs from the armband surged through my body and reasserted their control. Beyond weary, I sagged against the wall. Would he kill me? I couldn't run, couldn't fight. I had lost. I *was* lost.

"Just for future reference," he said, "if you're trying to escape, don't run down a blind alley."

The mocking tone should have ignited irritation, but that would have taken energy I didn't have to spare. Dull fear pulsed through me. He had paid a good tribute to Bezreth. I was his tonight. And I didn't have the wits or the strength to get away.

I closed my eyes. *Holy One, deliver me. Holy One, deliver me.* My lips moved silently.

He gave a heavy sigh. "We don't have time for this. You can't keep fighting me." He put a hand on my shoulder, and I flinched.

His hand stayed, unmoving but gentle. "Linette, it's me. You have to remember."

My eyes shot open. "I knew you?"

I studied him—the eyes that smoldered with an unreadable emotion, the angled planes of his face, the dark stubble of his jaw. Nothing connected. I shook my head. He thought I should know him, yet I didn't, and that added to the terror that roiled in my stomach. Still, I wouldn't cower. I met his eyes. "Who are you? When did I know you?"

His shoulders sank, and he backed up a step, giving me room to breathe. "Linette, I'm Kieran."

"Kieran?" The name rolled around like a pebble between my palms and dropped away. It meant nothing.

"You came with me to Hazor." Sadness mingled with regret in his voice.

Perhaps this was just a game he played.

Or a trick. A test to see if I had really broken with my past.

Had he heard my murmured prayers? Would he report to Bezreth that I wasn't faithful to the shrine-gods? A cold dread gripped my bones. "I don't know you."

He stared hard into my eyes. "*Caradung*. What did she—" He snatched my arm, stared at the wide bracelet, and swore again. In a swift, remorseless move, he pried the band from my wrist and threw it to the ground.

"No!" I dropped to my knees and scrambled for the band, clutching it in desperate fingers. Without it, I'd die. Was there still enough medicine for me to survive another day?

I braced my hand on the wall behind me and stumbled to my feet, suddenly aware of the flaw in my escape plan. I had to do more than get away from this soldier. I needed a supply of drug patches. "Please. Just take me back to Bezreth."

His eyebrows slanted as he scowled. "What are you talking about?"

"You have to take me back."

"Don't be stupid. I'm getting you out of Hazor. You aren't going back there."

My breath caught. Could this be an answer from the One? My means to be free of Bezreth and the shrine? This rough, scowling soldier? I gripped the armband tightly, the mangled edge cutting into my palms. Hope escaped my lungs with a groan. "The drug patches. I'll die without them."

He snatched the bent metal from my hands again and clenched it in his fist, then studied me through hooded eyes. "All right. I can get you drug patches. Here's my offer. If you want me to give you another, you cooperate."

I had little choice. I didn't know how to find my way out of Sidian, or how to find the drug patches I'd need to survive. Nausea rose in my stomach and I swallowed hard. "You have more?"

He never looked away. "Of course."

Even though his voice was carefully bland, all my instincts screamed that he was lying.

CHAPTER
12

SUSAN

SKIDDING AND SLIPPING on the damp rock, we scrambled back the way we'd come. I didn't know what the flying grubs would do to us, but I didn't wait to find out. Far ahead I glimpsed Lazul's light rod. "Hey, wait!"

Mark still had his light, but we'd never find our way around these caverns without Lazul. I strained to keep the man in sight— our last hope of escape.

Mark grabbed my hand and ran beside me. Maybe Lazul was planning to lose us in the tunnels. Too bad I had no breadcrumbs to drop.

Finally the Kahlarean slowed enough for us to catch up. He looked at us sourly. "I thought you needed to find that precious possession you dropped."

"Can we get back in there?" Mark asked tersely.

"No. Now that you've stirred up the grubs, they'll go through a whole life cycle. They'll cover the entrances with their webbing. They'll fight to protect their eggs. Thanks to you we can't use that cavern for a full season, and it's a major passage." He turned away and stomped toward his grotto.

I pulled a strand of sticky webbing from my shoulder and faced Mark. "You can't keep barking at him. We need his help."

He looked at the yawning darkness behind us, then at Lazul's disappearing back. "What's your plan?"

"I just think a little diplomacy would help."

We continued forward, staying far enough back to hold a whispered conversation. Mark threw another glance behind us, clearly torn about leaving the stone.

I reached for his hand. "I'm sorry about the portal stone." Losing access to this world forever held a finality he'd never faced before. I couldn't imagine how much it hurt him.

He switched his light rod to the other side and grasped my fingers. "You were right. I shouldn't have tried to recalibrate them in the first place. If I'd left them the way they were, you could have slipped through to Lyric, checked on Jake, and come right home."

So it was guilt troubling him, more than the loss of the stone. "Don't blame yourself. If the portal had stopped letting me through, like it did to you, I would have done the same thing. I'm just glad you're with me." And I meant it with my whole heart. This adventure didn't seem as dark and frightening as the last time I'd come through the portal. Mark was by my side. Together we could tackle anything.

He pulled me in tight for a one-armed squeeze as we kept walking. "Thank you. Now we'd better find a way out of these caves. Sounds like we have a long journey to Cauldron Falls."

We reached the intersection of several passageways where Lazul once again stood waiting. Mark unerringly strode into one of the tunnels, confident of the way back to Lazul's family grotto.

"Wait." Our reluctant Kahlarean companion tilted his head and listened. Beyond the faint trickle of water, the echo of footfalls approached.

"Friends of yours?" Mark asked.

Lazul shrugged. "Some of the soldiers stationed in these underhills." He brightened. "They could help you."

Mark stiffened.

"It might be better," I said quickly, "if we go on our way without bothering anyone else. Can you show us the shortest way out? We

102

really need to travel back to the clans." I took a few steps, hoping Lazul would follow.

Lazul gave us a hard stare. "I think it's better to let someone else take care of you."

My heart pounded faster, but I took a shaky breath. "Lazul, I have a little girl . . . about the same age as yours. We just want to get back to her, to our other children. Getting soldiers involved will take too much explanation."

Beside me, Mark held his breath.

Lazul sighed heavily. His puckered face made it clear we'd been enough trouble already. "Oh, all right. Follow me."

I tried to feel sympathy for him, but we'd only disrupted a few hours of his day. Somehow that didn't compare to the challenges Mark and I were facing.

Even with his disapproving trudge, Lazul moved almost silently. Though I strained to listen, I heard no further warnings of approaching feet. The soldiers must have gone off another direction in this warren of tunnels and caverns.

The Kahlarean led us around a bend and into a new tunnel that glittered with shiny rock chips that multiplied the light in dizzying refractions. What a strange world these Kahlareans inhabited.

"Just through there." Lazul pointed.

I stopped cold. The roof of the cavern lowered in a massive slab, leaving a passage so small we'd have to crawl. If it grew smaller, we could be trapped. Pinned. Helpless. Like when I'd been captive in a small Rhusican room. Claustrophobia crushed my ribcage. "No. I'm not going in there. Isn't there another way out?"

Lazul clenched and unclenched his fist around the light rod that he braced against the floor like a cane. "There are no grubs in there."

"That's not what I mean. It's so . . . all that rock overhead . . . and small . . ." It would be like crawling beneath a tilted anvil that could fall on us an any moment.

"Remember why we came." Mark squeezed my hand. "You can do this."

Lazul made impatient swishing sounds with his mouth. He exchanged a look with Mark. "I'll go first. Perhaps you should go last."

Being sandwiched between them only made me feel more trapped. My breathing sped up into tense hiccupping gasps, but I pressed down the panic. "Lead the way."

Lazul bent and wriggled ahead of me. I crawled along behind, silently praying crazy, broken phrases. *Oh, Lord. One more inch. Another. How much farther? Help me!*

An eternity of misery battled against my courage in the first few yards of that narrow passage, and I froze, unable to escape the vision of myself pinned in the dark under tons of rock.

"Almost there." Mark's gentle prompt interrupted my panic. Expanding my ribs in a deep breath, I pushed forward, knees scraping in my hurry. Then the cave roof sloped upward and we were able to stand again.

As the tunnel opened to another spacious cavern, light pooled around an opening ahead, and I rushed forward on shivery legs. A few more steps and we were blinking in the soft grey light of the open air. Breathing deeply, I took in the landscape stretched out before us. The mossy hills reminded me of the lands near Shamgar far on the other side of the clans, and a few spice trees with their braided branches dotted the horizon.

"Which way is Cauldron Falls?" Mark asked.

Lazul pointed. "About two days journey past the cup between those hills."

Hills? They were mammoth. True mountains, but with rounded green peaks and curving slopes.

"All right. We'll head straight that way until we find the Falls."

Lazul tensed. "No! You can't go that way."

"Why not?"

His eyes widened. "It's the assassins' enclave."

A shard of pain throbbed across my sword arm where a ven-blade had once poisoned me. Mark paled and pulled me closer, wrapping an arm around my waist. "Then how do we reach the pass by Cauldron Falls?"

Lazul stretched out his light rod like Moses's staff and pointed out a route that circled far below the two hills. "Go around. It'll take you longer. But no one dares go through the enclave."

"You'll get no argument from us," I said. "Thank you for all your help."

Mark looked grim but forced himself to sound cordial as he thanked Lazul. The Kahlarean bobbed his head a few times, then ducked quickly back into the cave, not bothering to hide his relief at being rid of troubling visitors.

"Okay. You heard him. We'll have to circle those hills." Mark rolled up the sleeves of his shirt, the color, buttons, and design anachronous in this foreign world. At least the bits of grub cocoon and dirt camouflaged the fabric a little. My sunny yellow blouse made me feel like I was wearing a bull's-eye. "Let's go."

I limped along beside Mark's aggressive stride.

He stopped and stared at my feet. "Where are your shoes?" His surprise held an edge of annoyance, as if he were picking Anne up from a friend's house and she had bounded into the car barefoot. Did he think I liked wandering around a strange world in my stocking-inged feet?

"On the rug by the front door. The portal didn't exactly give me time to pack, did it?"

"You can't hike across Kahlarea like that."

"If you'd been a little friendlier, Lazul and his family might have helped us. We could have used some other supplies besides shoes."

He stared at the light stick Lazul had given us, as if he'd forgotten it was there. His clear gaze swung to meet me. "Do you want to go back?"

Narrow tunnels. Kahlarean soldiers. Morphing grubs.

I shuddered.

"No thanks. I'll manage." I stripped off the damp socks and waggled my toes. "Besides, I just read a news story about how it would be better for our feet if we all went barefoot more. In fact, there's a whole group that is fighting for the right for people to work in offices and go into stores and restaurants without shoes. Podiatrists say . . ."

I kept chattering as we made our way toward the distant hills. Mark shook his head, and his smile grew.

I stretched my gait to keep up with him, fists on my hips. "What?"

He grinned. "Nothing." But his low chuckle kept up a counterpoint to my dissertation about the benefits of bare feet. As we hiked, I found the cushiony moss of these lowland hills was actually comfortable under my toes. There was something about this world that made me feel young, that made me almost enjoy bounding barefoot over the hills. The spires of the city of Lyric sang of beauty that was still close to the source of all artistry. The forest around Braide Wood refreshed wanderers with the scent of pine and honey-spice. The Grey Hills in their haunting sadness still murmured of hope and opened my heart to vastness as they stretched into the horizon. Even the harsh granite of Hazor stirred boldness and vigor. And Rhus—

My sense of wellbeing dissolved. Thank the One I was on the complete opposite side of the clans from that nation. Their green tapered trees, gardens, and fountains boasted a contrived beauty to rival any place in this world, but my memories held only horror and intense relief that I'd escaped.

Mark quickly settled into a ground-eating pace. This was another of the many times I wished this world had a written language, cell phones, or some other quick way to get a message to our friends in Rendor, Braide Wood, or Lyric. Relying on messengers seemed to work for them, but there weren't any messengers here.

I skipped a few steps closer to him, the darkening sky warning that we'd need to find shelter soon. "So what do you know about Kahlarea?"

"Besides the obvious?"

"I mean are there any scary monsters I should know about?"

He didn't answer right away. We crested a low swell of land and stopped to get our bearings. We'd be visible for miles around on this barren slope. How close could we get to the hills before being in too much danger? As far as I was concerned, anywhere within a hundred miles of Kahlarean assassins was too close.

"There were stories." Mark pointed toward a clump of trees far to our left. "Let's head there until morning. I don't like being out in the open."

"Stories?"

"Sure. You know. Living in Rendor with the Kahlareans right across the river, everyone had theories. Mostly, we just had to be careful of the usual. Rizzids liked to sun on the rocks. There were some bears and mountain cats, but they usually stayed far from the city. The ground-crawlers weren't so much of a problem because of the rocky soil. They're a lot worse in the lowlands."

"And those monster-flying-grub things?" Just talking about them conjured creepy crawlies up and down my back.

He ran a hand over his head. "Nope. That's a new one. Never saw those in Rendor or anywhere else in the clans. Let's hope they only live in that cave system."

"Amen." For a moment we walked in silence as I tried to banish the feeling of sticky grub filaments against my skin. "But you mentioned stories."

He sighed. "All right. Mind you, I don't know who started them. Probably some guardians who got a little punchy from too many patrols up by the Falls."

"Understood. Myths, legends. Might not be true. Go on."

"Well, you know how the assassins can move silently, almost invisibly?"

I glanced to our right where the gap between the mountains seemed to swallow light. I didn't answer.

"The story goes that as part of their training, they hunt a scolopendra. It's sort of like a centipede."

The tight thrill of fear forming in my midsection evaporated in a bubble of laughter. Here I was bracing myself for scary tales of danger. "You're not telling me that assassins train by chasing after bugs?"

SHARON HINCK

He was silent for a few seconds. "They say these are as large as lehkan. It takes days of stalking, total silence to approach them, and the armor of their bodies makes them nearly impossible to kill. Of course the bite is poisonous, but they also have clawed tentacles that can rip a caradoc apart."

I inched closer to Mark and matched my stride to his.

He slid a glance my way and gave an apologetic grin. "Remember, it's probably just a legend designed to keep kids from wandering. You know how fearless the people from Rendor clan are. The moms had to invent some sort of story to keep kids close to home."

"Well you've succeeded in creeping me out," I grumbled.

"You asked. Besides, we should be more afraid of the assassins who train by killing scolopendra than by the centipedes themselves, don't you think?"

I made a face at him. "That doesn't cheer me up. Is this really what passes for a fairytale among the clans? You're pretty dark and twisted."

That surprised a bark of laughter from Mark. "And what exactly would you call the Grimm brothers? Or Disney movies? Have you ever noticed how many moms are dead in those? Bambi is the worst."

I giggled. "I can't believe you're comparing Bambi to giant poisonous centipedes."

In spite of our attempts to joke, I was relieved when we drew into the cover of the forest. Night was approaching quickly, and I didn't like being in the open, whether scolopendra were fact or myth. Making camp didn't take much time since we had no tents to pitch, no heat trivets to set up, and no food to cook.

Instead, Mark showed me some berries – smooth as grapes, but with a mottled orange and yellow color that made them look as if they'd been tie-dyed. They had a heartier texture than most fruit, almost like a rich applesauce muffin.

"Try to get a little sleep." Mark said after we had eaten our fill. He sat with his back against a tree, and I settled beside him, craving his warmth, though the air wasn't particularly cool. Like everywhere else on this world, Kahlarea's climate seemed temperate. But with darkness falling, a different sort of chill prickled my skin.

I wanted Mark to keep his arm around me. His shoulder was my favorite upholstery, especially after he fiddled with the light rod, and it dimmed and went out. I realized a glowing light rod in this isolated place could attract unwanted attention, but I still hated to see the artificial illumination disappear.

"You can sleep." Mark's voice rumbled. "I'll keep watch."

How he could watch in the pitch black, I didn't know, but I closed my eyes, resting one hand against his chest, where I could feel his strong heart beat in a soothing rhythm.

When I next opened my eyes, the sky had lightened to the pigeon grey of predawn.

"You awake?" Mark whispered hoarsely.

I shifted away. "Yes. You should have woken me sooner. I could have taken a turn keeping watch."

He stretched his arm, rubbing kinks from his shoulder. "If you keep watch now, I could use a short nap before we head out."

"Sure."

He closed his eyes and was asleep in seconds.

I wasn't guardian-trained like Mark. I didn't have the discipline to sit still and alert. So I eased away from his sleeping form curled beneath the tree. I walked the perimeter of our small clearing, around the tree that looked like a corkscrew reaching to the sky, over to the braided spice tree, and from there to the patch of berries. I stopped to eat a few more, then ambled back to the tree where Mark rested on a bed of pine needles.

Turning, I circled back the opposite direction. There was no way to judge the passing of time other than the subtle changes in the light, but I wanted to give Mark a decent nap before we headed out. To fight the temptation of waking him, I set a slightly wider perimeter and circled again.

On my fourth or fifth lap, I heard a mewling sound, almost like a baby's cry. It stopped, then started again with a plaintive whimper.

Surely a baby couldn't have been left out here in the woods. Maybe it was the sound of a tiny caradoc lamb separated from its ewe. I glanced back at Mark, who was still sleeping hard.

The cry sounded again—so like a baby. My feet moved toward it. Just a quick look. I could always wake Mark if I needed him.

CHAPTER 13

SUSAN

THE MEWLING WAS close. I pushed through a thatch of tall ferns and came out into another clearing, where years' worth of pine needles coated the ground and tree branches stretched toward each other overhead. Nearby, a cluster of flattened ferns formed a large circle like the depressions marking places where deer had bedded down in the Midwest meadows back home. Did lehkan roam wild? They might have habits similar to deer. Too bad Mark wasn't awake to ask.

Listening, I stood motionless. Still no sign of a baby—human or otherwise. Time to head back. I shouldn't explore any farther on my own, anyway. I turned and retraced a few steps.

The tiny cry sounded again. I whirled in time to see branches of underbrush across the clearing stir in the dim light.

"It's okay," I crooned. "You're all right." I took a few steps forward.

The pine bedding shook as if an earthquake rippled beneath. What was happening? I grabbed a sapling for balance.

Suddenly the pine needles sprayed in all directions as a night-mare creature lunged upward in one fluid movement. My heart slammed against my ribs, desperate for escape as strange pincers reached toward me from an eyeless face. The serpentine shape continued to rise until it wove back and forth in a cobra's dance at the same height as my head. The most hideous centipede lurking in our basement was a cuddly pet compared to this.

I backed up in slow motion. "Mark," I croaked his name, but my lungs wouldn't expand enough for me to call out.

I inched another step away. "No, no, no."

The monster stretched to follow my backward progress. Its pincers clicked a bare inch from my face, emitting a weird chemical scent like the choking tang of chlorine and the cloying smell of varnish. Sideways jaws opened and viscous drool dripped from the fangs within.

I eased back another foot. If I turned to run, would it pounce?

Something crashed from a branch overhead, shoved me aside, and took my place in front of the giant centipede. I stumbled a few yards and hit the ground. Mark? No. This figure was smaller and wore the hooded mask and mottled grey of a Kahlarean assassin.

"This is my hunt," he hissed. He never took his eyes off the monster, but I felt the heat of his anger directed at me. "You find your own."

I rolled out of the way and ran back to Mark. He must have heard my body flailing through the underbrush, because he was already on his feet and rubbing his eyes.

I threw myself at him. "We have to help him. There's a . . . Back there . . . It's going to kill him," I gasped.

Behind me a roar rattled the branches, countered by a rebellious shout. More thrashing. Mark reached for the light rod, which looked puny and inadequate as a weapon. "Susan, slow down. What happened?"

An eerie whining sound rose in volume nearby and I thought better of my impulse to try to help the young assassin. I tugged Mark's arm, now pulling him away from the fern patch. "We'd better get out of here."

My irritated rescuer chose that moment to storm into sight. In one hand, casually hanging by his side, he clutched a curved blade with the silhouette of an Alaskan ulu knife. Maroon fluid dripped from the sharp edge. "Why did you interfere with my hunt?"

Mark quickly stepped between us. "We aren't out here tracking."

The assassin glared. With his small physique and bluster, he appeared to be fairly young. He lifted the other hand from behind him, and brandished the cruel looking pincer he'd severed from his foe. "I tracked him for half a season. I'm the only one getting credit for this kill."

Mark gave a stiff nod. "Of course. We didn't mean to interfere."

"Thanks for saving me," I said, trying to be friendly.

He only scowled.

Silently, three more hooded shapes materialized from behind trees. One of them addressed the youth, his flat tone a weird contrast to his words. "Well done, Trennor. You've made your first kill."

The youth pointed toward us with his dripping weapon, the adrenaline from the hunt apparently still fueling him. He looked ready to sever my limbs next. "She almost warned it off."

"Stand down." Even in the barely audible whisper of the older assassin, a rumble of authority ran through the air. "Return to the enclave and drain the venom. We'll distill it tonight."

The youth rocked forward on his toes but then gave a stiff nod and raced off.

In the time it took for him to dodge around a tree and out of sight, the three other men surrounded us in complete silence.

I pressed against Mark.

"What are you?" One of the assassins poked at Mark's chest with the tip of his dagger. At least it wasn't a spiral-bladed venblade. But we knew these three had a hundred silent ways to kill their prey. Over the grey cloth that covered the lower half of his face, wrinkles spiked from eyes as pale and cold as sleet. An elderly assassin? A teacher? Maybe we had a prayer of talking our way out of this confrontation.

Every muscle rigidly controlled, Mark matched the man's low tone. "Wrongly banished. We're traveling back to the clans. We mean no harm."

The man behind me patted my sleeves, my ankles. I flinched, but then followed Mark's example and didn't move.

He moved on and searched Mark, taking the light rod from him and returning to a position behind us. "No weapons, Master Voronja."

From beneath his hood, the master's pale eyes scanned us both and rested on my bare feet. "You travel light." Was there a hint of amusement in his breathy voice? The whispery speech made it hard to interpret emotion. "And in dangerous country."

Mark sighed. "The Council had little mercy when they banished us. But we—"

"Shall we practice our skills on them, Master?" The third man pulled a metal star from a fold in his tunic's cloth belt, and spun it on his finger like a toy.

"Apprentice, you were not addressed." There was no mistaking the angry hiss from the master assassin.

The apprentice quickly put away the shiny weapon and dipped his head.

My mouth was dry as gauze as I tried to swallow the dread lodged in my throat. Every second we spent with these Kahlareans increased our risk. I focused on Master Voronja. "I wasn't trying to warn that monster thing. I'm sorry if I interrupted your student's hunt. He saved me, you know. Please accept our thanks. We need to leave now to reach the river borders and seek a hearing with our clan."

Mark shot me an incredulous glance, probably impressed at how adept I was becoming at spinning a cover story. I didn't know if the banished were ever able to appeal the Council's edict, but hopefully the Kahlareans wouldn't know either.

"Then I can assist you." The master said in his raspy whisper. "We'll escort you on the shortest route."

"But that's . . ."

"Through our enclave. Yes."

Shock made me stumble back a step and bump into the young assassin behind us. "No we can't—" My protest died as a sharp blade pressed against my neck.

"Rahn, did I order you to draw weapons?" The elder Kahlarean bit out his question. He sounded like a harried schoolteacher whose patience was wearing thin. That comparison eased some of my fear . . . until it occurred to me that an assassin out of patience wasn't a comforting thought.

"Apologies, Master." The weapon withdrew as smoothly as it had appeared.

Beside me Mark had stiffened, but now he took a steadying breath. He'd been ready to dive into a battle unarmed against three assassins. Even now, he was barely holding himself back. I needed to diffuse this. Fast.

"I'm sure you and your students have important things to do." I tried a winning smile and all but batted my eyelashes. "We'll be fine. We got directions from someone back at Tremolite tribe, but we must not have cut far enough down from the enclave. We didn't mean to trespass. I'm sure you don't like being disturbed during your lessons. One time I accidentally drove onto a military base training area near our house because I didn't see the sign and—"

The elder Kahlarean winced and turned toward Mark. "Does she always talk this much?"

"We are trained to use only the words necessary," Rahn piped up.

I turned to glare at him. "Well I'm not in training to be an assassin, so I'll use whatever words I think are helpful."

Rahn's eyes widened, and he looked to his teacher in confusion.

A snuffle of laughter drew my attention back to the master. He shook his head slowly.

I cleared my throat. "Look, we really need to be going. Honestly, I don't know how many different ways I can apologize. I only went into the clearing because—" I gasped. "I almost forgot. I think there's a baby. Or a baby animal." I ignored the assassins and grabbed Mark's arm. "That's what I went looking for. I heard someone crying. We need to go look. Maybe the big centipede thing didn't get it . . ."

The faint baby's cry interrupted me.

I froze and darted my gaze around the clearing. "Did you hear it? That's what I heard before."

The young apprentice in front of us cupped both hands near his mouth and repeated the call, then snickered.

"You?"

He shook his head, but then glanced at his glowering master and stayed silent.

"Trennor used the call to lure his prey. Scolopendra feed on the small and weak." No traces of humor remained in the elder Kahlarean's face. "Small wonder it came out of hiding to attack you."

I drew myself up, ready to respond to that insult, but couldn't come up with a retort.

The master took a step closer to Mark and sized him up. "We don't allow unescorted strangers this close to the enclave. Only their corpses. Follow Rahn."

Mark's skin looked as wan as the morning sky. "Allow us a moment to discuss this change in plans."

The Kahlarean tilted his head, then slipped a metallic straw from a hidden pocket of his tunic. "You know this weapon?"

Mark's jaw tightened. "Yes."

The master gestured us away with his arm. Mark grabbed me and pulled me a few dozen yards out of earshot. The Kahlareans never took their eyes off us.

"What are our options?" I whispered.

"We go with them and get away later, or we fight them now." Mark's expression was bleak as he glanced at the distant mountains.

"Or we run." I eased us another yard from the three.

"That weapon . . . they'd dart us before we took two steps."

I shivered. "We need to pray."

Mark pulled his gaze away from the horizon and looked deep into my eyes. Love and appreciation kindled in his smile, and some of the hard lines of his face eased. "You're right." Ignoring the watching assassins, he rested his forehead against mine. "Holy One, we aren't sure if our mistakes have led us to this place, or if it was Your first will for us. But either way, we trust Your love and mercy. We have no weapons, but if You call us to fight, we will. We see no escape, but know You can provide one. Please show us what to do."

Cold sweat beaded on Mark's forehead where it pressed against mine. The grey mottled figures dominated my peripheral vision. But I shut out all distraction and asked the One to speak to my heart. The answer I sensed in my spirit sent a spiral of resistance through all my muscles. *This doesn't make sense.* With effort, I took a deep breath. *Yes, Lord. I'll go on any road. But promise me You're coming along.*

I looked up at Mark, and could tell from his frown that he had heard the same answer. "We go with them?" he asked.

I nodded. "I think so. Maybe the One will show us a way to escape later."

Mark's chest filled with new confidence and he managed a grin. "I never knew marrying you would be such an adventure."

I tried to smile. "Hey, you're the one from another world or reality or time, or whatever."

Guilt clouded Mark's eyes, and I regretted my wry comment. I put my hands behind his neck and pulled his head back down close to mine. "The One drew us here. He's our protector. That's not your job—not on your own anyway. What happened before . . ." Memories of the torture in Rhus burned through me in a sudden rush. I swallowed, mouth too dry to even whisper. "I don't blame you."

He studied me, searching my eyes for truth. I met his gaze openly, letting my love for him shine in my face. The swell of tenderness erased the power of my fear for the moment, and washed away the haunting memories.

"You're amazing, you know that?" His deep voice rumbled.

"No, you are." I winked. "So let's go be amazing together."

We walked back to the waiting assassins. With Mark's hand warm around mine, I could face them without dread making my legs weak.

"We accept your offer to guide us to the River Borders," Mark said with quiet courage.

"Yes, I heard." The master assassin tucked away his dart weapon. "Interesting way to make a decision. Rahn, take point." He stepped aside and gestured, revealing a glimpse of the venblade strapped to his wrist. "After you."

My eyes widened, and Mark and I exchanged a glance. Kahlareans must have much better hearing than we did. Or at least this one did. I thought we'd been far out of earshot. I'd have to be careful to guard every word—not one of my strengths.

Thank the One that He'd shown us what to do. If we'd tried to run or fight, we'd have had no element of surprise. *But how being led into an assassin's enclave is going to get us to Lyric, I can't begin to figure out.*

Familiar frustration throbbed inside my skull as I trudged after the two apprentices. How often had I seen the quickest and best path to solve a problem, only to watch circumstances throw up a barrier? Each time, I would beg God to explain why He asked me to go the long way around when He had the power to bring an immediate solution.

When Jake had battled leukemia, I knew God could touch the cells in his marrow and heal him in a millisecond. But if He chose not to do that, at least He could open up a space in the new cancer center in town. In full Technicolor, I saw the step-by-step best plan. But insurance wouldn't okay it. Every day in the hospital chapel, I alternated between raging against the pain God was allowing, and tearful pleading and bargaining.

I wanted the gift of the shortest and easiest path. Instead, He gave me the gift of holding me close and strengthening me for the hard path. It took me a long time to understand that both were gifts. And as I embraced the second, my need for the first lost its tormenting grip.

My notebook sketch had seemed to warn that Jake was in danger. Every impulse had driven me to the portal, to Lyric, and to helping him whatever it took. Instead, we'd been snatched away without weapons or supplies, dropped in a cave in an enemy nation, and delivered into the hands of assassins who, should they learn our identities, would no doubt kill us in a slow agony of torture and despair. With every step, our search for Jake grew more impossible.

Yet this is exactly when Your grace shines. As my feet kept moving across the cool moss, I chose not to imagine the difficulty of getting out of the enclave once we were taken there. With each footfall, I breathed another prayer. *I trust You. I trust You.*

An hour of hiking brought us to the foot of the imposing hills. The terrain had changed, and I began to hobble as more and more rocks jabbed my tender feet.

Mark stopped. "I know they're too big, but take my shoes. If you tie them really tight, they might stay on."

"Keep moving," the master assassin hissed.

Mark turned to confront him. "She can't go over these rocks in bare feet." My reckless hero, ready to raise the ire of a killer because he hated seeing me in pain.

Hooded eyes narrowed over the mask with unbending threat. "Move."

"Honey, I'm okay. Really." I scampered ahead to prove my point, and to draw Mark away from his suicidal impulse to throw a punch.

He caught up to me. "Hop on," he said, offering his back.

I hesitated, not wanting to be a burden.

"Let me help," he said quietly. "Please."

I wrapped my arms around Mark's neck and rode piggyback as we continued deep into a rocky canyon.

Around us rose sharp slopes coated with scree. The apprentices led us to the foot of a vertical rock face. I looked for a narrow tunnel or a hidden trail.

Instead, Rahn grasped an almost invisible handhold and began to climb.

I slid down from Mark's back. "No. You can't be serious. I can't manage that."

Master Voronja didn't argue. He simply slipped a venblade from its hidden sheath and pointed the twisted blade at me. "Climb."

CHAPTER
14

LINETTE

IF I ONLY had half a day left to live, I didn't want to spend it in these dim, littered alleys with their sour smells. Or with this rough, dark-eyed man who frightened me with his intensity.

His name had already escaped me, but my distrust of him grew.

"This way." His grip on my arm made the words unnecessary. He slid open the door of a hovel wedged into the angled gap between two taller buildings.

I held back. The small indoor space felt like a trap.

He shoved me inside and closed the door before sliding the lever for the lightwalls.

As soon as he let go of me, I rubbed my arm where his fingers had left bruising marks.

The light faded up to reveal a dusty common room with a few stark chairs and a single small alcove in the back.

A pack with a rolled blanket rested against the wall beside a sheathed sword.

He unbuckled the shoulder fastenings of his leather armor and tossed it aside. All his movements seemed brusque, angry. He crouched and pulled a wad of clothes from the pack and tossed it at me. "You can change in there." He nodded toward the back alcove, where a thin pallet filled half the floor space and a tattered curtain slouched at one side of the doorway.

I fingered the drawstring trousers and nubby sweater, but made no move toward the sleeping nook.

When I didn't obey, his eyes narrowed and he stretched to his feet. Dark whiskers shadowed his jaw. The scar over his eyebrow whitened as some angry emotion coursed through him.

I braced myself for a violent outburst.

Instead, he rubbed his shoulder and sighed. "We'll have to hide here until first light. I think I can get us out of the city then. But you can't travel like that." His gaze swept over my sheer shrine tunic and then he quickly looked away.

I felt vulnerable, exposed. A flush burned my skin, and I clutched the bundle of clothes, but still couldn't move.

"Messengers of the One," he muttered. "Linette, I'm helping you."

Not one cell in my body trusted him. "Then give me back my arm band." I'd never had it off for this long. I already felt weak, short of breath. How long before death claimed me?

His eyes hardened and he pulled the dented band from his pocket. "The deal is that you do what I ask."

Bezreth's words came back to me, hissing through my mind. "Do whatever he asks." My stomach muscles clenched, and I pressed against the door, trembling.

Raw pain tightened his features. He stepped closer. "Linette, did they . . . did you . . . I'm sorry I couldn't get to you sooner. I'd go back and kill them all if I could, but we have to get out of Hazor."

When I still didn't move, he reached for me. But instead of shaking me, or shoving me, he held me in an awkward hug. "I won't hurt you." He breathed the words against my face.

Was this his reassurance that he'd return my armband and provide me with new drug patches? The odd shakiness eased and my breathing slowed. The man's shirt smelled of finely woven caradoc wool and clavo and clean sweat. Familiar and soothing.

Moving stiffly, as if unused to being gentle, he coaxed me across the room. "Go ahead and change. Please."

I wasn't eager for his impatient and angry side to reemerge, so I stepped into the back alcove and pulled the curtain shut.

Soon I heard him shifting packs and checking weapons. I quickly slipped on the comfortable trousers and removed the shrine tunic. While I was pulling the sweater over my head, I heard the outside door slide open. Maybe he was leaving. I held my breath, then peered around the curtain.

A boy about Ria's age stood in quiet conversation with the general.

"Yes, I got her out. But she's not herself. She didn't even know me."

The boy shook his head. "How'd you get her to come with you?"

"I was . . . convincing."

"Oh, great."

"Nolan, is she going to be all right?"

The boy unslung a large cloth bag from his shoulder and handed it to the man. "Hard to say. I've heard the shrine girls have no memory before the day they enter—" He looked past the man and noticed me. "Oh. How are you?"

I pushed aside the curtain and took a hesitant step into the room. "Do you know me?"

"Your name is Linette. You're a songkeeper. You're terrible at the long-whistle and usually burn the stew and can't braid your hair very well. I helped you once, remember?" Large eyes peered at me from under dark bangs.

If this boy was right, I'd been about as useless in my early life as I had been in the shrine. I strained for something familiar but met a wall as blank and unyielding as the one in the alley. "He called you Nolan."

The boy grinned. "That's right. And he's Kieran. My father."

I relaxed a little. My captor wouldn't hurt me in front of his son, would he?

"So did you hear the music?" he asked.

"Music?"

Nolan nodded. "I asked the messengers to play outside the shrine at first light. They took turns. They were really worried. We thought it would let you know that help was coming."

Gratitude thickened in my throat.

Kieran tousled his son's hair. "It was a great plan." He watched me for a moment and then smiled at the boy. "I think she likes you."

"I'm likeable." Nolan ducked under his father's hand and pulled away.

Kieran laughed, and the surprising sound distracted me from my precarious situation. Until his eyes focused on me again.

"Get some sleep." He gestured toward the alcove.

Desperation gave me the strength to face him. "Give me my drug patch."

Nolan's mouth opened and he stared at me, then back at his father.

Kieran rubbed his forehead. A vein throbbed along his temple. "Nolan, we'll need some more food."

"But I—"

"Now."

The boy sent an uneasy glance my way. Then he pulled the door open and ducked out.

Out. Where I needed to be. Could I find my way back to the shrine? In my soft leather shoes, I slipped lightly along the far wall of the room and toward the door.

Kieran was faster. He reached the door before I did and hit the lever to seal us in.

I faced him. "You promised. Give me the armband." If I didn't stand up to him, I might be dead before morning. Even if he returned it to me, I'd need a refill patch soon.

"Linette," he said like a man barely holding onto his last thread of patience. "You aren't going to die."

So he had lied. He wasn't going to return my armband. My jaw hardened. "Is this how little your word means to you?"

He squinted at me. "Are you sure you don't remember who you are?"

I blinked. "What do you mean?"

"Never mind." He smiled and all the hard planes of his face softened. "You just sounded a lot like yourself there." The smile faded. "You trusted me once. At least I think you did."

He leaned back against the wall, arms crossed, almost languid. "Ask yourself. What do you remember?"

Pain pulsed along my forehead. I pressed the heels of my hands against the ache. "Don't change the subject. You're trying to distract me."

"Maybe. Partly." He waited.

Partly? But he also wanted me to remember. At least we had that goal in common.

I shook my head. "It's gone. I can't remember." My words sounded small.

He continued to slouch against the wall, blocking my exit. I'd felt safer with Nolan as a buffer. "Why did you send Nolan away?"

"You and I were heading for a . . . disagreement. He doesn't need to see that."

The small room closed in further. Tiredness made me waver on my feet, reminding me again that I'd been without the drugs for too long.

"Please let me go," I whispered.

A weary shadow settled on his face. He pushed away from the wall, guided me to one of the chairs, then pulled up a chair across from me. "Linette, I can't do that. You don't belong here. I've got to get you back to Braide Wood."

"How can you do that if I'm dead?"

He scrubbed a hand over his face. "Fine. You don't want to trust me. But what if you can't trust Bezreth, either? She stole your memories from you—your very identity. Did it occur to you that she lied as well?"

I struggled to focus. "Are you positive I can survive without the shrine band?"

"I promise I'll get you to the healers in Braide Wood."

Not the answer I needed. "So you don't really know."

"I know we'll all die if we don't get out of Sidian." Matter-of-fact. Uncompromising. And something else hummed in his low voice . . . a deep current of discouragement.

How was it that I could sense his inner pain? And why did that stir compassion in me? My resolve faltered. He was right.

I stood with as much dignity as I could muster. "Good night, then." I retreated to the alcove room and pulled the curtain closed.

When unfamiliar voices crept into my dreams, I stirred and then sat up quickly on my pallet.

"Let her sleep a little longer. She'll need her strength." The low tone was tight, pragmatic. The soldier named Kieran.

"What if she won't come with us? She seemed really confused," said a younger voice but similar in timbre. Nolan.

"I'll do whatever it takes." Kieran's flat words sent a cold twist through my stomach.

I heard Nolan stirring, moving closer to his father. "You're blaming yourself. It's not your fault."

"Don't," Kieran bit out. "I caused this. Bezreth took her because of me."

I chewed on my lip. So he'd been the one that sent me to the shrine-gods and the dark cells and Bezreth's control. And now he planned to drag me out of the city to die.

"Did she remember anything last night?" That was Nolan's voice, cracking on a few words.

"I don't think so. Maybe when the drugs wear off."

The drugs. I grasped my wrist. My lifeline was still gone. But I'd at least survived the night. I tested my memory. Kieran had stolen my armband. Before that I'd run from him down shadowy Sidian streets. Before that he had dragged me from the shrine and out of the palace. Before that were endless days in the rooms below the shrine. Before that . . .

. . . a grey, empty fog.

Bezreth must have been right. My current life began at the shrine. Everything before that was gone. And that meant she was likely right about the drug patches. I had to convince Kieran to give me back the armband.

"What if it's true?" Nolan's quiet question echoed my own. "You aren't going to let her die."

I held my breath. Kieran's answer was an impatient growl. The outer door slid open and slammed closed. Sweat beaded on my face. I brushed it away and realized my hand was trembling.

"He's gone," Nolan called softly.

I peered around the alcove curtain and smiled uncertainly at the boy. I had no more reason to trust him than his father, but he was at least less frightening.

"How are you feeling?" the boy asked.

As I stepped into the common room, my knees wobbled. "Fine. Where's my armband?"

Nolan glanced toward the door. Avoiding my gaze? "He's getting you more patches." Then he stepped closer and slowly moved his hand toward my face. When I didn't flinch away, he touched my forehead. "Fever." Concern darkened his eyes. "How good are the healers at Braide Wood?"

Braide Wood? The name felt as if it should be familiar. I squeezed my eyes closed and rubbed my forehead. Waiting for the name to conjure a picture, I tested the words again but found only a blurry wall.

Nolan sighed. "Sorry. Do you remember anything?" The gentle demeanor from the gangly teen endeared him to me.

"The music. You told your friends to play music."

Youthful pride filled his chest, and his eyes watched me eagerly. "Did you hear it? I wanted you to know you weren't alone. Did it help?"

"Yes. I heard. Thank you." Moisture in my eyes threatened to spill over, and I blinked a few times. "It helped me to remember that I didn't want to belong to the shrine-gods."

But I was still dependent on Bezreth for my survival. If I went back to the shrine, would she understand that I hadn't left of my own choice? Would she provide me with the drug patches I needed? Perhaps she'd give me enough so I could leave, since it had been so obvious that I didn't belong.

Nolan was still watching me. "What else do you remember?"

I took a few wavering steps toward the door. "Just that I need to go back."

The boy dodged quickly in front of me again. "I can't let you leave."

I sized him up. Wiry, but strong. At least stronger than I felt this morning. A sword rested beside a pack along the wall, but I couldn't imagine threatening him with that.

"Linette, we're on your side. Trust us."

Then why did he look so uncertain, so worried? I wavered.

He pointed to a small open door at the back of the common room. "Why don't you go get cleaned up? We'll be leaving soon. I'll find you something to eat."

I glanced around the room again, then surrendered to the inevitable. I couldn't attack him. I'd wait for another chance to get away. Meanwhile, I needed to save my strength.

After using the tiny washroom, I lingered to smooth my braids and splash cool water on my face. Last night I'd felt this same panic. Alone, trapped, in danger. And the reflex that sprang upward in me at that moment had been to talk to the One. So far, I had survived. *Holy One, You've rescued me from the shrine-gods, rescue me now from these strangers.*

I could hear Nolan moving around. The outer door slid open and quickly closed. Low voices murmured. After a deep breath, I stepped back into the common room.

Kieran tugged at a tie on his breastplate, then tossed the piece of armor to the floor. "That disguise won't work any longer."

Nolan helped him take off his gauntlets. "Should we wait until tonight?"

"No. The longer we wait, the more chance that they'll find us."

I rested one hand against the wall. "Disguise? You aren't really a general?"

Kieran's gaze snapped toward me. He studied me and frowned. "You don't look good."

Master of the obvious. "Maybe because you stole my armband? I tried to tell you—"

"We have to leave. Now." He grabbed a pack and tossed it to his son.

Nolan scurried to gather a blanket and made straight for the door. Kieran strode across the room and reached past me. I scooted aside, and he thrust a hooded cloak into my hands. "Put this on."

When I didn't move, he unearthed the armband from his tunic pocket and held it in front of me. "I tracked down a supply of the drug patches, and believe me, it wasn't easy."

I grabbed for it, but he pulled his hand back. "First make me a promise. It won't be easy getting out of the city. If I tell you to run, you run. If I tell you to duck and not make a sound, you do it. Understand?"

"Yes, yes." I was happy to put some distance between myself and the shrine, as long as I had the drugs to keep me alive. I could always choose a moment to escape Kieran later.

The scar near his eye twitched. "Can I trust you?"

"You're worried about my word? When you've done nothing but lie to me?"

His frown deepened. "No time to argue about it right now." He handed me the band, still dented from rough handling. There was a new drug-patch lining it, and I quickly pressed it around my forearm, then wrapped the cloak around my shoulders.

"The hood," he barked.

I didn't move fast enough for him, and he pulled up the hood to cover my head and shadow my face. He pushed a few of my stray braids back and tucked them under the fabric, his hand slowing for just a second. Then he turned away abruptly, grabbed up his sword and joined Nolan at the door. "Is it clear?"

The boy nodded.

"Let's go."

Nolan slipped outside, and I hurried to the door as well, to show Kieran that I was cooperating. Still, he grabbed my arm before letting me pass. "I can still take that from you if you try anything," he hissed. "Understand?"

I swallowed, my throat raw and sore. But freedom waited for me outside the door—freedom of a sort. "I understand." Yanking hard, I freed my arm and followed Nolan down the alley, not bothering to look back.

CHAPTER 15

LINETTE

THE EARLY MORNING passed in a blur of frantic running, confusing turns, and deserted back alleys. True to my word, I followed Kieran's directions, though I struggled to keep up with him and Nolan. Their tension infected me, setting off the pounding pulse of danger in my head. I saw no familiar landmarks, nothing that jarred my memory. That, plus the fever that continued to build hot and dry inside my skin, made the journey a bewildering nightmare. But no matter how confused I felt, there was no mistaking the sense of threat.

My steps became an uneven hobble, but I kept going. Finally, Kieran signaled for us to stop, and I slumped against the huge dark wall he'd led us toward. A short man with small eyes and a face like a rizzid stepped from an outcropping. Nolan handed him a bag, and the man pulled out a fistful of magchips, counted them, and beckoned us forward. In moments we edged through a hidden door and faced a rocky plain with the city at our back. Kieran kept moving, edging along the wall until we reached a sharp angle.

"Not that way." Nolan tugged his father's sleeve. "We'll be seen."

"I need to get closer to the main gate."

"Why?" the boy protested.

"Stay low." Kieran gestured to us both, ignoring his son's question.

He could at least explain where he was leading us. Dragging us all over without even bothering to—

My irritation fled as we rounded the corner.

A stone's throw away, heavily armored soldiers formed rows to welcome an arriving delegation of men and women in rough-woven clothes. With no regard for Nolan's hissed objections, Kieran glided toward a cluster of boulders, and we followed, ducking low to remain hidden.

I peered through a crevice, noticing an emblem on the tunics, a pattern of rolling hills. Crouched beside me, Kieran muttered a curse. "What is Corros clan doing here?"

I hoped he wasn't expecting an answer from me.

His head swung back as he scanned the walls then checked our surroundings again. "Wait here."

He was gone before either Nolan or I could argue.

I turned, riveted, to watch the entourage and Kieran's cautious approach. He ran lightly to a small grove of trees and disappeared from view. "Is he completely insane?" I whispered.

"No." Nolan leaned out to get a better view, while sliding a lethal-looking dagger from his boot sheath. "Only partly."

Did the boy think that if we were discovered he'd be able to fight armed warriors three times his size? They were both crazy. And I was the most foolish of all to throw in my lot with them.

I held my breath as the delegation and soldiers filed into the city. A blur of movement indicated that Kieran still hid in the under-brush by the trees.

Only when the final people stepped through and the heavy gate swung closed could I breathe again. I slumped with relief, collapsing against the boulder. But with the relief came a flare of anger. "So what was the point of that? Just escaping the city wasn't exciting enough for him?"

As the words left my mouth, Kieran returned, but he wasn't alone. He propelled a scrawny young man in front of him by twist-ing one of the man's arms behind his back and pressing a bootknife hard against his neck.

A few desperate mewling sounds escaped the man's throat.

"Always look for the stragglers," Kieran said to his son, as if instructing him on how to craft a field gauge rather than how to kidnap and terrorize a person. He increased pressure on the man's arm, eliciting a gasp. "Why is a group from Corros visiting Sidian?"

I sprang to my feet. "Stop that, you're hurting him."

He ignored me and let his blade press hard enough to break skin. The man's eyes flared and he squeaked.

I wanted to lunge at Kieran and pull him away, but a small slip of the dagger could do irreparable harm.

"Zarek offered help," the man choked out.

"What kind of help?" Kieran's voice was so full of menace a chill cut through the fever flushing my skin.

"Our plans . . . I can't . . ."

Another twist, another gasp. The captive squeezed his eyes shut, face contorted with pain. "To strengthen our clan. Weapons. Lehkan. That's all I know. All the resources have gone to Lyric," he added bitterly. "We've faced the most risk holding the border with Hazor all these years. If we can't get help from other clans, we'll get it here."

Kieran shifted his grip, cutting off the man's breath with his forearm. In moments, the prisoner slumped.

Appalled, I stumbled back a few steps, staring at my supposed rescuer. "You've killed him!" I should have stopped him somehow. Shouldn't have come with them. I struggled to think of a new plan, but my head felt tangled with waterweed, and the world swam.

"He'll be fine. But we need to move." Kieran tightened his baldric and adjusted the strap on his pack.

I knelt by the man and pressed my hand to his chest, feeling a reassuring beat of his heart. At least Kieran wasn't lying about that. Still, I scowled as I straightened, ready to blast him for his brutality. Instead, the ground seemed to waver and I closed my mouth, all energy focused on staying upright.

Nolan stared at the thick woods some distance from our hiding place, then he glanced back at me. "Oh, no. Look at her eyes."

Kieran's face swam into focus, inches away. "Linette, still with us? You're looking glassy."

I blinked. His eyes were dark pools, full of hidden currents. They stirred something inside me. This would be so much easier if I could trust him—if I could follow him, believing he was leading me someplace safe. But I didn't know whom to trust. I fought for another weak breath, my lungs laboring as if they'd filled with clay.

Kieran took my face between his hands. His palms were wonderfully cool, and I closed my eyes and imagined that he was drawing the horrible burning heat from my skin.

"What do we do?" Nolan asked.

I swallowed against the caradoc wool that had taken up residence in my throat. "The drug patch," I rasped. "It was too late. Bezreth said I would die."

Kieran let go of me, then shoved a gourd into my hand. "Not yet, you won't. Drink this."

Tart liquid filled my mouth and I choked it down. The orberry wine burned my throat, but maybe it would coax out a bit more strength.

Nolan wedged himself beside me and supported my elbow. "The patrols will be back any time. We have to run."

Kieran grabbed the gourd and didn't spare me another look. But he took up position on my other side, pulling my arm over his shoulders. "Let's go."

They propelled me forward, and I fought to keep my feet moving. Each step sent jarring pain up my spine, as if the rocky ground were charged with electricity like the wire of my cell. My head seemed to float outside myself, and brown, grey, and dark green shades swam past.

As we drew closer to the forest, I realized that the men were taking on more of my weight, half carrying me as they kept up an all-out run. Even Kieran was out of breath, and he stumbled a few times on the rough terrain.

He didn't let us slow when we reached the trees. Now a dizzying wash of dark branches, trunks, and underbrush swirled past us.

At last, Kieran stopped, letting go of me to grasp his thighs, doubled over and sucking in great gasps of air. I sank to my knees, grateful we had stopped moving, but now that I wasn't running, the earth seemed to spin beneath me.

"You're bleeding again," Nolan said quietly.

Confused, I held onto the ground for support and looked up. Nolan wasn't talking to me. He was looking at his father.

Kieran straightened and shrugged. "I'm fine." Dark splotches soaked through his tunic. His skin had the pale, drawn cast of hide stretched over a drum.

"Are you hurt?" I couldn't imagine what I could do to help, but my instinct was to offer aid.

The strain eased from around his eyes and a brief smile flitted across his face. "Nothing serious." He shifted his gaze to Nolan. "But we aren't going to get far like this. Change of plans."

Nolan nodded, but neither of them bothered to explain what the new plan was. They hauled me to my feet and kept walking. The haze of fever swallowed me, but thankfully it was only a short while until they stopped again. Nolan scooted ahead and pulled some branches aside, while Kieran kept me upright. A dark crevice appeared in the rock face, like the leering mouth of a shrine statue. Nolan slipped into the opening, and I shuddered.

Kieran pushed me in, following right behind me.

Nolan had already unpacked a heat trivet, and a soft glow illuminated the cave where we found ourselves. At its highest point, I could touch the ceiling, which curved steeply to the ground. Barely the size of a small common room, the hiding place was cramped and dark with the three of us and the men's packs and weapons. A blanket and some food scraps littered the stone floor near the back of the cave. I sank down, fingering the fabric.

"It's where he hid until he could get you out." Nolan shoved his pack under the sloped ceiling to get it out from underfoot. "Had to figure out a rescue plan."

Kieran eased his pack from his shoulders, wincing. "Which isn't going terribly well so far."

Nolan's teeth flashed. "We're all still alive."

His father snorted. "For now. Look at her. And we have to keep moving. I have to get to Lyric to let them know Corros is plotting illegal treaties with Hazor."

"Maybe if she rests a little."

I cleared my throat. "You don't have to talk about me like I'm not here." But the flare of irritation stole the last of my strength, and I let myself sink toward the inviting blanket, curling up and closing my eyes to shut out the spinning rock walls.

A hand slipped under my neck and the gourd of fermented orberry juice was pressed to my lips. I groaned and turned my head away.

"Drink it." Kieran's low command made me open my eyes. I took a few swallows.

He passed the juice back to Nolan, but kept holding me. "We're going to have to keep moving. The healers in Braide Wood would know how to help, but we need to go in the other direction so I can get to Lyric."

"We'll have to take her to Braide Wood first," Nolan said with uncharacteristic sharpness. "Lyric can wait."

Kieran gave his son a long look. "Whatever I decide, we'll have to move before she gets worse."

"Worse?" I held up the wristband. "I should be getting better. Just give me a little time."

He swallowed, and cords flexed along his neck. Easing my head down, he exchanged a look with Nolan. "Right. You rest awhile." He backed away and turned to unpack some supplies.

Now that I was still, questions shouted for attention in my mind like unruly children. "How did we know each other before? Why did you take me out of the shrine? Who is tracking you?"

Nolan crouched beside me, brushed his bangs from his eyes, and smiled. "He hasn't bothered to explain much, has he? It's not what he's good at."

Kieran blew out an irritated breath and ignored us.

"Is anything coming back?" Nolan settled himself more comfortably, hugging his knees.

I shook my head, but the movement sent fresh pain through my skull and I groaned.

Nolan touched my forehead lightly, then pulled his hand back. "You were—you are a songkeeper. From Braide Wood. I spent some time there once. Uncivilized place, really."

Kieran whipped a roll of fabric across the cave, hitting Nolan in the back of the head. The boy threw him a grin then turned back to me. "You also spent time in Lyric." His expression sobered as he watched me for a glimmer of recognition. "When people gathered at the tower, you helped lead the singing."

Nolan went on to tell me about mind-poisoning Rhusicans, a corrupt council member, and a threatened war with Hazor. The stories had a vague familiarity, like distant legends, but nothing in my memories could confirm them as fact. Still, his rambling recitation soothed. My muscles relaxed and my eyes drifted closed, but I fought hard to keep listening, to gather this information. To hear Nolan tell it, his father had heroically saved the entire city of Lyric.

Hard to believe. I squinted one eye open. Kieran had his back half-turned toward us, but I could still see his scowl. In his stained and torn tunic, unwrapping cooking gear, he hardly looked like the hero Nolan described.

"After the battle at Morsal Plain, he became the Restorer. So he wanted—"

The Restorer. I lifted my head. "'The Restorer is empowered with gifts to defeat our enemies and turn the people's hearts back to the Verses. We wait in the darkness for the One who brings light . . . '" Like a strong chord of music that expanded to fill the air, a flare of memory sang through me. The words tasted smooth on my tongue, familiar as a favorite meal.

Kieran stopped his rummaging and stared at me. Nolan's eyes brightened.

I winced. "That's all I remember."

"'The Deliver will come,'" Kieran said softly. "'And with His coming all darkness will be defeated.' And if He's paying attention, I'd say this would be a good time for Him to show up." He shifted to set a bowl on the heat trivet that lit the center of the cave. There wasn't real rancor in his tone, just the weary sound of a man who had been battling too much for too long.

Nolan grabbed a small bread loaf from the supplies near the packs and handed it to me. "Eat something. We have to keep moving."

I propped on an elbow, my head so weighted I longed to lay it back down on the hard ground. "Can't we just stay here for a while?"

Neither man answered me. Nolan stuffed another wedge of bread into his mouth. Kieran stirred the simmering bowl, then poured some into a wooden travel mug and handed it to me. "Drink it all."

Pungent steam rose around my face and I ventured a small sip. I remembered the flavor. Like the music and the verses, this taste teased a link with my past. Maybe I'd put all the pieces together eventually.

If I survived long enough. The fever seemed to be worsening. As I sat up to drink the rest, my head swam.

"Have to redress your wounds before we head out," Nolan told his father around a full mouth.

"It can wait."

Nolan ignored him and grabbed some bandages. "No, it can't. She can barely stand. What do I do if we're on the trail and you fade out too? I can't carry you both."

Kieran made a dismissive sound, but glanced at the side of his tunic that was dark and wet. "Well, get on with it then."

Nolan peeled the fabric away and helped Kieran pull the tunic over his head. Haphazard strips of cloth wrapped his torso, colored with red and brown. Bruises and raw gashes covered the skin of his shoulders above the bandages.

I gasped. "What happened?"

He shrugged one shoulder, then winced. "A small souvenir from Zarek. Could have been worse. Would have been if I hadn't escaped.

Nolan's quick thinking and some shrewd bribes gave me just the opening I needed."

Nolan shook his head and pulled the bandages free without taking time to be gentle. Fresh blood seeped from a deep cut on Kieran's side. A roaring buzz swelled in my ears, and I set the mug down, sinking back to the blanket as black sand filled my vision.

"Well, at least that hasn't changed," Kieran commented.

I surrendered to the fuzzy cloud and curled away from the men, the blood, the confusion. I must have dozed, because the next time I shifted my position and looked, Kieran was back in his tunic and belting on his sword. "Scout the trail," he said to Nolan.

The boy left his pack and slipped outside, as quick and agile as a minnow.

I sat up and pain pounded so intensely in my skull that I groaned. "I'm sorry. I can't go any further. Not yet."

Kieran seemed to tower over me as he looked down. "We don't have a choice. I have to get you to the healers right away."

"Why?" I wrapped my fingers around the armband. "We just need time for Bezreth's drug patches to start working again."

He crouched down, his face close enough that I could see the pallor under his stubble. "We can't wait for them to work."

"But why?"

He met my eyes squarely. "Because I lied."

My head throbbed. Lied? What was new about that?

"It's not one of her patches."

I stared at my forearm. "But you . . ."

"I had to get us out of Sidian. There was no way to get back into the shrine and get Bezreth's patches. But you don't want them anyway. They're what she uses to make people forget."

I felt blood leave my face. "They're what kept me alive!" My shoulders pressed back, braced against the sloping roof of the cave. "You have to take me back into town. I'll take my chances with the shrine."

Kieran crouched down and his dark eyes bored into me. "You know the One. Would you really serve the hill-gods?"

Unfair. Everything in me rejected the hill-gods. That piece of myself had broken through the fog. But did that mean I should trust Kieran and leave Sidian? Leave my only guarantee of survival? He just admitted he'd lied to me again.

"It's clear." Nolan poked his head into the cave.

Pain drilled behind my eyes. I rubbed them and groaned. I needed to make up my mind about whether these men were allies or enemies. But it was so hard to think past the throbbing in my head. Everything in my line of sight wavered like wisps of steam from a pot of clavo.

I pulled the armband off.

Kieran's hand closed over mine. "No. The patch isn't one of Bezreth's, but it will help with the pain."

Nolan stepped inside and nodded earnestly. "They helped my mother when she had the fever."

I tugged my hand free and frowned at the silver wristband. It was a sign of Bezreth's ownership of me. Of my captivity to the shrine. "I won't wear this."

"That's fine." Nolan dug in his pack and offered me a drug patch. "This will work without it."

Each beat of my pulse pounded against my skull. Maybe I was just exchanging one captivity for another, but if this would ease the pain . . .

I stuck the patch to the pale skin under my elbow and let my sleeve fall back into place. "You really think the healers at Braide Wood can fix me? Will they help me remember who I am?"

Kieran rubbed his forehead. "When there's only one option, you take it, and take it fast. We're out of choices. We aren't leaving you here. So let's go."

He wasn't very good at being reassuring. Nolan rolled his eyes, apparently thinking the same thing. Still, Kieran made sense. If Bezreth was the one who had stolen my memory, then the only option was to travel as far from here as possible, to reach these Braide Wood healers. I'd never manage alone.

Using the cave walls for support, I eased to my feet. "Well, if we're leaving, let's leave."

Nolan shot his father a worried frown, but picked up one of the packs and ducked back out. Kieran grabbed the heat trivet and levered it off. The cave fell into heavy darkness as he slipped through the opening, leaving me alone. The gritty smell of rock and dirt felt thick in my throat.

I could curl up on the hard rock and drift into sleep. Perhaps I'd never wake up, never have to face the horrible emptiness that filled my mind as my thoughts turned in any direction. Or I could risk a painful and dangerous escape with Kieran and Nolan on the slim chance that I'd find my memories, find healing, and find truth at the end of the journey.

The soft grey of daylight drew me toward the cave's entrance.

Holy One, I want to find You again. Do You want to be found by me? Will You guide me to someone who can help me remember?

A new hunger burned in my chest. However difficult the journey, and whatever I discovered at the end of it, I needed to know more about the One.

Bending made my head swim, but I reached down for the coarse blanket I'd been lying on, shook it out, and wrapped it around my shoulders. Then I forced my unsteady legs to move and left the cave.

As the rocks of Hazor spat us out, I still felt the teeth of Sidian inches from the back of my neck.

CHAPTER
16

SUSAN

IT'S AMAZING HOW an impossible challenge becomes possible when it's inevitable. I couldn't manage a climbing wall at my local gym, much less a Kahlarean sheer rock face with tiny handholds and no safety harness, but the assassins weren't interested in my qualms.

As I followed Rahn and Mark, my shoeless toes struggled to grip the small, smooth indents. Master Voronja and his other apprentice climbed behind me. At least if I fell, I'd take out a few assassins on my way down. I smiled grimly and pulled myself up another step. Thirty feet above the ground, my arms were already shaking, and the wall seemed to stretch upward forever.

Mark wasn't even breathing hard. Something subtle shifted in him each time he revisited this world. He was still my familiar husband from a Midwestern suburb, but he was also something more. The history of his family, his early guardian training, and his time on the Council all seemed to course through his muscles. Even in his jeans and chambray shirt, he looked like he would be more comfortable wielding a sword than driving a car.

"Not much farther," he called. "Don't look down."

Perversely, my gaze fell to the sharp stones below. Vertigo made the ground waver. I pressed my forehead against the rock, wishing I could burrow into it. When I glanced up to find the next handhold,

Rahn had disappeared over the cliff face, and Mark continued climbing, the distance between us stretching.

I had at least another twenty feet yet to climb. My heart jack-hammered so hard that I was afraid it would jar me off my perch.

A low hiss sounded behind me. "Keep moving." The master assassin's voice barely rose above a whisper, but the clear menace prodded me. Hyperventilating, I threw aside my slow, careful progress and scrambled as fast as I dared, just wanting to get this climb over with, whatever the outcome.

My fingers finally reached a flat surface, and I hefted myself up onto my belly. Mark's hands pulled me safely onto the wide ledge. As soon as I found my feet, I hugged him. "Too close," I gasped.

"Hmm?" he murmured against the top of my head.

"We're still too close to the edge." I kept my face buried against him, not wanting a glimpse of the long fall beyond the ledge. Even if we evaded the Kahlareans and escaped the enclave, I'd never be able to climb down from this dizzying height. The sensation of a trap closing tighter around my neck added to my trembling.

He chuckled and guided me further in. "Since when are you afraid of heights?"

A jolt of indignation helped me to get control of my rubbery knees and convince them to bear my weight. "That wasn't like cleaning out a gutter on a nice safe ladder. You've gotta admit that was scary."

"I'm admitting nothing." He turned me away from the edge. "You can open your eyes now."

His teasing helped the trembling leave my muscles. I drew a shaky breath and looked around. The polished rock face before us revealed the near-invisible seams of a door. The door matched the surrounding rock, but unlike the rustic caves where we'd entered Kahlarea, this entrance was metallic and mechanical. Mark nudged me and nodded toward a glazed plastic window, tiny as an arrow slit in a medieval castle. Bulbous eyes within followed our every move.

While the remaining two assassins slipped easily onto the plateau and to their feet, Rahn slid aside a recessed panel, pulled a small gadget from his belt, and pressed it against a lever.

Steel whispered apart, revealing a dim hall. "Who are these strangers?" A raspy voice asked from within.

The master assassin glided past us all and through the door. "Visitors. They may be helpful with our recent project."

I didn't like the sound of that. When Mark and I didn't move, Rahn grabbed my arm and tugged me toward the entrance. Mark bristled and wedged himself between the young Kahlarean and me.

Rahn tensed with the stillness of a snake about to strike. Hair rose on my arms.

"It's okay." I touched Mark's arm. "Come on."

My husband glared at Rahn, but released his breath, a potential explosion averted. Mark's normal easy-going nature was another thing that shifted when we were in this world. He was never this combative when negotiating a car repair bill or arguing with the city about our property tax increases. Of course, those sorts of battles weren't actually life threatening.

Realizing the magnitude of our danger again, my stomach clenched. I couldn't focus on that. We were here for a purpose. We had to get to Jake. One step at a time.

Watch, learn, and stay as friendly as possible.

We walked into a cavern illuminated by faint streaks of light-retaining mineral woven throughout the stone. Once we were inside, the Kahlareans removed their hoods and the grey fabric that covered their lower faces. Rahn padded ahead, his short form moving without a sound. Mark and I followed slowly, with the elder assassin close on our heels. The door hissed closed behind us, and my grip on Mark's arm tightened.

We passed between a few uneven natural rock pillars. Something blurry moved in my peripheral vision.

"Not bad, Clanon." A touch of humor colored the rasping voice of the master assassin.

Who was he speaking to? There was no one else in the corridor.

A cloaked figure stepped out from alongside one of the pillars. He gave a brief bow to the older Kahlarean.

I blinked. "How do you do that?"

The young Kahlarean ignored me and melted back against a cave wall, disappearing again.

I did a double take, and turned to the master assassin. "That's amazing. It's like he has an invisibility superpower. Can you all do that?" No wonder Kahlarean assassins had infiltrated Lyric and Braide Wood without discovery.

A flash of amusement lit the froggy eyes of the old Kahlarean. He rubbed knobby knuckles under his chin. "Distilling poison from scolopendra claw is not the only kind of distilling we do."

That explained exactly nothing, but I didn't really expect a Kahlarean teacher to be forthcoming with his secrets.

Mark gave a soft huff, and I glanced at him. His scowl had deepened, and I wanted to rub the worry lines off his forehead before he gave himself a headache. He clearly wasn't coaching himself to focus on anthropological curiosity like I was.

I didn't blame him. Men like these—perhaps even Voronja himself—had murdered Mark's family and friends. I nestled closer to him as we followed Rahn along a smooth hall, deeper into the mountain.

"I'm sorry," I said quietly. "This must be hard for you. Do you want to talk about it?"

His jaw flexed. "No."

"But sometimes it can help to let it out, talk about your feelings . . ."

"Not here," he ground out. He jerked his head in the direction of the Kahlareans behind us. "Not now."

I'd forgotten about our hosts' ability to hear so well. I pressed my lips together. We didn't dare risk revealing who Mark really was until we knew if they had set aside their long-standing vendetta against Markell, son of Mikkel of Rendor.

I did risk one more quick whisper to Mark. "Did you see that entrance? How are we going to find our way out of here?"

His only response was to squeeze my hand where it rested on his arm.

I drew in a strengthening breath. Mark had the gift of infusing courage and calm into me with one deep gaze into my eyes or the low timbre of his voice or the touch of his skin against mine.

Deeper into the cave, the hall expanded into a large arena. Sloping floors led down to a wide area, open except for a scattering of tall pillars that reached upward, some ten feet, some twenty feet. They added soft illumination to the massive cavern like giant glow sticks. Wide ramps led up from the central area to the level where we stood. The broad path that overlooked the arena held five equidistant openings to halls leading away from the center, and reminded me of the council chambers of Lyric. In Lyric, innocuous offices lay beyond each balcony door, but here I suspected that nothing so banal waited down the various halls.

At the moment, dozens of Kahlareans trained on the main floor like so many masked ninjas. Unlike guardians, who trained with swords and staffs, these men paired off in lethal dances of hand-to-hand combat with daggers. At one side of the cavern, other youths dove and rolled to evade syncbeam blasts. The master gestured us toward one of the overhanging balconies, and I was relieved we wouldn't have to walk through the main floor.

We passed through a short hall into a smaller room, the size of a small church under vaulted ceilings. Instead of stained glass windows, the only illumination came from more glowing veins in the stone walls, and sporadic light panels that cast a pale, somber glow. Low tables lined the wall to our left, and several Kahlareans worked over heat trivets, with steam rising from bowls and various gauges and odd tools littering the surfaces. To our right, more coved openings led to halls that appeared to lead deeper into the mountain—deeper into the mountain and deeper into danger. My nerves prickled with each step that took us farther from freedom.

One of the men at the tables turned and walked toward us with a spring in his step. I recognized Trennor, the angry youth who had killed the scolopendra. "Master, I've begun the distilling process. Can I choose a venblade from the armory?"

The elder Kahlarean looked up in a very human expression of exasperation. "You have ten days before the poison is ready. Ask me then."

I'd once wondered why Kahlareans used more traditional weapons when they had the incredibly lethal venblades at their disposal. If they had to hunt a monster scolopendra for the poison, it was obviously not easy to produce. Perhaps the use of a venblade was reserved for rare occasions.

Trennor bobbed his head, then turned toward Rahn. "I already cleaned the talon." He held out a scarlet claw, hung from a leather cord around his neck. Clearly his status had risen among the other students, and his mood was unquenchable.

"Congratulations," I offered quietly. "And thank you again for saving my life."

Beside us, Rahn made a snorting laugh sound.

Trennor scowled. "I didn't," he said indignantly. "Not on purpose. I just got you out of the way of my hunt." He cast pleading eyes at the master. "I didn't mean to save her life."

I bristled. "I'm only trying to be grateful." Someone should teach the boy some manners.

Trennor clenched his chinless jaw, making his cheeks puff out in anger and giving his face an even more froglike appearance.

Mark wrapped a hand around my shoulder and gave a soft squeeze. "Honey, this is an assassin's enclave. It's probably not a compliment to thank someone for saving your life."

Now Voronja snorted several chuckles. "Yet it's true his hunt inadvertently saved you and necessitated this visit." He pointed at Trennor. "So I find it appropriate for you to escort them while they are here."

Trennor let the talon drop from his fingers, and it dangled against his grey tunic. The skin around his eyes took on a greenish cast. "Master, no. Please."

"Take them to the eating hall. See that they have food, then find them a sleeping quarter. And ponder how each of your actions has consequences."

The youth's bluster deflated, and he gave us both a glare of undisguised malice. I almost felt sorry for him.

"We'd appreciate a meal, but there's no need for a place to sleep," Mark said to the elder. "We need to be on our way."

"Go with Trennor." The master used a tone that brooked no argument, then strode away, back toward the large training arena.

Uneasy, I looked at Mark. "Guess he told us."

Trennor shot us another sour look. "No one questions the master. This way." He gestured ahead to a hallway. Mark and I preceded him, with Trennor clearly as reluctant to be stuck with us as we were to go with him.

Suddenly a figure dropped from the ceiling in front of me. I squeaked and stumbled to a stop. The figure rose from a crouch, and I realized it was another small, young trainee. His eyelids drew together in a squint, and I suspected that the grey fabric covering his lower face masked a snicker.

"Ripon, practice hiding in some other corridor." Trennor glided past me and shoved Ripon aside. The boy scampered away with a wispy laugh.

As we followed Trennor, I kept glancing nervously at the roof of the hall. I began to expect Kahlareans to pop out of every shadow. "I still don't know how you manage to be so inconspicuous."

"Cub games," Trennor's disgust toward us expanded to include the less experienced trainees. He reminded me of my junior high son scoffing at our grade school daughter's homework. "They aren't allowed to use Rhusican blood until they've had twelve seasons of training."

The skin on the back of my neck prickled, and I reached for Mark's hand. He squeezed it, steadying me. I managed to keep my voice conversational. "Rhusican blood?"

Trennor led us into a large dining hall with long tables and benches that were empty at the moment. "Another poison we can distill. Sit there." He pointed at one of the benches, then stomped to a pass-through along one wall, and brought back a large platter of rolls, fish, and some odd-colored vegetables.

Fighting to keep my tone casual, I helped myself to a roll. "So what does the Rhusican blood do for you?"

He puffed out his chest. "You don't know much, do you? Everyone knows the Rhusicans can bend reality."

I bit down hard on the inside of my lip to stop myself from blurting out just how much experience I had with that Rhusican skill. "And you can do the same if you use their blood?"

"We can't fully duplicate the ability to create realities, but we can distort the vision and perception of others a little. Enough to seem invisible." Trennor grabbed a fistful of vegetables and stuffed them in his mouth.

"Resourceful." Mark leaned his forearms on the table. Now he was doing a much better job of showing casual, non-threatening interest than I was.

I chewed a small bite of my roll and studied the other food on the platter. How could Trennor eat the vegetables without teeth? I tentatively reached for a slender red stalk that was resting on top of the pile. It looked somewhat like a mix between a carrot and rhubarb, and was cooked to tender softness, so soft that it almost fell apart in my hand.

Trennor gulped and his narrow lips tilted up. "We trade for the best from all other nations. Syncbeams from Hazor, mental powers from Rhus."

"And from the clans?" Mark rubbed his chin.

Trennor's lids half-closed over his oversized eyes. "Your people have been much harder to trade with. But we have finally made some progress."

I tensed, waiting for his next revelation, but Trennor sprang from the bench and went back to the pass-through for a large mug of some steaming liquid.

"I hope he keeps talking," I whispered to Mark. "At least we're learning important things about the Kahlareans."

Mark's hand closed over mine gently. "I wish we weren't."

"Why?" I turned to him.

His deep, silver-blue eyes stared into mine. "They've let us see too much. They've let an indiscreet student run off at the mouth too much."

So? The Kahlareans had been careless. It was all to our benefit.

"Susan, they don't plan to let us leave."

The tightness in my chest contracted an inch further. I hadn't wanted to follow my thoughts along to that obvious conclusion. "I know. But we're here for a reason. We're going to find a way out of here, to the River Borders, back to Lyric, and to Jake."

He forced a half smile, but I still saw the worry lines around his eyes. Now it was my turn to pat his hand and change the subject. "It'll be okay. I wonder what weapons they're trying to get from the clans. I don't think they need swords or any other weapon the guardians use."

"You're right." Mark's baritone rumbled tight in his throat. "There's only one advantage the clans have had that the Kahlareans might want. The one thing they've been after for generations."

A fist squeezed my heart. I no longer had to remind myself to whisper, because I could barely coax a sound through my constricted throat. "A Restorer."

CHAPTER 17

SUSAN

"WE WERE SMART to rest for a night and build up our strength." I splashed water on my face from a tiny sink in our guest quarters, a room as spartan as the rest of the Kahlarean enclave. Blotting my eyes with my sleeve, I turned to Mark.

His crooked grin evoked crinkles around his eyes. "Right. Let's go with that. It was our brilliant decision instead of something we had no choice about." Lounging on the sleep pallet in the small, bare room, he rested a forearm on his raised knee.

I flicked some water his direction. "Really? You're mocking your only ally?"

He reached up, grabbed my arm, and pulled me down beside him.

My squeak turned into a giggle, and then into a low hum as his lips found mine. For a blissful minute, the rock walls, the enclave full of enemies, and the anxiety about Jake and the journey ahead all faded.

"Good morning to you, too," I murmured when he lifted his head. "Now, what's the plan?"

He snuggled me in against him and stroked my hair as I rested on his shoulder. "We talk to the One."

I nestled my hand into his. Mark bowed his head. Instead of a soft murmur, he spoke clearly. If Kahlareans were eavesdropping beyond the door, they could just pray along.

"Holy One who spun the universe and shaped the clans, guide our steps as we follow You today. Keep us safe and show us why You brought us here."

I squeezed my eyes tighter. "And, Lord, be with Karen, Jon, and Anne." Though each time I'd gone through the portal, I'd returned to find almost no time had passed for my children at home; when I pressed my bare feet against the hard rock floor, I felt the thick barrier of mountains between us, the danger, the enemies, the days of travel to get close to the Lyric portal, and my heart twisted. "I can't reach them, Lord. But You can. Take care of them, and help us return to them. And whatever is going on with Jake . . ."

My throat thickened and I swallowed.

Mark rested his head against mine. "Give Jake the strength he needs," he said, "and help us find him."

We sat together for a minute, letting the silence seep into our blood.

"Ready?" Mark stood, pulling me up with him.

"Um, sure." But ready for what? Did he have a plan in mind? A foolproof way to escape an enclave of assassins, cross miles of wilderness, and reach the River Borders?

He walked to the door and pulled a recessed lever. The door slid open.

My eyebrows climbed. "I figured we were locked in. I wouldn't have even thought to try the door."

We stepped into the hallway.

Crouched like an angry gnome, Trennor sat against the wall facing our door, hugging his knees and scowling in our direction.

I tried my friendliest smile. "Good morning. How are you? We slept well. Were you waiting for us long?"

Trennor's glare narrowed as he rose in a fluid movement. "The master will speak with you after his training cycles today. I'm to . . . take care of you until then." He leaned back against the wall, fingering the scolopendra talon hanging from a cord around his neck.

I was tempted to thank him again for killing the monster, but thought better of it. No need to irritate him.

Mark and I waited for Trennor to tell us what to do next. He shuffled one foot and shifted his weight, but apparently was at a loss as to how to proceed. It seemed Kahlarean boys possessed even fewer social graces than some human boys I'd encountered.

"We'd appreciate some breakfast," I said. "Could you show us back to the dining hall?"

He scratched at his ear. "Trainees only eat once a day. We don't have time to waste on more food than necessary."

Did he expect us to just stand around this hallway all day? I pasted on a smile. "But we're not trainees. We could use some breakfast."

He worried his lips from side to side.

If Mark and I were going to explore the enclave and search for escape routes, we needed to gain Trennor's trust . . . and get moving.

Mark cleared his throat. "Lucy here is a great cook. If you take us back to the kitchen, I bet she'd be happy to help with tonight's meal for the trainees."

Lucy? What kind of alias was that? I shot a glare in Mark's direction. "And Ricky will help me."

Mark lifted an eyebrow and grinned.

Trennor pushed himself away from the wall. "Fine, then. Good a place as any to keep you busy." He stalked off down the hallway.

Mark and I hurried to follow him. Trennor's annoyance at babysitting us reminded me of Karen and her teenage mood swings. I'd give anything to hear one of her sarcastic comments today. Or Jon and Anne arguing. An ache built in my chest, but I fought it down. I needed to focus. We had to find a way to escape.

We walked along the hall, turning again and again through subterranean passages. I wouldn't be able to find the way back to our room, much less the entrance.

"What causes the walls to glow?" I asked, my voice sounding loud after the silence.

Trennor let out a hiss that I took to be a sigh. "The darnite."

"Those blue threads in the walls? Must save you a lot of magchips, since you don't need as many light panels. It sure is beautiful."

Mark's brows drew together, and he stared at me as if wondering where my brain had gone.

In our partnership's division of labor, conversation was my specialty. And here, conversation might give us information we could use. I winked at him, then turned my focus back to our young Kahlarean. "So, Trennor, have you lived here long?"

"Yes," Trennor bit out, and stalked ahead faster.

He didn't seem to be warming to me.

As the boy led us forward, he shifted suddenly, hopscotching side to side. I realized he was maneuvering over flat stepping-stones. A channel of water, the same level as the floor, cut across the hall, flowing from and into rooms on either side of us.

Mark bent down and dipped his hand in the water. Ahead of us, Trennor was about to go around another corner.

"Where does this go?" Mark mouthed silently.

I balanced on two of the stone squares and crouched to stare at the water. How deep was it? Could we use the stream to find an exit?

"What are you doing?" Trennor had turned back.

I straightened. "The river looks beautiful in the light from the darnite. Is this the border river? I didn't realize it flowed through the mountain."

"It doesn't." Trennor gestured for us to start walking again. "We built these channels." His chest puffed up as if the plumbing system were all his idea.

If I played on his ego, maybe he'd keep revealing facts that Mark and I could use. "That's brilliant. So you've got constant running water."

Trennor scoffed and forged ahead.

So much for more reconnaissance. Mark offered his hand and helped me along the stepping-stones. He gave my fingers a squeeze before releasing me.

Trennor led us into the dining hall with its long table, and to the wall with the pass-through. He stopped at a door. "I don't think Anataz would like anyone messing with his kitchen."

"Is he your cook?" I asked. "Why don't you go ask him? Tell him I'm willing to help."

Trennor squinted, clearly troubled by the pressures of making decisions. "I can't disturb Anataz. He was one of our highest ranked assassins before he became too old for active duty. Just find yourselves some food quickly before he comes back." Trennor opened the door, and we went into the kitchen.

It wasn't a huge room, but it was at least twice as big as our kitchen back home. Across from us, a long counter ran the entire length of the kitchen. Various cooking utensils and containers lay on the counter in a haphazard way. To our left, the floor was covered with heat trivets on which huge pots simmered. The smell wafting from them was a cross between fishy chowder and burnt celery.

To our right, the water channel flowed along the wall, just below floor level, exiting the kitchen through a low rock archway. I glanced at Mark. He also made note of the channel, then quickly looked away.

"Help yourselves," Trennor said, waving his hand as he sat down on a stool by the counter. Mark and I searched the cupboards and a pantry-like alcove at the far end of the kitchen for any familiar breakfast foods, but there was no sign of bacon and eggs, or oatmeal, or even clavo; so we settled for some small bread loaves.

We edged away from the odorous boiling pots, but the other end of the kitchen was pervaded with a musty smell I couldn't identify. "What is that smell?" I asked as we munched on our bread.

"The vegetables are fermenting," replied Trennor. "That's how we make them soft enough to eat."

I peered at a stack of root vegetables on the counter. "Do they need to be peeled? I'd be happy to help."

Trennor rubbed his forehead. We'd apparently stretched his decision-making abilities to the point of pain. "I suppose no one would mind that." He gestured to some paring knives. "You peel them into the river. The current takes it out."

I gathered a handful of the long narrow roots and carried them to the river, blocking Mark from Trennor's sight long enough for Mark to pocket one of the knives.

He moved casually to the channel of water. "So this flows straight out to the border river?"

"What do you think you're doing in here?" hissed an angry voice. Mark and I turned to see a Kahlarean older than any we'd seen before standing in the doorway. Fine lines crossed his pale, chinless face, making him look like a turnip left in the sun too long. But his forearms rippled with lean cords of muscle as he lowered a massive crate to the counter with a thud.

Trennor stiffened, head bowed. "Th-th-the . . . guests needed food. I didn't want to disturb you, sir."

"Sorry for intruding." Fighting off the chilling reminder that we were surrounded by enemies, I tried a friendly smile. "We were just offering to peel some vegetables to repay the enclave's hospitality."

"Get out of my kitchen," hissed Anataz. He grabbed Trennor by the neck of his tunic and shoved him toward the door. Mark and I quickly followed.

"It's time for me to take you to the master, anyway," Trennor said sulkily. "Follow me."

Trennor led us up the hall and into the large main cavern. Once again, small groups of Kahlareans were engaged in combat drills. Between tall light pillars, I glimpsed young men leaping, climbing, and swinging from bars in a type of obstacle course. Their athleticism had a strange beauty to it, but they moved in eerie silence. I remembered the twilight attack outside the Lyric council tower, when Kahlarean assassins had seemed to appear out of thin air.

"How often do you train?" I asked.

Trennor barely turned his head. "All the time. Everything is training."

At one point Trennor moved over to the side of the tunnel, right up against the wall. We followed suit, and I was just about to ask why we had to be so far to the side when a whir of movement flashed past me. A running drill. The whole group was silent, but somehow Trennor had known they were coming.

We followed him through several stark chambers and into a room dominated by a still, dark pool in the center. Master Voronja squatted near the side, staring into the depths. This cavern had no lightwalls or pillars and was illuminated only by the fluorescent veins running through the rock in the floor, walls, and ceiling, and reflecting on the skin of the water. I stepped forward, feeling as disoriented as if I were walking through a planetarium.

With a quick bow, Trennor slipped from the room.

Mark stepped past me. "We appreciate the shelter last night, but we need to keep traveling."

The master pulled his gaze from the pool and beckoned us to come closer. The soft light highlighted fine wrinkles on his pale skin as he frowned. "We've given you safe passage, but before you leave, we need your assistance."

I tried to gauge the sincerity of the Kahlarean's expression, Mark's dire assessment of our situation still simmering in my thoughts. When in doubt, build relationship. I settled onto the ground beside him, tailor style. "Of course, whatever we can do."

"We don't have many interactions with the clans, but we have another visitor here, and we have some questions for him. But he's been . . . unhelpful."

I shot Mark a questioning look. His arms crossed, muscles in his shoulders and neck pinched with tension—it was clear that the strain of being around his lifelong enemies was wearing on him.

What else could we do? If we acted friendly and cooperative, we could keep our eyes open for any way to escape. "I'd love to meet someone else from the clans. And I'm happy to return the favor of your hospitality."

Mark made a low sound in his throat, but I ignored that.

The master's large eyes stared at me for a long moment. I didn't blink.

His expression didn't change as he rose. "Good. This way."

He led us around the edge of the pool to the back wall. As we drew closer, the faint outlines of a door became visible. Voronja pulled what looked like a thumb drive from a leather band around his wrist. He inserted it in a hidden crevice, and the door slid aside.

In the small, dim room, I could just make out a metal chair against the far wall and a low table nearby. A slim figure slumped forward in the chair, bound by arms and ankles. The Kahlareans may have been pretending we were guests, but there were no illusions that this man was anything other than a prisoner.

"Is he also one of the banished?" I asked.

"Far more important," the master said in his hoarse whisper. "Go ahead. Convince him to help us."

We walked into the room. At the sound, the man lifted his head, the threads of phosphorescence in the walls painting his face with streaks of light. Strands of fair hair fell back and beautiful clear eyes met mine.

Every ounce of oxygen froze in my lungs.

Jake.

CHAPTER 18

LINETTE

THORNY UNDERBRUSH REACHED out to snarl my ankles. Jagged rocks leered down from forbidding cliffs. In the distance, the strangled roar of a mountain cat issued a warning that I didn't need.

I was already in the jaws of a monster that gnawed my bones and tore at my muscles. The fever was eating me alive. Had Bezreth told me the truth? Shrine girls who tried to leave, who tried to manage without their drug patches, always died. Didn't they? I didn't want to die out here among the dismal rocks with no companions but two strangers—and while a stranger even to myself.

"Just a little farther." Nolan wrapped an arm around my waist so his shoulder could support some of my weight. "We'll find a place to camp soon."

Ahead of us, Kieran remained silent, as he had most of the day. He disappeared around a rocky outcropping, and Nolan urged me forward.

The fever burned up my spine, sending a dizzying pulse through my head. I focused on the effort of taking each step, and the struggle distracted me from the many blank places in my memories. Better to feel my body battling for life than dwell on the miserable emptiness of not knowing who I was.

"There. At the edge of that caradoc pasture." Kieran drew his sword and pointed to a shed in the distance. Slate with tattered edges roofed the deserted lean-to, and weeds half-buried it, making it blend into the scrub and rocks. "Wait here."

I sank to my knees, wondering if I'd find my feet again, but grateful for a chance to rest. The sky was deepening to dove grey, and the earth felt cool under my hands. Nolan passed a gourd to me, and I took a sip of tart juice and puckered my lips.

"Did I ever like this?" I handed the canteen back to him.

"No." Nolan shot me a quick grin, then went back to watching his father. "It's not popular in Braide Wood."

Kieran ran lightly, using a patch of tall ferns for cover as he approached the shed. He disappeared inside, sword at the ready, and a moment later emerged and waved us forward.

Nolan helped me to my feet, and we stumbled to the shed. Kieran gave me a hard, assessing look. "We'll camp here. Should be able to reach the Braide Wood border tomorrow."

I peered into the dark doorway and shook my head. If I stopped now, the fever might finish me, and they'd have to leave my body in this lonely shed. "Let's keep going. We need to reach help."

Kieran's eyebrows lifted, and he swiped a hand across his dirt-streaked forehead. "Are you remembering Braide Wood?"

A tight knot of discouragement twisted in my throat. "No. But staying here isn't helping."

"We can't travel at night."

"I can keep up." I stiffened my spine and glared at him. "Let's keep going."

His mouth pulled sideways and he looked at Nolan. "Let's make camp before we lose all the light."

Nolan propped me against the side of the shed and ducked inside. The last bit of strength dissolved from my legs, and I sank to the ground.

Kieran unearthed a drug patch from his pack. Before I could form words to continue my argument, he took my arm and smoothed the new patch onto my skin. "It's the last one. Maybe it'll take the edge off the pain and you can rest tonight. Tomorrow will be a rough one, but after that we'll have help." His eyes wore troubled shadows, made deeper by the worry that creased his brow.

I looked at the drug patch. "Once this starts to work, I want to keep moving."

His crooked smile held a mix of fondness and exasperation. "Maybe you could do it, but Nolan and I need a break. So will you try to rest—for our sakes?"

I managed a half-smile. "If you put it that way." His unexpected kindness confused me, but my head throbbed too much to sort out my questions.

Kieran helped me to my feet and into the hut. A small heat trivet on the floor formed a bubble of light. Nolan was tying a cloak over a window. "I think I've got it sealed up so no light will show from outside."

"Good work. But we shouldn't chance it for long. Let's get some food into her and then keep the trivet off."

I sat down, leaning against the musty wall of the shed. With my eyes closed, the low murmur of Kieran and Nolan's voices became a jumbled sound like water tumbling over rocks. I heard distant lehkan hooves pounding turf, and imagined someone riding across a wide plateau, but his face was blurry. Was my memory returning? More hooves beat in a harder rhythm, and I realized the sound was my own pulse beating against my skull.

Someone pressed a gourd to my lips. "Drink this."

No. It hurt too much. My throat felt as tired as the rest of me, and I couldn't endure the effort to swallow. I tried to push the drink away, but couldn't make my arms lift. Instead I just turned my head.

Arms supported me and tilted me toward the ground. Someone slid a pack under my head. The hooves returned . . . whole herds of lehkan galloping. They swirled around me, and I curled into a ball and faded into darkness as they ran.

I woke later, thinking I'd rolled onto a heat trivet. My skin burned, and I moaned and stirred but couldn't seem to move away from the heat.

"Shh." Something cool touched my face. A hand? A wet cloth coaxed a few drops of water into my mouth.

I managed to lick the moisture from my lips. I rubbed my eyes, straining to see anything in the blackness.

Scuffling sounds led to a sudden flare of light.

More sounds and a hoarse voice. "I told you, it's not safe." That was Kieran, the hard, angry man leading our escape. He was standing by the window, drawn, haggard, glaring at his son, who knelt by the heat trivet glowing in the center of the floor.

Even in my fevered daze, I sensed the anger building in the boy, ricocheting off the resolute stance of his father.

Nolan's eyes blazed as he sprang to his feet. "You have to do something. She's burning up." He tore his fingers through his hair, and his whole body shook. "Don't let this happen again."

Kieran pushed away from the window, and I wondered if he'd attack the boy or crush the heat trivet underfoot.

Instead, he groaned and pulled his son into an awkward embrace. "This isn't the same. It's not Rammelite fever."

Nolan squirmed, pushing his father to arm's length. "What do you know about it? You couldn't help her, either, and she died." His voice cracked, and he gave in to Kieran's grip and buried his face against his father's shoulder, his back shaking with sobs.

"I know. I'm sorry." Kieran held the boy tightly, murmuring again and again, "I know, I know."

Pain radiated from them both, shimmering like the glow of the heat trivet. A tiny buried part of me longed to comfort them. "I won't die," I whispered. But the sound didn't carry past my throat. Besides, I had no way of knowing if I was speaking the truth. I gave in to the dizzying pain and closed my eyes.

Nolan's low cries quieted to quivering gasps, then to a ragged silence.

"Holy One, we need you." Kieran's voice was raw and broken. "Linette needs you." He kept talking, but my mind drifted.

When I next opened my eyes, Kieran was grasping his son's shoulders. In the soft light of the heat trivet, I saw the tears that glistened on Nolan's cheeks. "Be strong for her sake," Kieran said firmly. Nolan's back straightened as if his father's words had poured new steel into his bones.

It was probably delirium from the fever, but the sight of the man and boy in the uneven light stirred a deep warmth inside my ribcage. For a precious moment, I wanted to form a song about tenderness and strength and longing and courage. Then the pain in my skull and spine swirled me away into confusing images and fever.

Much later, I opened my heavy lids and the shed was full of morning light. The cloak no longer hung over the window. I propped up onto my elbows and the fever gnawed into the back of my neck, making me groan. I rubbed my eyes and looked around. Weapons, gear, and the heat trivet had disappeared. The men were gone.

I was alone.

My heart lurched, and the quickening beat of my pulse drummed against the ache in my forehead. They'd left me.

I knew I'd been slowing them down, but Kieran had seemed determined to get me to Braide Wood. He'd said there were people there who could help me. I hadn't really understood why helping me was so important to him. Maybe he had something to prove.

I struggled to sit up. Even slow, careful movement made the ground sway.

Now he'd dragged me out into the harsh mountains and left me to die alone. I'd begun to trust him, even to care about the rough-edged man and his son. I groaned. I'd been so foolish.

What if Bezreth came after me? Could her people have followed us this far? Being dragged back to Sidian would be even worse than dying alone in this hut.

A soft scuffing sounded outside. I fumbled for a weapon, but the dirt floor was bare. The door slid open and Nolan bounded inside. When he spotted me leaning against the wall, he pulled up short and offered a shy smile. "You're awake."

"He left you, too? Oh, Nolan. I'm sorry."

His floppy bangs drooped lower as his forehead wrinkled. "Left?" He glanced around at the bare shed and his face cleared. "We needed water so I slipped out. Didn't mean to scare you."

"But where's Kieran?"

"Scouting ahead." Nolan passed me a damp gourd. "Maybe this will taste better than the orberry juice."

Water beaded the gourd, and I pressed it gratefully against the side of my face, telling myself that the relief flooding me was from the cool moisture and not from learning that Kieran hadn't abandoned me. I tried a sip, letting the liquid work its way down my dry throat.

Rapid, light footsteps sounded beyond the shed door. Nolan pulled out a bootknife and spun.

The door slid aside and Kieran slipped in. He noticed Nolan's weapon and gave an approving nod. Then his piercing eyes found me. "We need to head out. Can you stand?" He offered his hand.

I handed the gourd back to Nolan and clasped Kieran's forearm. His skin was cool, the muscles hard and ropey beneath my fingers. With a deep breath, I let him haul me to my feet.

The shed tilted and wobbled around me. "Stand, maybe. Walking I'm not so sure about."

A flicker of a smile lightened his grim features. "It's a start." He pressed his hand against the side of my face before I could protest. "You're a little cooler. Maybe the fever is breaking."

He was wrong. The gnawing heat was deep inside my spine, throbbing out into my limbs. But I said nothing.

Nolan grabbed the pack that had been beneath my head and headed out.

I took an uneven step toward the door, then paused to catch my breath, brushing my hair off my face. My braids were tangled. Several had broken free of their threads, and loose strands caught in the small beads of the other braids. I began to tighten one strand.

Kieran stilled my hands. "I never liked you in Hazorite braids."

I bristled. I hated when he referred to his knowledge of me. I resented that he claimed to know more about me than I knew about myself. I pulled away and glared at him, while I used one stray ribbon to cinch all my loose hair and the remaining braids together at the back of my neck.

He gestured for me to precede him out of the hut. Outside, he stepped closer again, supporting me with his arm. I wanted to flinch away, but after only a few steps, it was clear I needed the help.

"I know you can't remember right now." His voice was gruff, low. "And I know you're confused. Normally, I'd be the last person to tell you to blindly trust anyone, but . . ." He guided me over a rough pile of jagged rocks and onto a narrow trail.

I staggered a few more steps. "But you expect me to trust you."

Nolan was scrambling up a switchback ahead. Sparse angular trees guarded the slope. The very ground here felt angry and threatening.

He sighed. "Just let us get you home. You can sort out everything else then."

Home. Pain sliced through my heart. A place I couldn't remember. With the emptiness in my memory, would I ever have a home again?

Kieran's arm wrapped around my shoulders and pushed me forward. "Stop thinking. All you need to do today is keep moving."

The muscles in my back tightened, but I trudged forward. I didn't have spare energy to argue with him or to nurse my frustration and distrust. For now, it took all my strength to cover my pain. Each step pounded up through my bones and beat through my skull, until my body screamed at me to curl up in a ball. But if I didn't keep moving, I'd be endangering all of us.

"Could she follow us here?" I managed the hoarse question.

Kieran dipped his head lower, continuing to help me forward. "Who? Bezreth?"

I nodded, a shudder passing through me.

He stopped and turned me to face him. "I'll keep you safe. I won't leave you alone. She will never reach you."

Clinging to the words and to the determined set of his jaw, I managed to draw a deeper breath as we resumed the climb.

Ahead of us, Nolan darted over a peak, then reappeared, giving an all-clear signal to his father. He waited for us to reach him, then raced forward again. His boundless energy made me want to groan. Instead, I counted each successful step. One. Two. One. Two.

Time swirled past. Kieran's steadying arm faded from my awareness. Rocks and trees merged into a meaningless blur.

From far away, I heard a light melody. Nolan was whistling. I blinked, the pain receding a little. Still trudging, I raised my head and looked around. The pale grey emptiness overhead had lightened to the soft white of caradoc wool. The tune gave me a piece of life to grab onto. I hummed along, aiming toward Nolan's lithe form.

"Nolan!" Kieran's harsh whisper sounded close to my ear. The boy turned, and I felt Kieran shake his head, never breaking stride. "Quiet. It's not safe."

Nolan nodded, scanned the ridgeline above us and the trail behind us, and continued on.

"Can you remember everything that happened the past two days?" Kieran's low voice rumbled near my ear.

I stumbled, but he took more of my weight and helped me to regain my footing. "You mean do I remember how you lied? And all this hiking? Every step."

His shoulder moved in a low chuckle. "Good."

"Good?"

"Bezreth's drugs aren't stealing your new memories. So if I fill you in on things, I won't be wasting my breath."

I scowled at my feet. Irritating man. But conversation was distracting me from the pain. "All right. Explain. Why were we in Hazor?"

"A complex question," he said. "I know why I was there. You? Maybe Lyric and Braide Wood had become too painful for you. How's that for irony? Maybe you were escaping your memories." A note of sadness underlay his tone for a moment, but then as if the emotion were too uncomfortable for him, he shrugged and breathed a half-laugh. "Or maybe you thought someone needed to keep me in line."

I snorted. I'd only known him a few days, but I already knew that would have been an impossible task. "Start at the beginning. Tell me what you know about my life."

He paused to cinch his sword belt more tightly, repositioned his arm around me, and nudged me forward. "You were a scrawny little thing, and always singing. Lukyan told your parents you should be a songkeeper, and he taught you himself until you apprenticed in Lyric. Your clan is Braide Wood. A bunch of backward, stubborn farmers and woodsmen." But he couldn't hide the affection in his tone as he described the village and the people there. His quiet voice spun a beautiful story, filling my ears with bits of the everyday in a place that I now longed to visit.

One fact wedged like a thorn in my thoughts. Kieran said I'd served the One. Yet the One had clearly turned His back on me, allowing me to fall under Bezreth's control. Had my whole former life been built on a lie?

Each time we stopped for rest, Kieran shoved a gourd into my hand and reminded me to drink, while he slipped back along the trail to check for pursuit. He and Nolan had several whispered discussions, but I shut them out, too involved with my struggle against the fever that seemed to be eating away my bones and muscles in the same way that my time in the shrine had eaten away my memory.

They dragged me on one last grueling climb through the most barren rocks yet, and then an awkward scramble down a slope toward a wide meadow that stretched forward forever, and swept into a deep forest to our left.

When we reached the edge of the woods, Kieran drew in a deep breath. Some of the tension seemed to ease from his shoulders. "Almost there."

I shook my head. My legs were trembling. I couldn't go any farther.

Nolan hummed a line of a melody that felt strangely familiar and looked at his father. Kieran nodded, and Nolan began to sing. Even Kieran joined in, in a gruff rumbling approximation of the tune. The words broke free from some buried place inside of me. "Awesome in majesty, perfect in power . . ."

I didn't have strength to sing them, but the lyrics washed through my thoughts as we picked our way among the trees. Even with all the pain and confusion, hearing the music stirred a poignant joy inside me. One day I'd have to confront my anger at the One who'd abandoned me, but for now I let the beauty of the music comfort me.

"We're almost there," Kieran said when the song finished.

I was about to see my home. Surely the sight of my village would unlock all the memories. I'd find myself again.

We reached a ridge that looked down on rooftops scattered among the trees, where neat log homes nestled beneath sheltering branches.

Kieran let go of me and let me sink to the covering of pine needles. He watched me expectantly.

I returned his stare blankly. "What?"

His face clouded, but he quickly covered his expression and shot a warning glance at Nolan. "Never mind."

But cold realization expanded in my chest, threatening to drown me. He thought I should know these trees, this hill, the sweet spicy scent of the air. But it was all still blank to me.

CHAPTER
19

LINETTE

KIERAN DELIVERED ME to the healer's lodge. As soon as my body realized that the relentless hike was over, I fell into a hard sleep full of feverish nightmares and cold sweats. Gentle hands propped my head and poured bitter concoctions down my throat. A quiet voice sang through the night, weaving in and out of my dreams.

The next morning, a young woman knelt beside my pallet, holding a steaming mug. "Blessed first light. The crisis has passed." She offered me the cup. "How do you feel?"

"Better." I eased upward, relieved to find my muscles supported me. The twisting, burning pain inside my bones was gone, as if poisons had finally left my system. Yet when I gently probed my memories, they remained behind stone as thick and black as any wall in Sidian.

"You look stronger. I thought you might like some clavo."

I sipped deeply of the warm, spicy liquid, savoring the comforting flavors. "Where are Kieran and Nolan?"

"I believe they planned to leave Braide Wood at first light."

My stomach wrenched, and I handed the mug back to the young healer, unable to swallow any more. I'd been abandoned—again. Tossed aside like the peel of a mesana vine—a nuisance discarded without a second thought. Not that I would miss Kieran's abrasiveness, but Nolan had felt like a friend.

The woman watched me with concern. "Are you able to speak with a visitor? He's been waiting to see you."

I brightened and pushed to my feet, finding my legs wobbly but functioning. "Lead on."

After helping me dress, she guided me down a series of hallways to a bright open lounge. Small groups of people chattered and laughed, while others sat in quiet conversation with assistants, waiting to meet with a healer.

A white-haired man approached, leaning heavily on a walking stick, yet radiating joyous vigor with each step. "Well met, child."

I didn't move, still clutching the arm of the attendant.

He hobbled forward and swept me into a surprisingly firm hug. Confidence and courage seemed to seep straight into my skin.

When he stepped back, tiny wrinkles formed starbursts around his eyes.

"It's good to meet you." I managed a shy smile. "I'm Linette."

His smiling starbursts drooped, and compassionate tenderness moistened his eyes. "Oh, child, I know your name. I spoke to the One on your behalf every day while you were in Hazor."

Another person I was supposed to know. My throat tightened. Would I ever remember? Could I find a way to rebuild a life?

The man didn't give me time to dwell on my fears. "I'm Lukyan. The eldest songkeeper of Braide Wood. Let's walk outside. When we face a big problem, it helps to look at the big world the One has formed, to remind ourselves of His capability."

Lukyan leaned on his walking stick and offered his other arm to me. My first strides were tentative, but the weakness receded with each new step. He was right. The tang of pine air, the glimpses of wide sky through the trees, even the crunch of pine needles underfoot all lifted my spirits.

Slowly, his name registered. "Kieran told me about you. How long have you known me? What can you tell me about who I am? Do I have family here?"

"I knew you when you were a twinkle in your parents' eyes. At your dedication, the One whispered to me that His hand would be on your life in a special way. You were the youngest apprentice the songkeepers ever took on, and when your parents died—"

A small gasp escaped my lips. Another hope tore from me like support beams from a house. "I don't have family?"

He squeezed my hand. "The songkeepers have been your family, and the One has been your Father."

I mustered a grateful smile but felt another layer of loss. Why should I be grieving the parents I couldn't even remember? Yet I did grieve. And the songkeepers who had replaced my family. Would they welcome me and take me in now?

I turned onto a path that led toward wetlands lush with shrubs. A flock of moths burst out of a cluster of reeds and surprised a laugh from me as they danced away and glided over the water of a tranquil pond. A solitary heron posed in the distance, embodying stillness.

"This was your favorite place to create new songs," Lukyan said quietly. "Some part of you still knows that."

It was true. He had let me chose the direction, and I'd led us here. Hope flickered. Maybe I could resurrect all the buried parts of me. I settled on a log and waited for him to ease down beside me. "So tell me everything you know about me. What foods do I like? Why was I in Hazor? Where do I live? Who is Kieran?" *Why did he leave without saying good-bye? Why does he continue to haunt my thoughts?*

Lukyan's eyes widened, then quickly softened. "Kieran caused a bit of irritation among the staff at the healer's lodge when you were brought in. He insisted on staying beside you the entire night. He'd still be here now, but news from Lyric . . ." He pressed his lips together. "Not something you need to worry about right now. But he was needed there."

A small hollow space in my heart filled with warmth as I thought of Kieran watching over me. I might be lost and confused, but I hadn't been abandoned. It was good to know someone had kept watch, especially if Bezreth had sent soldiers to find me and bring me back.

Suppressing a shudder, I sought Lukyan's eyes again. "Who else do I know? Can you take me to other places that I might remember? Where did I live?"

Lukyan patted my hand. "When you left for Hazor, you gave your cottage to a young couple newly bonded. But Tara has offered—insisted—that she'll take you in when you're ready."

I looked over my shoulder at the lodge. "I'm ready."

He laughed. "Sweet Linette, you could give the healers the blessing of serving for a few more days. It makes them feel useful."

His wink made me giggle, but the sound felt unfamiliar to my ears. Had I been prone to laughter when I'd lived in this clan? Or had too much time passed since I'd found things to giggle about?

I shook my head. "I don't want to stay any longer."

"I understand." He rubbed his shoulder. "I experienced their overzealous hospitality a few seasons ago."

We stopped at the healer's lodge long enough for Lukyan to firmly inform them that he was taking me. Begrudgingly, they gave in, but I caught suspicious glances and whispered conversations just out of earshot as we left the building. I thought perhaps my caretakers were annoyed that we ignored their advice, but then I realized not all the whispers ran between healers. Even those there for care looked at me askance. Puzzled, I asked Lukyan about it as I followed him down the trail through the woods.

A hard expression flicked across his face, out of place among the laugh lines. "They've seen problems with memory before, caused by Rhusican poison. Your condition makes them uneasy." He watched me closely.

"Is that the name of the drug Bezreth gave me?"

His face softened into a sad smile. "It wouldn't surprise me if they have many things in common." Then he pushed his shoulders back and picked up the pace. "Well, whatever the cause of a problem, the answer is the same. Follow the One."

Finally the trail opened out into a village. I waited for a flare of recognition. According to Lukyan, this was the clan where I'd grown up, these were the trees I'd climbed, these were the people I'd served.

An old woman in a doorway called to her grandchild and held him close, sending a dark look my way. As we passed another small cottage, a door slid shut.

I looked at Lukyan. "What's wrong?"

"Not everyone understood your choice to go to Hazor. People fear what they don't understand."

Cold river water churned through my chest. "They fear me?"

"Oh, not anyone with a magchip in their light cube." He tapped his forehead and smiled. "They're just uneasy. Give it time."

Give it time. Give it time. The words mocked me in rhythm with each step I took. I had no choice. I couldn't set a course for myself when I didn't know who I was. I couldn't make others comfortable when I wasn't comfortable with myself. I couldn't explain my reasons for being in Hazor when I didn't know them.

Lukyan stopped in front of a large house on the edge of town. The door opened and a white-haired woman scampered toward us, grabbed my shoulders, and touched her forehead lightly against mine. "Oh, sweet child. It's so good to see you. Thank you, Lukyan. Those healers are too worried for their own good. What she needs is family"—she wrapped her soft hand around my slim wrist—"and some fattening up. I bet you're hungry, aren't you?"

She swept me into her home, and Lukyan called a good-bye. He wasn't staying? Panic welled, but there was no resisting the firm motherly arms that pushed me toward a large table.

"Sit, sit, sit." She hit her hand against her forehead. "Silly me. He said you wouldn't remember. I'm Tara."

A little girl ran into the room, whooping, chased by a boy about the same size. A slim woman with long dark hair came in from the kitchen alcove, holding a baby. "Oh, Linette, I'm so sorry. We should never have left Sidian without you. We knew things were getting dangerous. But Kieran can be so stubborn. We should have made you come back to Braide Wood with us."

I stared at her blankly. Tara caught one of the running children. "Linette, these rascals are Aubrey and Dustin. They belong to Talia and Gareth, who are both out hunting with Payton. And this is Kendra and her baby, Emmi. And . . ."

The rush of unfamiliar names and the new faces made me feel as if the floor were tilting. I cast a look at the door, tempted to flee back to the healer's lodge and throw myself on their mercy.

CHAPTER
20

LINETTE

FIVE TIMES IN as many days, I woke in the small back room of Tara's home and searched for some clue, some thread that would help me weave a picture of my past. Five times in as many days, I recited a simple prayer that Kendra had taught me, "As my eyes first open, may I open my heart to the One who painted first light across the darkness and allows me to see."

Five times in as many days, all I could see inside myself was an aching emptiness.

The same emptiness hovered throughout the day. I had become a phrase of melody with missing notes, caught in a clashing harmony that wouldn't resolve.

Tara's warmth and acceptance provided a welcome refuge from the suspicion and withdrawal of the village. Yet even under her roof, the awkwardness of my confusion made me want to hide in the room she'd given me. As the days passed, the knot of agitation in my gut built until I felt like I'd swallowed a millstone.

"Susan stayed here when she came," Tara had told me as she unfurled a woven blanket over the pallet. Her tone told me Susan must have been someone special to her. Another fact to tuck away.

"Aren't you glad we don't have to bother with those silly braids like we did in Hazor?" Kendra asked one morning as we dished up mugs of clavo. I smiled and nodded, but I wanted to slam the ladle to the table in frustration. Why did she insist on acting like I knew her? Didn't she understand? I had no memory of being with her in Sidian, no memory of being her friend.

At supper one evening, I listened to the swirl of talk around me, oblivious to the nuances, missing the jokes—unable to follow even simple conversation. My hand clenched around my spoon.

Payton chose that moment to turn to me, no doubt thinking to include me in the discussion. "We have more of the land cleared from the damage. Morsal Plains should be recovered in a few more seasons." He smiled expectantly, as if I'd understand and share his pleasure.

I shoved away my bowl of stew and pushed back from the table. "I don't know what any of you are talking about." Then, in the silence that followed, I fled to my room, ashamed of my angry outburst.

Huddled on my pallet, I fought back tears. Gathering up bits of information was not the same as remembering. I could learn names, but didn't know what I was supposed to feel toward a person, what experiences we'd shared. Tara's large family filled the home, but I still felt terribly alone.

I longed to settle into purposeful work, but a songkeeper who didn't know the Verses was worse than useless. I recruited Dustin and Aubrey to teach me, and began to relearn the rich and beautiful words. Lukyan visited often to explain the meaning. Still, I couldn't squeeze a lifetime of learning into a few days. It could take years before I'd be able to serve as a songkeeper—if the clan would even accept and allow it. I didn't know who I was, who I had been, or who I was supposed to be. I felt like one of the fabled wraiths that the children told me haunted a place called Shamgar.

My isolation deepened after the local guardians encountered a team of Hazorite soldiers near Morsal Plains. The guardians fought them back, but rumors circulated quickly that Zarek had sent them because of me, rumors I couldn't even refute with confidence. I felt surrounded by suspicion, and even Tara couldn't hide her worried glances in my direction.

One morning, I set out early to explore the woods that surrounded the village, with the same hope that propelled me each day. Perhaps today I'd recognize something. Maybe today would be the day I would find myself. Crisscrossing paths led to unexpected clearings and open prairies. Each new vista might provide a key—a glimpse that would jar open some better memories to replace my terrifying recollections of Bezreth. Besides, if I stayed under Payton and Tara's roof, I'd end up snapping and snarling at someone again, and they didn't deserve to have their kindness answered with my frustration.

I kept glancing over my shoulder. Had Bezreth sent the Hazorite soldiers to Braide Wood? Would she send someone else after me? How far did her reach extend? As those fears crept forward, I found myself wishing Kieran had remained in Braide Wood. He'd been short-tempered and abrasive, but he'd made me feel . . . protected.

Shaking my long hair free from my cloak, I followed a trail that led upward to a ridge overlooking the central homes of the village. Tall pines added a spicy scent over the subtle sweetness of honey-limbed bark and moist soil that cushioned my steps. I continued farther in the direction I'd been told led to the nearest transport. Lukyan had said he'd take me to Lyric soon. He thought that if I spent time at the tower, my spirit would find healing. I clung to any small hope these days.

Out of breath from the climb, I worked my way slowly along a steep part of the trail. Silence wrapped around me like caradoc wool. Out here, no one prodded me to remember. No eyes followed me—either with pity or suspicion. My shoulders relaxed, and I lifted my face to the soft grey sky.

Holy One, Lukyan says I knew You well. He claims you didn't forsake me, but I don't know what to believe. Forgive me for all that I no longer understand. And if you still want me, show me how to follow You again.

A twig cracked nearby, interrupting my prayer. I turned toward the sound. Although I couldn't remember personal encounters with them, I knew that predators roamed the outlying forests. They rarely troubled anyone during the light of day. Then my thoughts shifted to a greater danger. Vivid images of angry carvings and the screams of despair that waited beneath the Sidian shrine made my stomach tighten. Had Bezreth found me?

For a moment I couldn't move. But I'd rather confront the unknown than wait for it to spring out at me. I took a few tentative steps in the direction of the sound.

Pausing, I heard a soft rustling of leaves and pine needles. I followed the sound until the trees opened into a tiny space no bigger than Tara's kitchen. On a fallen log sat a young boy, perhaps five or six years old. Tousled curls framed his face, and his wide, clear eyes focused on something in the leaves a few feet in front of him. His hand stretched forward. When I saw what he was reaching for, my heart stuttered.

A scarlet-furred rizzid bared its fangs and inched closer to the boy. In the same way I remembered that water was for drinking and a tree was a tree, I knew that a rizzid was lethal.

"No!" I shouted. "Get back."

The boy's thick lashes lifted and his deep brown eyes met mine. He smiled gently, unafraid. The rizzid slithered the remaining distance. Before I could find a weapon or snatch the boy to safety, the creature crawled onto the boy's lap.

My breath caught in my throat, and I stood still, afraid to do anything to startle it.

The boy calmly stroked the rizzid's head. The animal's eyes closed, and a sound almost like purring gurgled from its throat. Then the boy set it on the log, petted it once more, and shooed it off in the same way I'd seen Tara send her grandchildren off to play.

I drew a breath, relief making me weak. Then I closed the distance and sank onto the log beside the boy. "You shouldn't touch rizzids. They're dangerous."

He blinked a few times and smiled at me again.

"What's your name?" I asked.

He still didn't speak. Maybe he was shy.

"My name is Linette," I said quietly. "Where are your parents? We're too far from the village. You shouldn't be out here all alone."

He stood and offered me his small hand.

I took it, soft and warm in mine, and scanned the clearing. "Hello? Anyone here?" I called out. Surely his parents had to be nearby. Or an older brother or sister who was supposed to watch him? I couldn't leave him here. I stood up. Tara would know him. She knew everyone in the clan and could return him to the right home.

Together we walked back to the trail and toward the village. His wide eyes took in everything around him with fascination, as if it were new to him in the same way these woods—that should have been familiar—were new to me.

On the ridge above the village, the lace of one of my boots came loose. I crouched to tie it, then smiled up at the boy. His gaze trapped mine, brown eyes deepening like quiet pools. His small hands reached out and clasped my face. As he touched me, memories seeped back in as softly as dawning light in the morning.

I recognized these trees. The tall pines stretching toward the sky were old friends. The sweet scent of honeyed wood reassured me I belonged. The trail seemed to ripple and settle, and now it felt familiar beneath my feet. I knew who I was and where I had been. I knew my heart again. Walls in my mind melted away, and an inaudible voice called my name.

Linette. Songkeeper. Beloved child.

I gasped, drawing in new memories with each breath. The sky visible above the trees seemed lighter. The sleeves of my tunic, softer. I ran fingers through my loose hair, and it no longer felt like a stranger's.

Childhood flooded back. Warm memories of my parents' hugs, gleeful races across open prairies, rambling invented songs that I sang to the empty marshes. Not all the memories were full of joy, but I embraced them all. My parents' tears when I left for my apprenticeship in Lyric, youthful quarrels with friends, a bad fall from a lehkan. Layer by layer, my life was rebuilt.

"Oh, thank You, Holy One!" I laughed with giddy relief. I couldn't wait to tell Lukyan and Tara. They'd been so worried. And Kieran. I shook my head. The poor man. All he'd gone through to get me safely back from Hazor, and I'd never thanked him.

But why had we been in Hazor? I remembered vague impressions of the painful days of traveling home to Braide Wood, and before that the wretched time below the shrine, but I couldn't seem to unlock the days before I'd entered that prison.

I tried from the other direction, skimming lightly over my childhood and apprentice years. The unfolding memories slowed. I remembered feast days, singing at the Lyric tower. I remembered much of my life in Braide Wood. But the last few years were still shrouded. I struggled for a moment, trying to push past the barrier, to unscramble the locks barring the door of those years.

I looked again at the child. Sadness glimmered in his eyes.

I drew him into a tender hug, then rested my forehead against his. I could grapple with the remaining lost memories later. The boy needed my help. I remembered the Braide Wood families now. Even with the strange gap in my memory, I knew enough to know that he wasn't from our clan.

"Where are your parents?" I asked again. "Where do you belong?"

It was amazing that he showed no fear, being left alone so far from the village. Perhaps he was simple-minded. He seemed unable to speak, always answering my questions with that same relaxed smile.

My earlier plan still made sense. I took the boy's hand, and we headed toward Tara's house. Somehow the One had used this boy's touch to restore my memory. To show me where I belonged. Now maybe I could return the favor.

I burst into Tara's home. She was kneading dough in the kitchen alcove, while hearty scents floated from a loaf on the glowing heat trivet.

"I remember! Tara, it's all coming back."

She clapped her hands together, sending up a small puff of flour. "Thank the One! Home cooking and time with friends will fix most anything." Her enthusiastic hug squeezed the breath from me.

In my excitement to share my great news, I almost forgot my small companion, who had trailed me into the home's common room. The boy tilted his head, eyes bright as he watched our celebration.

Tara released me and looked over my shoulder. "Who's this?"

"I hoped you might know. I found him in the woods near the ridge trail."

She cast me a worried look. "I don't understand. You found him?"

"He was all alone. I couldn't leave him. Has a new family moved to the clan?"

"No." Tara eased herself down to eye-level with the boy. "Were you traveling with your family? Did you get lost?"

The child touched Tara's temple, as if to brush away the worry that had tightened her features, but remained silent.

Tara rose slowly, wincing as she straightened her back. "Dustin!" Talia and Gareth's son tore in from the back room, then skidded to a stop and grinned when he saw a potential playmate. Tara tousled Dustin's curls absently. "Little one, run to the plateau and tell Tristan we need a messenger. Right away."

After Dustin reluctantly pulled himself away and headed on his errand, Tara lifted a fresh roll from the heat trivet, bouncing it from hand to hand. She broke it in half, and fragrant steam rose from the nutty center. She handed half to me and half to the child, then sat down and hefted the boy into her lap. "I know all the children from Blue Knoll. He could be from Lyric, but I still can't understand why he ended up here. Poor dear." She smoothed his curly bangs away from his eyes. His face betrayed no worry. Instead, he munched happily on the bread, then rested against Tara's shoulder.

"Everything will be all right." Tara wrapped her arms around the boy. "We'll figure this out." Then she looked at me, and her frown cleared. "So you remember everything now?"

I giggled, relief and joy welling up again. "Most of my life. The people I love. The One. His Verses. It's all coming back." Too excited to sit still, I wandered to the kitchen and poured a mug of clavo for Tara. When I returned, I set it on the table near her and perched back on my chair. "The strange thing is, the memories began to return after I found him. Do you think he has some sort of gift? Like a Restorer gift?"

The furrows on Tara's brow deepened. "I don't understand much about what you've been through, or what happened this morning. But couldn't it just be a coincidence that more recollections returned the same day you came across him? Or maybe he helped in the way some healers just help people feel better by their presence?"

No. It had been more than that. But I didn't know how to explain, and had no better theory to offer.

"Well, whatever happened, it's wonderful to feel like I know myself again. I still can't remember much about the last few years. But I'm sure it will come back."

A wave of sadness crossed Tara's face, but she hid it with a quick smile that dimpled her cheeks. "Welcome back."

What was that look about? What secrets about myself did she know that I still didn't? The small bread loaf suddenly felt like a hard lump in my stomach. I should be grateful for the parts of myself I'd recovered, but I couldn't help worrying about the parts that were still lost.

The boy surprised me by slipping off Tara's ample grandmotherly lap and padding over to me. He climbed onto my thin legs, and reached for my hand. He tapped a finger into my palm, and my hand closed quickly to trap it. He pulled it away and his body shook with silent giggles. As we continued to play the game, my worry melted. If this child could be so trusting and at peace in spite of being lost, I could surely trust the One for a few lost memories. I was safe in His arms. He'd let me remember what I needed to know.

A soft tap sounded at the door. Tristan must have sent a very quick messenger for Tara's use. "Come in," she called.

The door slid open and Lukyan limped in, leaning on his walking stick. His white hair was rumpled, his cloak uneven, and his face wore the confusion of someone waking up hard after a too-long nap. "I'm sorry to interrupt. I was speaking to the One and . . ." His gaze stopped on the boy in my arms.

Breathing hard, he walked toward me, eyes riveted on the boy.

I smiled. "My memory is returning."

He didn't answer me. Braced on his walking stick, he lowered to one knee so he could meet the child on eye level.

I couldn't read Lukyan's expression. Was it horror or awe? And what could bring on such intensity? Reflexively, my arms tightened around the child.

The boy didn't seem worried by Lukyan's strange tension. One hand still resting in my palm, the boy lifted the small bread loaf clenched in his other hand and offered it.

Lukyan's hand shook as he took the bread. Tears brought a shimmer to his cloudy blue eyes. "Thank you." The whisper scraped past his throat.

My brows knitted at Lukyan's reaction to the boy. "I found him by the ridgeline above the village. Tara said he isn't from any of the nearby clans. Do you recognize him?"

Lukyan didn't look at me, still absorbed in the child. A tremulous smile lit his wrinkled face. "I . . . I believe I do."

CHAPTER
21

SUSAN

UNDER THE BLUE-STREAKED threads of light in the cave walls, Jake's weary eyes took us in, then widened. The flare of recognition lasted the barest of instants before he pressed his lips together and nodded as if we were strangers.

I tried to gather my wits. "Wha—"

Mark's hand clamped around my arm and stopped me from running forward. A world of warning filled his grip, but I tugged against him, desperate to throw my arms around my son.

Mark's hold tightened, and he wrapped his other arm around me, squeezing hard. "Well met," he said to Jake. "Which clan do you claim?"

The corner of Jake's mouth lifted. "My people hail from Rendor"—his gaze flicked to me with a hint of warmth that he quickly hid—"and Braide Wood."

I pried Mark's fingers off my upper arm. He didn't have to leave bruises. I got it. It was safer for Jake if we didn't acknowledge that we knew him. "I've met a few people from Braide Wood," I said, hoping the Kahlarean master would attribute the warmth in my voice to memories of old acquaintances. Meanwhile, I devoured the sight of my son. He had filled out since I'd last seen him and carried a new maturity. But he also looked haggard and tired. How much time had passed for him in the month since we'd left Lyric? I couldn't begin to guess.

Mark turned toward Voronja. "We'd have a more productive conversation if you allowed us time alone."

The old Kahlarean smiled sourly. "No. You will have a productive conversation with me here."

Great. My son was a few feet away and I couldn't hug him. And how were we going to communicate without slipping and revealing anything dangerous?

"Were you banished as well?" Mark asked.

I stared at him, amazed at his ability to sound like he was speaking to a stranger.

"Not exactly. Do you remember when the former council leader Cameron was arrested several seasons ago?"

Several seasons? That meant close to a year had passed. I pressed my lips together, terrified I'd say the wrong thing.

"Some rumors reached our clan." Mark walked forward and sat on the edge of the table. As he tilted his head down to talk with Jake, the angle of his face matched Jake's so perfectly, I was sure the Kahlarean would notice the father/son resemblance.

"Apparently he has friends among the Kahlareans who arranged his escape. And my recent . . . visit here."

Conflicting emotions stormed inside my head. I was thrilled to see Jake alive, whole, healthy. This was exactly what Mark and I had prayed for, longed for . . . to find Jake. But this was the most dangerous possible place for a Restorer. Did the Kahlareans know who he was? What had he been facing, captive in this enclave, all alone?

We had to get him out of here.

"How long have you been a 'guest' of the Kahlareans?" I asked through a strained throat.

Jake smiled at me—the smile of a seasoned man, not a frightened young boy. "Not long. As you might guess, it wasn't a trip I would have chosen. But I trust the purposes of the One."

"He's been spinning some intriguing tales," said Voronja, head stretching forward as he followed our conversation. "But we didn't barter for him to hear stories. Cameron told us he could provide us with the blood of the Restorer. Apparently he lied."

"Imagine that," I said under my breath. Cameron was a snake whose poison continued to cause harm. But if the Kahlareans didn't believe Jake was really the Restorer, perhaps there was still hope.

Voronja loosened the straps holding Jake's arm to the chair, pulling back the loose tunic sleeve. Crisscrossing stripes of scars, some still a furious red, marked his arm. "He doesn't heal. And we've had no success with our experiments with his blood."

Rage burned the red stripes across my vision. I ran past Mark and to Jake's side. "What have they done?"

I wanted to touch his arm, to treat his wounds, to offer some kind of comfort. Instead, I took his hand, then rounded on the Kahlarean. "What kind of warrior tortures a boy for no reason?" Maybe their stupid experiments trying to turn Restorer blood into a weapon would give them all leukemia. Could there still be traces in Jake's blood? Could it infect the Kahlareans? The vicious wish surged through me.

Voronja's eyes narrowed almost to the size of human eyes. "We're the ones who were wronged. We've simply asked him how to find the true Restorer."

So now they'd torture him for an answer he couldn't give.

And was there a Restorer now? This was becoming a street-corner shell game. After Kieran had the signs, we'd assumed he would fill that role through his generation. Jake's Restorer signs had startled and terrified me. Now I didn't know whether to be relieved that he no longer had those gifts or worried because he could no longer heal. What did this mean for the clans? Was Kieran the Restorer again? Or someone new? Mark knew the Verses far better than I did. Was this part of the promise? Surely the need for help hadn't passed. Rhus, Kahlarea, and Hazor all posed unique dangers to the clans.

Lord, what are You doing? And what do You want us to do? Guide us.

I straightened. "Cameron is the one who sold you a false Restorer. You should be asking him where the real one is."

"Oh, we will," said the master assassin. "When we've found him." The anticipation in the old man's voice almost made me pity Cameron. Almost.

Mark cleared his throat, somehow maintaining a calm expression. "What interesting stories have you been sharing?" he asked Jake.

A sparkle caught in Jake's eyes as his chin lifted. "I've been telling Master Voronja about the One who loves all nations."

How could he talk about love, much less try to share it with his captor? Bloody and scarred and bound in a Kahlarean cave, his faith—his forgiveness—stunned and humbled me. I'd been proud of Jake when he scored three soccer goals in one game. I'd swelled with warmth when he'd shared his testimony at our church. I'd admired him with a fierce mother's pride as he'd endured the cancer treatments and still found strength to tease his younger sister and banter with nurses. But seeing the way he embraced his calling to follow the One, even in a place of danger and pain, strengthened and inspired a deep place in my heart.

"And even though Cameron delivered me to them for his own purposes, I think the One wanted me here."

I listened carefully to Jake's inflection. *Wanted.* Past tense. The One had sent him here for a reason, but clearly Jake didn't feel he had to stay any more. Because we'd come to rescue him? What was the One's plan? All I knew was that we had to get him out of here. "The purposes of the One are sometimes . . . mysterious," I said quietly.

Jake grinned. "Agreed. I've been thinking a lot about Alcatraz."

I blinked. Was that a clan name I'd forgotten? It took a moment to cast my memory back to the reference. Prison. Escape. Yes!

"By the way," Jake added conversationally, "I was surprised to learn that the assassin's enclave is so close to Cauldron Falls."

Still sitting on the low table, Mark straightened. "Oh, really? I didn't realize. We'd gotten rather turned around."

Mark's casual response sounded forced, but only because I knew him so well. I glanced at the Kahlarean, but he was still staring at Jake and didn't seem to have caught the nuances of the conversation.

Mark looked toward the door. "Have you thought of Huck Finn?"

"Yeah." Jake frowned. "But the Mississippi follows a pretty well-defined course."

Mark shrugged "Huck didn't know that. He just did what he had to do."

"What are they talking about?" the Kahlarean asked gruffly.

I squeezed the bridge of my nose. "I don't know." I didn't have to pretend ignorance. They'd already lost me.

Jake's gaze cut toward the Kahlarean master. "Sitting here has given me time to think about my favorite tropes."

I rubbed my temples. Tropes? Was it possible the torture had taken a toll on Jake's mind? Even Mark's brow furrowed as he struggled to make sense of that comment.

Then Mark's frown cleared. The side of his mouth twitched.

Voronja growled. "Enough wasted words. Will you tell us—"

Mark gasped and doubled over. All his muscles clenched as he groaned with a depth of pain reserved for childbirth or kidney stones.

A new panic coursed through me as I rushed to his side. Had the trip through the portal been too much and finally caught up to him? "What's wrong? Can you talk?"

He shook his head, body still curled around his middle.

The old Kahlarean moved in, too.

Suddenly, Mark straightened. His fist flew up, the hilt of his hidden table knife crashing into Voronja's throat. By the time I'd stumbled back a few steps, he had the Kahlarean pinned against the table. "Get his weapons. I can't hold him long."

Already, the Kahlarean was slipping downward, eel-like. I raced forward to help. Between us, we wrenched the venblade holster from his wrist, fighting to keep the blade from pricking either of us in the struggle.

Mark took him down to the floor, struggling to keep his grip on the man. He lifted the kitchen knife.

"Dad, wait," Jake yelled. "Don't kill him."

Both Mark and Voronja froze. "Jake, we aren't going to get far if I don't," Mark said through clenched teeth.

I plucked the knife from Mark's hand. Let the men debate about what to do next. I couldn't stand seeing Jake bound and helpless for another second. I used the blade to cut the straps holding Jake to the chair.

Jake stood slowly, wobbling as he tested his legs. Then he crouched beside his father. "Voronja is the one Kahlarean I've talked with here. If he dies, everything I've shared will be lost to his people."

Mark's hands found Voronja's throat. A lifetime of rage and fear shook his muscles. I couldn't be sure he was hearing Jake.

"Dad," Jake said again.

Something in Mark's eyes changed, and he hesitated.

Then, in a sharp flurry of movement, the Kahlarean twisted, broke Mark's grip, and sprang free. In the time it took for Mark to rise from his crouch, Voronja reached into a cubby near the door and faced us with a half-sphere geode in his hand.

Jake stepped between us and squared off with Voronja.

"Why did you tell him to stop?" the assassin asked, his knobby fingers resting on the lever of the syncbeam that could vaporize us all. "You had me at your mercy."

"Mercy," Jake answered. "Yes, that's the word. The One had mercy on me, and asks me to show mercy to others."

"So all those tales, they aren't just words? You'd die for them?"

Jake's chin lifted and an inner light touched his features. "My life is His."

Cords of tension squeezed my ribs until they threatened to crack. For once I couldn't find words to add. All I could do was wait.

The assassin stared into Jake's eyes as time stretched. Then he slowly lowered his arm. "You'll never be able to escape the enclave . . . without help."

Mark and I risked a few breaths, but still didn't move. Jake just grinned. "Any suggestions?"

Voronja's attention turned to me, and he sized me up. Then he pulled his hooded mask from his head and held it out to me. "My clothes will fit you."

Confused, I shook my head.

"Mom, breathe. It's another trope," Jake said as he took the hood from Voronja and slid it over my head.

"Good idea." Mark still sounded a bit shell-shocked. I touched his arm, the only comfort I could offer in the moment.

"Would someone explain it to me?" My words came out muffled as Jake slid the fabric mask over the lower part of my face.

Voronja pulled off his cloak.

Jake held it for him while the assassin bent to slip off his soft leather shoes. "You remember. The conventions in TV shows."

Mark spared a quick grin my direction. "Like if you're a prisoner, pretend you're sick to get the captor to let down his guard."

And Mark had once laughed at me for getting my ideas from Nancy Drew?

Jake helped the assassin untie the straps of his wrap-around shirt. "Or disguise yourself as one of the bad guys." He held up the shirt— black and form fitting. "It's not going to fit Dad or me."

No. He couldn't be serious. True, I had the smaller frame, but I was still a little taller than most of the Kahlareans we'd met. And most importantly, I didn't move like a wraith.

But Mark was helping Jake divest Voronja of the rest of his outer clothes. "Hurry and change. The hood will hide most of your face. Just keep your hands hidden."

Too desperate to argue, and fresh out of options, I pulled on the assassin's uniform. My fingers trembled as I tightened the draw-strings on the pants.

"Just think ninja." Mark dropped a light kiss on my nose, then turned to face Voronja. "What will your people do to you?"

Even in his uniform's dark under-layer, the elderly Kahlarean carried himself with dignity. "I'll need to be seriously injured to justify your escape. And tied well to give you time before I can free myself."

Jake beckoned to his dad, and together they tied Voronja to the chair, fashioned a gag from my shirt, and knotted it in place. Jake hefted the awkward syncbeam and met Voronja's eyes. "I'll remember you to the One. You and your people."

The man nodded, then closed his eyes. Jake clocked him on the side of his head with the geode, the sickening crunch loud in the small room. With his head lolling forward, Voronja's pale skin and knobby joints made him look old and frail.

Jake dropped the weapon, watching while a trail of blood slid down Voronja's face. "I hope that will be enough to convince them."

Mark handed me the arm holster that Voronja had worn.

I glared at him, squaring off for an argument. "I'm not carrying a venblade."

Appreciation flared in his eyes. "That's right. Keep thinking angry and powerful. Your posture almost looks Kahlarean now."

"It's not an act. Those things are way too dangerous."

"The sleeve doesn't look right without it. Someone could notice."

Jake stepped between us. "Forget the venblade. Just wear the holster with the knife."

Mark adjusted the lower part of my black hood, pulling it up to cover all but my eyes. He gently pushed a few last strands of my hair out of sight. "I know you're scared," he whispered. "You can do this."

Scared didn't begin to describe it. "Where are we headed?" The rock ledge that brought us into the enclave would be impossible to scale downward. I shuddered.

Jake gave me a one-armed squeeze. "Mom, weren't you listening? We're doing Huck Finn."

I shook my head, and the hood shifted, blocking my vision. I tugged it back into place. The fabric over my nose and mouth made me claustrophobic and short of breath.

Mark helped me adjust it again. "Do you remember the way back to the kitchen? Just get us there and we'll follow the water channel out to the river."

There were more things wrong with that plan than I could count. I was a poorly costumed assassin, about to guide my prisoners through confusing cave passages, when I'd never had any navigational abilities, all so we could jump into slimy cave water and swim into the dark unknown under a mountain of crushing rock.

I crouched and checked the straps of the soft-soled footwear I'd borrowed from Voronja. "Guys, we need to rethink this." If we just took some time to brainstorm, we'd come up with a more sensible plan. We had to.

Mark tugged me to my feet. "We have to move. We'll walk in front, but you have to make it look like you're in charge. Remember, you're a master assassin."

Suddenly the kitchen knife in my arm holster felt reassuring. I pulled the mask portion of the hood away from my face so I could take one last deep breath. One step at a time. Get to the kitchen. If I thought beyond that, I'd give up now.

Mark used Voronja's scrambler to unlock the door, then shot me a worried look.

I answered with a sharp nod. "Let's go."

CHAPTER 22

SUSAN

MARK AND JAKE moved into the outer room. Once again the reflective pool captured the threads of blue light from the curved cave walls and created dizzying patterns.

Jake crouched beside the pool. "Maybe we should see if there's a passage we could follow from here. I could dive down and feel for an opening."

Mark shook his head. "If we had scuba gear and some lights, maybe. But we have no way of knowing if we could hold our breath long enough to reach the next place with air. And if there's a current, we might not be able to get back."

Jake stirred the water. "It's not too cold. I could check it out."

I shuddered. Death by drowning was one of my worst nightmares. We were not going to dive into a dark pool and explore some narrow underwater passage that might close in and trap us. I grabbed Jake's arm and yanked him away from the pool's edge. "Forget it. Kitchen it is. At least there the channel had headspace with air."

"At least the part we could see." Mark said darkly.

"You"—I pointed at my husband—"stop being so negative. And you"—I swung my gaze to my son—"no more crazy ideas. This is going to be hard enough. Now lead the way."

Mark grinned at Jake. "She's getting the hang of acting like a Kahlarean master."

He snorted. "She's a mom. There are similarities."

I cuffed him on the shoulder, then spared a precious second to grab him in a tight hug.

"How did you know?" Jake asked. "How did you find me?"

"And what's happening in the clans? You said—"

"Later," Mark cut in. "We need to move."

A million questions chased around my brain, but Mark was right, conversation would have to wait.

We headed into the maze of underground corridors, and I followed Mark and Jake, trying to look like I was marching my captives to some important destination. I'd never been more grateful for Mark's sense of direction. After two turns, I was completely lost, but he never slowed. I recognized the channel where we crossed using stepping stones, but other than that, I had to put my faith in him. A row of young assassin trainees raced past us, so focused on their run that they didn't give us more than a glance.

I tugged my hood lower on my forehead. Anyone looking closely would surely see that my eyes were too small for a Kahlarean.

"Hurry," I whispered.

Mark led us to the arched opening of the large training area. "Don't panic now. You're doing great," he murmured. "Act natural."

Right. And how was I supposed to know what was natural for a Kahlarean master assassin? I peered into the arena. Our path followed the semi-circle of the cavern's upper level. We'd be as exposed as actors on a stage until we reached the right hallway and could retreat into the smaller darker paths. "We can't walk through here. Isn't there another way?"

Mark shot a quick look at Jake, who gave a small shrug. Apparently he hadn't roamed these caves during his captivity. We'd have to continue retracing our path to the dining hall. This was a terrible idea, but I didn't have any other suggestions to offer.

Jake's Adam's apple bobbed. Mark focused on the far side of the training hall and the opening that was our goal. I lifted my arm to gesture them forward, and felt the weight of the unfamiliar wrist holster. My heart pounded so hard the cave walls seemed to thrum

SHARON HINCK

with the beat. At least once we started moving again the trembling in my legs wasn't as obvious.

We took a few steps. Any second the nearby Kahlareans would come running—surround us, drop from the ceiling like bats, pierce us with dozens of venblades.

We took another cautious step. Mark dropped his gaze and moved forward with as quick a pace as would appear normal.

We made it ten more yards. The path that followed the semi-circle above the main floor of the arena seemed to stretch forever. I forced myself not to look to the side. Still I sensed the activity of the trainees: the near lethal hand-to-hand combat, the crackle of sync-beams, the swordplay, the balancing exercises. Perhaps all the chaos and activity would be enough distraction and no one would notice us. Another twenty yards.

We passed the first opening leading away from the arena. I wanted to duck down that hall and run, but this wasn't the exit that would lead us to our goal.

We passed the next opening leading from the arena, but Mark didn't slow.

How much farther? I vaguely remembered skirting most of the room when we'd come through here. I wanted to duck into the next hall. Anything to get away from our exposed position. My muscles tightened so much that I shrank in size. Good. That would aid my disguise. Even though I was smaller than Mark and Jake, the Kahlarean's uniform was still ill-fitting.

Too terrified to spare any more glances around, I focused on Mark's back and on keeping my footing on the slick, uneven surface.

A breath of movement registered behind me. "Master, did you dispose of the annoying woman? Will you require any more help from me with the other prisoner?"

Trennor! The folds of fabric over my mouth trapped my small gasp. Mark glanced back, and I caught a flash of panic in his face before he turned and forged onward. I ignored Trennor and quick-ened my pace. The youth scampered more quickly and pulled along-side me.

We reached another branching hallway and I waved toward it, hoping Trennor would take my gesture as an order to leave.

He didn't take the hint, but dogged our steps. "I've finished my courses today, so if you . . ."

I tried again to shoo him away. Ahead, Mark's shoulders hunched and he walked even faster, each long stride getting us closer to the right exit. Fifty yards to go.

Determination pushed aside my panic.

I caught up to Jake and gave a small push against his back. *Move, move, move.*

Light footsteps sprinted past all three of us. Trennor faced us, blocking our path. Ten yards from our goal. The scolopendra fang swung from a string around his neck. "Wait, you're—"

Mark barreled ahead, straight into Trennor. The shock kept him from calling out, but I no longer had hope that we could avoid the attention of others in the arena. With Mark half-charging, we pushed Trennor ahead of us and down the corridor. Mark slugged him and eased the boy's unconscious body to the rock floor before stepping over him. I sidestepped around him. "Sorry," I whispered.

"Hurry," Mark said. "They'll be right behind us." The tension of our careful walk snapped in a release of panic. No more time for disguises and subtleties. We ran for all we were worth.

Mark and Jake sprinted along the passageway. I swiveled my head to check for signs of pursuit, and when I faced forward, the hood and mask stayed behind, blinding me. Lurching into the wall, I kept running while clawing at the fabric until I could see again. Mark stopped until I caught up to him with stumbling steps. I grabbed his hand and we ran again, following Jake.

"Almost there," Mark said.

Breathing hard, I gave a quick nod. Just one old cook left to get past. Unless the dining hall was full of young, lethal assassins. I shook the thought away. We rounded a corner and burst into the dining hall, which was mercifully empty.

I dropped Mark's hand, rested my hands on my thighs and fought to catch my breath. The two men tore into the kitchen area, and by the time I caught up, Anataz the cook was on the floor.

"Okay, Huck." I glanced around the kitchen for inspiration. "What do we use as a raft?"

"No time." Mark stared at the channel of water where we'd tossed kitchen scraps a few hours ago. He grabbed my hand and gave it a squeeze. "We're going for a swim."

Opaque water disappeared into the darkness and the rock closed in around the channel. My throat closed as if I were already drowning, but there was no way back now.

Jake sat on the edge and slipped quietly into the murky water. Mark helped me to the edge and sat beside me. "Ready?" he asked.

I ripped off the entangling hooded mask and tossed it aside, then eased into the channel.

The water was cool but not icy. I thanked the One for the temperate climate of this world. In the darkness it felt like black oil against my skin. Swimming laps at our local YMCA had done nothing to prepare me for this, but I took off after Jake, with Mark following. The pale illumination coming from thin threads of darnite in the rock gave only enough light to be disorienting. From somewhere behind us, we heard a splash. "Let's go," Mark said. "They're following."

I launched into my best front crawl, desperation adding muscle to my flutter kicks. As the walls drew closer, the current spend up. I stopped propelling myself forward and instead concentrated on dodging boulders. I flew past one low outcropping, barely avoiding a concussion.

Would this channel close in even further, drowning us in the fierce pull of water and surrounding rock that cut off all air? Maybe this was how Jonah felt in the belly of the fish. All darkness, water, and slime. Terrified and buried.

Holy One, will You resurrect us?

The water propelled us even faster, and I held my breath, bobbing beneath the surface of the water now to avoid the lowering ceiling. When my lungs felt like they would explode, I thrust my face up for a gasp of air, but caught some water. I coughed and sputtered the brackish taste from my mouth. At least I caught a glimpse of Jake swimming strongly up ahead. I twisted to look for Mark behind me, but the force of the current tossed me sideways. Ricocheting along the narrow channel, I bruised my shoulders as I bumped the left wall of stone and then the right.

The next time I was able to surface, Jake's head was more clearly silhouetted. There was a hint of light ahead! Perhaps we were finally going to emerge from the mountain. Anything to get out from under the oppressive weight of tons of rock overhead. I craved the soft dove-grey sky and fresh air, trees, and grass. And I never wanted to see another Kahlarean.

I tried a few breaststrokes, fueled by new hope. Maybe we wouldn't be pulled into an airless tube of water, sucked into the bowels of the world to drown. After all, Kahlareans were pursuing us, and they wouldn't bother if this channel led to certain death. Maybe this river would set us free on land, where we would have a chance to get back to the clans.

Stalactites dangled inches above the water, and I quickly pulled my head under again. With my one hand in front, and one above my head, I gingerly tested for space before coming back up for breath. I'd rather break a hand than my skull.

The channel seemed to widen, although there was a strange dark emptiness in the center of the passage ahead. My body continued to race forward, carried by the current, and I saw Jake bob and surface and cut to the right. The image of my son being carried away on a current touched a primal fear. I stroked against the water trying to catch him.

Suddenly my eyes were able to interpret the space I'd thought was dull emptiness. It was a huge rock formation cutting the channel in two. I pulled harder, desperate to head to the right, but the current tossed me left and past the dividing point.

I'd lost Jake.

I turned, trying to swim against the current, but I was already yards and yards farther downstream. Where was the right hand branch going to carry Jake? And where was this left hand branch carrying me? And where was Mark? I could no longer see him behind me.

Hopefully these channels reconnected into one river. I definitely saw light up ahead. I concentrated on not choking on the churning water, bringing my head up in a regular rhythm to gasp in some air. Light framed an arched opening, but I couldn't see what happened to the water once it passed that archway and headed into the light.

My body flew out into space and plummeted.

The drop was only about twenty feet, but it felt as dramatic to me as the plunge of a cliff diver—without the grace. I hit the water with an awkward smack that knocked the last of my breath out of me, and I sank. As pebbles grazed my cheek, I got my feet under me and pushed upward toward to the light. For one dizzying moment I feared that I'd lost all sense of which direction was up, and that I was pushing myself deeper. But then I broke the surface.

The water eddied and pulled, and I swam weakly to the land across the river. I wasn't sure where I was, but I knew I wanted to be on the far side from the enclave's mountain. If this were the river that fed Cauldron Falls, I'd need to be on this side to reach clan territory.

I dragged myself onto the riverbank and collapsed, choking, gagging, but grateful to be alive, to have escaped the battering rocks, then the fall, and the million and one things that could have gone wrong. When I mustered the strength, I eased myself up to sit and stare at the opening where the water continued to pour from the mountain, waiting for Mark to emerge and tumble down.

I waited and waited, but there was no sign of him.

I wrung water out of my shirt and shook it a few times. *Don't panic. Mark and Jake emerged a little farther upstream. They're fine. You'll find them.*

Moving my focus from the cavern entrance, I squinted to study the river farther upstream. A dark shape floated in the water, and I gasped. A body? Had the Kahlareans caught up with Mark or Jake and murdered him? Or had an assassin found me?

I staggered to my feet and moved to the edge of the river. No, just a log. Relief washed over me, but lasted only a moment. I pushed wet, tangled hair back from my face and scanned the trees and river in all directions. Realization weighed down my spirit like my soaking clothes weighed down my body.

I was alive, but alone.

CHAPTER 23

LINETTE

"WE SHOULD LEAVE for Lyric today." Lukyan straightened, leaning on his walking stick. His eyes seemed abnormally bright, almost feverish.

Of anyone in Braide Wood, Lukyan was the one who had felt most familiar to me, the most safe. But his reaction to the boy in my arms scared me. I'd never seen him so agitated.

Tara brought him a mug of water. "So his family is from Lyric? In the name of all the clans, what were they thinking to leave him behind?"

He ignored the proffered drink. "No, no. Don't you see? He's—"

The boy slipped from my lap and tugged on Lukyan's robe. When the elder songkeeper looked down, the child gave a small shake of his head.

Lukyan stared at him quietly for a moment, then drew a deep breath. "We need to take him to the tower," he said in a calmer tone.

I longed to visit the worship tower, to commune with the One and feel the brush of his presence on my face. Perhaps, too, the last pieces in my memory would return once I could spend time there. But if the child weren't from Lyric, moving him there would make it harder for his family to find him.

Tara must have been thinking the same thing. She frowned at Lukyan. "So you don't know him? Then I'll care for him until we find his family. We don't want to take him too far from here. Whoever he belongs with, surely they'll be back to search for him."

"I'm not able to explain right now, but I'm taking him to Lyric."

My brows rose. Rarely had I heard such a sharp edge to his voice.

Tara planted fists on her hips. "You know how much confusion is going on in the city. I won't let you drag him to such a dangerous place."

Watching Tara and Lukyan square off was like seeing two gentle caradoc suddenly grow claws and fangs. The boy's chin dropped, and his shoulders curled forward.

Perhaps I'd grown some claws of my own, because protective instincts welled up in me, and I bristled. "Stop it! You're upsetting him," I said, more harshly than I'd intended.

Tara and Lukyan both blinked as they looked at me. I pulled the boy close and tucked him behind me. I was the one who had found him. I would make decisions about the next step. "I think—"

Scrambling sounds at the door interrupted. Dustin shoved the door aside and came running in. "Wade's been hurt. He was training first-years on the plateau and had a fall. Got trampled."

Wade. I tested the newly unwrapped parts of my memory. He'd been a childhood friend, a gentle, lumbering giant of a youth. A few weeks past, he'd come to see me and had seemed particularly sad that I couldn't remember my past life in Braide Wood.

Tara hurried to a cupboard in her kitchen alcove and pulled out a small gourd. "Have they sent for a healer?"

Dustin nodded.

"Well, I'd better go too." Tara grabbed her cloak from a peg, moving quickly for someone of her age. "Linette, you stay here and take care of . . . wait, where did he go?"

I spun. The boy had slipped away while we'd been talking. I ran to the open door and caught sight of him racing through the village, his little bare feet barely leaving an impression on the packed earth. Where was he going?

I took off after him, vaguely aware that Tara was following right behind. As we all headed in the same direction, I realized the boy was running toward the lehkan plateau where the guardians trained. How did he know where to run if he wasn't from our clan?

He had such a head start that I didn't get close until we reached the plateau where a group of young guardians clustered on the side of the field.

I tried to catch his hand to pull him away, but the boy slipped into the silent group without their notice. They moved aside as I approached. Wade lay crumpled on the ground, his trousers and the side of his tunic dark with blood. More worrying, his leg bent at an unnatural angle and seemed crushed beyond repair. I didn't have to be a healer to know he'd probably lose the leg.

"Oh, Wade."

Although his face was drawn with pain, he managed a crooked grin. "You remember me?"

Eyes stinging, I nodded. "What happened?"

"Showing the first-years . . ." He caught his breath. "How not to lead . . . a cavalry charge." He tried a shallow chuckle, but broke off as he gritted his teeth against the pain. "No more than I deserve."

I knelt beside him, my brow wrinkling. "What you deserve?"

"Failed again."

"I'm sure this wasn't your fault."

He winced. "I promised to protect their house. I failed."

Had the pain and shock made him delirious? "None of the other guardians were hurt." I glanced up at the circle of faces for confirmation. They nodded in agreement, as confused as I was.

"Jake. I failed Jake," he gasped out. "I told Markkel I'd protect him with my life, but . . ." He lost breath for more words. Shock and blood loss made his limbs shudder, and the movement elicited a deep groan. His eyes squeezed shut.

I had no idea what he was talking about, but his distress couldn't be helping his poor trampled body. "You've done fine. This was just an accident."

The little boy appeared at my side, pressing against me to ease closer to Wade.

"No, little one. Get back." I wanted to cover the boy's eyes against the heartbreaking sight of a strong, faithful guardian bleeding his life into the earth.

Before I could pull him back, the boy rested his small hand gently on Wade's forehead. The shuddering stopped.

Wade's eyes flew open. "I can't feel them anymore." His hand reached toward the mangled muscle and bone that had been his leg.

"Shh." I took his hand. "Just rest. Help is coming."

"Give the man some air." Tara elbowed her way past guardians, huffing from exertion. "And why hasn't a healer arrived yet? The lodge isn't that far away. Linette, get that child away from here."

The boy moved back, making room for Tara. After doing a quick assessment of Wade's injuries, she propped his head up a few inches and helped him drink from the small gourd she carried. "It'll help the pain."

I was watching Wade's face anxiously and at first didn't notice that the child hadn't withdrawn but had repositioned himself by Wade's legs. The boy looked up into the soft grey sky above us. I glanced up but saw nothing. Before I could draw him away, he placed both his small chubby hands on Wade's leg.

"No!" I snatched him away, horrified to see blood covering the tiny innocent hands.

One of the men gasped, probably as shocked as I was by the child's strange response to an injured man.

"Shades of Shamgar," another man murmured.

"Not possible."

The whole group stood unmoving, as if they were holding a collective breath. The ring of faces grew wide-eyed, but they weren't looking at the boy and me. They were all staring at Wade.

Following their gazes to Wade's legs, I squinted. Had I misjudged the injury? His leg wasn't as crushed as I'd thought. It must have been my worry or a trick of the light. Perhaps a divot in the soft earth had hidden part of the limb and made it seem more twisted than it had been?

Still fussing at Wade's head, Tara hadn't noticed the sudden tension and stunned silence of the men. "Look," she said with some pride, "his color is already improving. Now get a pallet. We'll need two men to carry him to the healer's lodge." When no one moved, she rose, ready to scold with all her grandmotherly fury. Then she, too, stopped short.

Wade moved his legs. "Hey, I can feel them again."

"What did you do?" Tara asked me.

I shook my head, too stunned to answer.

"He's been healed," one of the men said. His gaze settled on me. "But how?"

"It was the boy." A guardian apprentice spoke in a voice edged with accusation. "Look at his hands."

I used the hem of my robe to wipe the blood away from the boy's hands and found my voice. "He didn't do anything."

"It was him. I saw it," one of the men said. "Who is he?"

Tara watched the boy for a moment, worry deepening the lines between her eyes. "We don't know."

"He looks like a Rhusican," someone muttered.

"And you know the tricks they play."

I swept him up into my arms, confronting the semicircle of men. The child's head nestled against my shoulder, his curls soft under my chin. "He's just a lost little boy. You should be thanking the One that Wade's legs weren't hurt as badly as we thought."

"Agreed," Wade said loudly. He eased up to his elbows, waggled one foot and then the other, and laughed. He edged up the hem of his bloodstained tunic and touched his side, which showed no evidence of a wound. "Now someone go meet the healer and send him back to the lodge. We won't be needing him."

But the murmurs continued. "This isn't right."

"Get that boy out of our clan."

I tightened my grip on the child and began humming a quiet lullaby, hoping to drown out the harsh words of the men. My clan already distrusted me because I'd been to Hazor and because of my past confusion and memory loss. What could I say to stop this build of suspicion?

"Ask the songkeeper," someone said.

I lifted my chin, ready to answer, but then realized they were looking past me. Lukyan slowly made his way up the path from the village. The young men clamored to tell him what they'd seen and their fear that some Rhusican deception was at work.

"Did any of you talk to the One when Wade was trampled?" Lukyan leaned heavily on his staff. "As soon as I heard, I begged the One for His mercy."

A few nodded.

"So why are you all so surprised that he was healed? Why ask the One for healing if you don't believe He will answer?"

One young man shuffled his feet. "Sure, He answers. But this was different. That boy . . ."

"We all saw it," a first-year said, shooting a dark look toward me. "What kind of boy would touch an open wound? This was—"

"I'm your elder songkeeper." Even the guardians stepped back as all signs of frailty vanished in the blaze of Lukyan's eyes. "Have I ever led you into harm? Let me worry about the boy. You go back to your training, and praise the One for His gift to Wade."

Wade lurched to his feet, clearly tired of being the object of debate. "Let the songkeepers figure this out. Get back to your mounts. Where did my lehkan run off to? Poor thing needs some comforting. He's probably blaming himself for the collision and wants to know I'm all right." He winked at me.

Gratitude and warmth filled me, along with a fresh surge of joy at knowing I could remember people again. In the past days, I'd known I was supposed to love Tara and Kendra and Lukyan, and all the others of the clan. But love as an act of will wasn't nearly as satisfying as spontaneous love welling up over a foundation of memories. I loved these people, these prairie grasses, even the smelly lehkan.

Wade lumbered off to check on his beast while Tara marched along beside him, pestering him to let her check his wounds. He waved off her concern, and seemed oblivious to the sticky blood coating his trousers.

A sudden picture flashed in my mind of Kieran's wound seeping blood through his bandage, and how he'd mocked me for feeling faint. Today I'd been heartsick at Wade's injury and how his life would be forever changed without use of his legs. But I'd never felt dizzy or faint. Why had Kieran's wound troubled me so much?

Lukyan rested a hand gently on the boy's head. "It's almost time for the season-end gathering. I had thought the journey too hard on these old bones, but this is one gathering I cannot miss. We'll leave in the morning."

I looked over the curly head at my teacher's wrinkled face. "I'm coming too." It wasn't a question or suggestion. I'd found the boy, and I would care for him until we found his family.

Lukyan nodded slowly. "If you can pry Tara away from Wade, please ask her if I may invite myself to dinner tonight. I think we all need to talk."

That night the long common-room table was crowded, and Tara was in her element, bustling back and forth from the kitchen alcove. Payton occupied his place at the table's head. Lukyan and I sat on either side of the small child. We were far removed from the dark, speculative murmurs of the guardians, but I still felt protective. Kendra held Emmi against her shoulder on the other side of Lukyan. Across from us, Talia and Gareth sat beside their children, Dustin and Aubrey. Although Tara introduced everyone to the boy I'd found, Talia turned up her hard-edged nose and ignored him. Even with many of my memories restored, I couldn't recall a single warm conversation I'd had with her. She seemed to have inherited all of Tara's forcefulness with none of her maternal warmth.

"I'm ready to agree with you," Tara said to Lukyan, as she carried a caradoc roast to the table. "Some in the clan are still upset about what happened. It might actually be safer for the boy if you take him to Lyric. If his family comes looking for him, I'll tell them where he is and send a messenger to you."

A firm rap sounded at the door, and Wade stuck his head in from the doorway. "Mmmm. I knew you were making your famous roast. I smelled it all the way up on the plateau."

Tara sniffed, still annoyed that he hadn't allowed her fussing earlier. "Well, if you're inviting yourself to dinner, I'm glad you changed your clothes."

He chuckled and approached my side of the table. He lightly punched the boy's shoulder. "And how's our little apprentice healer?"

"He seems all right," I offered.

Wade scratched his sparse beard. "What's his name?"

I wiped a smudge of dirt from the boy's chin. "We don't know. He hasn't spoken."

Wade settled down beside me, his bulk making the bench sag. "Well you can't keep calling him stranger." He leaned past me and grinned at the child. "He's quiet as a baby caradoc. You could call him Caralad."

A herder's nickname for young boys who cared for grazing animals. I smiled as silent laughter lit the brown eyes that gazed up at me. "Caralad it is."

Payton invited Wade to thank the One for the meal and the blessings of the day. A flush crept up the guardian's neck, but he mumbled fervent thanks for the food as well as for the miraculous recovery he'd experienced.

As food was passed around, he leaned close and spoke in a low voice. "So you remember everything now?"

My heart warmed at his interest. With the puzzle of the homeless child and then Wade's emergency, the news of my memory returning had been pushed to the background.

I shook my head, probing those walls that still blocked me from accessing some parts of my life. "Before today, my life as I knew it began in the shrine in Hazor. Kieran told me some things about my past when we were traveling here, but it was like hearing about a stranger. And since I had a fever, most of what he told me is fuzzy anyway. But today it began to unfold. I remembered my childhood, my parents, the ache when they died, the joy of studying to be a songkeeper, the people of Braide Wood, the honor of leading worship in the tower as an apprentice in Lyric . . ." Again, I ran into the barrier, although it felt spongy and no longer like firm stone. "But there are still several years missing."

Wade puffed out his chest. "Well, you remember me again, so I'd say you've got the important facts back."

I giggled.

He leaned his bulky arms on the table and looked at me intently. "But you really don't remember the time we had to make camp at night on the way from the transport, and I fought the bear?"

Was he spinning a tale? Surely I hadn't made camp at night. No sane person would leave the shelter of a village too close to dark. I closed my eyes and felt around for any hints of that and shook my head.

"I'd be happy to fill you in . . ."

"Wade, have another slice of roast," Tara said quickly. She and Lukyan exchanged a look. What were they hiding? Couldn't I have a little time to enjoy all the progress that I'd made today without worrying about the remaining gaps?

I frowned at my plate. Lukyan reached over and patted my hand. "Child, be patient. The healers told us not to force this, to let you recall things in your own time. They said you'd remember everything when you were ready."

"I am ready." Frustration filled my chest, and I grabbed my mug as if cool water could drench the anger. Since arriving in Braide Wood, I'd been drowning in furtive glances, whispers, undercurrents I couldn't translate—even from the people I was closest to. The One had healed me through this special child's touch. But if that were true, why wasn't the healing complete? And why wouldn't my friends just tell me the missing pieces? The healers shouldn't be meddling. What did they know about the damage of Hazorite drug patches? I took a long drink and set my mug down with the thump.

A small hand reached for mine. Caralad's eyes met mine with sympathy, but then brightened as he smiled. He didn't have to speak. Love and encouragement flowed from his gaze. The tangle of unanswered questions melted away and my shoulders relaxed.

Kendra balanced Emmi in one arm and started a basket of small bread loaves around the table, then turned to me. "Will you take a message to Tristan for me? He's staying with Tag and her family."

I smiled. "Do you trust my memory?" I was only half joking.

She grinned. "I'll keep it short. 'Finish trying to solve all the clans' problems and come home.'"

Everyone laughed, but again I felt anxious undercurrents. Kendra longed to be by Tristan's side, but for some reason he felt Lyric was too dangerous. My only memories of Lyric were of glorious worship and festive gatherings, and I couldn't imagine what had happened in the past few years to bring so much change. In spite of the healers' advice to take things slowly, I needed to find out.

After the meal, Caralad settled in a corner of the common room, joining a table game with Dustin and Aubrey, while Kendra nursed Emmi in a chair nearby. I took advantage of the quiet moment to follow Wade outside to the porch.

He sank onto a stool and stretched his legs out in front of him, then gave a start when I pulled a chair over to sit beside him.

"So you and Lukyan are taking Caralad to Lyric in the morning?" he asked.

I nodded.

"I wish I could travel with you," he said. "I'll go to Lyric for the gathering, but the first-years are so unsettled by the accident that I need to stay here another day first."

I was glad he'd brought up the fall. "Wade, when you were hurt, you said you deserved it. What were you talking about? Who is Jake?"

He cleared his throat and glanced back toward the door. "Maybe you've remembered enough for today?"

Poor man. The healers didn't want him telling me about my past, but he needed someone to confide in. I'd seen the tortured guilt in his face, a pain worse than the trampled leg. "You don't have to tell me anything about the years I can't remember. Just explain what's happened in the clans since I've been in Hazor. I can tell everyone is upset, but they aren't telling me anything."

His shoulders relaxed and he tilted back to lean against the log wall of the house. "I guess that wouldn't break any stupid healer advice."

I laughed. "Good thing you didn't need their help today, with that attitude."

"Too true." He rubbed his leg and turned his foot from side to side, a bemused expression on his face. "What do you make of it? Why would the One heal me? And do you think the boy had anything to do with it?"

I leaned back beside him, looking out at the trees turning deeper shades of green and brown as the sky dimmed. "One answer is simple. The One healed you because He loves you."

"How could He, when . . ."

Good, we were getting to the root of his pain. I waited.

He let his breath out in a huff. "While you were in Hazor, things were going well. Jake—the new Restorer—" He shot me a sideways glance. "Well, that's a long story. But I was pledged to be his house protector. Then one day he disappeared. Mind you, that whole family has a way of disappearing and popping up unexpectedly. But I knew something bad must have happened, because Cameron disappeared at the same time."

"And since then you've blamed yourself?"

His round face tightened. "Of course. And now there's chaos in Lyric again, and rumors of another war with Hazor. The songkeepers are arguing about what it all means, the councilmembers are forming factions and debating how to protect the clans, Tristan and Kieran are in the thick of it all. And none of this would be happening if Jake . . . if I'd . . ."

I moved my chair around so I could face him. "So the blame for all the turmoil in the clans rests on your shoulders?"

A reluctant smile tugged the side of his mouth, and he rubbed his beard. "When you put it that way…"

"It sounds ridiculous, doesn't it? Because it is. The One is our strong tower. Not a Restorer, not the Council, not the guardians . . . even one as important as you."

He chuckled. "You always knew the right thing to say. I'm glad that hasn't changed." He leaned forward, the humor fading, and he took one of my hands between his large, callused hands. "Linette—"

The door slid open and Tara stepped outside. Wade dropped my hand and stood.

"Almost dark," Tara said quietly.

"Thanks for the meal," Wade told her. "Safe night to your house." With a clumsy nod to us both, he strode away as quickly as if a swarm of stinging beetles were chasing him.

I wasn't sure why he left so abruptly, but I savored the warmth filling my heart. "Tara, I think I was able to help him. I felt like a true songkeeper again."

"Hmm." She opened her mouth, but then seemed to decide not to comment. "Come inside. Lukyan wants to leave at first light. We need to pack some things for you and Caralad."

Contented warmth transformed into giddy excitement. Tomorrow I'd see the worship tower of Lyric. The sight would surely bring the last bit of memory back. I longed to gather with the other songkeepers and sleep on my pallet in the familiar songkeepers' lodge, and to see Tristan again, and to finally be able to thank Kieran for bringing me home.

My stomach gave a funny lurch. Of course I was eager to see Kieran. I'd never thanked him for getting me safely back home to Braide Wood. I only hoped that with all the political confusion in Lyric, Tristan and Kieran were staying out of trouble. I searched my memories of Kieran and shook my head. Somehow that seemed unlikely.

CHAPTER 24

SUSAN

"MARK! JAKE!" I shouted until I was hoarse, but the roar of the river threw the words back in my face. Each rustle of leaves jerked my attention, half in hope of seeing Mark or Jake and half in terror of the assassins, rizzids, or bears that could lurk behind any tree. The ongoing danger and isolation of the thick, dark forest beat against me with as much force as the crashing water.

Time to take stock and make a plan. I looked down at my mottled assassin's tunic and pants. The soggy fabric clung to me. Hours ago I'd longed to escape the caves and see the soft overcast skies, but now I craved a glimpse of sunshine from my own world. The constant atmospheric ceiling hung flat and oppressive, and without any sunlight or breeze, my clothes would stay damp for hours. At least I had Voronja's light, flexible footwear to give my feet some protection.

Since my best guess was that Mark and Jake had emerged farther upstream, I'd need to hike that direction to find them. Of course, there was also the possibility that the channel that had veered off to the right had carried them into a deep airless conduit and to their deaths.

Susan Mitchell, don't you dare let your thoughts go there.

Too late. A series of worst-case scenarios swirled through my mind.

I shook the water from my hair and corralled my wayward thoughts. I had to find my husband and son. I began making my way along the rock-strewn river's edge. Maybe physical exertion would help me shift my focus.

Keep moving. Find Mark and Jake.

This was a wild place and not well traveled. Back in the caverns, Jake had said the enclave was near Cauldron Falls. I knew the falls were about a half-day's hike upstream from Rendor, but was I above the falls or somewhere downstream from them? If I were between Rendor and the falls, wouldn't there be some sort of path? Perhaps I was in the unexplored wilds even farther upriver.

Doesn't matter where you are. Keep moving. Find Mark and Jake.

The terrain climbed, and my muscles soon grew rubbery from fatigue. I stopped frequently to scan the river for any sign of my husband and son, and to watch for Kahlareans on the opposite bank.

Over the rushing water, strange animal calls and rustling sounds carried from the dark tangled woods that crowded the banks. Each time I paused, my nerves stretched tighter. Each twig snap could be an assassin tracking me. Each strange howl could be one of the predators that lived in the wild outskirts of the clans. Too afraid to rest, I pushed onward.

My foot wobbled on a loose stone.

Pay attention, Susan. This would be a bad place to twist an ankle.

I focused on the uneven terrain until the sound of the river changed. I looked up to see a steep waterfall ahead. No cauldron shape welcomed the streaming water, so I couldn't be sure that this was Cauldron Falls. More importantly, a cliff blocked my path, sheer and impassible.

Panting hard, I cut inland, shoving aside thorny underbrush and searching for a way to continue upriver. In a minute the thick trees muted the sound of the water. No landmarks in any direction. If I kept scrambling through the woods, I'd be hopelessly lost.

Maybe I could find a way to climb the wet stone cliff. I hurried back the way I'd come, breathing a prayer of thanks when the river came into view.

I faced upstream again. The sheer rock face was as unforgiving as I'd remembered. I even dragged a few stones from the water's edge and used them as an improvised stepladder. But there were no ledges, no handholds, nothing I could reach to make any progress.

Fatigue caught up to me and I sank to my knees. "No! Lord, don't do this to me. Not again. Don't make me do this alone."

Tears felt hot against my face, my skin already damp from the spray of the waterfall. In the same way that a fresh loss resurrects old grief, this moment of helplessness battered me with memories of past battles: The terror and confusion that had choked me when I was first pulled through the portal. The waves of inadequacy that had churned in my chest as I revealed my Restorer status to the Council. The horrible loneliness of my captivity and torture in Rhus.

Wasn't there some vague theological theory that each battle, each wound, built new levels of faith and strength for future challenges? A truism that courage and confidence grew as they were tested? Only a few days ago, I'd been sitting in my living room chatting about the ways of God with Corina and Janet and Beth as we studied David. Someone had probably said something about trials building character.

"It didn't work!" I yelled up to the vacant sky. Instead of building confidence with each battle, I carried the scars of the past experiences and the moments I'd felt forsaken. My body was frailer. Even worse, fear had become a more ready companion because I knew more.

Despair welled in my gut, and sobs shook me. I knew how much pain a human body could experience, I knew how evil an enemy's intent could truly be, and I knew how lost and broken a mind could become under relentless attack.

What else do you know?

The gentle, inaudible voice interrupted my tears. I wanted to turn away—tried to allow the anger to deaden my heart. But the initial waves of emotion ebbed. I huddled on the ground, too drained by my own striving to do anything but squeeze my eyes closed and receive an Other perspective.

New memories swam past. The unexpected allies and friends that had brought joy and hope to even the most frightening paths when I'd first arrived in Shamgar. The healing and transformation in Kendra and Wade as they were freed from Rhusican poison. And on the day I'd tasted impending death at Nicco's hand, the glimpse of the Keeper of my soul ready to welcome me home.

What else do you know?

Strength trickled into my exhausted soul. I needed to affirm the truth out loud. "That You never left me. That I'd go through it all again if You asked." I stood up and rubbed the moisture from my face. "And that I'll never find courage looking inside myself. I need You."

I sighed, exhaling more of the frustration and panic from my muscles. For now, I'd have to entrust Mark and Jake to the care of the One. "I trust You. Help me trust You more," I whispered. "And guide my steps."

Since I couldn't find a way upstream, the woods were too dense and dangerous, and Kahlarean enemies lurked on the other side of the river, that left downstream. A few more tears threatened as I began the tedious effort of retracing my steps, but I sniffed them back. If I were anywhere close in my guesses, I could reach Rendor by nightfall. I'd led the Rendor clan out of Rhus; they'd offer me aid. They could help me search for Mark and Jake.

With that resolve, I made good progress and soon passed the place where I'd tumbled into the river. As I continued downstream, the gorge deepened, and soon I was hiking with my feet in the water, tall cliffs stretching above both banks. Stumbling over wet stones that had been polished smooth by years of pounding, I followed a bend in the river and the roar grew. Ahead of me, the river disappeared in a cloud of mist. The waterfall upstream had been a baby. This was the big daddy.

Shortly before the falls, the wall of stone flanking me gradually lowered and the banks widened, and I gratefully edged several yards from the rushing water. It seemed to reach for my ankles as if it longed to scoop me up and toss me into the churning waves.

Would I need to head inland to find a trail down the cliffs that guarded the cupped cauldron below? Maybe I could—

A shrill whistle shrieked over the sound of the falls. I froze, confused. Fire alarm? Siren? After a few seconds, I remembered. A signaler! Someone from the clans was nearby. I took a step toward the sound.

A heavy object barreled into me from behind, knocking me to the ground with a crash that stole all the breath from my lungs. The unknown weight landed on top of me, holding me down. Panic turned me into a squirming bundle of elbows and heels, but I couldn't get away, couldn't even see my assailant. Was a bear about to claw me in two?

The weight shifted, hands grabbed me and yanked me to my feet. I twisted my head, and almost laughed in relief. Not a bear. Not a Kahlarean. A fresh-faced young man in the garb of a clan guardian had tackled me.

Another ran forward, sword drawn. "Search for weapons. And careful."

"It's all right," I said, relief surging through me. I'd finally found allies.

The second youth raised the point of his sword to my throat. "Silence."

When his colleague finished searching me for weapons, he dragged me to a clearing. We stopped before a wooden shelter similar to the outpost I'd once visited at Morsal Plains. I'd heard about the guardian outpost at Cauldron Falls, the place where Linette's fiancé Dylan had been killed by Kahlareans with syncbeams, and where Kieran had discovered another incursion into the clans by assassins. No wonder these young guardians were jumpy. And I wore the clothes of an assassin. My relief muted, and I chewed my lip, wondering how to handle this.

"Look, I know you're probably first-years, but even so, you have to know I don't look like a Kahlarean."

They ignored me. "Chell, what do we do?" The guardian who had tackled me kept a firm grip on both my arms.

"She's trying to sneak into the clans. We should run her through."

"Or not," I muttered, keeping a close eye on Chell's sword.

"But she looks harmless." The younger man finally released me and stepped around to stand beside Chell and study me.

"What better trick?" Chell growled.

Time to settle this argument. "Guardians of the clans, well met. I'm Susan. The Restorer who rode against Hazor."

The youth's stubbled jaw dropped, his mouth gaping. His companion gave a bark of laughter, but my attacker soon closed his mouth and narrowed his eyes, assessing me. "Well met," he said at last, extending a hand. "I'm Dardon of Sanborn clan—"

Chell cut him off. "That's impossible. My older brother rode with the Restorer. She was"—his gaze skimmed me with disdain—"tall, strong, fearless."

"No she wasn't." My temper rose. "I wasn't. I knew I was inadequate for the call, but the One used me anyway."

"Not another word," Chell snapped. He turned to Dardon. "Don't talk to her. You know that's how the Rhusicans poison people."

My heart sank as I saw doubt enter Dardon's eyes. "Look, I realize I startled you both. I'll explain later, but my husband and son are lost upstream. I need help."

"See." Chell raised his sword point to my chest. "Her purpose is to lure us from our post." He strode away a few paces and scanned the view of the river through the trees.

"I'm not a Rhusican. I'm not a Kahlarean. I'm Susan of Braide Wood, friend of Tristan and Lukyan and—"

"The songkeeper?" Dardon's face puckered with worry. "Chell, if she knows the Songs . . . if she's telling the truth . . ."

Clearly Chell was the senior guardian. I needed to win him over.

"Chell, you're right. You can't leave the pass undefended. I just escaped from Kahlareans and they might come this way.

Chell scoffed. "You? Escaped Kahlareans? Dardon, take her downriver and send back reinforcements. Let the Rendor councilmembers figure out what to do with her."

"No! Can't you just use that signaler thingy to get help? We need to find Mark and Jake."

Both men froze. "Jake?" Dardon asked, eyes wide.

I squeezed the bridge of my nose. We were wasting precious time. I needed to organize a search. "That's what I'm trying to tell you. Jake. The new Restorer. We escaped the Kahlareans, but we've gotten separated."

Dardon looked impressed. "How would she know he's missing if she's not from the clans?"

"She'd know if she worked with the enemies who made him disappear," Chell said.

Kieran would love this guy. He had buckets of suspicion and more to spare.

A raindrop hit my nose, soon joined by others. Rain always fell after midday. Time was shorter than I'd realized to find Mark and Jake before nightfall. "Fine. Dardon can take me to Rendor. They'll recognize me and we can gather more help."

"I'm thrilled you agree with my decision." Chell turned to Dardon. "Don't trust anything she says. And just in case it is true that Kahlareans plan to cross, bring back all the guardians Rendor can spare."

Dardon grabbed a pack from the shelter and hoisted it over his shoulder. He took my arm and pulled me across the clearing. A small trail led downstream and he pushed me ahead of him. "Move," he said.

I seemed to spend more of my time in this world as a prisoner than a guest. So unfair. I walked quickly along the trail. Branches wove overhead, blocking some of the rain, but I was soon soaked again. "You wouldn't have a spare cloak, would you?" I tossed over my shoulder.

"Don't talk. Keep moving."

The young guardian was taking his commission seriously. "Which clan did you say you're from? Did you ever meet Tristan of Braide Wood? I was wondering how he and—".

Dardon shoved me, and I stumbled a few steps before resuming a steady pace. "Quiet."

Quiet? Anxiety about Mark and Jake twisted every nerve, and conversation was my only distraction. "How many times do I have to tell you? I'm not a Rhusican. I'm just Susan. My husband and son are lost somewhere above the falls, and . . ."

My voice choked off. I cleared my throat and blinked back the worry that stung my eyes. Weariness hit me in a heavy wave. I suddenly felt every punishing bruise inflicted by the violent ride through rocky channels and the fall into the river. My stomach ached from coughing up water and the emptiness of too many hours without food. Trudging onward, I shoved dripping hair off my face and sniffed. "I just want to know they're all right. They have to be all right." My voice sounded small. No wonder Chell found it impossible to believe I had been Susan the Restorer.

"Wait."

I turned. Dardon shrugged off his pack and rummaged for a moment, then tossed me a square of fabric. I shook it out. A cloak.

"Thank you." What had prompted his change of heart? I searched his face for a clue.

He shuffled a foot against the damp leaves and shrugged one shoulder. "Can we move now?"

It was amazing how much difference a small kindness could make. My muscles found new energy, and even the gnawing anxiety in my stomach eased. I picked up the pace. Dardon's attitude changed subtly too.

"Why were you traveling with no gear?" Instead of scoffing, his words held only curiosity and hint of concern.

"Good question. 'Take nothing for the journey—no staff, no bag, no bread, no money, no extra tunic,'" I said under my breath.

"What?" He stayed close behind me on the narrow path, following easily.

"I don't know," I said more audibly. "Perhaps the One knows that if I travel without anything else to rely on, I'll learn to rely more deeply on Him."

Dardon snorted. "You sound like a songkeeper."

That surprised a genuine laugh from me. "I wish." Lukyan had guided me through my confusion and fears. Linette had offered acceptance and friendship when others doubted me. The grace and love of the One shone in them. With our urgent escape, I'd had no opportunity to hear news from Jake about everyone I loved in the clans. Maybe I could finally get caught up. "Do you know Lukyan? The elder songkeeper of Braide Wood? Do you know how he is? Or Linette? She was in Hazor with Kieran. Do you know how they are?"

I glanced back over my shoulder to find Dardon's expression shuttered. "I . . . I don't think we should be talking until I know you aren't an enemy."

Why couldn't I have run into a guardian like affable Wade? If I saw Tristan again, I'd have to tell him the young guardians were doing a better job of being alert to threat. That was a good thing, but for some reason, the thought made me sad. In recent years the People of the Verses had been battered by enemies, confused by corrupt leaders, and seen their faith shaken by false Verses and unusual and short-term Restorers.

As we continued along the trail, I spent my time praying for them all, as treasured faces came to mind. Praying kept my mind off my aching limbs and empty stomach, but couldn't fully distract me from worrying about Mark and Jake. The One had drawn us through the portal into Kahlarea when we hadn't even known Jake's location. He'd helped us escape an assassins' enclave. I was alive and breathing against all odds. Why was it so hard to trust Him for the next need? When would His relentless faithfulness finally sink in deeply enough so that my first reflex wouldn't always be doubt and fear?

"Awesome in majesty, perfect in power . . ." I sang quietly as we followed the path. The melody of sacred Songs fueled me, and by the time wood and glass buildings came into sight, hope had strengthened in my heart.

The town wore scars. The scorch marks from syncbeams still marred many buildings. Several looked deserted. As we entered, many of the faces that peered out from homes looked haggard, their eyes haunted by trauma. I recognized the expression. I'd seen it each morning when I'd looked in my bathroom mirror.

"Susan?" A thready voice carried from under eaves where the last of the afternoon rain dripped slowly. A thin woman stepped out. Dardon watched me closely.

Miles of hiking . . . the tunnel from Rhus . . . the pebbled desert . . . the long journey back to Lyric with all the refugees . . . shell-shocked, no energy—or trust—for conversation. Children who didn't cry. Vacant eyes, trembling limbs.

Tears caught in my throat. "Aiyliss. It's me."

She took a few steps forward, arms open. A sob tore from my chest and I hugged her. I hadn't realized how much I longed to be with someone else who understood.

Words and tears poured from us both until I remembered Dardon. He stood watching, rubbing the back of his neck. "I . . . I . . . apologize for not believing you." Then he groaned. "And for knocking you down, and . . ."

I touched his shoulder. "You were protecting the clans. You did the right thing. Now can we get some help to search for Mark and Jake?"

He tossed his head back like an eager pup. "Yes. Of course." And off he ran. Aiyliss's neighbors gathered in front of her home, but after a brief reunion, she looked at my weary posture and shooed everyone away.

Aiyliss found me warm dry clothes and settled me at her table with a large bowl of clavo simmering on a heat trivet and a basket of small bread loaves. I breathed in the warm steam of the spicy drink and smiled my thanks as she sat across from me. "So tell me everything," I said. "What's been happening in the clans while I've been away?"

CHAPTER 25

SUSAN

A WEARY EXPRESSION tugged Aiyliss's lips downward. "We're rebuilding. So many homes and workshops were damaged when the Kahlareans occupied the town." Her eyes found mine. "But some things are harder to rebuild. How are you?"

While I held the steaming clavo close to my face, I wanted to give her a bright perky assurance that I was fine. Yet she deserved more from me. "It's been hard. Nightmares. Jumping at the slightest sounds. Loneliness because others don't understand."

Relief bloomed across Aiyliss's face, and I knew my deeper honesty had been the right choice.

"Yes," she said in an eager gasp. "At first the other clans sent supplies. Some builders and transtechs from other clans came to help repair homes. Jake made sure of that."

My mother's heart swelled a few sizes. How had my son developed the skills to rally support and lead squabbling clans? He'd never even negotiated successful truces between his younger siblings.

"But then rumors started." Aiyliss ladled more clavo into my mug. "People whispered about us because of the time we'd spent in Rhus." She shrugged. "Besides, the other clans had their own worries. We heard Zarek had abandoned his interest in peace with the clans, and the chance of war made all the clans along the border focus on preparing."

The last I'd heard, Tristan and Kendra were in Hazor with Linette and Kieran and some other songkeepers. "Do you know if all our people left Hazor safely?"

"I'm not sure." She frowned. "Some people think it was wrong for them to be there at all, and they deserved whatever Zarek did to them."

Loyalty spun into a flare of anger. "They aren't enemies. They've each sacrificed and served the clans more than—"

"I know. But you asked about what's happening. The Council in Lyric was in the middle of days of meetings when Jake disappeared. The worst possible time. And again, we're left without a Restorer. Unless that's why you're here?" She leaned forward, the light of the heat trivet catching the flicker of hope in her eyes.

I pushed up my sleeve, where darkening bruises gave ample evidence that I no longer healed instantly. "I came to rescue Jake. Somehow Cameron got free and gave Jake to the Kahlareans. They wanted a Restorer."

"Ever since Mikkel," she said quietly. Mark wasn't the only one from this border clan who carried deep scars from being targeted by Kahlarean assassins. He'd lost his father in a long-ago battle at Cauldron Falls, and perhaps worse, he'd lost his mother to assassins that were after him. All of Rendor had felt vulnerable long before the bargain that sold them to Rhus. Now they must feel doubly betrayed.

Aiyliss nudged the basket of bread closer to me. "Was Jake all right when you found him?" Compassion moistened her eyes.

I chewed my lower lip. "More or less. But he no longer has Restorer gifts either."

"Shades of Shamgar," she said under her breath, then covered her mouth and winced. "Excuse my language. The clans need a protector so much. And we need an advocate." A dull, bleak look fell across her face. "Has the One forsaken us?"

"No." I set my clavo down and lengthened my spine. "I don't understand the shifts in power, the changes of Restorers, and why things have been so hard for your people. But I do understand one thing. The One will never forsake you. You said that Rendor needs an advocate. You have One. Oh, and you have another. Me."

Although what I could do to help them was beyond me. I hadn't even been able to recover from my own trauma in Rhus. Now my brief flare of energy fled like the last few drops poured from a bottle.

Aiyliss reached across and touched my hand. "It's good to see you again. It's a gift to my home that you're here. Now I think you should rest."

A knock at the door saved me from needing to protest. As much as I was struggling to stay upright in a chair, I couldn't rest until Jake and Mark were safe. When Aiyliss opened the door, Dardon took a few tentative steps inside. "We have more than a dozen teams heading upstream to hunt for Markkel and Jake. I'll follow them now."

I pushed away from the table. "I'm ready."

Aiyliss shot a worried look toward the young guardian. "Susan, you won't do anyone any good if you collapse."

"It's true." Dardon tightened his sword belt. "We'll be moving fast to reach the outpost before dark. You'd only slow us down."

I wavered. The search teams knew the terrain and hadn't just spent a day escaping Kahlareans.

Aiyliss wrapped a gentle arm around my shoulders. "Let me show you to a pallet. I promise I'll wake you at the first news. Just wait."

Wait. My assigned task once again. "Wait" was a small lonely island that made me fume. For weeks I'd watched the calendar, looked for signs, wondered when I'd see Jake. "Wait" was the snarled terrain that had torn me in shreds before the picture in my journal came to life. Could I make the wise choice and be patient, trusting that the One would still protect my family?

Dardon shifted his weight from foot to foot in the doorway.

My shoulders sagged as I surrendered to common sense. "All right. But please . . . find them."

He dipped his chin in a quick nod and left.

With Aiyliss's help, I stumbled to a back room and collapsed. Too tired to organize my thoughts, all I could do was groan. "Find them. Help them. Find them. Help them." I fell asleep with the desperate prayer still on my lips.

A hand on my shoulder startled me. I shot from deep sleep to heart-pounding alertness and sat up so fast my head spun. "What?" I gasped.

"It's me. Aiyliss. You're all right."

I blinked in the gentle glow of dawn. As in many of the Rendor homes, large glass windows faced the river and offered a view of boulders edging the water and tall smooth tree trunks. Rendor. I was in Rendor. I was safe. And Mark and Jake—

"Any word yet?"

Aiyliss smiled. "A messenger ran ahead. Markkel and Jake found their way to the outpost before nightfall."

I grabbed her hand. "They're all right?"

She squeezed my palm. "I think so. I don't know everything that happened to them, but you'll be able to ask them soon. They're on their way."

I tossed aside the blanket and raced from the room, calling over my shoulder. "Thank you. Thank you for your help."

Bolting from her home, I followed the main road to the upriver side of town and found the path to the outpost.

A group of men emerged from the forest. Trousers, tunics. A few guardians with swords. There. A large man with short wavy hair flecked with silver, wearing jeans and a buttoned shirt that looked out of place.

"Mark!" My whoop carried over the sound of the river, and he jogged forward to meet me. I threw myself into his arms. "You're here. You're all right."

His lips found mine with the same joy and relief I felt, and a cheer rose up from the watching men.

Even while I soaked in the strength and love from his arms around me, I popped up my head to scan the group again. Jake laughed and strode forward with the others.

Relief made me sag. Mark's arms tightened for one more hug, then he held me out to assure himself that I was all right, too. His mouth twitched. "Back to stockinged feet again?"

I looked down. I'd been thrilled to shed my Kahlarean assassin disguise and wear the soft knit sweater and drawstring trousers that Aiyliss had given me. But when I'd rushed from her home, I hadn't taken time to find shoes.

"I stayed with Aiyliss. Maybe Dardon told you. I still have Voronja's shoes, though. Those should work for me until we get to Lyric. We're going there now, right? We never had time to make a plan past our escape, but now that you're safe we should decide what to do. And you are safe, aren't you? Are the Kahlareans tracking you? Will we need to stay here to help defend the city or—"

Mark's laugh was rich and deep, and then he stopped my babbling with another very effective kiss. It wasn't until I came up for air that I noticed a strip of fabric tied around his upper arm was stained reddish brown. "Were you hurt? Are you bleeding?"

He sobered. "A few Kahlareans caught up with us. Good thing we had some reinforcements."

My heart froze. "They wounded you?"

"Don't worry. Just a sword injury. Jake knocked the venblade from his hand before he could use it."

A shudder passed through me as I thought of how close they'd both come to lethal poison. I wanted to savor the relief of their safe return, but the truth was that danger still hounded us.

With Mark's good arm around me, we headed into town. The small contingent that followed us swelled as others of Rendor clan joined in welcoming Mark and Jake, a son of their clan and his son, the Restorer who had pushed back the Kahlarean occupation of their town. While the mood yesterday had been somber, today new hope lit the faces of the clan.

As much as I longed to talk with Jake alone and catch up on his life, I couldn't begrudge all the friendly chatter and the atmosphere of a family reunion. We stood in the street as more people came by to greet us. Mark fielded questions and asked about relatives and friends, but I noticed Jake speaking to a few of the guardians. His serious expression stood in stark contrast to all the swirling conversations. And it was Jake who finally cut short the party.

"Thank you for your welcome and your faithful presence on our borders." He spoke with confident warmth and the crowd quickly stilled. "But right now we have some clan business to take care of."

"The business of wiping out the Kahlareans." Dardon shouted, proudly clamping a hand on my son's shoulder as if the young guardian were responsible for Jake's very existence. "Markkel and Jake know the very nest of the assassins. It's time we destroy their threat forever. I say we attack today."

A mix of gasps and cheers rose from the group.

How easily we could be swept into a bloodthirsty enthusiasm for battle. I glanced at my husband. Fire sparked behind his eyes, but his furrowed brow revealed an inner struggle.

Jake stepped away from Dardon, shaking his head. "We need to prepare for travel, but not to attack Kahlarea. I've been told that the songkeepers have cancelled the feast day gathering."

From a cluster of young guardians, Chell stepped forward. "Of course they did. It's too dangerous to gather in Lyric right now. Who would protect the outlying clans?"

He had a point. Perhaps it would be best for all the clans to defend their borders, while we made our way to the portal and returned home.

Jake's eyes blazed. "Who has protected our clans in all the generations past? Who has guarded our borders while we met at the tower? The season-end gathering is not a hollow tradition. It's everything to our people."

The passion in his voice, his use of the word our . . . My chest contracted as my hopes for the quick reunion of our family evaporated. Would the One ask me to surrender my plans and pictures of our future? Perhaps even to leave my son here to serve this world?

Jake stepped onto a crate against a nearby home so he could see more of the congregating families. "To cancel the gathering is to concede that we don't trust the One anymore. That worship is no longer the first calling of every person who follows our Maker and Deliverer."

Murmurs and arguments built, along with restless stirring in the crowd. A cry to arms was more inviting to most than a call to worship. I didn't like either alternative. Mark saw my distress and drew me closer.

"Isn't this a decision for the songkeepers to make?" I whispered. Some whining, selfish corner of my soul wanted to tell the clans to solve their own problems and leave our family in peace.

My husband's squeeze on my shoulder was gentle, but his jaw was firm as he spoke to me quietly. "I don't know how to explain how wrong that decision was. What it would mean for the clans. This is worse than Cameron convincing the Council to create alliances with other nations or to manufacture syncbeams against the teachings of the Verses."

I almost understood. I'd spent enough time in Braide Wood and Lyric to have a sense of the healing, empowering, unifying strength of the One among His gathered people. But the Rendor clan members seemed as reluctant as I was to focus on those memories. Anger, stubbornness, and fear etched many faces.

"I have as much reason as any to wipe every Kahlarean from this land," Mark said, his rich baritone cutting through the scattered debates. The grumbling stopped as his clansmen hung on each word. "But our job is not to seek vengeance. Our job is to remain faithful, to obey the One . . ." He paused and his eyes met Jake's. "And to give the One time to unfold His plan for Kahlarea."

The breath left me in a gasp. My husband's entire life had been scarred by Kahlarean violence. His words shocked and humbled me. I'd never admired him more.

"What difference will our clan make, if none of the others are coming to the gathering?" someone asked.

Jake squared his shoulders. "We can't answer for them or control their choices. We can only do what we know is right. I have no idea how to convince the songkeepers and Council to honor the Verses, or how to persuade the other clans to come. Yes, the problems are huge. The danger is real. But we have to try. Rendor survived for a reason. " Nobility shone from him. He wasn't a reckless teen blundering into drama of his own making. He was a leader with a servant heart. I was his mother, and part of me still wanted to meddle, boss, and guide him; but listening to his firm declaration, even I was ready to follow him on any difficult path.

"Meet me here midmorning. We'll travel together," Jake said and stepped down from the crate. As people dispersed, I couldn't read their reactions. Would they pack a few supplies and return ready for the journey to Lyric? Or would we be traveling alone? Either way, a quick exit through the portal seemed further away than ever.

"All right." I reviewed the situation, ticking things off on my fingers. "We need to get to Lyric. We need to call for the feast day gathering. We need to help the Council and the guardians with a defense plan against an invasion by Kahlarea and Hazor. Anything else?"

A vulnerable expression flickered across Jake's face. "I don't have Restorer gifts anymore. That will complicate things." His hand moved toward his hip, and I recognized the gesture—reaching for a sword hilt, even though he wasn't wearing one at the moment. "And one more thing. Someone was helping Cameron. I don't know who we can trust in Lyric."

My toes curled against the bare ground and I looked down. "I guess I'd better get my shoes."

CHAPTER
26

LINETTE

CARALAD PLUCKED THE strings of the rondalin. A rich chord filled the air, and he beamed.

"He's a natural," said one of the Lyric songkeepers. We'd arrived a short while before, as the afternoon rains tapered away, and already Caralad had charmed all the men and women at the lodge. I only hoped the child wouldn't do anything unusual or frightening here, and that the warm greeting would last. Was I wise to have brought him this far? Lukyan had insisted this was the right idea, and the child certainly hadn't been upset to leave. Perhaps he sensed that his family was nearby?

I reached my arms around Caralad and positioned his fingers to bring a new chord from the instrument. Then I sank back, enjoying his discovery of the sounds while taking in the familiar songkeeper lodge. The large common room held a long wooden table down the center, clusters of comfortable chairs, and extra pallets rolled and stacked along the walls for the times when all the clans arrived in Lyric for feast day gatherings. Today only a handful of people were here . . . all familiar faces.

I asked Lukyan to keep Caralad entertained, and walked toward a woman I'd trained with years ago. She'd have answers to my questions. Now that I was away from the strictures of the healers in Braide Wood, I planned to learn about the last few years. Before I reached her, though, a timid knock drew my attention to the lodge doorway.

Nolan stood against one side of the open entry, as if clinging to the edge for support. His eyes took in the space nervously. His grip on the doorjamb relaxed when he spotted me. "Linette."

I changed course and headed toward the doorway. "Well met, Nolan! Come in."

He shook his head and backed away a step. "We heard you'd arrived in Lyric. Kieran would like to talk with you. Can you come?"

Kieran wanted to see me. My stomach gave a flutter. Silly of me. He probably wanted to meet with each of the songkeepers who had served in Hazor. Not that I'd have anything helpful to add, since my memories of Hazor began with entering the shrine. Reassured that Lukyan would take good care of Caralad, I grabbed a light cloak. The rains had ended, but I felt shivery and welcomed the added warmth.

I started to ask Nolan how he'd been, but he darted ahead, allowing no conversation. I followed him across the wide plaza in front of the worship tower. Beautiful white stone reached upward. Vaulted openings invited people into the huge space. Seeing the place where music had stirred my heart, and where mist had lowered and touched me with the tangible presence of the One, I drew a deep breath of remembered joy and peace.

"This way." Nolan headed toward a small alley between nearby buildings. I'd been foolish to hope that Kieran wanted to meet in the tower. Back when I'd known him, he'd always been blatant with his scorn for the Verses and the work of the songkeepers. Another reason I needed to calm the strange flutter behind my ribs. Kieran and I had no common ground. But I still welcomed an opportunity to see him, if only to fill in a few more gaps about Hazor.

Nolan and I emerged into one of the many small parks near the central plaza. Set a few steps down, twisting honeywood trees created walls of brown and green while clusters of blue ferns absorbed gentle splashing from the fountain in the center. No one else lingered in the small garden today, though Lyric should be crowded this close to the feast day. The strange emptiness weighed on me.

Kieran sat on a bench and stared at the water, but he turned sharply at the sound of our approach. Strips of fabric crisscrossed the arms of his tunic and the legs of his trousers, and he wore his sword and his bootknife, not typical garb for the city. As I searched my memories of years past, most of the images I had of him were similar. Usually alone, always ready to pack up and move at a moment's notice, eyes alert and piercing.

"Thank you," he said in clipped tones.

I inclined my head in response, but then realized Kieran was looking past me at Nolan. Heat bloomed up my neck. I already felt off-balance, and I hadn't even asked him any of my difficult questions.

Nolan shrugged. "She was easy to find." Then he shot me a warm grin before jogging out of the secluded park.

"He has so much energy," I said fondly.

Kieran snorted. "If we set him loose on Hazor, our problems would be over." His sharp eyes scanned my face. "You look well. No return of the fever?"

I smoothed a fold on my robe and sat beside him. "I'm fine. Thank you for getting me safely to Braide Wood. I'm sure I made the journey more difficult for you and Nolan."

He frowned. "And your memory? It's returned?"

I brightened. "Not at first. But I found a child in the woods . . . I know this will sound odd . . . but he . . . I . . . I began to remember."

Something like sympathy flickered in his dark eyes. "Everything?"

A subtle ache throbbed, and I rubbed my forehead. "No. And I hate this. I remember my childhood, the people I'd forgotten—but not the past few years. The healers told everyone not to tell me things, to let me remember on my own." An edge of frustration crept into my voice.

Kieran smiled. "And you're ready to rebel?"

I felt a sudden kinship with Kieran, the Braide Wood outsider. I raised my chin. "They're wrong. I need to know. You don't care about healers' orders. Will you tell me everything that's happened these last years?"

"I could." He crossed his arms, watching me closely. "I could tell you that Jake's still missing. Does that mean anything to you?"

I searched my memories and shrugged. "Wade told me he was a Restorer and disappeared, but I don't remember him."

The furrows on his brow deepened. "I could tell you all the political danger we're in, all the news, everything that's occurred, but would it make a difference?"

My shoulders sagged. "You're right. Even if you tell me everything, it won't be the same. It would just be words—someone else's story. I'll still have lost those parts of me. Never mind. It was a silly plan."

He shook his head. "It's not that I won't tell you. I just think you should be asking for more."

"More?"

"Linette . . ." He scanned the quiet garden, the windows of nearby buildings that looked down on us. "Do you remember the things I told you on the trail?"

I tucked a strand of hair behind my ear. "Not much. The fever made everything confusing."

"We were in Hazor because the One called me to be a Restorer."

I tried to keep the doubt from my face. "I wasn't sure I'd heard you right." I'd studied the Verses all my life. I knew the One used unlikely vessels. Yet it was still hard to imagine.

The side of his mouth quirked, then he sobered. "While I was the Restorer—and even since—the One has sometimes brought healing through me." He braced an ankle over his knee and adjusted the strap of his bootknife. All the reckless confidence I remembered of him seemed to have fled. "So," he said, "could I . . . Would you allow me to talk to the One on your behalf?"

The notion was as foreign as the idea of Wade teaching Tara how to spice her stew, or Tristan doing a three-peg weaving. I tried to nod, but a strange reluctance gripped me. Listening to him speak to the One would feel so . . . intimate. My pulse rushed inside my ears.

He shifted as if about to stand. "Of course if you don't actually want to remember . . ."

He was baiting me, and I knew it. But I couldn't stop a flare of temper. "Don't be ridiculous. I need to know. But you? You . . ."

The lines of his face tightened. "But me."

I hadn't meant to make him angry. "It's not just you. I'm uncomfortable around everyone. I remember bits and pieces but don't really know you . . ."

"And you can't imagine that the One would want to hear any request from me."

Behind the bitter edge of his words, I heard a current of sadness that confused me.

"The One invites everyone to speak to Him."

He turned away. "Break out the songkeeper proverbs. You are getting back to normal."

I'd disappointed him somehow. Why couldn't I seem to take a right step these days? I crossed my arms. "It sounds like you're the one looking for an excuse to walk away. Why did you even offer if you just want to argue?"

His eyes widened, then he laughed. "Fair enough." He held out a hand, callused and strong. I rested mine in his, my fingers looking fragile by comparison. His touch caused another strange twist in my stomach, but thankfully he lowered his head.

"Holy One, You made Linette. You know her heart and mind. I don't need to convince You she's worthy of Your touch. You give gifts simply because You love us."

His words surprised and humbled me. And he didn't speak with the formality I'd learned in my training.

"I also don't need to remind You how unworthy I am to ask You for this. I don't trust in my worth. I trust in You."

His hand squeezed mine. If faith could flow through skin, my courage would grow from the trust he imparted.

"Restore the rest of her memories."

Something rippled in my mind. What had been a wall became a gauzy curtain, the fabric of such a light weave that I could see through it. Slowly, even that thin barrier began to part.

Scattered images flew around me, and one by one as I focused on them, I reclaimed them. Strangely, the first that I captured centered on Kieran.

The clans had been threatened. I knew that now. I remembered how it felt: the rising terror at the sight of Hazor's cavalry stretched across the fields outside Lyric, the pang of watching from the wall as a lonely figure walked out to face them, the awe as mist gathered around the tower and the One protected us.

Memories from the seasons in Hazor also swept into sight: the thrill of being called to assist the Restorer, the efforts to share hope and light, struggling to support Kieran, battered by inadequacies.

From this distance of forgetting and reclaiming, I had more mercy on myself. I had poured my heart into serving. I could see now what I had been blind to then, that the One treasured my service, regardless of human measures of success.

I drew a deep breath, the peace of forgiveness opening my lungs. Would it be like this at the end of life one day? This view of my life through the One's tender eyes?

"Are you all right?" Kieran's gruff voice tugged me briefly into the present.

"Yes. It's returning." Tears choked me. "I'm seeing—no, I'm reliving it all." I couldn't spare more words. There was more to discover. Secure that I once again had access to all the memories of the work in Hazor, I cast further back. I remembered meeting Susan, sitting on the transport and explaining the clans to a woman who had come from some far-off place. Other new memories tumbled me forward. Being caught outside at night. The bear. Wade's injury. The weeks of helping Susan . . . introducing her to Lukyan, finding ways to support her in her difficult calling.

The song I'd been writing during those weeks. I remembered blushing as I talked to her about . . .

Dylan.

I gasped and my hands flinched.

Kieran held on. "What's wrong?"

"Dylan!" I gasped. How could I have forgotten all that love? All that longing? "But where has he been? Why did I go to Hazor without him?" I saw his wind-tossed hair, heard his easy laughter, tasted the giddy joy as we made plans. I'd been pledged and forgotten it? Forgotten him?

"Where is he?" I pulled away from Kieran and stood, glaring down at him. "Why hasn't anyone told me?"

Compassion muted the burning intensity of his eyes. There it was, that same expression I'd caught at odd moments from others. That strange, uneasy withdrawal.

"What? Tell me."

He stood and held my shoulders. "What do you remember?"

"He's a guardian." Even in my desperate scrambling for knowledge, I spared a smile. Tearing across the prairie on his lehkan, Dylan embodied confident courage. Stacking logs for the home he built for us, he exuded playful energy. Striding toward the transport stop for one of his guardian assignments, he radiated noble sacrifice. "I love him."

A muscle flinched on Kieran's face, but he continued to meet my eyes. "Keep following the memories. What else?"

Love swelled in my heart, filling me, strengthening me. The idea that I could have forgotten this was inexplicable. No wonder I'd felt so incomplete. Half of my heart had been missing. I beamed. "We're pledged. He went on patrol . . . just before Susan came to Braide Wood."

The curtain was completely pulled aside now. Almost all my memories had returned. All that remained was one corner where the fabric hid the last piece of knowledge, draped like a shroud. I closed my eyes and in my mind stepped closer toward that last corner. A chill brushed over my skin.

"No," I whispered. After all these weeks of struggling to remember any wisp of my past, I suddenly wanted to cover this cubby and leave it undisturbed.

"You don't want to remember." Kieran's quiet voice sounded resigned, weary.

How did he know?

"Even when you knew, you didn't want to face it. Maybe forgetting is a gift." This time he wasn't taunting or challenging me. Even so, his words made me want to prove him wrong.

"I will remember." Eyes still closed, I looked around at the swirl of happy memories, the beautiful parts of my life I thought had been lost to me. They stirred hope and strength. I was ready to be whole, to move forward. *Holy One, reveal the rest to me.*

The shroud melted away. I was in Markkel and Susan's lodging in Lyric, racing across the common room to meet Tristan. He was bringing news from Cauldron Falls. His haggard expression told me the truth—the truth that every cell in my body resisted hearing. Like a blow to my stomach, I heard his words again, as if for the first time. "I'm sorry. He gave his life defending all of us." I had crumbled then, Susan's arms supporting me.

My knees gave way now, too, as a sob tore from the deepest place in my soul. Once again there were arms to hold me, and some distant part of me was grateful. But there wasn't room for much awareness beyond the searing pain. Tears poured from me, and my shoulders shook as I cried so hard I came close to choking.

Sweet Dylan. Precious Dylan. I knew it all now. Our hopes, our plans. After he died, I'd often dreamt—beautiful, vivid dreams where we were together. When I'd wake up, the shock of realizing he was gone would hurt me all over again. This was similar, but so much worse. How could I have forgotten? And how could his loss hurt this badly when I'd only just remembered our love? But it did. And why would the One make me live through this horrific news more than once?

"I'm sorry." Kieran's simple words broke through the torrent of grief. I realized I was kneeling on rough cobblestone, clinging to his coarse-woven shirt that was wet with tears. He'd sunk to the ground with me, supporting me. Part of me wanted to draw comfort from his arms, but part of me resented him for causing this horrible pain.

"You knew." I pushed away. "Everyone knew. How dare the healers tell people to keep this from me? Why didn't you tell me?"

"When?" His eyes glinted. "When you didn't even know me? Or later when I was doing everything in my power to get you to Braide Wood, but it looked like the fever would kill you?"

His blunt assessment only made me more furious. I shoved away from him. "Then why did you ask the One to show me now?"

His shoulders sank for a moment, but then he raised his chin and the lines of his face hardened. "There are serious problems facing the clans. Bigger than any one person's grief. We need you." He rubbed his forehead. "I need you."

His quiet admission sparked a strange, twisting tingle in my chest.

Now that I was fully myself again, I remembered working with Kieran in Hazor. Assisting him had been a welcome distraction from grief . . . but also confusing . . . a bewildering blend of conflicting feelings.

How could I be so disloyal to the memory of Dylan? I scrambled to my feet. "I'm sure you'll figure out how to save the clans again." I welcomed the bitter taste of my words. It made it easier to pull away.

He launched to his feet, but I held up my hands, warning him off. "Leave me alone. I need . . ." What did I need? I couldn't untangle the pain. I couldn't find words for what I needed. I only knew I had to get away from Kieran. So I turned and ran from the courtyard. I half expected to hear a string of curses following me, but other than the soft splashing of the fountain, there was only silence.

CHAPTER 27

LINETTE

I DASHED TEARS from my eyes as I hurried across the central plaza of Lyric, trying to outrun the renewal of grief. The large buildings all seemed duller than usual, and even the soaring walls of the worship tower looked more grey than white. The dimming sky announced the approach of the evening meal, but I wasn't ready to face a lodge full of Lyric songkeepers.

As I passed an arched entry of the worship tower, my feet slowed. I slipped inside the empty building and walked the familiar floor toward the center. Even this late in the day, the soft glow through crystal windows reflected off the shimmering white walls. Many times, that trick of light had reminded me of the One's holiness and stirred my eagerness and joy. Today, that reminder almost made me withdraw.

How could I face Him? My muscles trembled with the need to shake my fist at Him. He wasn't protecting the clans. Enemies surrounded us. Our work in Hazor had failed. And He had stood by while Dylan died a senseless death.

Dissonant, jarring, my songkeeper training filled my head: the One was perfect. He loved me. I couldn't blame Him for all this pain and confusion.

I did.

Sinking to my knees by the round podium in the middle of the tower, I rested my elbows on the railing and buried my face in my arms.

"I should thank You," I said quietly, struggling to hide my anger. "You gave me what I longed for. My memories. But . . ." Forcing a tone of respect only closed off my throat. Restrained Linette, the faithful songkeeper. I knew all the right words, but my spirit was a clashing chord, all mangled sounds and broken strings.

Breathing hard, I slammed my fists against the railing, then glared up into the open space. "The Verses say You care. Are they a lie?" I barely recognized the hoarse voice coming from my throat. Not a joyful singer anymore, only a brokenhearted woman.

"You took Dylan from me. And still I gave up everything to serve You. Did it matter to You at all? All that hard work, all those seasons in Hazor. They didn't make any difference. We failed. So why did You send us?" I was shouting now, and the rage in my voice frightened me.

I drew in a sobbing breath. "Did I fail You? Did Kieran? Is that why so much went wrong?"

My whole body sagged under the feelings of betrayal. I wasn't sure if I had betrayed Him or He had betrayed me, but the loss was an abyss, a dark pit that swallowed any meaning, any hope, any faith. All my life I'd turned to the One with my problems. Where could I go when He was the problem?

Nowhere.

I clung to the railing as if it could hold me back from the gaping emptiness in my soul.

Soft mist formed around me, the gentle touch of the One falling on my skin with no hint of rebuke or rejection. Peace called to me, coaxing me to unburden my heart. Slowly I dared more questions. "Why did You take Dylan? All this time I've tried to be strong, to believe there was some purpose only Your mind comprehended. But what if his death was random? What if You were looking away? What if You aren't even there?

"And Hazor—I couldn't help Kieran or the people . . . and You let me be taken captive."

A shudder moved through my body, and only the supportive mist and my grip on the railing kept me upright on my knees. "Why? Even Lukyan can't explain it. Have You rejected me? You let me forget everything. Even You."

The last words came out as a gasp, the horror of that emptiness hitting me in the core and knocking the last breath of air from my lungs. "How could You allow that? How could You let me forget You?"

I never forgot you.

The words resonated so strongly in my heart, they were nearly audible.

Tears ran down my face. "I know. And You brought me home. But I don't think I can bear the hurt all over again. How do I move forward without Dylan? How can I serve You when my heart is full of doubt?"

Now that I'd begun, I barely stopped for breath. "And the clans are in danger. Holy One, I've been so tangled in my own problems that I didn't even ask Kieran about it. What are You planning to do to protect us? What do You want from me?"

I braced myself—ready for explicit directions, ready to embrace some new danger or difficulty.

Love.

The chief calling every clan member learned as a child. Too simple. I needed more details, specific guidance, steps of action.

Love.

"Of course I love You and seek to offer love toward others . . . but what do You want me to do?"

The mist thickened around me, soaking into my pores and stilling my fretful questions. As if a hand pushed aside the complex pattern of pieces on a table game, all my worries scattered in His presence.

As gently as a lullaby, yet as piercing as a guardian's signaler, He spoke to me again.

Love.

I bowed my head and let the music of His voice swirl through my soul. A last strand of my rebellious mind protested. "It's not that simple, not that easy."

Never easy, but enough.

New tears welled in my eyes, less stinging now. "Yes," I whispered, my anger spent. "Make me a vessel of Your love. Teach me, show me."

The ache of loss still pulsed through me. My concern for the homeless boy still throbbed in my heart. Worry about the nations threatening our borders troubled me as well. Yet the many needs lost their power to overwhelm me. A deep passion to draw the clans' focus back to the One burned in my bones—a familiar sensation, but somehow new and fresh, too. Back in Hazor I'd longed for a sense of purpose, and now He'd stirred that in me. Wrapped as I was in the sheltering presence of the One, faith returned. He would guide me in how to love Him and others in each of those situations.

As the mist lifted, I stood and raised my arms, reaching for His presence. Music welled in my heart and I sang a new song as the One provided the words.

May each beat of my heart sound in worship
Like drums calling people to praise;
May my voice and my life bring You glory,
Joining songs that the mountains raise.

My voice was breathy and tentative, without the strong, clear tone a trained songkeeper should have. But I'd never sung with more truth. My very bones hummed a harmony. As I sang, images flooded my mind. The hand of the One protecting me, drawing me safely from Hazor. The faces of young messengers and women of Sidian absorbing the Verses. I saw Dylan, on his lehkan, turning his head in a moment of surprise and delight, as the One Himself beckoned. Dylan galloped to meet Him, toward a land of indescribable beauty and light.

For You've guided the days of Your children;
You carry us home from afar,
And my soul is restored in Your presence—
I seek only to be where You are.

Rejoice in the One who delivers,
For He lifts up the broken and weak.
You call me to serve You in love;
Your face will be all that I seek.

New tears flowed down my cheeks, but they were tears of mingled grief and resolve. As my love and trust rekindled, I longed to sing with more strength. My lone voice was so small in this grand space.

But Lukyan had taught me long ago that the One could take the smallest melody and build a strong chorus around it, if the music were true. The smallest life could produce magnificent worship when it was placed in His hands.

The mist was gone; the sky through the windows above was darkening. I drew a deep, steadying breath and stepped back from the podium. My calling awaited. I'd do all I could to fill this space with others for the season-end worship. I'd continue searching for a family for Caralad. I'd offer love to each person the One brought across my path, knowing that He would show me what that love should look like for each unique need.

Emerging from the tower, I'd only taken a few more steps when a shrill sound rose from the side of the city that faced Corros Fields. I stilled. A signaler. The pattern of staccato blasts indicated the most urgent of warnings: invasion.

Heart in my throat, I ran toward the lodge. I needed to get to Caralad and Lukyan. I'd only taken a few steps when another signaler sounded, then abruptly cut off. What was happening? Shopkeepers dashed into the street, leaving their empty stores, clamoring to each other for answers.

"Linette!" I heard my name called over the chaos. Kieran raced up to me, sword drawn. "Take cover in the guardian tower. Safest place. I've already sent Nolan there."

I shook my head. "I have to get the boy I'm caring for. But I'll take him there."

He spared a terse nod and ran past me toward the far walls of the city.

I pushed my way past a group of anxious people in the main square and hurried toward the lodge.

A handful of first-year guardians charged from the training tower and raced past in the same direction Kieran had taken, a pitifully small band of reinforcements for the guardians on watch. Lukyan had told me that after Jake's disappearance Lyric had been deserted by the guardians and first-years of other clans, breaking the system of interwoven assignments blending guardians from various clans into a cohesive force in Lyric.

At the songkeeper lodge I met a sealed door. "Let me in! It's Linette!" I pounded the metal with one hand while fumbling for the release lever with the other. Locked. When had songkeepers ever locked their common room door?

"Out of my way," an irritated elderly voice echoed from inside. The door slid open. Lukyan leaned heavily on his walking stick, glowering at the handful of songkeepers clinging to each other near the door.

Caralad nestled in the arms of one of the women. Thankfully, he didn't seem upset by the panic around him. When he saw me, he squirmed free and ran to me.

"We need to move to the guardian tower." I had to shout to be heard as another signaler sounded near the front gates. "Kieran said it would be safer."

Lukyan nodded, his face creased in sadness rather than fear. "Lead the way."

"We aren't going out there." Havid stepped out of the group. "Especially not if she tells us to." Her eyes skimmed over me coldly.

I had hoped the distrust wouldn't follow me from Braide Wood. What had Havid told the other songkeepers that had stirred up this sudden animosity in the short time I'd been out? Frustration almost overwhelmed me. I gathered Caralad into my arms. "There isn't time to argue. You don't have to trust me. Trust Lukyan."

"Why? He's not a Lyric songkeeper," another woman said shrilly.

So the factions had extended to the songkeepers as well as the guardians. They should be appreciating the fact that Lukyan had made the journey from Braide Wood when many of the other clans refused to send their songkeepers for the feast.

I wavered. As a young songkeeper, I'd been taught to bend, to serve, to cooperate. Taking a stand in opposition of the Lyric songkeepers went against my nature. But if Kieran said the guardian tower was the safest place, then I believed him.

"Lukyan and I are going to the guardian tower. I hope you'll come with us." Still cradling Caralad, I offered an elbow to Lukyan. He took my arm, and we walked outside. I didn't look behind me, hoping at least a few of the others would follow. Instead the door slid closed with an angry thump.

I turned my focus to protecting the boy as the signalers abruptly stopped their clamor. "We'll be all right," I whispered in his ear. Lukyan's steps wobbled, and his weight on my arm increased. I led us along the sides of the buildings; the open square felt too exposed. Our progress was painfully slow, but at last we reached the guardian tower.

Nolan met us in the entry hall, nervous energy shimmering from him in waves. "This way." He led us to a back room, pushed aside a storage rack of weapons, and revealed hidden stairs. "You'll be safe down there. I've got to go help my father."

I grabbed his arm. "Wait. Did he ask you to join him at the wall?"

Nolan's gaze skidded away. "He needs my help." He tossed his bangs to the side in a gesture half sullen and half defiant.

Kieran wouldn't want Nolan in the middle of the danger. But how to stop an eager youth from a reckless path? "You can't leave us here. We need at least one person who can fight."

Shifting his weight from side to side, Nolan frowned, indecision playing across his face. Lukyan leaned hard on his staff and began coughing, then raised a weak hand when he'd caught his breath. "Linette, we can't keep a young warrior from the battle. Even if it means we are left defenseless." He turned his head toward me so Nolan wouldn't see the sparkle in his eyes.

I hid a grin, then gathered Caralad close. "Don't be afraid," I said to him, although the boy hadn't shown a glimmer of fear. "If enemies break in here, I'll find a way to protect you."

Nolan made a sound of exasperation and cast one more look toward the hall. "Fine. I'll stay with you. For now." He waved us down the stairs, then slid the storage rack into place to hide the entry again and followed us, holding a light cube high enough to let us see our footing.

A cold chill breathed across the back of my neck; a flash of memory took me back to the steps beneath the shrine in Hazor. I'd fought hard to regain my memories, but there were a few I longed to forget.

Soft, chubby fingers touched my cheek. I looked down at the boy in my arms. Caralad's dark eyes met mine with compassion beyond his years. "Everything will be all right," I said firmly.

He smiled.

At the foot of the stairs, Nolan led us into a space the size of a large common room. A wall to the left held racks of swords, boot-knives, baldrics, and leather gauntlets. A deep cubby on the right held shelves of supplies. Straight ahead of us I glimpsed a bathroom through an open sliding door. Rolled pallets were stacked around the room, and a low table in the center held several heat trivets. "What is this place?" I asked as I lowered Caralad to his feet.

Nolan turned on the heat trivets, filling the room with a softer light than his cube. "The guardians call it a beetle nest. You know, like where stinging beetles hide below ground if they're threatened."

We pulled some pallets closer to the table and sank down, except for Nolan, who kept prowling the room. "Even the first-year guardians don't know about this one." He paused by the rack of weapons and pulled out a knife to examine. If I didn't keep him occupied, he'd dash out to fight beside Kieran.

"Are you hungry? It looks like there's plenty to work with. I could make some supper."

Food managed to distract him. I kept him busy helping me prepare a meal, although his constant fidgeting warned me I wouldn't be able to hold him long. Even while we ate, his hand kept straying to his bootknife, and his gaze slid often to the door.

When Nolan had sopped up the last bit of his stew with a piece of bread, he uncrossed his legs, and pushed away from the table.

Before he could stand, Lukyan lifted a hand. "The Verses for the day."

Nolan hesitated, then sank onto the pallet. He'd seen and heard enough about the One to honor our traditions, but his scowl made it clear to all of us how much he objected to hiding here instead of fighting alongside his father.

I didn't blame him. I wanted to know what was happening. If I didn't have Lukyan and the two boys to care for, I'd have followed Kieran to the city walls to find out what sort of invasion we faced.

Caralad, seated beside me, patted my arm. Then he stood, circled to the other side of the table, and settled down beside Nolan. His presence softened Nolan's scowl as Lukyan led us in the creed. Caralad remained silent, but his face glowed as the rest of us quietly spoke the words. We reached the last part of the creed.

"We wait in the darkness for the One who brings light."

Never had the words felt more true. We huddled in a beetle hole with enemies advancing. What battles were being waged at the walls?

Lukyan continued reciting the day's Verses, but broke off midsentence as another coughing fit grabbed him—this time not feigned. He wheezed as he tried to catch his breath, and I rushed to his side, touching his face to check for fever. His skin was cold and clammy, muscles on his neck straining as he struggled for air. He pressed his hands to his heart as if coaxing his lungs to work again.

"Perhaps . . . you . . . will have to . . . recite." His mouth lifted, but then grimaced and he doubled over.

"What do you need? How can I help?" I eased him to a blanket on the floor and offered him water.

His gaze grew unfocused. "Not . . . time . . ." Then his lips moved without sound.

"Nolan, give me your bootknife."

Already alarmed at Lukyan's struggle, the youth's eyes grew even wider at my sharp command.

"Now!"

He pulled out his dagger and handed it to me, hilt first. "What are you—?"

"I'm going to find the Lyric healer. Lukyan needs help."

"I could go," he offered. "If you tell me where to find him."

"Her. I know her, so it will be quicker for me. You need to protect Lukyan and Caralad until I get back."

Lukyan shook his head, but another coughing fit left him too weak to argue. Nolan swayed from foot to foot, but finally nodded. He grabbed one of the swords from the storage cubby and escorted me up the stairs. Once he was sure that no enemies lurked in the guardian tower, he motioned for me to leave our hiding place. "He'll kill me if anything bad happens to you," he muttered.

Anxiety shadowed his face as he ducked his head down in a familiar uneasy gesture.

I took a moment to lift his chin and meet his gaze. "I'll be fine. Take care of them. You can do this."

His deep brown eyes shone with determination. He squared his jaw in a gesture so like his father that I caught my breath. *Holy One, this boy is so precious. Keep him safe. Keep them all safe.*

Then I ran.

CHAPTER
28

LINETTE

WITH EVERYONE HIDING from the threatened invasion, the plaza was deserted in the evening dusk. Instead of the warm glow of light walls spilling into the street through inviting door-ways, every home turned a closed and fearful face at anyone foolish enough to venture out. Touching Nolan's bootknife secured in my belt, I gathered up my songkeeper robe in my other hand and raced even faster to the healer's home.

My frantic pounding on the door produced no response, so, ignoring ceremony, I slid the door aside and entered. Scanners and bandages littered a nearby table, as if the healer had been called away in a hurry. Of course. She was probably at the battle. I wouldn't divert her from her important work. I only needed her to tell me what herbs could help Lukyan.

Footsteps scraped outside and I spun, fumbling for the dagger.

A young Lyric guardian stumbled inside, clutching his arm. Seeing his eyes move to my knife, I hastily sheathed it and pulled out a chair for him, glancing helplessly at the herbs and containers filling the shelves. "She's not here."

He nodded. "She's at the wall. Corros side. She sent me to wait for her here."

Torn between Lukyan's need and the wounded man before me, I picked up a rolled bandage and passed it from hand to hand. "I need to find her. It's urgent."

He waved me away with his good arm. "I know where she keeps the orberry wine. I'll be fine. Go."

Halfway on my run to the far side of the city, I realized I should have asked him the status of the battle. Well, I'd know soon enough. The eerie silence of empty streets gave way to growing sounds, muffled by the tall protective walls of Lyric.

Shouts. Clangs. Wails.

Once I cleared the buildings blocking my view, I saw a few lookouts stationed on the top of the wall. I ran up a narrow stairwell, startling a young messenger at the top of the steps.

"Have you seen the healer?" I asked, my chest heaving for air.

He moved aside. "Out there somewhere."

I hurried to the curved parapets and peered out at the wide fields between Lyric and Corros, hoping I could locate her green tunic.

Under the dimming sky, lehkan charged in a chaos of spinning, snorting movement. I spotted Tristan and a cluster of his men, all mounted, all frantically holding back a much larger group of soldiers on lehkan.

The large cavalry could only mean Hazor. My blood chilled. I wanted to turn away from the lethal slashing of swords and the angry shrieks, but I scanned for the emblem of King Zarek in the distance. I had to know. After all this, would I still fall back into Bezreth's hands?

I couldn't let fear distract me. Squinting, I leaned forward, and my gaze slipped to the guardians on foot, fighting closer to the wall. Even though my purpose was to locate the healer, I found myself searching for someone else.

I spotted him not far from one of the hidden doors in the wall beneath me. Dark hair, lithe movements, sword darting with the skill he'd used when he sparred with Zarek.

Kieran was too reckless. He fought as if he didn't care if he lived or died. My fingers squeezed the smooth white stone of the parapet, and I tasted blood as I bit my lip. Our last conversation had ended with me shoving him away, blaming him for the pain my memories caused. Would he die with that unfair accusation echoing in his heart? *Holy One, not now. Please. Spare him.*

With a few more breath-stealing clashes, he disarmed the man in front of him, then spun in and slammed him in the head, knocking him to the ground. I finally got a look at the enemy's tunic.

The unconscious attacker wore the emblem of Corros.

Scanning the battlefield, my heart screamed a denial at what I witnessed. The men riding Hazorite lehkan were all from Corros. A neighboring clan. Our own people.

As the horror sank in, Kieran dragged his opponent toward the wall. He disappeared from sight just as another man charged toward him, sword raised.

At the far end of the field, one of the Corros riders pressed a signaler, and the screeching call drew the men back. The sky was darkening swiftly, and the attackers withdrew. The Lyric guardians also disengaged from battle, those on lehkan riding to pastureland outside the city, and those on foot making for the door.

The scramble of movement beneath me jarred me back to my purpose, and I hurried down the steps to find the healer. As people swept past me, keeping my feet took all my effort. Then I spotted her, examining a man supported by two other guardians. I pushed my way closer.

"Take this one to my house." She turned and waved a few more limping men away from the wall, then pushed her hair off her face with a harried gesture. "Return to your homes. I'll send an apprentice to you soon."

She brightened when she saw me. "Linette! Well met. Have you come to help?"

I shook my head. "Lukyan is ill, having trouble breathing. I know you can't come right now, but is there anything I can do to help him?"

A flash of sympathy warmed her face, but even while she gave me directions about which herbs he needed, she scurried from person to person, assessing and barking orders. "Send a messenger to me if he doesn't improve by morning," she tossed over her shoulder and hurried away before I could thank her.

"Linette? Messengers of the One, what do you think you're doing?" Kieran's angry shout spun me around.

He was scraped, torn, bloodied, but alive.

I dashed forward and threw my arms around him. "You're not dead."

He stiffened, then patted my back with jerky movements. I retreated, flushing, reminded of how I'd shouted at him in the garden.

"Where's Nolan?" he asked sharply.

"Safe in the guardian tower. Lukyan is sick. I needed to find the healer."

He gave an exasperated huff and turned toward the wall. The young guardian he'd disarmed earlier sat in a limp heap, wrists bound in front of him. Grabbing the man's arm, he propelled him to his feet. "Move." He frowned at me. "You, too."

We made our way back to the city center, stopping at the healer's home briefly so I could gather the proper herbs.

When we clambered down the steps to the beetle hole, Nolan faced us, sword at the ready, his arm trembling only a little.

Kieran shoved his prisoner over to the wall and clamped an arm on his son's shoulder. "Thank you for keeping them safe."

The boy grew a few inches and nodded, while Caralad looked up from where he knelt beside Lukyan. I hurried over with the herbs, crushed them in the bottom of a mug and poured water over them. Lukyan's breathing had already eased. Perhaps Caralad's healing gifts had helped. But I was glad to have a concoction to offer as well.

My own breathing began to steady along with my mentor's. We weren't going to be run through by Hazorite soldiers or Corros traitors. At least not tonight.

Then heavy scuffling echoed from the top of the stairs. The weapons rack.

Our hiding place had been discovered.

CHAPTER
29

LINETTE

BOOTED TREAD SOUNDED on the stairs, and Tristan stepped into view. He zeroed in on the table. "Any food left?"

"Took you long enough to get your mounts settled," Kieran grumbled.

Tristan unbelted his sword and propped it against the wall. "They did well today. We've held the walls. For the time being."

"Is it Hazor?" Nolan's eyebrows pulled together as he threw a glance at the man slouched against the wall.

"Worse," Kieran said tightly.

Tristan sank to the floor beside the low table and reached for the bowl of leftover kasaba mash. When no one would elaborate, Nolan shifted his weight. "Do you plan to tell us?"

Lukyan pushed up on his elbows, then managed to sit, resting his arms on the low table. "Don't blame them, Nolan. Some events are so wrong that even giving words to them is a terrible burden."

Tristan shot Lukyan a glance. "You know?"

"The Verses speak of a time of rebellion." His voice held a tremor. "I've seen the time approaching."

Kieran strode past me to snatch a bread loaf. "I hardly think this is some mystic destiny unfolding. Just Cameron causing more trouble." Since my spontaneous expression of relief at the wall, he had apparently decided to ignore my existence. I did the same and passed a bowl of dried berries across the table.

Tristan scooped up a mouthful. "But I wouldn't have believed I'd ever see clans fighting each other right outside the walls of Lyric."

"And on the eve of the season-end gathering." I looked at the prisoner, pleading for him to deny it. "You would attack your brothers and sisters who keep the worship tower for all the clans?"

"Lyric has hoarded the power for too long, songkeeper." The man's lips curled. "And when Tabor and Blue Knoll join us, Lyric will be ours."

I sensed Kieran's sudden stillness. He exchanged glances with Tristan.

Then, as if their captive realized he'd said too much, he clamped his jaw shut and scowled at the floor.

The small room seemed to close in further. More clans fighting each other? Dark spots flickered on the edges of my vision until I remembered to breathe. I gasped in some air. "It can't be true. It can't."

Lukyan's shoulders curved forward as sadness weighted him. Tristan shook his head but kept eating. Caralad turned to meet my gaze. Silent tears rolled down his cheeks.

My battered heart twisted. Our talk was upsetting him, even if he didn't understand. I gathered him close again and settled him in my lap.

"Who's he?" Kieran asked.

"She found him," Nolan piped up. "In the woods."

Tristan's chin came up. "In Braide Wood?" The bristles on his face seemed to stiffen in distrust. "He's not from our clan."

I rested my chin on Caralad's soft curls and wrapped my arms more firmly around him. "Kieran, this is the boy I told you about. He started my healing. And that's not all. Wade's leg was crushed, and Caralad fixed him."

"A healer? A new Restorer?" Tristan asked around another mouthful.

Kieran studied the child. "But where does he belong? What has he told you?"

I gently wiped away the trail of tears on Caralad's cheeks. "He doesn't speak." I avoided looking at Kieran, but knew he was rolling his eyes. Well, too bad. I might be too trusting, but I'd rather be compassionate and naïve than cynical.

I looked around the cramped room. "I suppose we should head back to the songkeeper's lodge if the danger is past."

"Too late." Kieran leaned against the wall near the stairway. "It's already dark. We'll stay here until morning."

I sighed, suddenly feeling the effects of the long day of travel followed by my emotional time at the worship tower, not to mention my race across the city. I wanted to curl up on the floor and sleep. Instead, I brought out more food for the men and began to roll out pallets on the limited floor space. Lukyan could have the spot along one wall, and I'd put Caralad and Nolan beside him—

"Get away from him!" Kieran's shout made me turn.

Caralad stood right in front of the prisoner, his hand reaching out to offer a bread roll. Kieran grabbed Caralad roughly and swung him out of reach. I raced forward, snatched the boy away, and glared at Kieran. "Leave him alone. He was just being kind."

Kieran's eye twitched and he squeezed his forehead. "Linette, he's—"

"My fault." Tristan lurched to his feet. "Shouldn't have left him here. The local guardians have returned by now. I'll take our prisoner up to them."

"I had some questions for him." Kieran gritted the words out through his clenched jaw.

Tristan hauled the man from Corros to his feet. "I'll take care of it. We'll make plans when I get back."

I adjusted Caralad in my arms so I could see if he was frightened by Kieran's rough actions. Instead, the boy was beaming—beaming!—at Kieran as if recognizing an old friend.

Kieran's eyes narrowed. "Are you sure he's not from Braide Wood clan? He looks familiar."

Caralad rested his cheek against my shoulder, but continued to stare at Kieran with a wide grin. That settled it. The poor child must be simple.

Lukyan suddenly began coughing again, and I let the subject drop while I prepared him a mug of clavo steeped with herbs. After Tristan left with the prisoner, Kieran unwound enough to take off his sword and sit down. As he relaxed his continual alertness, dark shadows smudged the skin beneath his eyes and he kept rubbing his temples.

I quietly asked Nolan to entertain Caralad, then heated more clavo and brought a mug to Kieran. I eased to the floor beside him. "This might help."

He frowned.

"Your headache," I added.

He flashed a crooked smile. "This feels familiar."

I shifted, moving to go clear the table, but he grabbed my arm. "I don't need you taking care of me. Maybe you thought that was your job in Hazor, but—"

"Maybe we need you to take care of us." I pried his hand off my arm. "Maybe the clans need you. And maybe you'll have a better chance of helping us when your head isn't throbbing and you can think straight." I stormed away to finish clearing up. Lukyan made a sound almost like a chuckle, but when I looked at him, he appeared to be dozing, chin propped on his fists with eyes closed.

The clavo didn't improve Kieran's mood much. When the dishes were washed, I distributed blankets and settled onto a pallet, singing softly to Caralad until he fell asleep. Eventually Nolan and Lukyan joined him in settling down to sleep.

"Was anyone hurt?" I asked softly. Kieran had ignored the pallets and sat in the doorway, leaning back against the frame, angled so he could watch the top of the stairs.

He shrugged. "You don't repel an attack without injuries. I think they were testing the defenses. Could have been worse. Will be tomorrow."

"And you think Cameron is involved?"

"He's convinced his clan that they—and he—should be in power. And the Council—the ones who are left—are useless as always." He sighed. "Get some sleep. Nothing we can do tonight."

I dimmed the lightwall, curled up beside Caralad, and pulled a blanket over my shoulders, forcing my breathing into a slow and steady rhythm. The harder I tried to sleep, the more my mind wrestled with the dangers facing the clans. Power struggles weren't unprecedented. Years ago two clans had withdrawn from the People of the Verses, but Markkel had managed to reunite them with the rest of the clans, and their balcony in the Council was no longer dark and empty. But to violently attack another clan? And during the end-of-season gathering, when the focus was supposed to be on worship? I closed my eyes and remembered the comforting presence of the One when He'd spoken to me in the tower. Everything in the world seemed to be fracturing, but He was my tower. Focusing on His goodness, I asked Him to quiet my heart and renew my trust.

Eventually, Tristan came back downstairs. By then I was nearly asleep, and too warm and settled in my nest to rouse. My messages to him from home could wait until morning. The gentle murmur of Tristan and Kieran's low voices rose and fell as they discussed guardian assignments and strategies. I must have dozed, because some time later their topic had shifted.

"When are you going to do something about it?" Tristan asked.

"Leave it," Kieran answered. "The clans are in crisis. I don't need complications."

Tristan snorted. "The clans are always in crisis. Don't be a coward."

I expected to hear the scuffle of a fight breaking out after that taunt, but Kieran just sighed. "It will never work. Look at me. She deserves better."

Tristan lowered his voice, his next words barely audible. "She deserves someone who will protect her and cherish her and think about her obsessively . . . and we both know who that is."

I bit my lip and slipped the blanket off my ear so I could hear better. Who were they talking about?

When Kieran didn't respond, Tristan tried again. "It's obvious she feels the same. Why can't you allow yourself a little happiness?"

"I don't care what you think you've seen. She loves Dylan. I can't compete with that. And even if I could, I wouldn't."

She loves Dylan? They were talking about me? Kieran and me? Tristan was crazy, although not for the reasons Kieran was stating. He was the one who deserved better. Someone stronger, someone who could stand beside him the way Kendra did for Tristan.

"Look, I'm happy for you and Kendra," Kieran said in a low rasp, "but I think becoming a father has made you a little touched in the head. Just because it worked for you doesn't means it's the right path for me."

"You're a father too," Tristan answered quietly.

"Yet another reason to drop the subject. Nolan needs me. That's enough responsibility."

I coughed and rolled over, pulling the blanket over my head, hoping they'd stop talking. It worked. Heavy silence covered the room. I clenched the fabric in one fist, twisting it in time with the tortuous twists in my heart. Of course I cared about Kieran. He'd been the One's chosen Restorer and I'd been honored to help him. And yes, Tristan and Kendra had sometimes teased me about Kieran as if they'd seen more than friendship. And yes, if I were completely honest with myself, those confusing feelings I'd grappled with during our seasons in Hazor were probably . . .

Love.

I twisted the blanket more tightly. Why? Why had Tristan given voice to this? I'd been able to hold it at bay—in Hazor, and today when my memories and feelings had returned. Why had Tristan unlocked that door?

Kieran had made it clear that he didn't feel the same. *That's enough responsibility,* he'd said. He was right. I'd be nothing but a burden. He was older, experienced, a leader, a father, a warrior. I spent my life creating music and teaching the Verses. We couldn't be more mismatched. Silent tears ran down my face. At least he didn't know I'd heard.

As if the restless night hadn't been bad enough, I woke in the morning to angry voices. Kieran, Tristan, Lukyan, and even Nolan talked over each other.

"If we lead a small band to beat them back . . ."

"We must invite all the clans . . . maybe the Council—"

". . . and I'll do reconnaissance and tell you . . ."

They sounded like they'd been at it awhile and hadn't bothered to wake me. Or perhaps they'd just forgotten about me. I'd faced some difficult new days, but this was a day of despair and shame. Our clans were supposed to gather in worship today. Instead we were making battle plans. I moaned and felt a small hand press against my forehead. Caralad sat beside me, as if guarding me from the argument. His gentle touch comforted and strengthened me, and I sat up, pushing my hair away from my face.

"We have to go to the worship tower," I said loudly.

The men turned to me with a mix of hopeful, quizzical, and exasperated expressions. I rose, wishing I didn't feel so rumpled and disheveled. "It's the feast day. We cannot neglect our worship. And we can't take arms against our brothers."

Tristan rubbed his short beard. "We could call for a parlay, but with Jake missing—"

"All the more reason." I pressed a hand against the wall for support. The clans were understandably devastated at having yet another Restorer snatched from them in a time of need. Jake had had such a sweet, strong spirit. Back in Hazor I'd often talked to the One on his behalf, knowing the monumental challenges he faced. "When did he disappear? The emblem I made for him . . ."

"I was never able to deliver it. I'm sorry." Tristan's eyes softened. He rummaged in his pack that was propped near the doorway. After pulling out the crumpled cloth, he offered it to me. "When we arrived back in Braide Wood, I learned about the changes happening in our clans. Cameron had escaped, Jake had disappeared, factions were forming, Hazor was once again strengthening its forces near the borders."

I smoothed wrinkles away from the carefully stitched waterfall. All those days in a fog of lost memories, I'd lost so much time, so much understanding of the dangers and problems. "What's been done?" I asked.

"All we could," Kieran snapped. "But we have new decisions to make, so why don't you save your questions for another day—if we even survive to see another—"

Tristan elbowed Kieran hard, shooting him a glare. "I tracked Jake myself, and still have my best guardians looking. We won't give up."

Kieran grabbed his baldric and slipped it over his shoulder, every movement as sharp and angry as if he were sparring. What had I said to set him off now? "This feels familiar," I murmured.

He looked up from settling his sword at his hip, surprise startling a wry smile from his lips. "Sorry. Not your fault."

Tristan wiped his hands over his face and shook his head. "You two will have to get things untangled later. Linette, what did you mean about the worship tower?"

"We have to begin the call to worship."

"She's right." Lukyan pushed to his feet.

Kieran tightened the strap on his bootknife, then straightened. "How does that even make sense? Most of the songkeepers from other clans haven't come for this gathering, and we need people to watch the walls."

"Remember what happened when Hazor tried to invade?" Mist had fallen over Lyric while the people gathered to sing, the power of the One striking terror into the hearts of our enemies, protecting our city.

"I was a little busy," Kieran said dryly.

Remorse flooded me. Of course his memories were different. I walked to Kieran and placed a hand on his chest, where Zarek's soldier had impaled him on the field of battle. "The clans all owe you so much. We haven't forgotten your sacrifice. You of all people know we . . ."

He stared at my hand until I pulled it back. Finally, he met my eyes. I could read the conflict that tore at him. All his life he'd fought against a world that seemed to oppose him on every side. Even so, the One had called him, and that call had changed him. He longed to trust, to yield, to serve. But every instinct in him urged him to rely on his own plans.

"Maybe there's an answer in the middle," I said quietly.

"Such as?" He trudged up the stairs, and the rest of us followed.

Holy One, show me the right path. "Lukyan can go to the song-keeper's lodge and ask those who are there to come to the tower. I need to go to the worship tower immediately."

"You won't be safe there," Kieran tossed over his shoulder.

I scurried to keep up as we entered a large training room in the guardian hall. "The safest place to be is in the presence of the One."

Caralad grasped my hand and nodded.

"Fine." Kieran looked too irritated to argue. "But Tristan and I—"

His plans were interrupted by the shrill sound of a signaler.

"Again? It's barely first light." Tristan jogged to the doorway and tilted his head, then paled. "That's not coming from the Corros side of the city."

CHAPTER 30

SUSAN

AS WE CRESTED the berm near the transport station and Lyric came into sight, a flood of memories pounded at me like the relentless force of Cauldron Falls. My knees buckled, and I stumbled to a halt, clutching at the hooded cloak Aiyliss had given me. The last time I'd arrived here I'd led a haggard band of captives, newly released from the nightmare of Rhus—weeks ago by my world's time, seasons ago by this world's, and a lifetime ago by the terrain of my soul.

Again I walked at the head of Rendor clan, but today the large contingent strode purposefully. Moved by Jake's impassioned plea, they walked with a confidence that, unlike my own, seemed to grow as Lyric drew nearer. Looking out toward the curving walls, I shuddered, unable to take another step until Mark's arm wrapped around my shoulders. "Are you all right?" he asked quietly.

How often had he asked that question in the days before we'd come here? He didn't deserve all the worry I'd caused him. I ignored my bruises and aches, lengthened my spine, and managed a smile. "Lyric takes your breath away, doesn't it?"

Not a lie. When I'd first seen the city, the towers had reminded me of gothic cathedrals. But instead of sharp spires and dark lines, here all the shapes were curved. The white pearlescent wall drew a rippling pattern around the whole city, with beautiful scallops adorning the top of the entire expanse. The huge entry tunnel dipped down below the wall, and then a wide ramp led up into the city, glowing with iridescent crystal.

I wanted to run away, skirt the city and head straight for the grove. The rumors and bits of information we'd gleaned frightened me. What if Cameron had taken over the Council again? What if a Rhusican sowed poison throughout the city? What if Kahlarean assassins infiltrated and attacked? The dangers that might face us turned my feet to lead.

Jake drew alongside us, one hand resting on the sword Rendor clan had provided. Mark wore a similar one. Though the clan had offered me one as well, without my former Restorer skill, it wouldn't have done much but weigh me down. Instead, I'd accepted a boot-knife and adjusted the Kahlarean venblade holster to wear at my ankle.

"Beautiful, isn't it?" my son said. "Not just the buildings, but what it means. When I first saw it, the words for a song came to me. Couldn't help myself."

I indulged in a motherly hug and brushed his hair back from his face. It had grown long, in the custom of many of the clans. His tunic covered the horrible scars on his arms, but his cheeks seemed hollow and too thin, his eyes too weary. "Will you be all right? When I think of what they did to you . . ."

His weariness disappeared as he smiled. "Mom, you helped me through it."

"Me?" I shook my head. "We should have tried to come back sooner. I feel like we abandoned you."

"The One used your suffering to bring truth to Rhus. When I was afraid, when I doubted, I remembered that."

His words humbled me and challenged my perspective. This wasn't the time to dwell on whys or what ifs. Mark and I were here for a reason. We'd come to rescue Jake. Against all odds, we'd accomplished that. And the One had also rescued Mark. My husband had looked into the face of his enemies and shown mercy. And I . . .

I still had fears to confront. I squared my shoulders and faced the walls—and any obstacle that lay beyond—determined that on the other side, my family would be restored.

Jake turned and scanned the group behind us, then studied the nearly empty city entrance. "The roads should be full of gathering clan members. We've got to find out what's happened."

Without waiting, he strode forward, the rest of us falling in behind. A guardian several stories above us on the wall watched us for a few seconds, then turned. The shrill warning of a signaler sounded.

By the time the noise stopped, a contingent of guardians had charged from the entry, fully armed.

"Hold back," Jake called to our group. He walked forward, hands a careful distance from his sword belt.

One of the guardians pushed to the front, waving to his companions to stand down.

Tristan! He looked as rough-hewn as I remembered, and a bit harried. But warmth lit his eyes as he offered his arm to Jake. "Well met, Jake of Rendor."

As the men clasped forearms, Mark and I stepped forward, so I was close enough to hear Tristan's next quiet words. "It's about time you showed up. The clans are in about the most danger I've seen—and that's saying something."

"So I've heard," Jake said. "Sorry I couldn't escape sooner. But the One sent help." He moved aside, and I tossed back my hood.

Tristan's eyebrows rose, then he grinned at Mark and me. "Back again? And where did you find our lost Restorer?"

"Cameron sold him to the Kahlareans."

Tristan bit back an oath. "Kieran suspected something like that. Cameron disappeared at the same time as Jake. But it's hard to believe he'd stoop that low."

Not hard for me. But I pushed away both my animosity at the mention of Cameron's name and my relief at finding he had disappeared. More political and military discussions loomed ahead, but at the moment I had other priorities. News in Rendor had been sketchy and so polluted with rumors that I needed some reliable updates. "How is Kendra? And everyone in Braide Wood?"

Tristan's grin returned. "We have a daughter. Emmi was born in Hazor, and we returned to Braide Wood before the truce with Zarek fell apart. They're safe at home."

"Congratulations!" I sprang forward and hugged him. The startled guardians waiting nearby lifted their weapons. His deep laugh reassured them, and they lowered their swords while I badgered Tristan for details.

He ignored my questions and scanned the area. "Later. There's no cover out here."

He hustled us into the city, but I wasn't going to be deterred that easily. "So you were still in Hazor when the baby was born? How long was the labor? Is Kendra doing well? Oh, and how are your parents? Are the fields at Morsal Plains recovering? Is Kieran still working in Sidian?"

Tristan rubbed the back of his neck and cast a glance at Mark, who covered a laugh with a cough. What was their problem? I was trying to be efficient and get some questions answered quickly.

In spite of our urgent pace, I took in the wide plaza in front of the worship tower with appreciation. The huge arched entries on all sides invited everyone inside. But where was the sound of drums? Where were the voices raised in praise?

A slim figure moved across the plaza, blonde hair catching my eye. Linette! A small boy held her hand. A young cousin from Braide Wood at his first feast day celebration? It looked like the child would be disappointed, since clearly no gathering was occurring.

I grabbed Mark's arms and tugged him as I veered in her direction, waving to catch her attention. We'd only moved a few feet when a man ran toward us from between the guardian tower and the council building. Mark's hand reached for his sword, and he reflexively blocked me with his other arm in the sort of parental seatbelt move we'd often used when hitting the brakes on our van.

I peered around Mark. "Kieran! You're back from Hazor. How did that go?"

He spared a glance at me and raised an eyebrow, but then ignored us as he stopped in front of Tristan. "We've diverted an outright attack. Corros has agreed to send a delegation to an emergency Council session."

"Good work," Tristan said, his face betraying his surprise that Kieran had managed a negotiation.

He shook his head. "They had a condition. That Cameron will speak for them."

Nerves flared up my spine. The man who had tortured me, betrayed the clans, sold my son . . . How dare the Council allow him that respect?

Kieran turned his focus on Jake, scowling. "You picked a fine time to disappear."

Jake's jaw muscles flexed. "Wasn't by choice. Looks like we picked a good time to return."

Into the near palpable tension between them stepped Linette. "Jake! Well met." Her gentle features lit up with relief.

Jake's skin flushed, and he clasped both her hands. "I talked to the One about you each day. How did the work go in Hazor?"

Her smile drooped. "We tried."

Kieran's hackles rose, and he edged between them, facing Linette. "I thought you were going straight to the worship tower."

This time *my* hackles rose, but she just tilted her head as if confused by his sharp tone. "I visited a few homes of friends first, letting them know we plan to go ahead with the morning worship. But we're on our way now."

I knelt to get on eye level with the boy. "And who is this fine young man?"

The full warmth of Linette's smile turned on me. "We call him Caralad. We don't know his actual name. I found—"

"Save the reunion for later," Kieran said tersely. "If you're still determined to start the gathering worship, get to the tower and stay there. Tristan, we need your most trusted guardians to escort the Corros delegation. I've sent Nolan to the Council offices to notify the councilmembers."

"Mark and I can go with Linette to the tower."

"Wait," a feeble voice quavered from near the worship tower. We all turned, and my heart swelled at the sight of Lukyan's bushy white brows. "I must request a different important meeting."

I stepped forward to meet him, lending my arm to support the bent frame of a body that had been used for years in service of the One. "Well met," I said quietly. "Of course we all want your counsel."

He smiled at me, and the smile felt like a benediction.

Kieran shifted restlessly. "Maybe you could go with Linette to the tower and—"

Lukyan planted his staff with force. "I must speak with Susan"—his gaze shifted to my son—"and Jake." The corner of his mouth shifted and he stepped in front of Kieran. "And you, Kieran of Braide Wood."

Kieran shook his head. "Maybe after we—"

"Now!" The elder songkeeper's voice held thunder that belied his frail appearance. "Join us at the worship tower."

Tristan slapped Kieran's back. "We'll wrangle the Council together. Go have your talk."

Kieran shot him a glare and clamped his jaw, but stalked toward the nearest tower entrance.

I walked beside Linette as we followed. "We heard in Rendor that the gathering was cancelled. Is it true?"

"Not if I can help it," she said.

She'd always reminded me of a fine-boned warbler, but whatever she'd experienced since I'd seen her last had given her a core of determination and strength that today put me in mind of a falcon.

Jake had taken my place at Lukyan's side, and we slowed our pace so they could keep up. Although he was helping the elder songkeeper, my son's gaze strayed often to Linette. My brow puckered. Was she another tie that would make Jake unready to return to our world? Hadn't we come here to bring him home?

And what if I have another purpose? the One whispered to my heart.

I pushed the thought aside. I couldn't face that question right now.

The vast worship tower was empty. My heart sank and my gaze sought out Linette's. At least a few of the local songkeepers ought to be here—no matter what threatened outside the city. Our feet echoed on the polished stone floor.

"So empty," Jake said sadly.

"Not empty." Linette faced us, lifting Caralad into her arms. She looked up at the space over our heads.

Kieran rubbed the back of his neck. "She's right."

A hint of reverence shaded his tone, forcing me to do a double take. Had aliens taken over Kieran's body?

He focused on Lukyan. "Why this meeting? Make it fast."

Okay, maybe not.

Mark grabbed a wooden armchair that rested near an entrance and brought it to Lukyan, who eased himself down and gestured for us to sit. Mark sank easily to the floor and I sat beside him, my bones protesting, still sore from the battering of our escape in the river and from camping last night. Linette gathered Caralad into her lap, and Jake settled beside her. He whispered something to her that made her giggle. Kieran scowled and knelt on the other side of Linette, as if ready to spring into battle at any moment.

His scowl faded when she turned to him. "Where's Nolan?" she asked quietly.

A hint of warmth tinged his features. "Running messages for us here in town. Don't worry, I won't let him out of Lyric."

She smiled and shook her head. "But I'm guessing he offered."

Kieran's low chuckle echoed in the mammoth space.

Now it was Jake's turn to shift impatiently. "Lukyan, I need to present myself to the Council and testify about what's happened."

Kieran nodded. "Having the new Restorer back will do a lot to hold off civil war."

My chest swelled as I thought about how my son had held the clans together in the past few seasons. It was bittersweet to look at Jake as a leader instead of my little boy, but I was so proud of him.

Pain flickered across Jake's face, and he pushed back a sleeve to show his unhealed wounds. "Except I'm not anymore."

Kieran's eyes widened, and Linette made a small sound of dismay, but Lukyan seemed unsurprised. The old songkeeper drew a slow breath. "And you worry about why the One would withdraw the gift?"

"His service here is finished." I said hopefully. "We can all go –"

"We're facing a civil war," Kieran said to Lukyan. "Some of our own clans are allying with our enemies, and who knows what allegiances Hazor and Kahlarea and Rhus have built with each other against us? And now we have no Restorer? I have a city's worth of questions for the One."

Lukyan shook his head. "There is something more important to discuss."

Our voices all rose in protest.

"What could be more important?"

"We must convince the . . ."

"Can we rally the guardians from . . ."

Whichever way this discussion moved, and whatever plans we made, I wanted to be clear that our involvement was temporary. We were not going home without Jake this time, especially now that he was no longer a Restorer. But arguments swirled, and no one listened to me.

Lukyan tapped his walking stick a few times. "Don't you see? The answer, the important answer, is right before you."

He captured our attention, then reached out to rest his hand on Caralad's head. The boy smiled up at Lukyan, and the old man's eyes watered. After a long pause, he pulled his gaze away to look at the rest of us. "The answer is this child."

CHAPTER
31

SUSAN

I'D EXPECTED ENCOURAGEMENT from Lukyan, perhaps a brief speech to remind us to trust the One. His focus on the little boy at this time of crisis left me confused and even disappointed. Was he being metaphoric? Was this some sort of parable? We needed concrete direction for immediate problems. Did the elderly on this world suffer from dementia?

Even Linette seemed startled. She tightened her grip on Caralad and studied Lukyan with a worried gaze.

Kieran sprang to his feet. "We have to get Jake in front of the Council—what's left of it. If you don't have any new information for us . . ."

"He's not from the clans," Lukyan said quietly.

I stared at the boy again. "He doesn't look Rhusican or Hazorite or Kahlarean. If he's not from the clans . . ."

Mark stiffened. "Are you saying he's from . . . where we come from?"

A poor lost boy from our side of the portal? I leaned toward Mark and whispered, "Are we meant to take him back with us?"

"No. You don't understand yet." Lukyan looked at the boy as if for permission to say more. "It's time to turn to the Deliverer for help."

"Which we'll do when he shows up one day." Kieran shifted his weight.

Lukyan frowned at him. "He is here."

Kieran turned, quickly scanning the round walls of the tower. There was nowhere for a man to hide.

Linette caught on first. "Caralad? Is it possible?"

Lukyan gripped the arms of the chair, his limbs as gnarled and weathered as the wood that held him. "If my only reason for thinking this was the voice of the One in my heart, I would understand your doubts. I'm an old man. Perhaps overwhelmed by my zeal as my days approach my final gathering, or perhaps confused by age and weariness." His alert eyes and wise smile made a mockery of those doubts. "But this child fulfills every prophecy. 'When three Restorers gather—'"

"Wait," I interrupted. "I thought that was part of Cameron's scheme."

Lukyan nodded. "You remember well. His false verses spoke about the time when several Restorers would come in quick succession, marking the end of the time of the Restorers. He twisted the true Verses. They speak of three Restorers at the season-end gathering, but not to do away with the gift of Restorers. Instead this will be a sign of the Deliverer, the fulfillment that all the Restorers pointed toward."

Linette soaked in his words, her expression rapt. "But the Verses are talking about something generations from now. They promise that even our enemies will know the words of our songs before the Deliverer comes."

Kieran groaned and sank back down.

She frowned at him. "What?"

"Think about it." Resignation shaded his words. "Our work in Hazor."

She gasped. "Of course."

My temples throbbed as I tried to fit the pieces together. Kieran and Linette had spent many seasons sharing the Verses with the people of Hazor, but did that count? Did that fulfill the promise? Maybe Lukyan was seeing pictures he wanted to see in a Rorschach blot of prophesies.

Lukyan's rheumy eyes sought mine. "Many of Rendor clan have told me that you did more than lead them out of Rhus. You shared the truth of the One with the Rhusicans."

Had I? It was true that when Nicco had torn around in my psyche, using my memories as his demented playground, he'd stumbled onto Someone he couldn't comprehend. In his own way, he'd been curious. But did that really mean that truth had been revealed to all the enemies?

I shook my head. "Even if our interactions with surrounding nations fit the prophecy, this couldn't be the time of three Restorers. As far as I can see, the clans no longer have even one."

Jake nodded. "After my capture by the Kahlareans, the Restorer gifts left me. I see that as a mercy. They couldn't succeed in their schemes without the blood of a Restorer. But now I'm not even sure whether I'm meant to provide leadership in Lyric any longer."

"I'm sure now that Jake's service to the clans is done, we're meant to return home," I said firmly.

Lukyan pointed an arthritic finger in my direction. "One." Then his arm swung to Kieran, who was still frowning. "Two." A gentle smile tugged at his lips as he pointed to Jake. "Three. This has never happened before."

My stomach tightened, strange currents skittering through my nerves. Could it be? Could we be observing the moment of fulfillment of the clan's most cherished prophecy? It would be like joining shepherds on their visit to a Bethlehem stable, knowing that the culmination of grace in all of human history was unfolding. I couldn't begin to untangle the theological implications of how the One was unveiling His plan for this world, but a small thrill ran through my stomach and my pulse quickened.

I looked at Caralad. Could he be the promised Deliverer, or was he just a lost child? Or worse, could he be a ruse from an enemy to sow confusion? Gentle eyes blinked back at me. If he were the Deliverer, why didn't he speak? And how could this little boy help the clans?

I reached for Mark's hand. Sitting awkwardly on the floor beside me, his eyes were wide, fixed on Caralad with an expression of awe. I wanted to give in to the tentative hope that the others were experiencing, but a part of my heart sank. My plans of disentangling our family and getting home slid further toward the horizon. How could Mark leave his world if he believed the promised Deliverer had come? How could I ask him to? And what would Jake's role be now? The familiar ache of being torn between two worlds throbbed in my chest.

Silence and confusion held us all captive for a moment. Finally, Kieran stood. I expected him to drag Jake away and hurry to the Council tower. Instead he crouched in front of Linette and the boy and offered his arm. Caralad's eyes twinkled as he gripped Kieran's forearm in a traditional warrior's greeting. Kieran held his gaze, then turned to confront the rest of us. "I'll be the first to say that the One's prophesies have not looked the way we expected." He raised an eyebrow in my direction, no doubt remembering what he'd originally thought of Tristan's suggestion that I was a promised Restorer. Unexpected and then some. "But even though that caused frustration and confusion, the One did what He promised."

Kieran was telling the rest of us to have faith? I rubbed my eyes and fought back a wave of vertigo. Meanwhile, Linette's face lit with gratitude. She briefly touched Kieran's cheek. A small gesture of appreciation or something more?

Jake sprang up and cleared his throat. "Lukyan, I agree this is important, but I do need to speak to the Council – what's left of it."

Kieran straightened and nodded. "And we have to meet with the Corros delegation quickly and see if we can prevent all-out civil war. Let's all go to the Council tower now. We'll bring the boy along, but this isn't the time to tell anyone who he might be."

Linette set Caralad on his feet and rose to stand beside him. Her chin tightened as she confronted Kieran. "I'm staying here. The clans have never needed the feast day gathering more than today. The best way to call others to worship is to worship."

Kieran bristled, ready to argue, but as he stared down Linette, the planes of his face softened. "Maybe you're right. Do you know of anyone else who plans to come?"

Beyond the arched entryways on all sides, the streets were empty. Linette's shoulders drooped. "Everyone I've spoken with is afraid or angry. Lukyan, what about the other songkeepers?"

Lukyan shook his head, suddenly looking every one of his years. Using the arms of the chair, he struggled to stand. "But I will try again. You should begin the first gathering day songs. I can care for the boy."

Caralad smiled at Lukyan, but shook his head. He turned away from all of us and knelt at the railing of the center dais. His small face tilted upward.

Linette picked up one of the small drums used for the call to worship. "It looks like I'll have company. He can stay with me. I'll begin the songs."

"And we'll come back to join in as soon as we can," Jake promised her.

"I could stay, too," I offered. I hated imagining Linette and the boy alone in this huge tower, futilely inviting the clans to gather. Sitting through negotiations with a clan that was threatening Lyric held no appeal. And to be honest, I couldn't handle seeing my husband and son growing further entrenched in life here.

Mark helped me to my feet. "We'll both need to inform the Council about what we learned in Kahlarea. Jake will need our support."

He was right. Still, my feet dragged as we left the tower.

Cameron was representing Corros, stirring up the strife. Meeting with the Council meant facing him. I wasn't sure I could do that. His evil went far beyond his initial cruelty toward me. His schemes had hurt Jake.

I clung to Mark's hand. Beside us, Jake strode toward the Council tower with all the confidence of a leader. He didn't look reluctant to confront Cameron.

Maybe I could also stay calm for this parlay and hold myself together when I saw Cameron. Or maybe I should sharpen my bootknife.

CHAPTER
32

LINETTE

AS THE OTHERS left, I carried my drum to a doorway, the solid floor of the tower seeming to waver under my feet. I had good reason to feel unsteady. Danger stalked Lyric from within and without. Why would the One send a helpless boy to a time like this?

My gaze sought Caralad where he knelt beside the center dais, his tender face tilted upward. Could he really be destined to become our Deliverer? He looked so ordinary, so defenseless.

I thought of the reaction of Wade's men. Fear and suspicion like that would put Caralad in danger. He needed a family to keep him safe until his destiny was confirmed. Perhaps Lukyan and I would find a couple who could give him the protection he needed.

Deeper determination strengthened my arm as I began beating the rhythm of the gathering call, my palm drawing a welcoming invitation from the taut leather. I couldn't understand all the ways of the One, but I could still trust Him, and I'd do all in my power to help Caralad. And right now, I'd worship, even with a voice of one.

The drum wasn't my usual instrument, but I did my best. Still, the doors of homes across the plaza remained closed, the streets empty. If we could just gather people, surely the conflicts and disputes would shrink in the presence of the One who created us all.

I moved to an archway on another side of the tower and tried again. The rhythm sounded as weak as a shallow pulse. In past seasons, the combined songkeepers from all the clans had created a compelling tide of sound that almost carried people toward their time with the One. The empty tower made me ache. The longing for those times of worship filled me—not my own puny wish but a deep longing stronger than myself. The One longed for His people. He invited. He called. He welcomed.

I raised my voice and began the traditional greeting song.

Called by the One,
Draw near.
Maker and Protector,
He is here!

I moved to yet another entryway and sang out to the city.

Why did I persist? Even if some of the Lyric clan heard and joined me, they were only one of the twelve clans. Unlike Lukyan and me, many of the other clans had ignored the feast day pilgrimage, too worried about rumors of imminent attack. Even if messengers reached them to reassure that it was safe to come, it could take days to gather.

Keeping the rhythm steady, I walked to the next of the eight archways and began to sing again.

From the direction of the guardian tower, a small group made their way toward me. Hope rose and I fought to keep my rhythm from rushing. As they grew closer, I saw waterfall emblems on tunics. Of course! Rendor clan—those who weren't needed for the emergency Council meeting.

Deep voices sang softly, joining the call.

A few doors slid open, revealing faces of Lyric families taking note that feast day was being honored after all. Bit by bit a trickle of local families moved out into the street. Some of the children wore torn and dirty tunics, not their best clothes. After the feast day had been cancelled, no one had bothered with their usual special preparations. But now, one by one, transtechs put aside their gadgets, grandmothers left their three-peg weaving, and tradesmen arrived with toddlers riding their shoulders. A mother cradled an infant, a grandson supported an old woman, and a husband and wife held hands and leaned against each other as they approached.

As people entered the tower, a few raised their brows at the sight of a lone child kneeling by the dais. Others smiled. How would they react if they heard what Lukyan believed about him?

Prodded by some protective instinct, I moved to Caralad's side. Normally, once all the visiting clans gathered, the songkeepers activated the dais that rose and rotated, helping us lead the songs. Since I was alone, I saw no reason for that pageantry. Instead, I put away the borrowed drum and picked up a rondalin. We filled a meager circle around the dais, but I was grateful for each person who had answered the call.

Before I could begin the next song, Lukyan limped into the tower followed by several songkeepers. Even Havid and Royan, with their pinched and sour faces, trailed the group. I hid a smile. Apparently, once they knew that the feast day gathering was proceeding, those two didn't want to miss their opportunity to be prominent. They brushed past Caralad and picked up their instruments, stepping onto the round platform.

Lukyan looked so weary. The trip from Braide Wood had already exhausted him, then the stress of alarms, hiding, not to mention the coldness and distrust of the local songkeepers. The past few days had taken a great toll. I hurried to take his arm, guiding him to his place. I was grateful that the others began the next song. My throat was hoarse from doing the call alone.

With no regard for Caralad's safety, Royan slid the lever to activate the dais.

I reached a hand for the child, offering to help him onto the platform, but he simply eased back and continued to kneel with his gaze fixed to the windows far above us.

Lukyan leaned heavily on his walking stick as the dais rotated slowly. "Thank the One for a few more voices," he whispered to me under the music.

"What do you think is happening at the Council tower?" I asked him. "Will the negotiations succeed? Do you think they'll all come join us soon?" Longing flooded me again as I pictured the quarrelling clans reaching enough of an agreement to join the gathering. The morning worship was always a tender time of confession, forgiveness, and new unity. We'd never needed that more.

The elder songkeeper lengthened his bent body, riveted on Caralad as our platform circled past. "The One holds our future. Let us place our needs in His hands." He smiled at the families surrounding us. "May the One stir our hearts beyond rote songs and responses."

The faces below us reflected the mixture of feelings welling in my heart. Uncertainty at the problems beyond the tower walls. Sadness at the sparse numbers. Gratitude at the One's invitation to meet with Him in this special way. Eagerness to hear from Him.

I strummed my rondalin, adding another layer of depth to the rising music, and joined my voice to the song. One emotion rose above the rest: love for the One who loved us first.

CHAPTER
33

SUSAN

MY MEMORIES OF the Council tower were far from fond, and my heart clenched as we entered the austere building. Our footsteps echoed against the hard, bare floors and crashed back from the obsidian walls. A foreboding sound.

Kieran marched straight to the Braide Wood chambers, while Jake veered off and followed the curved hallway toward the Rendor offices.

I hesitated. From my first visit, I'd been embraced by Braide Wood and claimed it as my clan. Should I join the Braide Wood representatives?

Mark's arm around my shoulder decided for me as he guided me to follow Jake.

Rendor's outer offices were empty. Unlike other times I'd attended Council sessions, today there was no pageantry. We didn't wait for the somber chimes to call us in. Jake and Mark didn't leave their sword belts in the outer office. We just crossed the clan office, pushed aside the next door, and strode into the central Council area.

The Rendor balcony already held several councilmembers who had been part of the group that traveled with us. Mark and Jake immediately entered a conversation with them, adding to the agitated murmurs throughout the tower. Twelve balconies encircled the massive room, with ramps leading down to the center. A few of the balconies remained dark, even token representation withdrawn. The clan sections that were lit had conspicuously empty seats.

On the far side from us, Kieran joined Tristan and several others from the Braide Wood delegation. I was glad to see they both wore their swords. This attempt at negotiation could easily devolve into armed combat.

As much as I'd hated the tedious bureaucracy of the Council in my past encounters, today's disorganization was worse. No clear leader guided the discussion, and tense voices rose and fell while no one seemed to be listening to anyone else.

Finally, I dragged my gaze to the Corros balcony. Men and women were arguing animatedly, and I spotted a few Hazorite soldiers with the group, but there was no sign of Cameron. Relief washed through me. Perhaps I wouldn't have to deal with him after all.

My focus skimmed past the Lyric balcony. A dark-haired man in a Council tunic had his back to the assembly, shoulders pulled back, arms gesturing with arrogant authority as he addressed the other Lyric councilmembers.

Ice seized my stomach, and I sank into a chair in the back row, trying to swallow.

How could I have forgotten Cameron's pompous voice announcing himself as the chief councilmember of Lyric? Even though he was speaking for the Corros delegation, he had planted himself with Lyric in the place of power, surrounded by several Council guards.

Why was anyone loyal to him after all the evil he'd committed?

As if hearing my thoughts, Cameron tugged on his tunic and strode confidently down the ramp to the center. The noise of discussions around the tower quieted. "As the most recent chief councilmember, I will open this emergency session of the Council. Corros clan has been offered help from Hazor in exchange for allegiance—"

"Traitor!" The shout came from someone in the Braide Wood balcony.

I grinned. Not everyone was ready to listen to the snake.

Cameron smoothed back his glossy, tar-colored hair and smirked. "I'm only here to present their position to the Council. Much like

Shamgar of the past, they have not received help from the other clans and have good reason to look elsewhere."

"Why did Corros ask you to represent them?" A woman from Blue Knoll leaned on her balcony railing and called out the challenge.

"They understand that I have also been treated unjustly by this Council, by Lyric, and by the clans."

"That's enough," Jake said under his breath. He clapped the shoulder of a Rendor clansman that he'd been talking with and pushed past a few others to stride down the ramp.

"Should we go with him?" I whispered to Mark. Even as I asked, I realized I needed to stop thinking of Jake as my little boy. He was a man with his own calling, his own suffering, his own courage. Watching his destiny unfold stirred a strange conflict in my soul. I felt joy and gratitude, yet strangely bereft at the same time. My role had changed so much, and I wasn't sure I could let go.

My husband leaned forward, keeping a careful eye on our son. "Let's give him a moment."

He was right, but I frowned. Why was it so much easier for Mark to accept each new season in our children's lives? What was wrong with me that I wanted to cling?

A sudden silence gripped the room. I was delighted to see the flicker of shock when Cameron saw my son—alive and back in Lyric.

"The only injustice you've received is a lack of trustworthy guards to keep you from causing more trouble." Jake took a place near Cameron, subtly usurping the center of the shiny black floor.

"Ah, the self-proclaimed Restorer returns after abandoning his people when danger threatened," Cameron sneered. "Seems to be a pattern with those mythic leaders—the ones in whom poor misguided people put their faith."

To my shock, a rumble of resentful agreement circled the room. How unfair! Each Restorer had suffered and most had died to help the clans. The cost had been huge. None of us could solve every problem or remain indefinitely . . . but to accuse Jake of abandoning the clans when he'd been kidnapped—

"The Restorers were revealed by the One." Jake's voice carried easily to the top row of each balcony. He spared a disdaining glance in Cameron's direction. "You proclaimed yourself king against everything the Verses teach."

The tower fell silent again, and Jake snatched the opportunity to continue. "I'm here today to testify that once again Cameron has consorted with enemy nations. He sold me to the—"

"I accepted the role of king because the people needed a strong leader who would not abandon them. Someone who could help the clans take their role among the independent nations around us."

Cameron was a psychopath. Surely the delegates in the tower would shout him down and order him dragged out.

Instead, many councilmembers sat forward in their chairs, or leaned on their balcony, listening with rapt attention. A few heads even nodded.

"Some of the clans aren't ready to take their place in the modern world. That is their choice," Cameron continued. His arrogance and condescension made my stomach sour. "But is it fair to hinder struggling clans who do have the courage to move forward in new alliances? Corros is grateful for the assistance that Hazor has offered them. And Lyric is ready to become a center for those more enlightened clans."

The picture his words painted began to make sense. Why not allow such treaties? It would keep everyone happy. A cloudy lethargy soaked through me.

Mark grabbed my hand. "Susan," he whispered. "Something's wrong."

I shook myself and gauged the reactions around the tower. The councilmembers seemed drawn in, entranced. They were acting like—

"Rhusican poison," I whispered. *Holy One, help us!* My breathing shortened and stuttered as I clutched Mark's hand.

Cameron kept speaking, holding everyone in thrall. Jake held his ground, but frowned in confusion. He opened his mouth and then closed it without speaking.

I scanned the balconies again, studying each face.

Then I spotted him. Deep in the shadows of the Lyric balcony, hidden by a hooded cloak, a man stood with gaze fixed on the center of the tower. He was smiling.

His face had haunted my nightmares since my captivity in Rhus. Nicco.

The Rhusican who had violated my mind and assaulted my memories again and again, until I was a broken shell.

A whimper escaped my lips and Mark pulled me close. "Susan, what is it?"

I wanted to close my eyes. To will myself away. But if I looked away from Nicco, would he disappear? Was he a paranoid delusion caused by trauma? I was afraid to speak, afraid to attract Nicco's attention.

"Lyric balcony," I managed to whisper.

Mark followed my gaze. "I see him. Is he a—"

"Shhh." Too late. Nicco pulled his attention away from Cameron and saw me. The distance across the wide tower seemed to compress. Nicco's teeth bared as his smile grew.

Horror flooded me. I fought for air. *Susan, focus. Think about your purpose here.* Support Jake's testimony. Help the clans past this crisis. Bring Jake home.

Don't go back there now. Don't panic—

I bolted for the door and escaped into the outer office, gasping for breath and trembling.

Mark followed and surrounded me with his arms. Then he turned me, pressing me against his chest. "Holy One, we need You. Be our defender," he whispered.

His prayer steadied me, but I still struggled to speak.

"Susan, talk to me. What's wrong? We can stop a Rhusican. We've done it before."

I pushed away from him and choked out my words. "Not *a* Rhusican. It's him. Nicco. The one who . . ."

I wrapped my arms around my stomach and doubled over. Waves of nausea coursed through me. I couldn't do this. Couldn't face him. Couldn't face the memories of that trauma—

Mark grabbed my shoulders and pulled me up to face him. "Susan, you're stronger than this. Jake needs our help. The clans need us." His harsh tone almost hid the thread of compassion that warmed his eyes.

But the firm reminder was what I needed. I drew in a breath that filled my chest and lifted my chin. "When we can't go back . . ."

"We go forward." The corner of his mouth canted upward. "That's right. I can't understand all that happened to you in Rhus. But I know this: you won. You showed Nicco the One, and he let you leave. You rescued Rendor clan. My clan."

He was right. The horror of that captivity was real, and I didn't need to feel shame for being slow to recover. I might bear the scars for the rest of my life. But as bad as it had been, the One had never left me. I was standing here today.

"The One is bigger than Nicco," I said quietly. My voice trembled, but my heart strengthened. "The One is greater than all of Rhus. He's stronger than my worst dread."

Admiration shone in Mark's eyes. "And because He loves us, we can trust Him."

I drew every ounce of strength from our moment together just before the outer door slid open.

A storm gathered across Mark's face and I spun to see who entered.

Nicco tossed back his hood. Auburn curls framed his face, and his smile chilled my bones. "Medea's pet. I've missed you."

Mark stepped in front of me, his hand clenched on the grip of his sword.

"Wait." I moved beside Mark. This was my battle to fight. "Nicco, what are you doing in Lyric?"

He shrugged. "Helping an ally."

"You chose the wrong ally. Cameron is using you. If you really want to help your people—"

He laughed. "Always so concerned about my welfare. Does he know? Does he know how much you care?"

The dangerous scrape of steel on leather told me Mark had drawn his sword, but I kept my eyes on Nicco and lifted my chin. "Mark knows that the One cares about each soul. Even the enemies of the clans. Even the enemies that can't recognize truth when they crash into it."

Mark's anger burned hot enough for my skin to feel the heat, but at least for now he held his ground. Behind us, the drone of Cameron's voice was interrupted by a shout and the chaos of over-lapping outbursts. Nicco rubbed his eyes and pinched the bridge of his nose.

I tilted my head. "Sounds like your pal Cameron is losing con-trol of the Council. That's all right. Jake will explain everything to them."

Instead of trying again to provoke Mark or torment me, Nicco winced. He seemed strangely disinterested in the noise erupting from the Council chamber.

"Cameron isn't your real reason for being here," I said softly. "And it looks like you've been away from home too long."

That drew a flare of rage from Nicco's eyes. "You think you understand us."

I held my ground. "You're still curious about the One. You came seeking Him."

He pressed the heels of his hands against his temples, pushing hard against whatever chaos swirled through his mind. "A whim. A useless one."

Pity tugged me. A strange sensation when all I wanted to feel was hatred. Or was Nicco simply manipulating my thoughts? I looked at Mark.

Every tendon in his jaw was tight, each muscle in his body rigid. He held his sword ready to run Nicco through if I gave him any signal. No confusion in his feelings.

Nicco backed up a step, worrying his head side to side. He was clearly in pain, and I doubted he had enough control to twist my reactions at the moment. And the longer we kept him occupied, the more time we gave Jake to bring reason and truth to the Council.

Holy One, what do I do? What do You want?

The Rhusican was evil. Selfish, corrupt, frivolous.

"And such were some of you . . ." The verse nudged my heart. Without the One, I was no better.

"Useless," he moaned again.

"Maybe not so useless," I said quietly. "But this isn't the place for what you seek. If you have the courage—"

"Courage?" Nicco pulled his hands away from his head and straightened, arrogance puffing his chest even though lines of pain still tightened around his eyes.

"If you have the courage to come with us to the worship tower," I continued firmly, "I believe your curiosity will be satisfied. But from what I remember, you were afraid of anyone you couldn't control."

"Susan," Mark said under his breath. "What are you—"

Nicco laughed. "Anything to stop the boredom. These people are empty-headed. Easy to sway."

Jake's beautiful baritone voice carried through the open door. "Awesome in majesty, perfect in power." He sang the words to the ancient song, and one by one others joined him. Deep rumbling warrior voices, gentle soprano councilmembers, some off-key, some breathy, but all beautiful.

Nicco frowned, then shrugged. "Show me this tower."

I turned to Mark. "Let one of the Rendor councilmembers know. The worship gathering has begun, and the Council should all come. They can finish negotiations later."

Mark shook his head. "You've seen how he twisted minds in the Council tower. What if he . . ."

I rested my hand on the tense muscles of Mark's sword arm. "Let the One worry about what Nicco is able to do at the worship tower." I managed the confident words without a quaver in my voice, even while my stomach twisted and burned and my nerves screamed at me to run.

The song finished. We couldn't risk letting the Rhusican back into the Council meeting. I finally understood why the One had brought me here. Nicco wouldn't let anyone else introduce him to the One. And no one else had a better chance to dissuade him from helping Cameron ruin the clans. "Mark, now is your chance to tell the Council. I'll take Nicco to the tower and meet you there."

Nicco smirked. "She wants to be alone with me."

His juvenile attempt to cause trouble was so obvious, it stirred only a flicker of annoyance. Even Mark, whose fury had been so palpable, ignored Nicco.

Instead, my husband lowered his sword and gave me a worried look. "Are you sure about this?"

I glanced at my worst enemy, and then smiled back at my dearest love. "I'm fine. Go talk to the Council."

CHAPTER 34

LINETTE

STANDING IN THE worship tower at my assigned spot on the dais, I listened as waves of music rose and fell. Caralad continued to kneel by the railing, also soaking in the melodies. Images from the past season spun through my mind. Loss and joy, forgetting and remembering, doubt and certainty. Through it all, the rich music of the One's love had carried me.

I wished more people were here for this reminder of His goodness. So few had gathered here today, my heart threatened to break. But my disappointment quickly faded under the overwhelming presence of the One. With His help, I'd create music that lifted hearts to Him, however many or few people could hear.

Although we'd begun late, we followed the full traditional pattern of gathering day. After hearing the One's invitation and rejoicing, we knelt and bared our hearts to Him. Some songkeepers didn't like the songs of confession, or the times of silence and tears. I loved it. When the One showed me where I'd been blind to my own selfishness, I didn't feel crushed by despair. Instead, I felt relief as I acknowledged how much I needed Him. How much I longed for a Deliverer.

I glanced at Caralad. As others bowed their heads in remorse, he continued to smile up at the grey light that seeped through the windows and embraced the walls.

Expectant silence formed throughout the tower. Looking out, I spotted Susan. A hooded stranger stood beside her, glaring uneasily around the room.

Lukyan stepped forward and took a slow breath, wheezing tightly. When this feast day was over, I would insist that he visit a healer. Even braced with his walking stick, he wavered on his feet. I eased closer to him, ready to support him if needed, as he recited a long portion of the Verses. Finally he finished with the declaration, "The Verses of Life."

The small crowd answered, "One without end."

A musician near the dais introduced a tender melody on a wooden flute. As we began the next song, more people appeared in the archway that faced the central plaza. My eyes widened as dozens of councilmembers made their way toward the center of the tower. Had the meeting ended so quickly? I recognized people from several different clans, then spotted Tristan and Kieran. Neither looked at peace. That didn't tell me much, since Kieran always wore a worried frown.

Jake walked forward reverently, then stood behind the group encircling the dais. He caught my gaze and smiled. Near him, Markkel scanned the room then spotted Susan and moved toward her. Markkel took her hand, and Susan rested her head against his shoulder.

The spirit of the room shifted with the arrival of everyone from the Council meeting. Expressions of distrust and disagreement were as evident as a sour note in a melody. The clans were fracturing. Our enemies no longer needed to conquer us. We were destroying ourselves.

I kept singing, layering the lyrics with the cry of my heart. *Holy One, heal our clans.*

The last notes faded. Time for another songkeeper to recite Verses.

A hush filled the tower, like the silence when a mother waits for her baby's first cry or a child listens for the comforting footsteps of his father.

In the momentary quiet, a clear, soaring voice began to sing. Startled, I glanced at all the songkeepers. This wasn't one of the traditional songs.

The others on the dais were also looking around, confused.

The tone was so pure the very walls of the tower seemed to vibrate. The melody skipped, jumped, rose. Lukyan slid the switch that slowed and then stopped the dais. It lowered back into place, and when it settled, I was directly in front of Caralad, who still knelt with his face lifted.

He was singing. The most extraordinary music I'd ever heard lifted from his small throat.

The light has come.
We see His face.
His love is our true
Resting place.

My shock was so great that at first I barely heard the lyrics. Others around the tower craned their necks to see who was singing.

Oblivious to the way he was disrupting the order, Caralad continued to sing.

The Maker's love was cast aside;
A shroud of grey proclaimed the rift.
And every day the heavens cried,
Awaiting the One's promised gift.

He returned to the chorus and my fingers found a chord on the rondalin. Whatever his purpose in introducing this new song, I would try to learn it, to follow.

The light has come.
We see His face.
His love is our true
Resting place.

My focus was down on my strings when I heard several gasps. A girl in the crowd pointed to the windows high above us. A woman screamed and fell to her knees, gathering her children close.

Light sparkled on the marble floor, as if the songkeepers had all held up brilliant lightcubes at the same time. I looked up and hit a wrong string. I quickly squinted and shielded my eyes, forsaking my accompaniment. Something terrifying was happening. The grey sky beyond the windows was tearing apart like overworn fabric. I instinctively looked for Kieran, but he was no longer where I'd last seen him.

Everything in the tower glowed. I stepped off the dais and put a sheltering arm around Caralad. He paused for a breath and offered a tranquil smile that steadied me. Then he stood and raised his arms, singing the chorus again. The song floated over the sounds of panic throughout the tower. His words were so exultant that I knew if this world were about to fracture apart, the arms of the One would carry us all safely to the next.

Standing beside Caralad, I fought back my terror under the brilliant light and sang with him, finding a shaky harmony.

The light has come.
We see His face.
His love is our true
Resting place.

People around us began to elbow their way toward the doors, even those who had been huddled on the floor. A few looked to the songkeepers for answers, but even the worship leaders were pale and trembling. All but Lukyan stepped off the dais and hurried away.

Caralad and I finished the song, and I set aside my rondalin. What should I do next? I knelt beside the boy. "What does it mean?" I whispered.

Someone pushed through the crowd and grabbed my arm.

"Come with me." Kieran barked the order. "We need to see what's happening."

"Wait. Help Lukyan." The tower had nearly emptied, and the elder songkeeper sagged against his staff, alone on the dais. I scooped up Caralad, and Kieran supported Lukyan, leading us to one of the arching entries where my friends were clustered.

Tristan, Jake, Markkel, Susan—all stared up at the sky, shielding their eyes. Past the torn grey that slipped away like running water, a vibrant color glowed. The blue of a feathered moth, but much sharper. A blue like none I'd ever seen. A clean, rich, deep blue of holiness.

"Is it an invasion?" Tristan pointed at the fierce glowing circle that stood out against the wide expanse of blue. "Do the Hazorites have a weapon that could do this?"

Kieran scanned the streets. Those who had been at the tower ran for their homes as if a roof could protect them from the world tearing apart. "Nothing I've heard of. It would have to be a massive syncbeam. But it doesn't seem to be targeting anything."

Markkel shook his head, open mouthed and dazed. Inexplicably, Susan gave a breathless laugh. "It's all right. It's only the sun." Despite her reassuring words, she also seemed awestruck by the huge change above us.

I glanced around. "Where is the stranger who was with you?"

Susan inhaled deeply, as if happily drawing in the unusual light. "He ran away after Caralad's song." Her smile turned bittersweet. "At least he heard it."

Markkel pressed his forehead against hers. "And who knows what that song will do?"

Tristan circled us impatiently, waving an arm at the sky. "So can any of you explain this?"

"The song did," Jake said. The confidence and strength in his voice helped me push back my fear. He faced us all and smiled. "The grey shroud, the mark of separation, the daily rain. And now . . ."

Lukyan wavered, bent, and sank to his knees in spite of Kieran's efforts to hold him. "Now the light has come." Lukyan's voice trembled with both awe and conviction. His wrinkles stood out like weathered rock under the terrifying brightness.

I crouched beside him. His breath sounded tight and shallow. "We need a healer," I said.

"No," Lukyan gasped. "Protect the light."

I glanced at the sky again. What was he talking about? How could I protect the searing light?

Across from me, Kieran knelt, supporting Lukyan's shoulders. "He means the boy."

Our gazes met. If Caralad were truly the Deliverer, as Lukyan believed, he'd need protection. But where would he be safe? We had to find a family to care for him. Perhaps Tristan and Kendra? Or Markkel and Susan? Could that be why they were here again? Maybe they could take him somewhere far away until he was old enough to announce his identity.

Lying back against Kieran, Lukyan reached for my hand. He saw the worries that played across my face and wheezed in another breath. "You must keep him."

"Keep him?" I shook my head. "I would love to, but he needs a family. Stronger, wiser people to protect him."

"You don't have to do this alone." Lukyan placed my hand in Kieran's, his gaze riveted to Kieran's face. "Will you protect her house?"

Kieran's eyes widened, then resolve tightened his jaw. He gave a nod of recognition toward Caralad, but avoided my eyes. "I've already pledged to be the One's house protector. I'll guard them both."

Lukyan sighed with a half smile, and a second crackling breath slipped from his lips. Then his chest stopped moving, his eyes fixed, unseeing, on the strange sky.

Kieran's hand tightened around mine. Susan pressed her fist against her lips. "No, not now." She stared at Lukyan as if she could will breath back into his body, then with a small cry, she buried her face in Markkel's shoulder.

Panic stiffened my arms, and I pulled away from Kieran. I grabbed Caralad with shaking hands. "Heal him. Please. We need him more than ever."

Caralad's brown eyes were pools of compassion. Ancient eyes that understood.

I nudged him toward Lukyan. Caralad had healed Wade. He'd returned my memory. If he were truly the Deliverer, he could restore Lukyan.

Instead, the boy gently closed Lukyan's eyes, touching him with somber affection, as if he'd known him for a lifetime, instead of only a few days. Then Caralad turned away from Lukyan and hugged me.

Sorrow groaned from deep in my chest. I wanted to shake him, demand he do something, but instead I clutched him, allowing his small arms to comfort me.

Nearby, Susan cried softly, and Markkel murmured soothing words. While Tristan and Jake held a quiet discussion about our next steps, Kieran eased Lukyan into his arms and lifted him.

"We'll take him to the songkeeper lodge," Kieran said quietly as he led the way. I was grateful he had decided a course of action for all of us. Numb, lost, I managed to hold Caralad's hand and walk in our quiet procession to the nearby building. By now the streets had emptied, and I wanted to hide as well—hide from the searing light that seemed to expose even more of the brokenness and chaos that reigned in Lyric, and in my own heart.

Our arrival added to the dismay of the songkeepers who paced the common room, wringing their hands and arguing. Grief etched their faces when they saw Lukyan's lifeless body, but so did guilt. After all, these same songkeepers had resisted Lukyan's efforts to hold the gathering and had only reluctantly joined me in the tower.

Havid rolled out a pallet and Kieran gently laid Lukyan down.

"Was it the broken sky? Is that what killed him?" Royan asked, shooting an accusing glare toward Caralad.

Kieran straightened. "The One called Lukyan home."

"But what are we supposed to do? What do we tell the people?" asked another songkeeper.

I picked up Caralad, needing the comfort of his warmth, the touch of his silky hair beneath my chin. Kieran looked to me, and I realized he was waiting for me to answer. I was just beginning to absorb the responsibility I'd accepted by agreeing to care for Caralad. Giving counsel to the other songkeepers seemed impossible. Lukyan would have known what to tell them.

Holy One, guide me, please.

"We will teach them the new song." My voice was steady, truly a gift from the One. "The light has come. The promises of the One are unfolding, and He will guide our clans."

The admiration that shone in Kieran's eyes warmed me.

"But what about—?"

"How will we—?"

"Why did—?"

Worried questions from the other songkeepers pelted me like stones.

"Take care of Lukyan," Kieran said, interrupting their queries. He guided me toward the door. "We'll come back when we're able."

Again I felt a wave of gratitude that he was making decisions. He hustled our group back out into the vibrant street and away from the questions I didn't know how to answer.

"Thank you," I said softly.

He raised an eyebrow. "You know how I feel about songkeepers. No sense letting them badger us."

I smiled. "Should I be insulted? I'm a songkeeper, too, you know."

"I haven't forgotten," he said, rubbing his forehead. Was the harsh light making his head hurt? Or was it the promise Lukyan had demanded from him? A frisson of regret skimmed through my chest. The poor man didn't want to be saddled with responsibility for Caralad and me. He was still adjusting to being a father to Nolan.

I looked behind us. Markkel and Susan were talking with their son; Tristan stood nearby, keeping an eye on the surroundings, hand on his sword. For the first time, I realized Kieran's son was missing. "Where's Nolan?"

"I sent him to find as many messengers in Lyric as he could. We're sending them out to let all the clans know it's safe to come to Lyric. That the threat of civil war is over and Corros has reached an agreement with the other clans."

"They have?"

"Not exactly. Let's just say I was being . . . optimistic." He shrugged. "A Rhusican was influencing the meeting, but Susan drew him away. Markkel and Jake then convinced the Council that attending the tower worship was vital, and the debates could be postponed."

I looked at him, askance. "So what will happen when even more angry, worried people from other clans arrive tomorrow?"

Kieran shielded his eyes and looked up. "My guess is that everyone will be so preoccupied with the changes to the sky that other arguments will be forgotten. And Hazor, Kahlarea, Rhus . . . they were behind a lot of the efforts to fracture the clans, and they'll have their own problems now, too."

He led us to a small park behind the guardian tower. Plantings of ferns surrounded a small fountain, and a circle of trees shielded weathered wooden benches from the street, providing privacy. Not that privacy was hard to find today. People had disappeared into buildings like groundcrawlers into their tunnels. Uneasy, I dared another glance at the glaring light above us and wondered if we should follow that example.

I sank onto a bench, and Caralad squirmed from my arms. He ran to the fountain and splashed happily, watching droplets sparkle as they fell back into the basin. Just like any other boy. How could he also be the Deliverer?

The others watched him, their expressions reflecting some of the same confusion and questions, but none of the hostility or suspicion that Caralad had received in Braide Wood and Lyric.

"Child, what are we supposed to do?" I asked him. He smiled at me, but didn't speak. He just returned to his carefree play. A flare of irritation throbbed in my head. His voice worked. We'd all heard him. Why wasn't he answering?

I turned to the others. "Why would the Deliverer come as a help-less child? Why won't he explain his plans?" My voice quavered. "And why did the One take Lukyan from us when we need his wisdom?"

Susan settled on a bench nearby. "Where we're from, the One sent His Deliverer as a baby." A thread of sadness slipped into her tone, and she reached up for Markkel's hand. "Then He—"

Markkel coughed and shook his head. She met his gaze and they exchanged some sort of silent message, because she nodded and pressed her lips together, offering me an apologetic shrug.

Jake sat on the edge of the fountain, dangling his hand in the water. "The important truth to focus on is that this is good news. Even if we don't fully understand the details, the Deliverer has come. And Lukyan lived long enough to see this day."

I managed a bittersweet smile. "You're right. Every day of his life he longed for this moment. He would want us to celebrate." I opened my arms, and Caralad ran to me. Smoothing the curls back from his forehead, I studied his face again. What a wonder that I was touching the long-promised Deliverer. He was real! He was here!

Kieran came to sit beside me, blocking my view of Jake. He tousled Caralad's hair absently. "We have another problem."

Tristan rolled his shoulders. "You mean besides the messages you sent promising that Lyric is safe when nothing is safe?"

Kieran narrowed his eyes. "Aren't any of you paying attention? It's time for the rains."

He was right. Past time. Every single day, the rains marked each afternoon, providing water for homes, for fields, for travelers. I stared at the pool around the fountain, wondering how long that precious water would last. "What will we do?"

Markkel cleared his throat. "Susan's home has a sky like this. Rain falls, just not each day. The way things are done may need to change. Seasons may shift. Temperatures may range more. But the song said this is a sign of blessing, so you can trust it will not bring harm."

"Except for people's panic," Tristan growled. "We'll need to set up guardians to prevent hoarding. I take it we can resume the Council meeting?" He looked to me.

I made a quick decision. "We'll begin the tower worship again tomorrow, after more clans have arrived."

He nodded, as if accepting the orders of a commander. Tristan had always been kind to me, but treated me like a perpetual first-year. Untried, weak. His ready acceptance of my suggestion startled me.

"Then let's get the Council gathered as quickly as we can." Tristan walked a few steps toward the main square.

I rose to follow, but Kieran rested a hand on my shoulder. "We'll catch up with you at the Council offices," he said to the others.

Jake frowned and seemed about to protest, but Markkel whispered something to him and guided him away. Susan's gaze shifted between Kieran and me, and she gave me an encouraging smile. "Let me take care of Caralad for a while, so you two can talk."

A flare of protectiveness rose up, and I began to object, but Caralad ran to Susan, jumping as he neared her. She swooped him up and spun him, laughing.

I stepped toward them, not willing to let him out of my sight.

Caralad waved good-bye, eyes sparkling.

His joy was contagious, and I let my worry slide away . . . until they all left us and I turned my gaze to Kieran. His expression was grim and closed—the look of a warrior about to engage an opponent in lethal combat.

CHAPTER 35

LINETTE

I'D OFTEN VISITED this small garden near the worship tower in years past, but today it looked as strange as a foreign land. The bright light from what Susan had called a sun enlivened the color of each leaf and flower. Then the air moved, another unfamiliar sensation, brushing over my skin like a touch. Leaves overhead flickered and danced. The play of light and shadow was dizzying.

"Markkel and Susan say this is normal where they come from?" I breathed.

Kieran snorted. "I don't find much that's normal about them." He prowled the perimeter of the garden, scanning each entrance as if we were a walled city expecting attack. Who was he watching for? Everyone in Lyric seemed to be hiding indoors as if it were night.

A sudden thought struck me. "Do you think this light will continue all night?"

He shrugged and sat down on the bench, leaving as much space as possible between us. "I guess we'll find out."

A long heavy silence stretched, broken only by the droplets of water in the fountain and the swishing of air moving through the leaves once again. Would I ever get used to that strange wonder?

Kieran abruptly grabbed my hand.

I startled and had to fight an impulse to flinch away. As branches shifted overhead, shadows moved across his hand, the hand that

Lukyan had joined with mine so recently. The poor man had been coerced into a pledge to help me. As if I hadn't caused him enough trouble in Hazor. What must he be feeling? Trapped? Angry?

I finally pulled my focus upward, and my gaze traced the scar across his forehead. My fault as well. I hadn't heeded Kieran's warnings to stay away from Zarek. He'd never told me what he'd suffered at the king's hands before escaping and rescuing me. Did he blame me?

There were thousands of things I wanted to say, yet nothing I knew how to put into words. "I'm sorry," I finally managed.

"Sorry?" Kieran had been staring at our hands, but when he met my eyes, his were hard and remote.

"I'm sorry that Lukyan made you pledge . . . to . . . that is . . ."

"I suppose you'd prefer Jake," he said sourly.

"Jake? What does he have to do with this?"

His eyes narrowed to that assessing glare that saw so much. "You don't . . . care for him?"

"Of course I do. He sacrificed a lot to help our people, when he isn't even from here."

"That's not what I mean."

He wasn't making any sense. I shook my head. "I don't understand."

He studied me for another moment, and slowly the angry edge faded from his expression. His lips moved as if they wanted to smile, but then he sighed. "And then there's Dylan."

I struggled to follow the conversation, distracted by the feel of his rough calluses against the palm of my hand, the warmth of his nearness. Maybe I should just start over. "I know I've caused you a lot of trouble in the past. I'm trying to apologize."

This time he couldn't hold back a wry smile, even though his eyes still held a brooding shadow. "Oh, you've been trouble. I won't deny that."

There was an undercurrent in his voice that I couldn't translate. I tried again. "I feel badly that Lukyan made you promise . . . I don't know how—"

"How you'll stand having me underfoot? Because I will be."

A strange flare of hope spun through my heart. Did he really want to be—

"Caralad is the Deliverer." Conviction and purpose pulled his spine taller. "I wouldn't trust anyone else to guard him."

The hope fizzled, and I pulled my hand away, bracing against the solid wood of the bench. Kieran was committed to Caralad. I was the inconvenience that came along with that promise.

"What did you want to talk about?" I said flatly. After all, he was the one who had insisted we remain behind. Why was I trying to communicate with a man who was about as forthcoming as the stones beneath our feet?

He groaned, braced his elbows on his legs, and pressed his forehead against his fists. "Shades of Shamgar . . ." He muttered something I couldn't hear. "I wanted to know if you're all right . . . with Lukyan's request," he added awkwardly.

Kieran was always six steps ahead of everyone else, full of strategies, ready with confident statements. His uncertainty was odd . . . and endearing. I had an urge to comfort him, as I would Nolan. I quashed that desire and let him flounder.

When I remained silent, he straightened and glared at me. "Can we do this? Can you see us . . . together?" He made a helpless gesture.

What would it be like to see Kieran every day? My imagination wove a happy picture of a cabin beneath a honey-limbed tree in Braide Wood.

Oh, Linette, foolish girl. Kieran would never fit that life. My eyes stung.

He grabbed my shoulders, dark eyes piercing deep into my soul, uncovering my secret longings, searching for hints of . . . what? What was he looking for?

"Fine," he bit out. "Someone has to show a little courage here. I've told myself a million times that this could never work. You're too gentle, too young. Yet you invade my thoughts like stinging beetles I can't chase away."

My eyes widened. Realization spiraled upward through my chest, sparkling across my heart.

"You're a songkeeper, for pity's sake," he continued. "And you never give me any sign. How can I even ask?"

"Ask what? So far, you've been giving me a list of everything wrong with me."

Another gust of air tossed a strand of hair across my eyes. I reached for it at the same time as Kieran. He won, tucking the hair back, then leaving his hand against my cheek. My breath quickened, moving past lips softened in surprise.

"Linette?" His voice was rough and throbbed like the tower drums, stirring me with a compelling invitation.

He complained I'd never given him a sign. Perhaps he wasn't as perceptive as I'd always believed. I had to at least match his courage. I smiled and dared a small nod.

Now his eyes widened. Shock, disbelief, and then joy flared. He moved suddenly, like the skilled warrior that he was, claiming my lips.

I stiffened for a moment, then melted as his arms surrounded me. I met his embrace, clinging with an abandon that finally proclaimed what I'd been afraid to admit, even to myself. Time spun away, and all the sparkling light and stirring air of the garden took up residence in my soul.

His chest rumbled with a half-sigh, half-moan, and he pulled away, holding me at arms' length.

From inside my happy fog, my lids only half open, I watched the play of emotions in the man I'd loved for so long. He frowned, suddenly worried. "Are you sure? You're not just going along because—"

I laughed. I couldn't help it. How could he still be uncertain after the song we'd just sung together with our kiss? Giggles dissolved me.

His frown deepened, so I kissed him again, quickly, firmly, then said, "I love you, Kieran of Braide Wood."

Had I really blurted out those words?

I must have, because his slow smile lifted every hard angle of his face. "And I love you, you maddening songkeeper—may the One help us both," he added under his breath.

Lyric was in chaos, plans needed to be made and leadership reestablished. But we lingered for precious moments. I rested in Kieran's arms as we talked quietly. He told me about how his feelings had grown and how he'd feared he was wrong for me. I admitted the love I'd fought to suppress while we were in Hazor. Our conversation was as much a confession—and equally as sweet—as the songs I'd sung in the worship tower that morning. Brought into the open, our various fears and doubts lost all power. The new sun glowed down on us as a tender benediction.

"I wish Lukyan could sing our life-bond song," Kieran said, slowly drawing us back to reality.

In spite of a heart full of joy, I found there was still room for a corner of sadness. I'd miss my teacher so much. "I wonder how he knew?"

"He wasn't as dense as you've been," Kieran grumbled.

I pulled away and tried to glare at him, but only managed to giggle. Then I sobered as a new thought struck me. "What will Nolan say?"

Kieran grinned. "How can you ask? He adores you. He treats you like a mother already. The whole time we've been in Lyric, he's badgered me nonstop to visit Braide Wood and see you." Now it was his turn to turn sober. "I wanted to, but we were making trips into Hazor near Corros to learn about their plans, and I was working with Tristan to find Jake."

He almost managed Jake's name without scowling. The reminder of his ridiculous jealousy made me smile. "I know. Saving the clans, as usual. What would we do without you?"

He shook his head. "You used to be in awe of me, you know. Back when I was a Restorer."

"Really?" I tilted my head. "No, no memory of that. Maybe a few of my memories are still lost?"

He chuckled as he stood, offering me his hand. "Come, songkeeper. We'd better catch up with the rest. By now Susan has probably invited enemy armies for dinner, and Tristan has likely reassigned guardians to all the wrong places."

I rose, reluctant to leave our sanctuary. "I want to be sure Caralad is all right. Maybe I can convince him to tell us what we're supposed to do next."

"And," he added, "I want to find a songkeeper to oversee the life-bond. Today."

As we walked from the park, I stared shyly at the ground. "Today?"

"Yes." Now that his earlier uncertainty had fled, he sounded positively dictatorial.

And not one tiny parcel of my heart disagreed.

In a quiet evening ceremony, as the sky faded to a more usual shade of dusk, we stood beneath the windows of the worship tower. Kieran and I knelt at the rail, hand in hand, and Lyric's eldest song-keeper proclaimed us joined. The reclusive and mysterious man rarely involved himself in normal songkeeper activities, but Markkel apparently knew him from past encounters and had convinced him to come.

Tristan stood behind Kieran, grumbling that Kendra should be there. Markkel and Susan watched fondly, and Nolan sang along to the life-bond chorus gleefully. Caralad blessed us with his gentle smile, then stepped back to hold Jake's hand, as if he sensed that Jake needed comforting. My heart was so full that affection spilled out to all the precious people in my life. But as my focus returned to Kieran's face, the love welling in my soul poured out in a torrent. His steady gaze promised me trust, loyalty, and an adoration deeper than I'd ever known. When we rested our foreheads against each other, our breaths mingling, I silently asked the One to help me bring joy to each of Kieran's days. When we stood after a last Verse, the light in my husband's eyes felt like the One's reassurance that He had heard and answered that request.

Although we didn't know what to expect of the sky as we left the worship tower, darkness fell as it always had. However, the nighttime still held a surprise. My breath caught at the sight of thousands of pinpoints of light adorning the black sky, a new marvel in a day full of wonders. We stared at them a long time, my hand clasped with my husband's, Nolan and Caralad on either side of us, before we all took refuge in spare councilmember apartments that Markkel had somehow arranged.

Between the wondrous events of Caralad's song and the transformed sky, and the amazing revelation of Kieran's love for me, I fell asleep in his arms with a joyous new melody singing through my dreams.

"You even smile in your sleep," Kieran murmured as first light pierced the window of our room. He was propped on an elbow, looking down at me with so much warmth that I immediately felt as if our pallet were stuffed with heat trivets.

I stretched, then wound my arms around his neck, pulling him closer. "You give me a lot to smile about. Let's just stay here all day."

He burrowed his face in my neck, the dark stubble on his cheeks tickling my skin. I sighed happily, but after a quick nuzzle he pulled away. "I wish we could. Except you've called for another feast day worship, and I've told the clans it's safe to come to Lyric. Time to face the music."

"So to speak." In spite of the problems ahead, I laughed.

The happy glow remained as I wandered into the common room. Susan sat alone on a couch, sipping clavo. "I made a big pot," she said, gesturing toward the kitchen alcove.

I ladled some of the simmering liquid into a mug and joined her on the couch, tucking my legs under me.

"Congratulations again," she said with genuine warmth. "I wondered how long it would take him to stop getting in his own way."

I blushed. "It seems everyone knew what he was feeling except me."

"And him," she said with a chuckle. She touched her mug lightly against mine. "To men who are worth the wait."

I drank, savoring the gentle burn as the clavo warmed my throat. Much better than the bitter stuff they made in Hazor. "So what are your plans? Will Jake be staying here?"

Susan pressed her lips together, and worry painted her eyes as she cast a glance toward the back rooms. "We were sent to save him. Once we did, I thought we'd all go back to our world. It's complicated. I guess a lot will depend on what happens today."

When I'd first met her, her constant drive was to find a way home. Neither of us could have imagined her other visits to our clans, or the challenges they would bring her family. Compassion welled and I set my mug aside and rested a hand on her arm. "I'm sorry. I can't imagine how difficult it is to think about returning home without him."

"Don't get me wrong," she added. "I'm glad for the time here. I faced my worst memories, fears that had haunted me. And they've lost their power." A sad smile lifted her lips. "And I've gotten to know Jake as a man, not just my little boy. I'm trying to set aside my own picture of the future . . . to be willing to let go."

"Each time you've come, you've helped our clans so much. You've chosen to suffer for the sake of our people."

"Mark's people too," she said softly, staring off into space.

I realized she was afraid, afraid for their life-bond, their future. I took her hand. "His world is with you. You believe that don't you?"

She shrugged one shoulder, fighting back tears. "I don't know what to believe. I don't know what Jake will decide, and that's hard enough. But what if Mark . . . ? I don't like not knowing."

I squeezed her hand. "Lukyan would say that this is the place our faith is tested. In the not knowing."

"I'll miss him," she said quietly.

How would we move forward without Lukyan? I'd never needed his wisdom more than now. A quiet sob grabbed my chest, and Susan pulled me into a hug as we let our grief flow.

Kieran strode into the room, adjusting a buckle on his baldric. When he saw us crying, he stilled, looking like he wanted to back out of the room. "What happened?"

"Lukyan." I sniffled.

His tension released as understanding softened his face. He walked quickly to me and brushed a soft kiss against the top of my head.

Susan scrubbed tears from her cheeks and breathed a soft laugh. Kieran frowned in her direction. "What?"

"Nothing. I'm happy for you both. It's just a little disorienting."

He rubbed the back of his neck and looked almost sheepish. "Not just for you."

I shared my clavo with him. "We were talking about Susan's family, and how today will affect their decisions."

Tristan walked into the room, catching the end of the conversation. "The news we've gathered so far tells us that people are scared."

"Never a good thing," Kieran said darkly.

"But if our uncertainty drives us to seek the One, it might be just what the clans need." I turned to Susan. "And we can definitely hope that the One will grant you clearer guidance at today's worship. I wonder how much to explain to people about Caralad."

"I think for now, the fewer who know, the better," Kieran said.

I padded over to the common room window and pushed aside the curtain. The sky held new wonders yet again. This morning vibrant shades of pink and red streaked the horizon just above the scalloped walls. I caught my breath. "What's happening?"

Caralad entered, rubbing his eyes. He joined me by the window, and I picked him up so he could see. Markkel came in shortly after, his hair wet from the shower.

Susan peered out the window beside me and smiled. "It's the sunrise."

Markkel's brow furrowed. "Red sky at morning, sailors take warning."

"What sort of warning?" Tristan asked. Kieran moved closer to me, hand closing over his sword.

Markkel shook his head. "Never mind. Could mean rain. A storm."

"Rain would reassure a lot of people," I said cheerfully. "It's time to head to the worship tower." Foreign proverbs probably held no sway in our world, and I was too full of love and hope to expect the worst.

CHAPTER
36

LINETTE

"HE'S NOT ALLOWED in the worship tower." A local Lyric songkeeper frowned at me, blocking my way at one of the open archways. His face could have been a carving on Sidian's wall, hard and cold.

My arms tightened around Caralad as if I could protect him from this rejection. "Everyone is welcome," I stammered. Several dozen songkeepers bustled around the tower, tuning instruments, moving large drums, preparing for the new feast day. The activity slowed as they overheard our confrontation. I wanted to be happy the group had grown so much since our call went out yesterday. I recognized songkeepers from Sandor and Blue Knoll and other clans.

But as their eyes turned toward me, my face heated with embarrassment.

Only Kieran's hand on my shoulder steadied me. Markkel, Susan, Jake, and Tristan had gone to the Council tower and planned to join us here later. But Kieran had refused to leave my side, so he and Nolan had come along to help me prepare for the morning worship.

Royan crossed from the dais to join the discussion. He ignored Kieran, even though they'd served together for so many seasons in Hazor, and couldn't meet my eyes, either. "We are all in agreement. He disrupted the traditions of worship yesterday. The damaged sky must be a sign of the One's anger—caused by this child's actions."

If the eldest Lyric songkeeper involved himself more in the leadership of the local songkeepers, he surely wouldn't agree, but he wasn't here. And Lukyan wasn't here to explain, either. The responsibility pulled my shoulders back. "You don't understand. He's the—"

Caralad placed one of his small, plump fingers against my lips. One could argue his song had revealed his identity, but he hadn't spoken since. He wasn't ready to clarify or explain who he was.

Havid approached us. "You can still fill your place as a songkeeper this morning. Just find someone to watch the boy away from here." At least her tone was gentler than the others. She even smiled. "And the songkeepers discussed something else this morning. They have assigned a new eldest songkeeper for Braide Wood. You."

The words would have thrilled me under any other circumstance. I loved the people of my village and would be honored to serve them as Lukyan had taught me. He'd prepared me for the task. But right now I couldn't think beyond the shock of the songkeepers barring Caralad from worship.

"If you won't allow him into the worship tower, then I'm not welcome here either," I said quietly.

Havid's eyebrows drew together. "Don't make this into a conflict. You understand the importance of our traditions."

The whole purpose of our traditions was to prepare us for the Deliverer. Now he had arrived, but no one recognized him. And if he wasn't ready to explain, what could I say?

Havid leaned closer. "People are worried about the sky. They blame him. Is he an agent of one of our enemies? Sent by Hazor to destroy the daily rains? Or a Rhusican creating a huge illusion so they can invade?"

My stomach lurched. This line of thought could lead to more than rejection. Caralad could quickly be in danger. I caught more malevolent and suspicious glares coming our way.

Kieran's hand left my shoulder and drew his sword in one effortless motion.

"No!" I wheeled on him. "This is the worship tower!"

"You have every right to stay if you want," he said quietly. The nearby songkeepers backed away.

"Not this way. Let's go." My chin lifted, and I hitched Caralad higher on my hip. I glanced back at the soaring windows overhead, heart aching that I wouldn't be here for this crucial feast-day gathering. Perhaps Caralad would have shared another song . . . one that would have healed our clans. Would the mist fall? Would the One breathe strength into His people?

I led us back out to the plaza, Kieran and Nolan following. Halfway to the Council tower, my legs gave in to trembling at what had just happened.

Kieran sheathed his sword and lifted Caralad from my arms. "Well, that was fun," he said dryly.

"I didn't know what to do," I said in a small voice. I sought comfort in Kieran's face and saw something I'd never expected to find directed at me: respect and admiration.

"The Deliverer chose a good mother. You have the instincts of a she-bear."

Beside him, Nolan snickered. "I told you she was tougher than she looked."

"Remember that." I squared my shoulders and looked at the three men who were now my family. My gaze rested on Caralad. "I've studied the promises my entire life, but he's so different than we all expected. No one recognizes him. He doesn't explain. He—"

Kieran tapped my nose. "A certain songkeeper I once knew would have said the One's timing is not ours." Then he rolled his eyes. "Did I just quote the Verses? You're a bad influence."

Caralad's shoulders shook with silent laughter. He sobered as he turned his head to stare at the worship tower. He didn't have to speak to express the pain of being refused entry.

"Maybe we should tell the Council who Caralad is," I said. "Maybe they will have a plan."

Kieran barked a short laugh. "You've addled my brain, but not enough to believe that."

"But what are we going to do?"

"Don't you already have your answer?" Nolan piped up. "You're the new eldest for Braide Wood."

"I think Nolan's right." Kieran hefted Caralad higher and settled him on his shoulders. "But first let's go find out how much of a mess the Council is making of things. The others might need our help."

A gust of air caressed us, whistling between the buildings, as if the sky breathed like a living creature. Overhead, white mounds of mist, like heaps of caradoc wool, slid across the expanse of vibrant blue. I reached up a hand. If I could touch them, would I feel the presence of the One in a tangible way, as I did when the mist lowered in the worship tower?

Kieran smiled at me. "It seems we have more new things ahead." On his shoulders, Caralad also reached up. His face seemed to drink in the sunlight. Then the large piles of mist gathered, took on grey edges, and covered the brightness, before chasing across the sky and leaving shimmering blue once again.

We could have stood there all day watching the changes overhead, wondering at what we would discover next. But Kieran strode onward to the Council tower. He lowered Caralad back to the ground when we reached the entryway, and I took the boy's hand.

The wide rotunda inside was empty and silent. At least no one was storming out in protest. Perhaps the quiet signified the meeting was going well. As we neared the curved hallway, two men stepped from the hall, muttering to each other and shaking their heads.

Hazorite soldiers.

My skin turned cold, and I forgot how to breathe. Had Bezreth sent them? Even now she wouldn't let me go.

Kieran moved in the space of a heartbeat. He drew his sword with the lethal whisper of steel sliding free from leather. Nolan pulled his bootknife and held his ground.

I gathered Caralad close and retreated enough to get a wall against my back.

The two soldiers turned from their conversation toward Kieran. Every line of his face was tight and hard, the scar across his temple throbbing red, sword raised and ready.

The two Hazorites opened their arms in a shaky gesture of conciliation.

"Kieran, wait! They aren't armed," I managed to squeak.

"What are you doing here?" Kieran's voice grated in the large lobby, the muscles of his arms rigid as he held his stance.

"A tr-treaty," one of the men answered.

Kieran still didn't relent, his eyes narrowed.

"Zarek sent us to appeal to your Council . . . after what happened to the sky."

"You couldn't have come from Sidian that quickly." Kieran's sword caught a glint from the lightwall, each dent and nick a reminder of the many encounters he'd survived.

"N-no . . . we were in Corros." The younger man's eyes were wide, his skin pale.

Kieran's jaw flexed. "Stirring up civil war between the clans."

More footsteps approached from the curved hallway. I tucked Caralad further behind me.

Tristan strode into view, took in the scene at a glance, and rolled his eyes. "Stand down, Kieran. The Council is sending them back to Zarek with a message."

Kieran lowered his sword slightly.

I frowned. "The Verses forbid treaties with the surrounding nations."

Tristan crooked a grin my direction. "Not exactly a treaty. More of a nonaggression promise. From them." He turned toward Kieran. "Since you're here, we could use your help. The Council is about to decide what to do with Cameron."

"They've made a mess of things each time they've dealt with him." Kieran sheathed his sword and stepped aside. The two Hazorites skittered past.

Ignoring them, Kieran gestured Tristan back toward the Braide Wood outer office, pausing to clap Nolan on the back and offer an approving nod. I tightened my grip on Caralad's hand and followed them, happy at the way Nolan's shoulders straightened at his father's silent praise. Kieran was a far better parent than he gave himself credit for.

In the Braide Wood office, I hesitated, studying Caralad's pure and innocent face. I'd had few occasions to attend a Council meeting, but I knew enough to want to protect the boy from all the contention and selfish agendas that seemed to rule.

Tristan slid the door open, and my decision was made for me as Caralad skipped forward, tugging at my hand as if eager to watch.

I swallowed a sigh. He was the Deliverer. He'd eventually need to observe the people he'd come to deliver, even if he'd have to deliver them from themselves.

We joined the rest of the Braide Wood delegates in the balcony where Kieran quickly made his way to the front. A few of the councilmembers frowned, but several grinned, no doubt anticipating excitement.

Across the wide tower, I caught sight of Markkel and Susan in the Rendor balcony.

I edged forward to see the floor of the chamber and the two men presenting to the Council.

"Jake has admitted he's no longer a Restorer." Cameron brushed lint from the front of his tunic, subtly drawing eyes to the bands marking him as chief councilmember. "Maybe he never really was. And if he lied about that, how can you trust his bizarre accusations?"

Jake stood near him, arms crossed. His fair skin was a bit flushed, but he remained calm. "Are you saying only a Restorer can speak truth? Then we couldn't trust a friend . . . or a councilmember."

Chuckles echoed throughout the chamber.

"I'm saying no one should trust you." Cameron faced off, spittle flying as he grew more agitated. "I've guided these clans safely through crisis after crisis while you romped through the woods with rebel guardians and then disappeared. And now when I've forged peace with our neighbors across the river, you concoct these ridiculous stories."

I'd seen the scars on Jake's arms. Learned from Susan about his captivity in Kahlarea. In front of me, Kieran braced against the balcony railing, anger building through his muscles.

Jake laughed. He turned away from Cameron and raised his gaze to the balconies surrounding the central floor. "You've heard the witnesses; you know the truth. He has no more Rhusican allies within this chamber to sway your minds. All that remains for you to decide is how to protect the clans from him."

"Protect the clans?" Cameron sputtered. "I'm the only one who stood between the clans and ruin. This whelp has no place leading the Council."

Jake smiled sadly. "On that point we agree."

I gasped. I'd seen firsthand how Kieran struggled when the role of Restorer was removed. Did Jake feel useless now? Forsaken by the One? I scurried up to the balcony's edge, ready to protest, but Jake was still speaking.

"I cede the floor to the other chief councilmembers from each clan." He walked calmly up the ramp to the Rendor balcony.

Kieran's hand moved to his sword. "What is he doing?"

I touched his arm, hoping to temper his protective response. "He's trusting the representatives of the clans, as he should. Wait and see."

Turning away from the action, he met my gaze. I half expected him to mock my naivety, but he released a slow breath. "All right. But if Cameron—"

"Banishment!" Shouts rose from each of the balconies in turn.

Unanimous. A harsh and unrelenting judgment that most would find heartbreaking, but would it be enough to protect the clans? Cameron had woven allegiances with surrounding nations.

Veins stood out on Cameron's forehead, his complexion blotchy as he faced the rejection of the people he'd bullied and deceived for so many seasons. He lifted a hand, still able to command attention. Silence fell over the room, and he sneered. "My concern has only ever been for our clans, but if my presence causes so much distress, I will bear the sacrifice and leave our lands. I have one humble request. That my banishment be across the River Borders."

It was my turn to clench the railing with mounting anger. "Kahlarea? Why would he want to go there? And how dare he dictate terms?"

Several burly guardians marched down to the chamber floor and grabbed Cameron, tying his hands. Seeing him bound came close to satisfying my longing for justice, but his confident stance made me fear his schemes would continue.

To my surprise, Kieran grinned and stepped back. "Let's go. Jake doesn't need our help anymore."

I didn't understand his shift in mood, but I was only too glad to leave the Council to its work. As we turned to go, Jake called out from the Rendor balcony, "One more thing. I believe the Council must reaffirm that our borders are closed to all Rhusicans."

The cheer from every balcony followed us out the door.

We gathered with our friends some time later in the marble-floored lobby of the Council tower. Susan was hugging Jake. "I didn't dare hope," she said, pulling back, then squeezing him again. Next she hugged Markkel, happy tears glistening in her eyes. When she saw us, she laughed. "Isn't it wonderful?"

Kieran rolled his eyes at her giddiness. "Corros is no longer rebelling and Hazor is retreating, but we aren't clear of problems."

She refused to be subdued by his reminder. "The Council will deal with the rest later, but they're dismissing soon so everyone can return to the worship tower. Oh, and Rhus also sent a messenger promising to stay away from our lands."

"Why?" Distrust shaded Kieran's tone.

Susan beamed. "The sky. They think the clans caused it. They're terrified. It's wonderful. Not that they're terrified . . . that's not wonderful part . . . but that they aren't threatening the clans anymore. Best of all, Jake is coming home with us."

I quickly focused on Jake, but his smile was steady as he nodded. "The Council doesn't need a young leader with no special powers."

"Oh, Jake," I whispered. "I'm sorry."

He met my eyes, his expression open and clear, with only the slightest hint of regret. "It's okay. I did what I came here for. I thought I'd never want to leave but"—he glanced past me to Kieran, then back to me—"I have no more reason to stay."

On a sudden impulse, I reached into the pocket of my song-keeper's robe and pulled out the fabric emblem of Rendor. "Back in Hazor I made this for you—to remind you of the strength of your clan. Now it can remind you of your time here, and all that the One accomplished through you."

Jake smiled, blinking a few times. "Thank you."

Markkel patted Jake's back. "The clans will be safe now."

Safe? His words drew me back to all our unsolved problems. I wasn't ready to celebrate. "Did they really let Cameron choose his banishment? What if he has more schemes?"

Markkel fought back a grin. "He's being escorted to the Kahlarean border, just as he requested."

I shook my head. "He formed allegiances with them. He's getting off too easy."

Kieran chuckled and hefted Caralad up to his shoulders. "Cameron doesn't know that the assassins' enclave is eager to see him. He sold them a Restorer who wasn't. That's going to make them cranky."

I should have pitied Cameron, about to arrogantly plunge into Kahlarea unaware; but I felt only relief and a sense of satisfaction. He had designed his own demise.

Susan leaned against Markkel, still smiling. "I've never heard the Council so united. They pledged to never again cancel the season-end gathering."

From outside, the drums began the invitation. Susan sent a puzzled look my direction. "Wait. Why aren't you at the worship tower?"

A pang pierced my chest, but when I watched Caralad, perched on Kieran's shoulders, my heart had no room for pain. His small feet, clad in soft leather boots that had once been worn by Tara's grandson, dangled across Kieran's chest, and I squeezed his toes. I was able to recount the conflict with the songkeepers without even a tremor in my voice.

Susan's eyes went wide. "'He came to his own, and his own people did not receive him.'" She sounded like she was reciting from her people's Verses. Then she brightened. "But you did. Part of me wishes we could stay to see him grow up."

Wonder filled me again. What would it be like to watch the Deliverer grow? Would he teach me more new songs? Would the people of Braide Wood get past their suspicions and fear of him? Would he eventually explain the plans of the One?

I looked at Kieran's rugged face, his firm jaw and strong shoulders. What a gift that I wouldn't face those questions alone.

I shook myself and turned back to Susan. "When do you plan to go home?"

Markkel sighed. "We'd planned to find you to say good-bye and slip away during the worship."

I smiled. "Since I'm not needed in the tower this morning, we can come with you."

We walked slowly. My throat thickened with tears as we passed the worship tower, and the blend of voices carried on the air. But we soon made our way down quiet streets to the walls closest to Corros Plains. A few guardians remained on watch but didn't stop us from using one of the small doors to leave the city.

The mossy hills held a sheen under the new light. I turned and looked back at Lyric. The sun touched the white walls and made them glow. The rippling shapes created contrasts of light and shadow. Everything in the world looked different today.

As we walked silently toward a small grove, Markkel, Susan, and Jake fell behind, speaking quietly. Caralad ran ahead, Nolan loping behind him. The boys detoured toward a field where shy caradoc grazed in the distance. "Don't scare them," I called.

Lingering remnants of sorrow at giving up my place in the tower fled. Back in Hazor I'd felt inadequate, and when my memory was lost I'd felt even more useless. Yet today I'd been given Kieran, Nolan, and Caralad to love and care for—a purpose to embrace. And a calling I could only fulfill in His strength.

Caralad waved at me and bent down, lifting a fluffy white bundle. A caradoc fawn lost from its mother. He carried it closer to the herd, and one of the shy creatures lifted its head and ambled toward him, butting its head against him when he set the baby down on the moss.

Kieran laughed. "He really is a caralad. I wonder what other surprises we have ahead."

I slipped my hand into his. One last uncertainty had been tugging at my heart, especially after watching him draw his sword, ready to fend off the Hazorites. "Will you be happy in Braide Wood? Raising the boys, being a true part of the clan . . . no more adventures?"

His laugh was deep and full-throated. "No adventures? Every second with you is an adventure. And now we have Caralad to defend. No guardian ever protected a more vital house."

The air stirred, prompting the leaves of the nearby trees to rustle with a joyous abandon. Soft hints of music wafted from Lyric. A strand of my hair blew across my face.

Kieran caught it and tucked it behind my ear, then took the moment to kiss away my doubts. "I'll wake every morning thanking the One. Now let's say good-bye to the others so we can take the boys home."

EPILOGUE

Susan

HOW COULD I not leave a piece of my soul in this world? I loved the clans. I'd fought for them, bled for them. But each time I was here, my heart pulled like a magnet, drawn irresistibly toward home.

Ahead of us, Caralad romped in the fields. Kieran and Linette conversed quietly, hand in hand. Jake knelt to retie his boot, and I tousled his hair. "Are you ready to go home?"

He straightened. "I'm trying to figure out what to say to the kids."

I bit my lip to hold back a laugh at his description of Karen, Jon, and Anne, as if he were far older. The truth was after all he'd experienced in Lyric, Rendor, and Kahlarea, he had matured far beyond his years.

"You can start college now. Although I'm sure it will take some readjustment." I may not have to let him go to the People of the Verses, but I still faced letting him go into our world. My throat pinched at the thought, but the memory of the One's unceasing provision settled my soul, reminding it to find joy in His plans for my family.

Jake cast a look back toward the walls and tower of Lyric. "Maybe we'll visit again some day."

Mark shook his head. "We lost one of the portal stones in Kahlarea. Once we leave here, it will be for good."

"I'm sorry." I leaned my head against his shoulder, wishing I could draw out some of the pain and loss he was feeling. "Especially now. I wish I knew what it will mean for this world now that the Deliverer has come. And how his life will unfold. Wouldn't it be amazing to be here?"

He kissed the top of my head and gave me a quick hug. "It's time to go home. My life is there now."

We quickened our pace and soon found the place deep between the trees where a slim invisible space drew us with the pull of static electricity.

The others gathered close. Kieran and Mark clasped forearms. Linette and I hugged.

Jake fought back emotion as he said his good-byes, then he slipped effortlessly between two trees and disappeared.

I knelt to say good-bye to Caralad, staring deep into his eyes, wondering if I would find answers to all the mysteries his presence had raised. He didn't speak, but his steady gaze gave me comfort. Then Mark squeezed my hand and took a step toward the portal.

Just before I followed him, Caralad pressed something into my other hand.

Clinging to Mark, I followed him between the trees.

The grove, the fields, and Lyric in the distance all disappeared. The transition this time was smooth, and after a gust of wind that came from all directions at once, we found ourselves in Jake's basement bedroom.

After a deep breath of relief, I looked down to see what Caralad had given me just before we left.

Smooth and grey and unassuming, a portal stone rested in my hand.

The End

Day of the One

Based on the poem, "A Day of the One"

Composer: Cameron Banks
Text by Sharon Hinck

Soprano 1: There was a time, time rich with days be - fore the sad and lone - ly songs were

Soprano 2: There was a time, time rich with days be - fore the sad and lone - ly songs were

Alto: There was a time, time rich with days be - fore the sad and lone - ly songs were

S 1: sung.

S 2: sung.

A: sung

T: There was a day____ rich with time be - fore men fought and bee - tles

B 1: There was a day, a day rich with time be - fore men fought and____ bee - tles

B 2: There was a day____ rich with time be - fore men fought and bee - tles

Day of the One

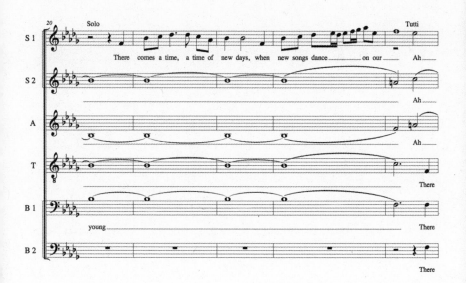

Day of the One

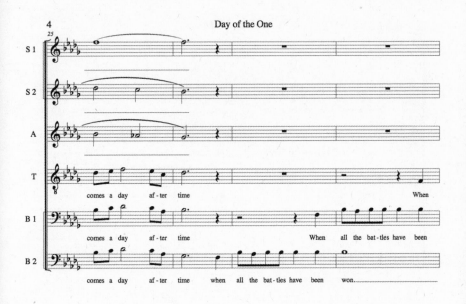

Day of the One

Day of the One

GLOSSARY

caradoc: Docile herd animal with soft, shedding coat that is used for weaving and creating textiles.

clavo: Spicy tea with a rich flavor and near-healing properties; favorite hot beverage of the clans; usually brewed in a wide wooden bowl over a heat trivet and ladled into mugs; Hazorite version is much stronger and bitter.

Council: Governing body of the People of the Verses, comprised of chosen representatives from each clan; meets in Lyric and makes decisions that affect all the clans.

cover-and-ambush: A children's game similar to hide-and-seek.

darnite: Blue mineral that produces light, embedded in the walls of Kahlarean caves.

guardian: Member of any clan who trains for military/protector role, which includes serving the Council and the people, training for and engaging in battle, and patrolling the borders.

grenlow: A Kahlarean fish, similar in size to a sardine, that swarm once each season in the fast-flowing streams near the River Borders.

Hazor: Nation across the mountain border of the People's clans. Hazorites worship the hill-gods and sacrifice their children to those gods. Zarek is the current king and rules from the capitol, Sidian.

heat trivet: Flat panels or tiles that glow with heat or light. Various sizes are used to provide surfaces for cooking and illumination. They are a smaller version of the technology used to create the light walls common in homes.

Kahlarea: Nation across the river that borders one side of the People's lands. Kahlareans are pale, with bulbous eyes, and their assassins are feared everywhere for their stealth and ability to hide and appear from nowhere.

lehkan: Animals used for riding. They look similar to elk, with fierce antlers and soft llama-like fur. They are ridden under saddle and guided by leg commands.

Lyric: Central city of the tribes. The Lyric tower is the place where the One meets with the People in an especially tangible way. Lyric's walls are white and form a scalloped pattern as they encircle the city.

light rod: Used by Kahlareans in caves – a staff about five feet in length that emits a soft glow when activated.

long-whistle: A thin metal musical instrument popular among messengers.

mesana vine: Dark maroon, parasitic plant that grows in harsh terrain. The pith is fibrous, salty, and edible, though far from tasty.

orberry juice: A tart juice made from small orange berries that grow on low-lying shrubs along the edge of Morsal Plains.

orberry wine: Fermented, intoxicating version of orberry juice that is especially popular in Hazor.

Perish: A table game of strategy, played with two sets of small stones, usually black and white.

Rammelite fever: Progressive, fatal illness that causes joint pain and ongoing bouts of high fever, thought to be caused by a small parasite found on plants in low-lying swamplands.

redbud: A wildflower that grows on the plateaus near Braide Wood

Restorer: A leader sent by the One to save His people, traditionally a guardian. Once called by the One for this role, the Restorer develops heightened senses and strengths of various kinds, and heals rapidly from most injuries.

Rhusican: A person from Rhus, a nearby nation; usually attractive, with reddish-gold hair and vibrant aqua or green eyes. Rhusicans have the ability to read and affect minds and to plant poison in people's thoughts that can influence their behavior and even cause death.

rizzid: Lizard-shaped creature about the size of a squirrel, red-furred and poisonous.

rondalin: Stringed instrument similar to a Celtic harp, but round in shape.

THE SWORD OF LYRIC

SHARON HINCK is a wife and mom who has enjoyed many adventures on her road with God, although none have involved an alternate universe (thus far). She writes "stories for the hero in all of us," about ordinary people experiencing God's grace in unexpected ways. Known for their authenticity, emotional range, and spiritual depth, her novels include contemporary fiction as well as fantasy, and have been recognized with three Carol awards and a Christy finalist medal. She has also contributed non-fiction articles to dozens of book compilations and magazines and has written devotions for *Mornings with Jesus* for many years.

With an undergrad degree in education, she earned an MA in Communication from Regent University. She spent ten years as the artistic director of a Christian performing arts group and has been a church youth worker, a ballet teacher, an organist, and a freelance editor. When she isn't wrestling with words, Sharon enjoys speaking to conferences, retreats, and church groups. She and her family make their home in the Midwest, and she welcomes visitors to her online home at *sharonhinck.com*.

ACKNOWLEDGMENTS

My precious family – Ted, Joel, Kaeti, Josh, Jenni, Jennelle, Kyrie, Mom and Carl – you each inspire me daily. Your love and support make my writing possible.

I'm deeply grateful to the prayer team members who have joined this project with their intercessions over the years (Patti, Joyce, Amy, Chawna, Rosemary, Cheryl, Kathy, Sue, Stacy, Nancy, Ginny, Michelle, Nina Ruth, Ruth, and Becky); to the Book Buddies; to critique partners (especially Amy and Chawna for in-depth feedback on the full manuscript); to early readers (Mom, Jenni, Ted, Liz, Hannah, and Joyce); to various writing buddies (such as Brenda, Chawna, Michelle, Carol, Jonathan, John, Erica, Beth, and Stacy) for awesome insights on select chapters; to the Church Ladies; and to my other patient and encouraging extended family and friends. I also want to thank Cameron Banks for generously sharing his musical talent.

Huge appreciation goes to my agent Steve Laube, who has always been a champion for these stories, and to my editor Reagen Reed who made them better. Thank you to everyone at the marvelous Enclave Publishing who made this new story possible.

Most of all, thank you to the One who has loved me enough to pursue me.

scolopendra: Huge centipede-type creature with poisonous talons, hunted and harvested by Kahlareans to distill for their venblades. Killing one is a rite of passage for an assassin trainee.

songkeeper: A person who leads worship, composes songs, encourages people, and promotes the faith life of the People.

stinging beetles: Nonpoisonous but prone to inflicting uncomfortable stings, these flying scarabs are common along the River Borders near Rendor. They are the size of large dragonflies, and the yellow and orange beetles are more likely to attack humans than the blue and green varieties.

syncbeam: Long-range, focused energy beam used as a weapon.

three-peg: A weaving technique where yarn is wrapped in patterns around a small three-pegged loom to create a variety of textiles, including sweaters and bed-covers

venblade: Small dagger used by Kahlarean assassins; a reservoir in the handle injects poison into the blade to cause paralysis in the victim.

waterweed: A dangerous plant found along river banks, its tendrils entangle moving creatures and can cause drowning.